Skinfull

Hannah Bradby

Published 2005 by Onlywomen Press Limited, London, UK

ISBN 0–906500–83–4

British Library Cataloguing in Publication Data
A catalogue record for this book is available from the British Library

Typeset by RefineCatch Limited, Bungay, Suffolk, UK.
Printed and bound in India by Gopsons Papers Limited.

Skinfull

a title encapsulating two novellas:

Skinfull   *page 1*

Underneath the fairy lights   *page 133*

Skinfull

Maya

Maya shakes her head, despairing at her own leakiness. After 10 years of menstruation why couldn't she anticipate her own bodily cycles? But each month she lived in denial until caught unawares. "Roll on the menopause" she mutters as she rolls up her sheet. Her monthly reminder of what a disapproving teacher had once referred to as her "excess of femininity". Wiry red hair, long fleshy limbs and a generous mouth, that never seemed to fit together harmoniously. Maya saw her body, hair, clothes, voice and manners as constantly letting down her true inner self. Her ungainly body detracted from the quiet scholarly, demure and elegant person of no specific gender that she wished the world would see. Her sense of awkwardness had been exacerbated by her arrival in Glasgow three months earlier. And she just didn't quite fit here. She had come to take up a job that seemed ideal when she had been interviewed, but which turned out to be all wrong for her. Her boss didn't like her and she had no friends. Bal had potential, but hadn't yet turned into a real friend.

Sighing, Maya rubs at the stain under the cold tap. She spreads the sheet out in the patch of sunlight, hoping it will have a bleaching effect through the dirty windows. Then she turns her attention to plaiting her hair tightly and pinned it firmly to her head. Infuriating tendrils will have escaped by lunchtime. Taking an apple, she sets off for work at a reluctant pace in the knowledge that she'll probably just miss the last bus that would get her in before her boss.

1

Maya and Balvinder

Half an hour later Maya arrives at the Shakti Family Centre, constructed from steel cables, plate glass and blonde wood which looks light and airy in among the heavy granite buildings from Glasgow's heyday of trade and empire.

"Morning Shuggie."

A brass plaque welcomes the visitor in English, Punjabi, Hindi, Arabic, Urdu, Cantonese and Polish. Shuggie, sitting in his glass-fronted cubby-hole, twitches his "Daily Record" and buzzes open the security door.

"You're looking a bit peely-wally, pal!" Balvinder is already behind the reception desk.

Maya just grimaces at her, not feeling up to discussing her bodily state.

"Is it your monthlies?" asks Bal too brightly.

Maya looks over her shoulder to see if Shuggie is listening.

"Don't worry about him. He's studying the form at Ayr." Balvinder lifts her chin and shouts towards the cubby hole, "Evens both way, every time, pal!"

Shuggie shrugs.

"Is the big K in yet?" asks Maya.

"No, no. She phoned to say she'd a dentist's appointment. She'll not be in until later. How about I buy you an early lunch? Once Shuggie's back from the bookie's? In the meantime, I'll brew you up some ginger tea. My ma would say you're needing your insides heated up."

Maya takes her sluggish body to her desk in the corner of the open plan room and admires her view south over the Clyde towards the dome of the central mosque and the high-rise blocks of flats in the Gorbals.

"Power, remember!" Balvinder deposits a steaming mug next to the keyboard, the contents of which perfume Maya's nostrils.

"Eh?"

"S'what Shakti means. Strong like a woman." Balvinder smiles sympathetically. Maya leans forward as her innards cramp up.

Before her job interview, Maya had searched the web for the meaning of Shakti and found that any Asian women's group that wasn't called Saheli seemed to be called Shakti.

Her interview presentation had been about involving local community groups in deriving images of gendered power. One of the interviewers had asked what Maya thought the relationship between power and empowerment was.

"Umm. Making people's lives better through boosting their self confidence?", Maya had tentatively suggested. Now she was actually in the job, Maya felt like the least empowered person alive, thanks to her fractious relationship with Mrs Kapadia. And the possibility of empowering anyone else seemed remote.

By eleven thirty, Maya and Balvinder are in La Perla.

"Glasgow's best café," pronounces Balvinder as she slides into a booth. She doesn't bother consulting the menu since she knows her order by heart.

"Sausage, egg and tattie scone roll please. And a frothy coffee," Balvinder orders. Maya is gazing in amazement at the long laminated list of things that can be put inside a roll. After a pause, Balvinder adds, "And the same for her too. And a Ben Lomond Volcano for afters. Thanks very much." Turning back to Maya she says, "That'll see us both right."

The rolls arrive at speed and Balvinder bites in with relish, expertly keeping the egg yoke contained within the roll. Maya doesn't want yolk on her chin so asks for a knife and fork to dissect the roll. Inside, the bread is stained amber from the flat patty of unnaturally pink sausage meat. As Maya pokes it out of the roll, Balvinder explains.

"Lorne sausage. I have to send parcels of it down to my cousin Kam in London 'cause you don't get it down there. She says you can't get a decent roll and sausage any where."

Maya nods, her scepticism as to whether the word decent should ever really be associated with roll and sausage remains unspoken. She cuts up the tattie scone and egg, mopping up the runaway yolk with the inside of the roll.

"How odd to eat a scone wrapped up in a bread roll. Carbo-load-a-go-go" she thinks aloud through a mouthful. But Balvinder is already wiping her mouth with a brittle paper napkin.

"You're not one of they bleeding-heart vegetarians are you?" Balvinder asks, seeing the square sausage abandoned on the side of Maya's plate. But she doesn't wait for an answer.

3

"My cousin, well her husband thinks she's a vegetarian. She is. Mainly. Apart from the roll and sausage. Has to be flat. And square. It's only 'cause she misses Glasgow so. Anyway, I have to get the Lorne parcels delivered by special courier so they can arrive when her husband's out at work. She has an old frying pan that she cooks them in, with the kitchen windows wide open. Then she'll make a strong curry to cover the smell."

"Two Ben Lomond Volcanoes!" announces the waitress setting down two cut glass dishes containing what looks to Maya like entirely inorganic, inedible material: two blobs of white ice-cream dissolving into a pool of orange liquid. The scummy mess is topped off by a brown coconut-dusted blob. Balvinder is excavating with relish.

"Usually I just have the Ben Lomond. But the volcano is bound to be good for a lassie in your condition. The Irn Bru will stave off the anaemia!" Getting no reaction Balvinder prompts, "Seeing how it's made from girders. Eh!"

"What is it called?" Maya unwillingly betrays her ignorance.

"Irn Bru. You can get it down in England now. But it's a pure Scottish drink. In fact they make two versions – one for us and one for the English folk. The one for the Scots has twice as much sugar as the one they take down south," Balvinder reports, flashing Maya a beam of nationalist pride. "My pal who works in the Barrhead bottling plant told me."

Maya picked up the brown blob which was, at least, dry and seemed safer than the fizzing scummy orange gloop. Biting through the chocolate crust into white foam was like eating super-sweet fairy liquid bubbles.

"Mmm. Pure dead brilliant," Balvinder scrapes her bowl clean. "Do you no fancy your ice-cream float? Shall I eat it? Otherwise we'll have some explaining to do to the waitress. She makes these herself you know!"

No wonder Balvinder's face had got fatter over the last three months, thinks Maya watching her scrape another bowl clean.

"So where did you say you stay?" Balvinder asks.

"No. I've moved here to live now."

"Aye. Well I guessed you weren't Scottish like, with your posh accent. But where's your house?"

4

"Oh. Down by Queen's Park."

"Who do you stay beside?"

"Umm. I've only met one neighbour. She's old but dyes her hair black. She's always knocking on my door to open jam pots or change fuses. I've never met the other neighbours on the stairs, just seen them out of the windows taking their kids or dogs to the park."

"But are you married? Or do you stay with your ma and pa?"

"No. My mum lives in London."

"Does she mind you being so far away?"

"I don't think so. In fact she'd probably rather I was further away. Guatemala or the Cayman Islands."

"Does she no like you then?"

"No. Well. Yes. But she likes hot countries."

"Aye. Not much chance of that here. Heat I mean."

Maya's mother, Hilary, had been horrified when Maya had announced her intention to move to Glasgow.

"But it's so white there," she had exclaimed, "and so cold". Hilary's consistent desire that her daughter behave like an exotic and oppressed product of the colonies was wearing.

"Well, I'll seem blacker by contrast won't I mother?" Maya had retorted. And to get them off the subject of skin colour she continued, "And anyway, according to the city guide, Glasgow is often warmer than the south-east. But wetter."

Annoyingly, her mother had been right about Glasgow being cold and white. The grand proportions and sash windows of the tenement buildings, even her modest one, kept the indoor temperature cool and the lack of black people, compared with Stoke Newington, was odd. Maya's best friend, Maureen Oshanti, had made clear her reluctance to visit. During a school trip to York she had felt so conspicuously black that she had sworn never again to travel due north from London.

Balvinder is draining her coffee cup. "Did you work before you came here?" she asks.

"Yeah. I was in a schools project."

"What, like a teacher?"

"Kind of. But better. No admin or discipline. I helped the children decide how to renovate their playground and then we

5

did it together. It was actually my old primary school. It was funny drinking tea in the staff room at break time."

Maya had thought of herself as good at routine. Good at getting up in the morning, working through what needed to be done. She was used to a sense of satisfaction at the end of the day, having completed her day's work. She was used to being able to keep colleagues happy with her progress. That was what it had been like in her previous jobs. And at college. But not now. Not here. Not with Mrs Kapadia.

"What about your brothers and sisters? Where do they stay?"

"I haven't any. It's only me."

"Oh." For a moment Bal is stuck for a question. "What's that like?" she asks as the waitress places the bill down on the lemon-yellow formica table.

"I'll get this." Maya searches for a fiver and three pound coins in her purse, rather than answer Balvinder's impossible question that suggests both incredulity and pity.

Heather

"Mummy. Quick! My poo is trying to jump out of my bottom!"

Baby balanced on hip, money belt firmly attached, Heather struggles against the sliding compartment doors into the little toilet cubicle. How to wipe the child's bottom, without dropping the baby down the toilet and slipping a disc again?

"Lucky it didn't touch my pants, Mummy!" exclaims the child after regaining her seat in the compartment, satisfied that she would not, after all, be forced to change out of her favourite Barbie-pink pants. "I'd just better not to do a wet fart now, eh mummy?" She smiles up towards her mother, showing her new freckles, developed in the Mediterranean sun despite the liberal application of total sun block.

Heather nods and hopes that none of the other passengers of the SNCF cross-country train speak too much English. Her daughter's scatological chat seems to have done nothing to disincline the man opposite from doting on her daughters and making loud comments to his neighbours. Heather cannot decide if the man's comments about "les bels enfants avec les

6

têtes d'anges" are more or less annoying than being leered at herself.

At last, around Lyon, when both children sleep, Heather closes her own eyes to avoid eye contact with the overly admiring man. When she had been younger she had felt invisible as a proper grown-up; too young to have worthwhile professional opinions and too visible as a sexual object. As a lone traveller, she had never managed to transform her aloneness into an air of mystery and independence. She had never learned the trick of camouflaging her origins to external view and knew that she was easily identifiable as coming from the comfortable, middle-classes. Always a soft target. Among other blessings, motherhood had delivered her from that over-visibility. Pushing a pram brought immunity from wolf-whistlers. But perhaps her invisibility would have come anyway as her hair greyed?

Maya

Maya leans gratefully on the warm fryers, looking in through the greasy window at the lumps of protein on display. She feels far too menstrual to cook tonight, but needs comfort food. Balvinder had recommended this chip shop on the grounds that it changed its oil at least once a week. Outside it is raining, so all the people queuing for food are crushed in front of the fryers and the windows are translucent with condensation. Visible through the wet windows is a gold blur of the sign on the opposite side of the wide avenue – Queen's Park Café. Maya had gone in one Saturday, hoping for a cappuccino, eggs Benedict and a read of the Guardian, only to find that despite its alluring name, it was a standard pub. All the men at the bar had turned to watch her as she ordered a coffee. Dry-roasted peanuts had to substitute for soft eggs. The filter coffee had sat stewing in its Pyrex jug too long. Maya had tried to look at ease in her own company, sitting at a little round table. But since the pub had no windows or newspapers there was nowhere to look except for the televised football match or the faces of the drinkers watching the football match. The screen was positioned so that Maya could study the viewers' faces as they watched the progress of Kilmarnock versus Dundee. Not one man's gaze broke from the soccer action as Maya examined each face. They winced, gasped and shook their heads in unison, like muppets. Maya had tried watching the screen. She wanted to see what kept the drinkers rapt. But she couldn't. And then the match had ended and some bloke had lurched towards her table smiling. Rather than face the inevitable, "You're not from Glasgow are you?", Maya had skidaddled.

The queue shuffles forward as two couples leave with warm paper parcels under their arms.

Maya had endured work that day, longing for five o'clock. Mrs Kapadia had arrived in the afternoon, chewing on cloves to numb her sore gums where the dentist had been at work. At least pain had dampened her usual enthusiasm for thinking up new plans for Maya to execute. At last, home time had arrived. Balvinder's brother had collected her from the front door as usual. But as soon as Maya had left the Shakti building, she found that her flat no longer seemed such an attractive refuge after all. No-one except her mother ever rang and since Balvinder was her only nearly-friend, no-one called round, except for the neighbour with tight jam lids. Once Maya closed her front door behind her, she was there, on her own, for the evening.

Another shuffle passes down the queue.

"Haddock and chips please." Maya likes the delicate flavour and fine flakes of plaice best, but feels haddock would be a less conspicuous order. She is wrong. Complete incomprehension meets her request so she tries again.

"Haddock and chips? Please?"

"Fish. We have fish," replies the boy in the greasy apron.

"OK. Fish."

Maya listens to the customer behind her order.

"Fish supper, please. Heavy on the salt."

Balvinder

"Here's your lovely wee girl, hen. She's beautiful." A glint of a gold tooth smiles at me from a pasty, friendly face. She shows me a little dolly of a baby. Perfect. I smile in slow motion and wonder what she's talking about. And who is she? She is mopping me down with a J-cloth and warm soapy water. A male face looms over.

"OK?" Since it's clearly required, I nod. Although the fact that I can't speak might indicate otherwise. He moves off and I realise that his green pyjamas probably mean that I'm in hospital. I'm wheeled off down some corridors and parked in a dark ward. Pasty-face hands me the bundle of baby and leaves. Women keep offering things: tea, painkillers, toast. But no-one tells me what to do with the bundle. So I just continue to clutch her.

Around me, other bodies are snuffling and murmuring. The lights are off, but there's activity on all sides – crying, feeding, adjusting inco pads, changing nappies. Groaning is coming from a woman in labour, she's crying out for help. She's told off for disturbing the rest of us. I was making those noises a few hours ago and I've survived. But I can't help her. I can't even stay awake. But what if the baby cries? What if she stops breathing? I wish she would wake up. Then I'd know she's alive. But if she does what will I do? I can't get out of bed. My legs don't work. The groaner is given a jag and quietens down. My eyes close.

Hospital morning starts when the fluorescent lights are switched on. Half an hour later, we're allowed tea and pills and shift-change inspection starts. The drawing of pastel-coloured curtains doesn't stop sound travelling.

"Have your bowels opened?" asks a midwife.

"Yes," a whispered voice from behind the curtain.

"What colour is your discharge?"

"Red," the quiet reply.

"Like liver or like blood?" persists the midwife.

"Ummm. Light red," a tiny whisper.

"Any clots?" the midwife rings out.

Pause.

A giggle starts in my belly. The midwife is the prime clot. My stitches close down the laugh.

A barely audible, "No."

"Any unpleasant smell?"

No audible reply.

"OK. You're ready for discharge."

"What does that mean?" asks the little voice.

"You can go home."

Last night's groaner, Julie-Ann, is waiting for a "Caesarian

9

section for her naughty baby who won't turn around."
Julie-Ann sits in bed looking expectant and nervous with her
Mum holding her hand, while the rest of us tuck into our
bran flakes and bananas. They're keen to get you to shit here,
that's for sure.

A tall glossy woman is preparing to go home. Her smart
husband arrives early to miss the traffic but the paediatrician
who has to discharge their baby can't be found. Glossy
woman is complaining as she rubs Clarins special cleansing
and lifting lotion for mature skin into her neck.

"Was like a bloody war zone trying to sleep in here. If we
ever have another I'm going private."

The midwife explains that she has bleeped the paediatrician but the ante-natal and post-natal wards have just been
merged due to falling birth rates and a lack of trained staff so
everyone's rushed off their feet.

"Surely falling birth rates should mean less work," points
out the husband sourly.

Julie-Ann and her mum go out to the front door for "a wee
ciggie." Julie-Ann has her Ellesse track suit jacket clutched
over her babydoll nightie. Imagine braving east winds and
the gaze of the public on the flesh of your thighs just for a fag!
The orderlies arrive to fetch Julie-Ann for her section. I tell
them she's away for a smoke out front but they leave to find
another body to deliver to the surgeon. The midwife greets
Julie-Ann's return tetchily and gets her into a hospital gown
– one that shows her bum at the back. Julie-Ann stays put in
her bed.

"I'm to look at your stitches." Her badge says, "Janine
Dunlop. Midwifery assistant". "Has the baby fed?"

I shake my head. Have I failed already? Janine consults the
clipboard on the end of my bed.

"Breast or bottle?" she asks.

"What?" I don't understand.

"Do you want me to give her a bottle?"

I nod. Well the baby can't eat branflakes can she?

"I'll take her off while you sort yourself out," Janine nods
towards my stomach.

I see some blood has leaked out onto the upper sheet.
Shame fills me up while Janine wheels the baby off in her fish

tank cooing at her. What a relief that someone who knows what they're about is caring for the baby. But I'm gutted that it's not me calling her "my wee darlin".

Heather

Arriving into the Gare de Lyon, Heather finds the bus that takes her and the children to Gare du Nord, from where the Waterloo-bound Eurostar departs. Four hours later, crossing London in the taxi she gazes out of the window, enjoying the feeling of getting closer to home after a month abroad. Heather tries to identify what makes the boulevards and pavement cafés of Paris look elegant, open and designed for good living, whereas London looks so much less of a city, more a suburban, unplanned sprawl, even in the centre. Compared with Paris, New York and her own beloved Edinburgh, London just doesn't look like a metropolitan centre. Even Glasgow has more dignity and aplomb. At King's Cross, she gets her sleep-crumpled infants into their sleeper train compartment. She lays them down on bunks and stashes the luggage underneath.

"Mummy, I've got a sweaty eyeball," mumbles the child rubbing her eye sleepily.

"Back to sleep now sweet-pea," Heather soothes.

"Lick my eyeball clean Mummy."

Heather declines this invitation and strokes the child's forehead.

"Is it Tuesday now Mummy?"

"No. Tuesday is tomorrow."

"Is it tomorrow now?" the child tries again.

"Not yet. When you wake up again it will be," Heather tries to keep her voice soothing.

"Tuesday sounds like sweeties. And I'll see Daddy on the Tuesday day won't I?"

Heather nods and closes her eyes, hoping the child will follow suit. She too is longing to see Doug. He'll be indulgent and doting after their long absence and she will wallow in his tender ministrations. Little fingers are trying to pull her eyelids apart. Was it wrong to wish one's children asleep so much, to love them best when they are unconscious? Had her mother felt the same about her? Had her mother ever actually put her to bed, or had it always been Mrs McFadyen? It was

11

Mrs McFadyen that Heather could remember singing the Skye Boat song in the gloaming.

When the train pulls out fifteen minutes later, the rattley motion lulls the children. Heather sighs and pulls two miniature bottles of rum and a tin of coke from her rucksack, mixing them in the complimentary hygienically wrapped plastic beaker. She rehearses recounting to Doug the complete disinterest shown by train staff and passengers alike as she staggered onto the train, carrying two dishevelled children and a rucksack. She hasn't shaken the inter-railing ethic of travelling light so as to be able to flee potential rapists and pursue departing buses and trains. Perhaps if she exhibited fewer competencies and stood on the platform surrounded by bags and crying children, people would arrive to her aid? But perhaps she'd have to be twenty-something and blonde instead of forty-something and greying? The rum is just scrambling her thoughts comfortably when the baby wakes and Heather has to wriggle about to accommodate them both on the bunk with her nipple in the babe's mouth.

"Lucky baby. Rum and milk" she murmurs.

Balvinder

Lucky sods as can walk have all had their turn in the shower and it has flooded again. Water is leaking out under the door. The midwifery assistants won't clear it up since it's not their job and the cleaners have finished their morning shift. Janine, the mouthiest, makes it clear that she shouldn't be working today since "it's no right" and "it's no safe". It seems that there's only one midwife on duty and she's just newly qualified. Janine says that "Bernie wouldn't stand for it".

At half eleven the food trolley arrives and plates are delivered to our beds. Or at least to the other women's beds.

"Where's mine?" I ask the woman with "catering and hospitality services" embroidered across her left breast.

She consults her food-spattered list and announces, "Minority dinners up shortly", before pushing her trolley out of the swing doors. Ten minutes later a plate of steaming lamb curry sitting on a pile of basmati rice is delivered to the table at the end of the ward. The smell perfumes the air, stronger even than the odour of disinfectant. I have to suck back my spittle.

12

I'm just unstrapping my piss bottle from the side of the bed
to get the food, when Janine brings it over to me.

I'm not offered a sweet, a drink or fruit but at least I'm not
eating the soggy plastic-ham like the other women. My head
is filled with the scent of haldi, jeera and kali mirch, as I
swallow the food down. Ma's face hovers in my mind. Her
dimples are sucked in, like when she's about to explain how
women must suffer. I fill my face with meat and push the
thought of her away. Belly filled, I slide down the bed,
rearranging my catheter gingerly. The baby's blanket is rising
and falling as she sleeps on. I sleep too.

Maya

Escape from work at last. I push out of the plate glass and
steel doors, wave to Shuggie in his booth and breathe deeply.
Mrs Kapadia has decided that we need a thermometer to track
"our" fundraising efforts. So this afternoon I had the humiliation of sticking together bits of A4 paper to make a five foot
strip and drawing in two black lines and a bulb coloured in
red. Mrs Kapadia says that I cannot colour in red between the
black lines, to represent the two thousand pounds that have
been promised by prominent local business man, Mr Qureshi,
until the cheque clears. (Balvinder tells me that Qureshi and
his uncle, the curry kings of Glasgow, are credited with bringing pakora to Scotland, and their sons are much in demand as
husbands).

Fine drizzle cools my cheeks, over-heated by the excessive
office temperature that is necessary to keep Mrs Kapadia's
gold-sandalled feet warm. Only Bal is brave enough to turn
the thermostat down and she wasn't in today. The other
volunteers don't risk Mrs Kapadia's sing-song mocking tones
asking who is penny-pinching and giving her chilblains.

"If we are stuck in this freezing country, we must at least
keep our blood warm, hai na?" she asks, handing round the
crystallised stem ginger.

I don't know what I was expecting from this job. Certainly
not Mrs Kapadia and her demanding ways. Not close scrutiny
from a well-upholstered woman who knows best about everything. I suppose I imagined it would be like the women's
group that Mum used to attend – Dalston Dykes and their

13

Daughters, or something. God knows why Mum was there. Must've had a lesbian phase I suppose. I used to hang about at the back of the decommissioned synagogue where they met and play giggly games with the other children. It always seemed co-operative, well-organised and friendly. There was apple juice and flap-jacks to keep us kids happy. I'm not sure what Mum was up to while I was giggling and eating ... examining her own cervix and comparing stories of oppression I suppose. Then Mum got a new boyfriend and decided that joining his squash ladder would spark the gender revolution more quickly than worthy discussion with her feminist sisters. So instead of going to the synagogue we drove to Hampstead Squash and Rackets Club where I drank cola from the drinks machine while Mum perfected her drop shots. There were no other children. And then she dropped the boyfriend too.

The damp will make my hair frizz up. Ugh. Still. Why should I care? It doesn't matter how crazy-frizzy it gets since there's no-one for me to impress in this town. I think of Balvinder's beautiful smooth curtain of shiny hair, recently done in a "Diva-cut" framing her face, with an off-centre parting. Apparently her Mum went crazy.

"At least I didn't get the fringed Diva," Balvinder told me glumly.

"Would that have been worse?" I asked.

"Have you ever seen a Sikh with a fringe?" was Bal's curt response. She slept at her older brother's house for a week to keep out of her Dad's way, specifically out of the way of the beating he would have given her.

Thursday is programme change day at the cinema. I'm heading along Argyle Street towards Renfield Street, stopping at Tesco metro to buy luxury eat-out-of-the-pot fruit salad, a bag of cashew nuts and a raspberry fruit crush. It's a quarter to six, so if I hurry I should be able to watch two films before bedtime. And I won't have to worry about my English accent, sitting quietly in the dark.

Balvinder

The evening shift brings Bernie the senior midwife on duty. She's nothing like Bernard Matthews or Bernard

Manning. Bernadette McGinty has got some definite ideas about breast-feeding. I'm trying to explain that I'm not really a fit mother but I'm silenced when she pinches my left nipple between her fingers and shoves it in the baby's mouth. Baby sensibly keeps her eyes shut and is reluctant to suck. So Bernie shoves the nipple in again.

"You've got some neck!" I finally manage.

"You've a wee baby who needs to put on weight fast," she replies, keeping the baby's head pushed to my boob.

The only safe place to look is out the window. After a couple of minutes, the baby is sucking hard. Bernie backs off. But she's still talking.

"You need to keep that baby wrapped up properly. She's only at thirty-five degrees. She needs to be swaddled whenever you're not holding her."

Bloody cheek. I want to tell the interfering cow that it was Janine that dressed the baby this morning, not me. But the baby has just fallen off my tit and Bernie is busy getting her on again. And the tea lady said I'd done really well to give birth to such a lovely baby. The baby gets sucking again and Bernie goes off to harass a new arrival.

I pull the sheet up to my neck and over the baby's head. I wish I could reach my dupatta. Peeking under the sheet, I watch the baby feed. She's got a big load of my boob sucked into her mouth, not just the nipple. Her wee mouth is stretched wide to make a seal. With her eyes shut and her furry hair she reminds me of pictures of baby rats from a biology lesson. But cuter.

She runs out of energy and lays in a wee dwam with milky stuff leaking out of her mouth. I feel quite chuffed. Fancy me making her look so dreamy. Her mouth twitches into a smile then fades. My face is grinning like a soppy twat, so I scowl quick in case Bernie notices. I fall asleep with the baby rat snuggled up, waking up through the night to repeat our new feeding trick.

Maya

Maya emerges from the cinema after watching the only two films that she hadn't already seen; an action movie featuring helicopter chases, and a cheesy chick flick where high school girls find true love despite the grave disability of being cleverer than the available men. She feels unsatisfied and slightly nauseated, as though she'd binged on too many sweeties. And the question of what to do tomorrow night, now that she's seen every film being screened, is preoccupying her. Maureen Oshanti, her London bosom-buddy, who phones her every Sunday night, had told her to join an evening class.

"That's what lonely spinsters do, Maya. That's what adult education classes are for."

"Reenie, evening classes are full of housewives looking for the mental stimulation that they used to get at work. I need the stimulation that I'm **not** getting at work. I won't find friends, just babysitting work," Maya had protested. "And," she had added to anticipate Maureen's next suggestion, "I don't like kids much."

Maureen remembered their attempts to learn Spanish and Arabic before a gap-year world-trip and had admitted defeat on this, but decided that Maya should take up a sport instead.

"You need a team sport to make friends. How about football?"

"I've no co-ordination Reenie," pointed out Maya.

"True. Carpet bowls? Orienteering?"

Maya opens the door of her flat, to be greeted by stale air. The dismal loneliness of her existence bears down on her. A letter lying on the hall floor, written in her mother's showy copperplate, exacerbates her feeling of failure. She steps over it to make a hot water bottle and mug of Horlicks to take to bed.

Sitting under the duvet and sipping the drink that her grandmother used to make her when she couldn't sleep, Maya feels that she does indeed have all the trappings of a lonely spinster. Her feet edge the hot water bottle into a comfier position and she resolves that tomorrow she will develop a proper social life.

Heather

At half past six the train comes to a halt in Glasgow Central station. Heather packs up around the children, putting off waking them until the last minute. And suddenly, there's Doug taking up too much room in the skinny compartment, scooping up both children and the rucksack, leaving

16

Heather with only her money belt to carry to the car. The children cover Doug in kisses and eventually, when they're at home and installed in front of their favourite Morph video ("as amusing as plasticene can get", a babysitter had dryly remarked), Heather is able to get close enough to kiss him. Mucous-membrane contact restored, she starts to tell him all the significant kiddie-doings that he has missed while she and the children have been in France. The baby's first attempts to walk, and which lullaby she favours. The child's ability to order strawberry ice-cream in French and pride at having wiped her own bottom. Only Doug could really share the true delight in these pieces of micro-news.

Heather's late arrival to the all-encompassing experience of motherhood meant that she had witnessed her child-bearing colleagues losing the ability to speak about anything but their offspring. When she found herself pregnant in middle age, she had vowed to keep talk of her children to a minimum in her professional world and to discuss the details of her daughters' staggering achievements only with her co-parent and the grandparents. When first married, Heather had told herself that the desire for children was simply narcissism. Every time the news reported a meteorological disaster, famine or armed conflict, she congratulated herself on avoiding bringing new people into the world. Passing the age of thirty and having achieved success in her work, Heather found herself using her contraceptive cap rather less carefully than before. During a stay at the Lochalsh Hotel to celebrate their wedding anniversary, Doug noticed that she'd left the cap at home altogether. During the subsequent discussion (over an excellent joint of local lamb), Heather realised that she did, after all, want to be pregnant. She wasn't sure if she wanted children, but to experience pregnancy had become a priority. After another few years, during which they had ruled out IVF, two pregnancies had happened, one very soon after the other. And Heather had been plunged into the world of her children. She wondered why had no-one told her about the excellence of children as a post-work relaxation regimen? Better than squash, massage or hill-walking because the insistent and short-term nature of their demands pushed all else aside.

The debriefing with Doug comes to a close with the arrival of number one daughter in the kitchen.

"I'm ravishing Dad" she announces.

"You are, my petal" he agrees. "The prettiest princess."

"No, Dad," she shakes her head impatiently. "Ravishing hungry."

After two mugs of milky coffee, some of Doug's speciality fried eggy-bread-and-jam sandwiches, and a careful inspection and watering of her window boxes, Heather's fatigue begins to descend. The baby is asleep in her cot and Doug has taken his other daughter to the playpark. Heather can see the tops of the swings where they were headed out of the bedroom window. Their third floor flat is level with the tops of the Chestnut trees that line the park that they overlook and the candles are just coming out.

The big bed, that often accommodated all four of them, is in a pool of morning sunshine. But before folding herself under the duvet, Heather can't resist looking through the pile of mail awaiting her, stacked on the tall boy in the hall. Ignoring all the official correspondence, she finds three hand-addressed envelopes. The biggest envelope contains an invitation from Annie, a school friend, to attend her wedding reception in the Braidhead Hotel, Queensferry. Heather loves any excuse to go east and an opportunity to see what her contemporaries have done with their lives is not to be missed. But she probably ought to visit her parents too. The re-used envelope is a round-robin from her brother who lives out an alternative lifestyle in the Findhorn Foundation. And the third is a summons to a board meeting of the Shakti family centre. Heather feels cheated by this third missive; although addressed by hand, it is really a work letter. It should have been sent to her University address and she should not have had to think about it until tomorrow. Heather has long adopted a strict work-hygiene practice as resistance against the long-hours culture of her University. She avoids letting work leak into the evenings or week-ends as far as possible. Now that she is head of department and the youngest female professor in the University, she feels a duty to set an example. When she leaves the department at the same time as the administration staff in the evenings, some lecturer invariably

"jokes" about it being "alright for some to knock off early".
Before the children, she had felt steadfast in her sense that it
was right to resist the competitive exhaustion that academics
seem to relish. Now it felt harder to maintain. Just by having
children she was letting the side down, demonstrating a lack
of loyalty and dedication. She didn't feel the same sense of
guilt about time out to care for her elderly parents, since this
duty seemed inevitable and not a flippant lifestyle choice like
childbearing.

Heather shoves the Shakti letter into her briefcase and
takes her brother's epistle to the bedroom. Reading the news-
letter in bed affords some guffaws at her brother's wide-eyed
account of the joys of therapeutic clay gargoyle-throwing,
macrobiotic nursery snacks and the spirituality of genital
massage in the communal sweat tent.

Balvinder

With the morning tea delivery comes the menu-selection
card. The tea lady asks if I want halal meals again? I can't
answer. The lamb curry I ate yesterday was Muslim food. No
time to explain the difference between Sikh and Muslim ideas
about meat as she burbles on.

"I ticked it for you yesterday sweet-heart, because you were
asleep yourself. And you need to eat after what you've been
through. And I know you like your curries because my sister
is married to one of your sort. Lovely lad is our Hamza. So
polite."

Getting no response, she hands me the menu card where
the options are: "hot meal of the day"; "salad of the day";
"vegetarian meal of the day"; "halal dinner"; "kosher dinner".

"What's the vegetarian dinner?" I ask.

"Usually it's like the ham salad but with egg or cheddar
instead."

Limp lettuce with plastic, dayglo orange cheese or halal
meat? It's too hard. I can't make my mind up. Sikhs never,
ever eat halal food. Well, according to Ma and the aunties
they don't. They say it's against our religion. But then drinking is against our religion too. But it doesn't stop the uncles
getting steaming on Tennants and Teacher's.

The tea lady is coming back round to pick up the menu

cards. I can't face salad. But I can't eat halal either so I tick the kosher box. I expect the tea lady to accuse me of fraud – being both a Muslim and a Jew. But instead she congratulates me.

"Aye, they Jewish meals are even nicer than the curries, hen. We staff aren't allowed the curries or the koshers for our meals any more. Manager says they cost the hospital three times the ordinary meals we produce in the kitchen. They're vacuum packed see, bought in from restaurants. One of the chefs is away on his halal training the now."

She takes the menu card away and with a cheery sashay of her hips moves back to her trolley.

"There's an upside to being a darkie eh! At least until that chef finishes his training," she calls as she moves out of earshot.

Stupid honky. It's all upside as far as food is concerned.

Perhaps it's less bad for a Sikh to eat kosher than to eat halal? What would my Ma say? Or my auntie Harjeet? I've no idea what Jewish folk eat. There was a Jewish lad in our primary school. We only knew because he was excused morning assembly, unlike us Asian kids. He never got any grief for being Jewish, despite being a speccy geek-type. The Catholics and Protestants were always too busy hammering each other to bother anyone else.

Still thinking up a razor-sharp come-back to shout up the ward at the tea-lady, when the rat sneezes. Her face screws up then a tiny mini-achoo comes out and she opens her eyes and looks amazed at herself. I laugh aloud. Fancy her being able to sneeze already. Her eyes gaze about. They aren't blue. But they're not brown either. Sort of milky mud colour.

"That baby will go right off your milk if you eat any more curry," Julie-Ann is squeaking at me across the aisle. "Then you'll be on bottles like the rest of us."

Silly bisum! How does she think babies manage in India? Julie-Ann's mother pronounced breast-feeding to be "a piece of nonsense" and proved herself to be a match for Bernie. Julie-Ann's daughter only weighs 3lbs – a "Superkings" baby. Her premmie baby clothes are tiny. Julie-Ann's mother thinks my six pounder looks like a sumo wrestler – not altogether feminine.

Oh how I wish my Ma was bustling down the ward

delivering a tiffin tin. Like all my aunties got when they delivered their butter-ball babies.

Maya

Reaching her desk before Mrs Kapadia gets to work, Maya considers her jobs for the day, most of which amount to telephoning strangers to try to convince them to meet her in person, to give her an opportunity to persuade them to give her money. As happens every morning, unless Balvinder is there to distract her, Maya is confronted with her utter unsuitability for her job. She was not the first-choice candidate, feels hurt by this knowledge and blames her mother for the hurt. Given her lack of experience in fund-raising or project management, Maya imagines she was short-listed for the job because according to her application form, she could have been properly Asian. Maya curses her mother's hedonistic search for exotic authenticity that led to her birth on Indian soil. But she can't blame her dear devoted grandparents for their surname. Paul could be an ordinary enough WASP name. If it wasn't combined with Maya. But despite her name and birthplace, Maya Paul has never been Asian enough. Her mother has always been disappointed that Maya didn't inherit the smooth black hair, and Moghul profile of the tabla player who was her father.

Maya fingers a garnet-studded locket around her neck and re-focuses briefly on the list of names dictated by Mrs Kapadia yesterday: Mr Karogi, travel agent 945 6736; Mr Bashir, MP 445 9865; Mrs Imran, diplomat's wife 227 4515; Mrs Jacob, business man's daughter, married to a minister 357 3969. Maya met the other two candidates for her job at the interview, both graduates like her and much more properly Asian than her; one from Birmingham and one from Bradford. So properly Asian in fact that when they were offered the job, their families intervened to prevent an acceptance. And so Maya, the third choice candidate had got it.

Maya chews the chain that holds the locket round her neck. Her grandmother had given it to her the last time she had visited her in Leamington Spa. The lumpy unattractive locket contains a lock of Hilary's baby hair, which Maya finds rather yucky. But she values the necklace because it only left her grandmother's neck when sea-bathing during their annual holiday to Hunstanton, when it was carefully placed inside her spectacles case.

Sighing and letting go of the locket, Maya grasps the telephone and, trying to summon up the understated calm of her late grandmother, steels herself to dial the first number on the list. Her morning is to be spent talking to people whom Mrs Kapadia thought she knew about a project that no-one has yet defined. Maya knows she is a useless fund-raiser. She tries not to feel apologetic since the job description had not mentioned this type of work when she applied. Only after a fortnight of working at Shakti, did it became apparent that Mrs Kapadia's ideas about what Maya should be doing differed from what had been discussed at interview. Referring to her job description does not help since Mrs Kapadia is not used to being gainsaid. And Maya knows, from listening to Mrs Kapadia's feisty discussions with the board of managers, that she can justify anything with reference to the Shakti family centre's mission statement: "To improve the transferable skills, social networks and quality of life of women, and their families, who could suffer from racism." Maya takes a breath and starts on a familiar script.

"Hello Mr Karogi? ... I'm calling on behalf of the Shakti family centre, managed by Mrs Kapadia, who sends you and your wife her very best wishes ... Yes, she returns your greetings ... I wonder if I could tell you about some of the work that we're doing here? ... It'll only take a couple of minutes."

Heather

Heather starts the transformation from mother to professor. After a month of clothes that could absorb mashed banana and yoghurt, she steps into a dry-clean only wool skirt, white T-shirt and tweed jacket. A squirt of "eau dynamism" and an application of "old rose" lipstick complete her costume. The children are in the kitchen with Doug, getting to grips with baked beans, sausages and mushrooms. Heather avoids their stickier extremities as she kisses them good-bye. As she's putting on her coat, Doug calls through from the kitchen.

"Mr Cromarty phoned last week. Wanted to know whether

you'd be going across to a preview night of some play. You'd better phone them today."

Heather's heart sinks slightly with the return of mild guilt about her parents, from which she had slipped free while on holiday. She had gone to France by train partly to make sure she couldn't be easily recalled should her father develop pneumonia. Air travel with her children was always ghastly anyway. She found it too easy to imagine the horrible details of air traffic accidents whenever she flew with the kids. She suppresses a groan to save Doug from hearing it. The joyless duty that binds Heather to her parents is quite unlike what keeps Doug's family together – alcohol and fried food he says. Although they hurl top volume dog's abuse at one another periodically, Doug's family don't harbour their resentments, whereas Heather's family is all about avoiding difficult topics. Doug keeps himself removed from Heather's parents by maintaining the language of respect that he had needed as a teenager with no prospects when courting Heather. He has never addressed his in-laws by their first names, even when invited to do so by Heather's father. Since Doug's status has not improved much since those courtship days, he continues to treat Heather's parents as his seniors.

"OK love. Thanks for not telling me last night." Heather unlocks the front door and puts her keys in her coat pocket.

"And I'm at the climbing wall tonight. So you'll get the weans?"

"Aye. No bother. Cheerio."

Half an hour later, Heather enjoys the heavy clunk as her office door closes behind her. Getting out her almond crois-sant and takeaway latte, bought to counter the shock of returning to work, she starts up her computer. A quick scan down the list of 400 e-mails that have accumulated in her absence to pick out the friendly or interesting ones. Once she's worked through those, it's on to the post and now a reply to the Shakti letter in her brief case becomes unavoid-able. She thinks about asking the department secretary to do it, but she's only putting off what should be a quick job.

Dear Mrs Kapadia
Board of management meeting, 23rd April

I am pleased to accept your kind invitation to chair the above meeting. Thank-you for giving me adequate notice. Perhaps we could meet beforehand in order to agree an agenda? I would be pleased to come to the Shakti office on 14th April at 3pm.

Yours sincerely, Heather Cromarty

At ten o'clock she props the door open to make herself available to passers-by in the hopes that she won't lose touch with the students. The current buzz is about plans to sell the crumbly old building that houses the students' union to developers as a means of reducing the University's deficit. Heather has promised the Student-staff Liason Committee that she will draft a letter of protest to the Vice Chancellor's office. But first, a more urgent letter needs to be written. Heather reaches for the Basildon Bond writing pad, kept especially for the task, and unscrews the cap of her favourite fountain pen to update her parents on the aspects of her holiday that they will consider of note and excusing herself from the preview night at the theatre.

Balvinder

They've noticed that I haven't yet had a visitor. Janine offers to wheel the telephone to my bedside. She suggests the drain bottle attached to my scar is perhaps stopping me from getting to it? She's right. I do feel a right plonker carrying the glass jar along the corridor, showing off my pee and my pus to everyone. It's bad enough when the midwives swill the bottle's contents and discuss whether enough liquid has dripped out of me yet. And I don't like to leave the baby alone in her fish-tank cot. Someone might steal her. Come to think of it, that would solve a lot of problems. Worse, someone might swap their bald, lardy baby for my pretty little rat.

But the problem isn't that I can't get myself to the phone. The problem is who could I call? No-one knows I'm here. Ma thinks I'm visiting cousin Kamaljit in London. Kam has promised to phone my folks to cover for me, but she thinks that I've gone camping with a boyfriend. She made me promise to "be careful" and asked whether he was Sikh. I told her he was white. "Ah well. Could be worse!" she replied, sighing.

24

How much longer before they kick me out of here? And will they make me take the wee rat with me? Janine says her eye colour won't come out for another three weeks.

Maya

Another day of fund-raising and being mocked by Mrs Kapadia. Maya has failed in so many ways. She's not authentically Asian enough for the board and not frivolous enough for Mrs Kapadia.

The Kapadia family money comes from cash-and-carry warehouses that supply the corner stores of the central belt of Scotland. Mrs Kapadia does not work at Shakti for the financial recompense, indeed she does not claim her salary as director. She wanted the position because she felt that it might justify her socialising and networking and, since her boys have left home and are not yet ready to marry, she has time. The sons mock her little tea parties and constantly up-to-date knowledge of the latest marriages and separations of people and businesses. Mrs Kapadia knows that women's problems in the Asian so-called community need to be presented by a very respectable spokeswoman. And she feels she more or less fits the bill. Any lack of orthodoxy in her behaviour is compensated for by enormous wealth and her husband's global family business, with holdings in Canada, Hong Kong, Tanzania and Mauritius.

Mrs Kapadia would have liked Maya to be her companion on a round of meetings and launches where she talks up the cause in the families where she wields influence. The cause of Asian women does not easily excite interest in wealthy social circles in Scotland and Maya has no personal contacts among the powerful or rich to exploit.

Mrs Kapadia, with the support of the board of managers, had obtained start up money for Shakti from the Lottery fund. This had been used to locate and rent the Shakti premises and make the initial appointments, on the understanding that local statutory welfare service providers would meet the running costs of the family centre. Just before Maya had arrived, social work withdrew the promised funding as a result of their own budget being slashed. So Maya became the only employee of Shakti (apart from Shuggie the caretaker), and

25

there was no money for the planned crèche, multi-lingual library, or internet café. Mrs Kapadia had persuaded the board that, following a business model, they should use the salaried member of staff to generate the short-fall in cash so as to run all the projects they had been planning. Maya had arrived in Glasgow, prepared to get a group of pre-school children and their mothers involved in painting murals and making mosaics in the outdoor play area, and expecting others to establish a crèche, English-language class, drama group and writing co-operative. It was disappointing to learn that Shakti had, in effect, been reduced to whatever she and Mrs Kapadia could make of it. Only her mother's delight, should she return to London, keeps her in Glasgow.

Today Maya works on past five, causing Mrs Kapadia to comment that probably Maya has no-one to go home to.

"Perhaps I should introduce you to some nice young men, Maya? Oh no, but you can't cook roti can you?" Mrs Kapadia quips, raising a smile of amusement from the volunteer ladies staffing reception.

"Mr Macdonald won't be pleased if you're in here late," she continues more quietly for Maya's hearing only. "Don't upset him, otherwise we'll even be clearing up after ourselves."

Later, when Shuggie does his evening round locking the windows, he tells Maya to bring him the outer door key to the pub opposite, whenever she leaves.

"No bother. I'll be there until eleven tonight, anyroad."

Alone in the building, Maya wonders what to do until eight o'clock when the dancing class that she's dared herself to attend begins. She thinks about going home to eat, but knows that once she reaches the refuge of her little flat she won't have the courage to re-emerge. She had made a deal with herself, using her grandmother's methods of persuasion: she will attend one session of the Clydeside country dancing club and, as a reward, she will allow herself the luxury of buying a copy of Vogue tomorrow. She isn't prepared to think about whether she'll go to a second class the following week just yet.

Maya settles down at the keyboard to eat her banana and oatcake supper while catching up on recreational e-mails. She doesn't dare write to Maureen Oshanti between nine and five since Mrs Kapadia would not hesitate to come up behind her and read her screen. Open plan offices as social control. According to Shuggie, managers in a local firm had the employees' e-mails screened for mention of their own names. Three people passing derogatory comments had been sacked. Maya feels acutely aware of the message she'd sent to Maureen several days ago which referred to "Mrs K my over-bearing witch of a boss". To be found to have insulted her would have left Mrs Kapadia victorious and affirmed in her assumption that Maya did not have the wit or breeding to cut it as a serious player. Deleting messages didn't remove them from the hard-drive and Maya had no doubt that if it suited Mrs Kapadia's purposes, she could get incriminating material fished out of the digital dustbin.

Maya has a message from Reenie@conde-naste.com in her mail box. Wishing to prolong the pleasurable anticipation of words from her best mate, Maya goes to make a cup of tea. From the week they both started at St. Mildred's middle school, Reenie and Maya's friendship was marked by their names being run together as Maya'n'Reenie which rapidly became pronouned Maiareeni and which they adopted as their joint name whenever they met someone they didn't trust. Maya's mother Hilary loved Maureen since she was black and therefore utterly authentic, but also middle class, the daughter of two doctors, so Hilary didn't have to make any concessions. Maureen's parents' on-call rotas meant that she spent a lot of time at Maya's house. It was during the fifth form when they were meant to be studying for exams that Maureen began to disentangle herself from the double-persona Maiareeni and formulate her future in fashion journalism.

Maya's mother never bought any other periodical or newspaper, but however little money they had, she always bought Vogue. Maya had frequently resented Hilary's refusal to sacrifice her own luxury-reading, but developed the habit of reading it nonetheless. And Maureen picked up the habit too. She loved the glossy inconsequence of Vogue's vision of the world and she decided to join it. She visited the Conde Nast offices and showed the deputy editor a selection of her writing, some published in the school magazine, and explained that British Vogue desperately needed a black face to retain credibility.

Maureen had sharp good looks reminiscent of a young Grace Jones. She also wrote in succinct, punchy, well-constructed and punctuated sentences.

The Vogue deputy editor was about to go off on maternity leave and needed someone to sort out her bookshelves and filing cabinet to make room for her temporary replacement. She said Maureen could undertake this labour, unpaid, for a fortnight, as work experience. And this was an enormous privilege since, it was explained, this golden opportunity was usually only offered to the finalists of Vogue's annual writing competition. Maureen accepted, without telling her parents and after a fortnight the deputy had gone off for an elective Caesarean – too frightened and too posh to push. Maureen survived another month, still unpaid, by making her knowledge of the office workings (coffee and herbal infusion rota, smokers' rooms, length of lunchbreak acceptable on a Friday etc), available to the maternity cover deputy editor.

By now Maureen was attending the meetings where writing was distributed among the staffers. Hesitation from anyone to volunteer to write two hundred words publicising a novel on ecological themes by a former popstar, gave Maureen her chance. Her first published copy appeared on page 159 of Vogue six weeks later accompanied by much celebration from Hilary and Maya. When Maureen was offered a small wage, she faced her parents' displeasure and told them of her embryonic career. Although her parents had hoped that she would follow them into medicine they didn't prevent Maureen from pursuing the Vogue job. Her ability to gain top grades in all her school subjects made medicine a possibility that she could return to and they hoped journalism would be a passing phase.

During Maureen's initial months as the office junior she learned to dress like a Vogue-girl. This involved wearing a single outstanding piece set off by a lot of black. The piece might be a pair of jeans, a skirt or a shirt recently released by a reputable designer and not yet written up in the fashion press. Once copies of the piece were appearing in Top Shop, the Vogue-girl's original must be discarded for the next new thing. To Maya, these clothes looked unremarkable, if well cut, but then she had not doggedly acquired the syntax of fashion like her friend.

As part of solidifying her decision to attend the beginners' dance lesson, Maya had telephoned Maureen to ask her to supply a suitable outfit. She missed being dressed by Maureen. In London they had always enjoyed the dressing up as much as the subsequent going out. In Maureen's hands, Maya's deep-brown eyes, bright-red hair and Rajasthani warrior-nose looked like a fantastic exotic mix, rather than the peculiar inheritance from her mother's sex tourism. It was something to do with the confidence with which Maureen put together outfits and applied make-up. Usually reticent, stepping out with Maureen, as Maiareeni, Maya enjoyed the head-turning effect that they had together. Linen-clad advertising men who had drunk too much tequila frequently offered to cast the girls in their next shoot.

E-mail from Maureen

Dear Doll-face
I fed-exed up a frock for your dancing class. Should look fantastic. So now all you need to do is learn to dance. And get a new job by the sound of it. Why can't you tell your boss to phone her own cronies if she wants money off them? Because you're too timid I guess. So why not look for the money from elsewhere? There must be some council fund or charity or EU money that would allow you to get on with your worthy work?
XXXXX Reenie

Maya smiles. Maureen assumes that since Maya's work is altruistic, someone must be prepared to pay for it. But persuading people to give over their cash for fashion products must be easier than fund-raising for constructive work with marginalised communities. The transaction is cut-and-dried when you buy a magazine or a frock. You don't expect anything else. Just the product. All the people that Maya phones will donate only if there is little risk attached to their reputation and plenty of attendant glory.

The frock that Maureen sent hasn't arrived yet. So Maya would be wearing her denim skirt and Blundstone boots, chosen to help their wearer to blend in rather than stand out.

With another two hours until the lesson starts, Maya decides she might as well do some searching for suitable funding bodies. Her efforts in phoning round for funding have raised barely enough to cover the rent for two months. And the idea of applying for money from an impersonal, faceless bureaucracy appeals. She has had enough of failing to appreciate the delicate tangled social networks of patronage, the complexity of what could not be mentioned to whom, in which Mrs Kapadia is constantly coaching her, but with no hope of success. At least the lottery fund or a charity would simply turn down her request, rather than wanting to know the religious mix of potential project users. Wouldn't they?

Balvinder

I'm still in the hospital gown and using up the ward's supply of sanitary towels and nappies. The midwives must feel dead sorry for me since they haven't told me off yet, unlike Mrs Iqbal in the next bed. She's been chided for having too many visitors, some of them even – shock horror – outside visiting hours! Having too much family is obviously more annoying than having none. Yesterday, Mrs Iqbal's seven year old daughter stayed sitting with her mum, on her bed, gazing at her new sibling when the Dad went to fetch an auntie. At least Janine didn't nip Mrs Iqbal's head while he was away out. But as soon as he got back, she set about him. Neither of the adult Iqbals understand, much English, which left their wee lassie translating Janine's criticism of their irresponsible behaviour for her parents. The daughter's Punjabi version of "What if Mrs Iqbal had been rushed off to theatre with post-partum haemorrhaging? Who would have looked after your daughter?" was pretty approximate. And it certainly didn't stop the Iqbals from pulling the same stunt again today. Later, over the drugs trolley Janine was complaining to another nurse-type.

"These people don't take proper care of their girl babies." Then she caught my eye and smiled sheepishly. I tried to look dignified.

What would she know? My baby rat is no more of a problem because she's a girl. She'd be one hundred per cent problem if she was a laddie too. Ma always calls Jasvinder,

Harminder and me her pearls and rubies. That's why she has to protect us.

The tea trolley swings into view with its load of tepid tannic brew. It could do with some adrak and laichee to liven it up. But at least there's a plate of kitkats. It's worrying how excited I am by a chocolate-flavour-covered waver. Maya would tell me off for eating a nestlé product. But it's either that, or stealing Mrs Iqbal's Quality Street once the lights go out tonight. And I would, even though they're out-of-date stock from her uncle's shop, if it wasn't for my tubes. I'm hungry all the time. I go to sleep thinking about Ma's mukki ki roti, served with saag and loads of butter.

Maya

"Now, if you have only been coming to these sessions for a couple of months, please sit down, and we'll begin our inter-mediate class. So for the advanced group only, the Tobermory eights and reel written especially for us by our lovely band leader – Hamish."

Applause and stamping break out around the room. The compact dance teacher motions for silence and everyone quietens for her next announcement. As she draws breath to continue with the lesson a voice pierces the low chat of the dancers with a nasally exaggerated highland accent.

"He's a lovely tune-smith but he cannae hold a note! Is that no right Hamish?"

Hamish who is sitting on a stool, holding his accordion turned towards the voice coming from near to Maya, on the PVC-covered banquette that runs around the perimeter of the room. Hamish's face remains impassive as he replies to the heckler.

"Aye, but I'd rather be a tuneless teuchter than a dancing Paki."

Maya slides down on the seat a little, bracing herself for further hostilities. Everything had just got OK. She'd borne the acute awkwardness of arriving at the lesson knowing no-one. Having been one of the first to arrive she had sat at a sticky table and tried to read her newspaper. Mostly she'd just felt relieved. When she had taken the Shakti-building key to Shuggie in the pub he'd told her to "Watch yourself down by

31

the docks hen." She'd only located the little building between
a car salesroom and sheet metal rolling premises because
she'd followed a woman with floaty hair who looked like a
dancer. As the woman was unlocking the security door, Maya
had admired the reflection of the sun on the river as it sank
towards the water.

As she had opened the inner door, floaty-hair told Maya she
was the teacher and explained that the building was so
unprepossessing because it was all that remained of a tenement that had been knocked down. The landlord hadn't
wanted to move when the tenements were being cleared.
Since he owned the place the demolition workers knocked
everything down around him and for thirty years people
bussed back in from the outlying schemes where they'd been
re-housed to drink where they'd always drunk. Once inside
the teacher went to get ready at the back of a long dark room.
The only natural light came from three frosted windows
above head height.

After ten minutes the fluorescent light had come on behind
the curly wrought iron that fenced off the bar in the corner.
Other people had started arriving and buying drinks and
Maya armed herself with a glass of wine. It came out of the
brown screw-top five litre bottle and tasted oily.

As the dance class had started, the thirty-odd people who
had gathered were instructed to change their dance partner
every ten minutes or so, and it became clear that there were
plenty of other absolute beginners. The teacher, who introduced herself as "Flora, and yes my surname is Macdonald,"
had talked them through the dashing white sergeants, strip
the willow, and the gay Gordons. For each dance they had
walked through it once, then danced through it with the
band stopping intermittently for the teacher to correct those
who had got lost and finally, once through without stopping.
As she had circled round the class Maya felt as though she was
meeting a parade of people even less suited to dancing than
her, which was comforting, but surprising given her own
clumsiness. One man was so nervous that his earlobes were
dripping sweat, another could not make eye contact and
another, initially chatty, then got the impression that Maya
might be a feminist, and could no longer speak to her. Maya

had danced with a brusque woman who said she was fed up with short incompetent men, so had decided to dance as a man herself. And a plastic surgeon who found every mistake that he made a tremendous joke and who had Maya snorting at the absurdity of their joint lack of co-ordination.

But now, suddenly it seems she's misunderstood the gentle pleasure of trying to step, jump and turn in time to music played on the accordion, penny whistle and snare drum. Maya looks at Flora, expecting some kind of reaction, but her creamy complexion is relaxed. She smooths her crushed-velvet bias cut skirt over her thighs and continues with the lesson.

"Thank-you gentlemen. Enough boys' banter. We'll start. Take your partners please. Jonty, could you and Jenny now demonstrate the turning pass and the pas de pas?"

The heckler chuckles as he calls "On yourself Hamish" and turns towards Maya on his way to the bar in the corner. Her face must reflect her alarm at the repartee, since Hamish's abuser reassures her on the way past.

"It's alright. I'm just kidding him on. Can I get you a beer?"

"Oh. Sorry. Thank-you. No." Maya's mortification makes her armpits sweat.

"Och go on. Just a wee swalley."

"OK then. Can I have a pint of bitter please?" Maya asks, since she certainly doesn't want any more oily anti-freeze wine.

"They'll only have seventy or eighty shilling here. So we'll have none of your real ale nonsense."

"Sorry." Maya was embarrassed to find herself apologising again. "Either is fine. I mean lovely."

When the heckler returns from the bar Maya's hot embarrassment had passed and she realises that she is probably only as red faced as all the other sweaty dancers.

"It's close in here isn't it?" she comments as she sips carefully on her treacley pint of eighty shilling.

"Have you had a skinfull already?" asks the Heckler.

"Sorry?"

"Have you drank too much?" he explains.

"No, I just get hot easily. Sorry" says Maya flushing crimson again.

"You're right. It is stuffy. The class used to be in the old Palace dance hall. More air there. High ceilings. It had a sprung floor and an orchestra pit. But it got closed down after a fire. Insurance job. This place is pretty pish-poor by comparison. My knees always hurt from dancing on they concrete floors."

"Is that why you're sitting this one out?" asks Maya.

"Aye. I know this dance already," says the Heckler.

"But I thought it was just written especially," says Maya, surprised.

"It was, but eight year ago now. Her up there," he indicates Flora the teacher "she always goes on about Hamish writing it. She thinks it adds class to the proceedings." A pause as the Heckler drinks his beer. "Did you really think I was going to have a square go at him?" he asks pointing his thumb towards Hamish. Maya nods and tries not to start blushing again as the Heckler chuckles to himself. "You've not much faith in humanity have you?" he says more soberly, once his mirth had passed.

They sit next to one another drinking their pints. People have been arriving through out the evening, and the room is now packed with eighty or so bodies. The Heckler exchanges insults with various passing dancers and gives Maya a guided tour of the idiosyncrasies of the regulars. There is Richie, an excellent dancer who made all his partners look fantastic. He uses the dance class as a dating service, and the Heckler points out three women on the floor that he has previously courted. Richie's attention is currently focussed on a woman described by the heckler as "yon dainty lassie" whose previous experience of dance must have been ballet judging by her poker-rigid posture and pointy-pointy toes. And there is Birgit, married to an expert on sea-loch salmon farming of international renown, who spends a lot of time away up the west coast. Birgit's flat is where parties always end up and is where, in the roof-top hot tub, Richie was discovered snogging Bryan. Bryan is not, to Maya's eye, an elegant dancer, but thoroughly competent. He was one of the original eight people who had come to the first ever lesson of the Clydeside Country dancing club ten years earlier.

"And I'm Shiv" says the Heckler when he's run out of other people to describe.

"Have you been here from the start?" asks Maya.

34

"No, I was still in short trousers then. I started about four year ago" says Shiv.

"What made you start?" enquires Maya, hoping he won't return the question.

"To win an argument," replies Shiv. "A fool of a man at my work fancied himself a bit of an expert on India. He'd been trekking in the Himalayas a couple of times and picked up a bit of Hindustani. Reckoned that he understood anyone with a dusky complexion. Kept wanting to talk about Ayurvedic thought and how to cook an authentic curry. So I told him that I only ate tatties, neeps and haggis and my hobbies were Highland dancing and caber-tossing. And then since I'd made the claim I thought I'd try it out. Well the dancing and the haggis anyway. Haggis goes very nicely with a chana dahl. And I'm a natural at the dancing. If I say so myself. I'll show you if you like."

Shiv pulls Maya up to her feet and they find an empty patch of floor in front of the bar. The class was learning an elaborate version of the "Canadian Barn dance", while Shiv walks Maya gently through the basic version.

Balvinder

"No, no, no Ma. No! Don't!"

It's my own voice, shouting that wakes me. And another noise. A baby crying. And the night shift woman who is shaking my shoulder.

"You're having a bad dream love. Wake up and feed your baby."

I try to pull the baby past my catheter tube across the bed. That wakes me up alright. And then I realise that Ma doesn't know anything yet. She just thinks I'm a slightly wild, spoilt daughter. How am I going to tell her? Will I have to tell her? Will I become one of those outcast girls, who have gone too far, not even mentioned in the gossip? What to do?

Heather

Brightness bathes Heather as she pushes her offspring across Queen's Park to Noah's Boat Day Nursery. The sunlight seems to un-scrumple the sleep-deprivation wrinkles around her eyes a little. The baby's routine of dawn defecation, followed by an hour of gurgley singing takes its toll. She muses on the sagacity of taking her perfect babies to a nursery named for an apocalyptic survivor as they approach the windows painted as an underwater scene.

Comfortingly, her daughter barely finds time to kiss her goodbye as she rushes off to the messy-play corner. And a fish mobile immediately takes the baby's attention. Heather finds it remarkably easy to put her children out of her mind as the rituals of the working day follow one from the other. Buy two papers, one Scottish and one written from London. Read front page while waiting for the train. Get through the headline news before alighting in town. Pick up fruit and sandwich en route to the office. In the building lobby, dodge the crowd of undergraduates massing for a 9 o'clock electronics lecture. Take lift to 17th floor, unlock office, fill coffee machine, switch on computer. Deal with e-mails, then try to ignore any new arrivals. One super-efficient colleague never opened up her e-mail until the end of the day, but Heather's control isn't quite so steely. What if there's a lovely message embedded in the dross? An invitation to speak in Florence or Hawaii? The award of a book contract or research grant? News from a favourite former student? No such excitements today. Just the usual agendas and minutes from committees, requests for help from students up against submission deadlines, adverts for cheap inkjet cartridges and correspondence about reviewing journal papers.

Heather settles down for a day of steadily working through her list of administrative and teaching tasks in their order of urgency. Providing not too many people arrive at her door she would clear her "to do" task today and be ready to write two lectures tomorrow, deliver one the following day and then make a start on revising her book proofs. Progress on the proofs would be held up by the Shakti board meeting. The last meeting had been tense as differences in the priorities for the centre emerged among the staff and the management board. Mrs Kapadia had won the day, since there wasn't an alternative plan being put forward. Heather reminds herself that if she can manage to keep a group of University lecturers behaving like a more or less united Department despite their divergent goals and ambitions (or lack of them), a family centre, albeit with a formidable director, should be no problem.

The only job to which Heather cannot allocate a priority rating is calling on her parents. It's both urgent and easy to postpone. Heather assures herself that she cannot possibly visit them until the proofs and the board meeting are done. Thankfully their sense of time is pretty hazy at present. And even if they had noticed how long had elapsed since her last visit, they would be too polite to mention it. Calling on her parents is the one area of domestic life that she cannot delegate to Doug.

Balvinder

Crunch time. Balvinder takes her mobile phone from her bedside cupboard. The catheter and drain bottle have both been removed. The baby is asleep in her cot. Balvinder had fed her, topped and tailed her under Janine's tuition and put her to sleep, all snuggled up in the approved manner. Being washed has completely knackered the little rat so she didn't even have the energy to have another snuffly feed.

Hiding the phone in her hand Balvinder locks herself in the toilet. No way is she making her phone call public to the ward. She's heard too many details of the other women's lives as they sit in the corridor asking for supplies of sanitary towels, nappies, nighties to be delivered or reminding hopeless husbands to take Jodie to Brownies and Tarquin to his flute lesson. The most painful piece of inadvertent, unavoidable eavesdropping was poor Michelle from the bed opposite, trying to find somewhere to stay when she and her tiny baby were discharged. The social worker had arrived and drawn the curtain around the bed. Michelle and her edgy, chaotic-looking boyfriend were told that the baby could not live in their flat, or share an address with the boyfriend at all. A care order was threatened. Michelle was trying to avoid going to the supervised accommodation the social worker had "busted my backside" to find. Balvinder cannot bear the thought of being pitied as she pitied Michelle. Even though she has even fewer options than Michelle. Thankfully, social services are not yet involved. In fact no-one even knows she has been pregnant. Punjabi suits hide bulges and no-one takes their clothes off with the lights on in Balvinder's house.

She knows that mobile phones are forbidden in hospitals, but suspects this might be a scam. Probably the nurses just didn't like people using them so they pretend they interfere with "life-saving machinery". Like antibiotics and alcohol. Balvinder's cousin, Jaspal, has just qualified as a dentist and likes his beer. Jaspal boasts that Punjabi Ramgaria Sikhs could hold their drink better than anyone. He also claims that doctors introduced the myth that antibiotics should not be taken with alcohol in order to stop prostitutes being treated for syphilis from losing their inhibitions and spreading the disease. Given his genial disposition, perhaps Balvinder can stay with him? She has his mobile number in her phone. No. Jaspal is a mummy's boy and he wouldn't be able to help telling his mother. And then her Dad would find out. Who else? Myriam from school? She lives in her own flat, and works all day in investment banking. But Balvinder's father would assume that Myriam's brothers got her pregnant and murder all five of them.

Can Balvinder phone her mother? Dad will be out at the cash and carry just now. Could Ma talk him round some how? Maybe, but not quickly. What if one of her sisters answers the phone? Balvinder has never had a secret from either of them. At the start she had thought about doing a pregnancy test but where would she have hidden it? Even her knicker-drawer was shared with her two sisters. And, even if she could have disposed of the test-stick, what would she have done with the knowledge? How could she have known but not told them. So when she didn't feel sick, she convinced herself she couldn't be pregnant. Ma was always so sick in pregnancy. She'd been advised against conceiving again, when she gave birth to Balvinder's youngest brother weighing less than she had done at the start of the pregnancy. Now, if she phones home and her sister asks "How are you?" Balvinder doesn't think she could avoid everything tumbling out.

Knocking on the toilet door.

"Are you in there? Your wean's crying. She needs you."

When Balvinder won't respond, Janine opens the door using an allen key on her belt.

"Sorry to barge in hen" says Janine as she catches Balvinder's thunder-brows.

"You can't expect us to run after your baby. Especially now your tubes are out. She needs you. You're her mammy."

Balvinder feels sick and defeated. Her baby's face in the Perspex cot is scrumpled up like a walnut and red from shouting.

Maya

I wake up from a deep sleep with that strange dislocation when for a few seconds you don't know where you are. Then I remember I'm in Glasgow at the start of a weekend, having seen all the films in town, and feel glum. And then I remember I have a friend. Shiv. He walked me to my bus stop and waved me off with "see you next week". I'm not a failure anymore. I roll over wrapping the duvet tightly round my shoulders. The weekend of empty, structureless time stretching before me doesn't seem so endless, knowing I'll be dancing next week. I've got a hobby! I can go to the library and find a book about Scottish dancing, borrow a CD of the tunes. I can chase up the delivery of the frock from Reenie.

Heather

"Hello Mother. It's Heather. Your daughter."

"Hello. Yes, Hello. Hello Heather. How are you?"

"I'm fine. I got back from France, with your grand-daughters the other day."

"Of course. And how was your trip?"

"I wrote to you about the swimming pool. We all swam every day."

"Splendid."

"And there was a lovely vineyard out the back."

"Aaah."

"And we visited a couple of cathedrals."

"And was the weather kind to you?"

"It was lovely mother. Plenty of sunshine."

"Not too humid?"

"Not at all."

"And was the villa clean? Not too stoury?

"No, it was positively hygienic – tiled throughout."

"Well that will have pleased you."

"And how is father getting on?"

"Soldiering on dear. Soldiering on. Would you like a word with him yourself?"

A long pause as the phone is fumbled across from one pair of rheumatic hands to another.

"Heather. How lovely to hear your voice. Are you well? Oh, you will have told your mother that already. How's work? Tell me that."

"Work is OK. Same as usual. There's a big debate about whether to sell off one of our city centre buildings. Seems like a good idea in some ways given our muckle great deficit."

"Aye, but that's a short term solution to a short term problem."

"Solutions of any term are welcome at present father."

"You can fill me in on the details when you visit us. In the not too distant future I hope."

"OK father. Bye-bye the now."

Balvinder

Bernie says that I've got to go home tomorrow. There's no reason to stay. My wounds are not leaking anymore. The rat has put on weight and can keep herself at 37 degrees. Apparently she and I have bonded.

"So," announces Bernie standing with the trolley telephone next to my bed, "you'll be wanting to talk to your family then."

And she's right about the baby. I have bonded with her, if that means that I can't imagine leaving her behind now. So phoning Ma is out of the question. I won't be allowed home with a baby. So I call cousin Kam.

"Where are you Bal?" she shrieks at me. "Why aren't you answering your mobile? I've been frightened. Are you OK?"

"Yeah fine," I say.

"You have **got** to phone your parents. They've not said anything yet, but I know they're wondering why you don't come on the phone. Where are you anyway?"

"Um. With friends," I said unconvincingly.

"Well go home soon Bal. I can't cover for you any longer. I'm going to that wedding in Derby next week. Your aunties'll be there."

So I don't think I can go and stay with her.

40

Without giving myself the chance to swither any longer, I phone the only other person I can think of: Maya. She'll not be horrified by my having a baby. I get her at Shakti and she promises to come and see me in hospital.

Maya

Why would Balvinder not tell me what was wrong? She said she was fine, but in hospital and could I visit her. Her voice was a bit tight, not giggling. So I'm taking the afternoon off to visit her. I tell Mrs Kapadia who looks slightly puzzled.

"I thought she was visiting relations down south" she says.

"No, she said she was in the Southern General Hospital, but that she's not ill."

Mrs Kapadia raises one eyebrow.

"But of course you must go to her. Go now. No problem."

Maybe Bal's Dad hit her after all. Perhaps her Mum's unwell. I'll go and pick up a glossy magazine and a crossword book, in case she needs entertainment.

Maya and Balvinder

So Maya follows the instructions that Balvinder had given her on the telephone and makes her way to ward six of the Southern General Hospital, just south of the river Clyde. And she follows Mrs Kapadia's instructions in getting a box of luddus en route. And only as she gets within three sets of swing doors of Balvinder does Maya realise that she's in a maternity hospital. She finds Balvinder looking paler and thinner than before, in the corner of a room shared with five other women. Her eyes have smudgey dark shadows underneath. She's sitting on a bed, wearing the same clothes as the last time Maya saw her at Shakti. Next to her, wrapped up in white cotton sheets, frayed from being boil-washed in the hospital laundry, is a baby.

"Hello Balvinder," says Maya, gaze fixed on the baby.

"Hello Maya," says Balvinder grinning.

Maya is uncertain what to say next. So she states the obvious. "That's a lovely baby." She inflects the statement up at the end so it becomes a sort of question.

"Yes" replies Balvinder "you're quite right." And she looks

down at the bundle and wonders aloud "Would you like to keep her Maya?"

"Is she yours to give away?" asks Maya.

"I made her," says Balvinder with surprised pride.

"Why didn't you tell me you were pregnant before?" asks Maya, feeling that this conversation is not going quite right.

"I didn't tell anyone. Not even myself really."

Bernie the pro-breast-feeding midwife spots a visitor at Balvinder's bed and hurries over. She needs to release beds today. There's a queue of women at term plus ten days who need to be induced. She knows that Balvinder doesn't know where to go with her baby, but she's loath to get social services involved. This would mean that Balvinder would be occupying a bed for another few days and the last two unmarried Asian lassies on the ward had given their babies up for adoption. The last time Bernie asked the social worker, neither baby had been found a suitable family. So, with the baby's best interests at heart, Bernie hopes that Balvinder will keep her and judging her to be made of stern stuff, behaves as though this will happen.

"You must be here to take Bal home," Bernie states unequivocally.

"Ummm," says Maya redolent with equivocation.

"Just in case you hadn't managed to bring baby clothes, I've got some here. And you can borrow this blanket to wrap her up," and Bernie is swaddling the baby up in a NHS-stamped honey-comb baby blanket.

So Maya finds herself carrying a plastic bag of second-hand baby clothes and a dozen disposable nappies, following behind Balvinder calling "goodbye" to the other mothers on her way out of the ward. Maya continues to follow-on out of the hospital and into a taxi.

"Where do you live Maya?" asks Balvinder.

Maya gives the address, pays the driver when they arrive. She lets Balvinder into her flat, puts on the kettle and makes tea while Balvinder feeds her baby. Sitting on the kitchen work-surface, she sips her tea, watching Balvinder nursing in the only chair. Then the baby is tucked up in Maya's recess bed.

"Thanks for having me to stay Maya," Balvinder says.

"Oh. You're staying ...?"

"Yeah. I've got to. I've nowhere else to go. My Ma'll kill me. If my Dad doesn't get to me first. You don't mind do you? You'll be out at work all day anyway. You're not ashamed of having me here?"

"Ashamed? No? But there's not much space. And I don't know anything about babies," Maya says truthfully. As the only child of an only child there wasn't much opportunity to learn about child-care techniques at home.

"I know how to look after babies. I just didn't know how to avoid making her." Balvinder's eyes drop in embarrassed defiance.

"Do you know who her father is?" asks Maya.

"Yes."

"Does he know?"

"Know what?"

"Know about the baby?"

"No. He doesn't even know I was pregnant."

"Why not?" asks Maya.

"How could he? I never saw him again. I never got out to a gig again. Dad stopped my library visits." Balvinder winds her dupatta more tightly round her shoulders and head. "Look Maya. I'll cook all your dinners for you. And I'll clean up your flat. It'll be no bother having me here."

But she is clearly too exhausted to do anything. Maya cooks pasta and tomato sauce which they eat in front of the telly. Then as Maya is clearing up she finds the box of luddus in her bag that she had intended to give to Balvinder in hospital. She puts them on a plate and serves them with another cup of tea.

"These are from Mrs Kapadia. She said you'd like them."

"Did you tell her about me?" Balvinder's eyes have widened out in alarm.

"I said I was visiting you in hospital."

"But did you say about the baby?"

"Balvinder! How could I have done? I didn't know about the baby until I got to the hospital."

Balvinder bit into a luddu and as the orange mixture crumbles down her front she weeps. And the baby starts whimpering from the bed recess, so Balvinder climbs in with

43

her. They are both asleep half an hour later when Maya peeks around the curtain that divides the bed from the kitchen.

This leaves Maya to sleep on the sofa wriggled down into her four-season sleeping bag. She lies thinking about her Granny who had bought her the bag. And who had coped with Maya when she had turned up as Hilary's unanticipated baby. As a girl Maya's favourite Granny-told bedtime story had been about her arrival from India.

"And your mummy handed me a parcel wrapped with a red cotton towel. And she said 'Look I've made you into a Granny.' And I unwrapped the blanket and inside I found a sweet baby who smiled at me."

"And did you love me Granny?" Maya remembers asking. Her grandmother's scrupulous honesty had got in the way of the affirmation of sentimental love that Maya craved.

"No, not immediately. I was worried whether I could remember how to fold a nappy. But very soon I loved you so much, I was quite taken by surprise."

"And where did Mummy get me from?"

"From a city of Princes and Palaces. Grandpa and I used to call you our little Maharani."

Maya had outgrown this story and wanted more details of her arrival into the world. Hilary had never told her mother much about Maya's conception and birth, both of which had happened in India, so Granny was in no position to expand the story. Just after Maya's twelfth birthday, Granny had had a stern word with her daughter — something which didn't happen very often. This prompted Hilary to tell Maya a version of her story. Having enjoyed her own performance, Hilary repeated it a dozen times before tiring of her own inventiveness. Maya was used to sifting fiction from Hilary's fantastic accounts of her life. She weeded out the least likely elements of the story and cross-checked the rest with what little Granny knew. And then she told her story to Granny who told it back to her at bedtime. Reenie was the only other person to whom Maya had told her story. She felt possessive about it, jealously guarding the minimal secrets of her own origins.

So to find herself witnessing the beginning of another life was odd. She ought to feel sympathy with the small fatherless stowaway in her bed with Balvinder. Empathy even. But she just felt annoyed. Maybe Granny felt the same when Hilary sprang a baby on her. It probably wasn't in Grandpa's retirement plan to house a bastard child every holiday and many weekends.

But Balvinder wasn't even really a friend, let alone family. Maya couldn't look after Balvinder's baby. Bad enough to unwittingly become an eyewitness to the baby's early days. Would the baby want to retrieve the evidence later? Maya would love to find a reliable witness for her early days. The sooner she could get Balvinder out of her flat, the less use she would be to the baby later. What would practical, organised Maureen do in this situation? She would never have allowed this to happen to her. Maureen assumed that people were going to take the piss as a matter of course. She would have avoided getting drawn in. Her protective barriers were more effective than Maya's. Reenie would find Maya's predicament amusing.

"Well at least you're not lonely now" she imagines her friend telling her as sleep finally overtakes her.

Heather

I've closed my office door and I'm getting ready to leave when Mary knocks and pushes the door opening.

"I have to leave my studies Professor Cromarty" she announces without any preamble. She goes on to explain that her mother has just been made redundant from her call-centre job and that her father is a long-term invalid. Mary has to take on extra shifts at Asda to keep herself and her parents. Yes, she says that she's applied to the hardship fund and is in receipt of her full allocation of loans. She has only three modules to complete in order to graduate with BA honours. As a graduate she could earn more, even at Asda, and I suggest three different strategies to gain extra time for doing the assessments, and at the very least I urge her to suspend from her studies rather than to withdraw altogether. Mary refuses all of my suggestions. It seems that she's made up her mind that circumstances have defeated her and she's almost relieved that her inevitable failure in the face of insurmountable odds has arrived at last. By now it's a quarter past five. Mary shows no sign of noticing my end-of-interview cues. I've shut my diary, closed down my computer and drawn the blinds but she has just began to describe her father's symptoms again. If I don't leave the building within five minutes I risk reaching the nursery after closing time. When there was a bomb-scare in town I arrived late and found my two wee lassies fair chuffed with themselves, sitting on the nursery manager's knee, eating rich tea biscuits and watching a Winnie the Pooh video.

If only Doug hadn't accepted a day's work covering for a friend today, he would have collected the children already. Mary is recounting the injustice of her mother's redundancy once more. I agree for a second time that it is very unfortunate. Mary has no intention of following my advice, but wants me to bear witness to her troubles and give my blessing to her decision to quit. But I can't condone her pulling out of her degree, especially when she's so close to completion. And I cannot offer her a cup of tea or any more sympathy now.

"I am sorry Mary. I must go and pick up my children. If you'd like to talk over your options again, come back tomorrow. Between ten and twelve noon is the best time."

The poor lassie shrugs, sniffs and says goodbye.

I run to the lift and while waiting for the unbearably hesitant descent decide to get a taxi to the nursery and hang the expense. Of course there are none available on the street and I've walked all the way to the station by the time one passes. But I make it to nursery in time. I ring the bell and get buzzed in to the hallway lined with low rows of coat pegs. As I open the shoulder-height door-handle I'm greeted by number one daughter.

"Thanks Mummy! You came later than Rosie's mum. I got a shot on the pooter!" My little angel is using the cursor keys to push Noddy around toy town to find Big Ears. According to her weekly report she'll be graduating to mouse skills next week. The baby gives me a gratifyingly fruity gurgle as I lift her out of the playpen. With a yeasty warm baby on each hip we call "awlevoi", approximating for the "aurevoir" that we learned on holiday, to the nursery workers busy clearing up. I kiss the tops of their heads as I strap them into their double buggy. We get outdoors and discuss our supper options as we walk towards home. "Pasta and poo-poo" suggests my big girl and chuckles at her own wit. The baby joins in. I look forward to soft-boiled eggs, carrot sticks and raisins, followed by bathtime, a Shirley Hughes story book, snuggles and an enormous gin and tonic with Doug when he gets back from the restaurant.

Balvinder

Taking in a Paisley-pattern bed quilt and hand-painted stencils of sea-shells around tongue-and-groove panelling, I know I'm not in hospital. I'm totally blank. Clunk. A heavy door swings shut and the panelling reverberates. I remember that I'm at Maya's. Seeking refuge as a fallen woman. That's what Sister Agnes would have called it. But it was the white girls, the Catholics that she was always warning about the sins of the flesh. She thought us heathen headscarf-wearers were safe from fornication. How far have I fallen?

Maya

Mrs Kapadia is working from home nursing her chilblains, giving Maya the requisite ninety minutes to find someone to speak to at the city council housing department. Maya wonders whether it is intentional that only the very dedicated and persistent can find their way through the system to a human who is willing to listen. While on hold for the sixth time, listening to a Barbara Streisand ballad, she reminds herself of Hilary's utter lack of shame about using her single mother status, if it meant getting a sought after local GP or a place in the after-school kiddie-care scheme. Maya fingers the shopping list that Balvinder sent her out with that morning. Balvinder was not prepared to leave the house, so shopping is Maya's job. Already the possibility of returning home to an empty flat to make a quiet supper and feel lonely seems like a nostalgic fantasy.

A bored housing officer, who, if not willing was at least prepared to listen to Maya, finally arrives on the line. Maya is resolute and insistent that Balvinder is the council's responsibility to house and that if they fail Bal will be at risk from her wrathful parents. Eventually Maya extracts an agreement that

47

the officer will visit Balvinder at Maya's flat and that, should she seem to be eligible for re-housing, Maya could visit the flats on Bal's behalf. Maya puts down the telephone and makes for the toilet. She had needed a pee for the previous forty minutes but couldn't risk going back to the beginning of her telephone trail through the council housing department. Washing her hands, she sees her own reflection. She's fiddled and ruffled her hair until it stands out like a crazy halo. When younger she had thought that on reaching adulthood she would manage a smooth and glossy look. But even when she spends money on smoothing serums and hair waxes advertised by supermodels, she remains dishevelled.

Maya returns home via Allison Street, where the shopkeepers practise competitive banana discounting to lure the customers in to stroke and sniff their crates of mangoes, lychees and guavas. She hands Balvinder's shopping list to the grocer since she doesn't know what mooli, aatha, paalak, moong dahl or haldi are. She does better with chilli peppers, aubergine, paneer, basmati rice, and lime pickle. For once Maya feels relieved not to show too much of her father's Rajasthani appearance. Being taken for an ignorant white girl seems preferable to being pitied as a stupid half-caste.

The walk home, with the laden plastic bag-handles cutting into her palms, seems too far. And once gaining her door way, there's two flights of wide stone steps to get up, before she can set down the load. In the kitchen, Maya finds the baby sleeping on a pillowcase in the bottom of the cardboard box that had previously housed her personal papers. Balvinder has rearranged the furniture so that the television is in the kitchen and can be seen from the bed recess. "Home and away" is on.

Balvinder sets to work transforming the contents of the plastic bags into a beautiful meal; yellow dahl, green paalak and snowy white rice, dotted about with the red chilli oil of lime pickle. As she eats, Balvinder questions Maya.

"So I didn't know you was born in India. It says on your passport".

"Well I didn't know until my mum told me," replies Maya defensively, feeling that Balvinder is in no position to complain about secret origins, given her hidden pregnancy. Maya is lying anyway since Hilary was always reminding her about her Indian blood, as if repetition would give Maya black pride.

"Anyway, what difference does it make?" asks Maya.

"None. It's just funny that you're an Indian-born whitie and I'm a Glasgow-born darkie."

Maya is not pleased that Balvinder has discovered her birthplace. From experience, she has learned to say that she is from Leamington Spa. It avoids people's annoying expectation that she have some understanding of or affinity for India just because her mother carelessly gave birth to her in a small Rajasthani city. Given Maya's dearth of reliable knowledge about the circumstances of her birth, it seems a reasonable untruth.

Getting the conversation back to Balvinder's problems, Maya announces that the housing officer will visit the next day.

"I can't live in a council house," says Balvinder.

"Why not?" asks Maya

"Our people just don't. And anyway who would do my shopping? Can't I just stay here?"

Maya doesn't feel able to utter a brutal "no". Instead she says, "I'll be here for the interview and I'll check out the flats for you."

Balvinder just shakes her head and climbs back into the bed recess clutching the baby. Maya clears away the plates and withdraws to the other room. It looks as though her bookcase and her shoe-boxes of postcards and letters have been sorted through. Her scrap book lies open in the middle of the floor, showing out-of-focus pictures of Maya's grandparents on a windy Hunstanton beach, taken by Maya aged eight years. Lying across and obscuring the pictures was a tea towel, wet, probably with some baby fluid. Maya's frustration wells up in a rage against Balvinder. She picks up the tea towel and goes back through to the kitchen to remonstrate, but mother and baby are sleeping again. Maya puts the tea towel in the washing machine and goes to run a rose oil bath for relaxation.

The old pink bottle of "Superior bath essence", favoured by her grandmother was empty save for a dribble. It had been the main method by which Maya conjured up a comforting

49

olfactory memory of her Granny and she had been hoarding it. Rose oil "Superior" had long-since gone out of production, as Maya had discovered from asking in a number of pharmacies. Maya supposes angrily that Balvinder must be feeling very relaxed as she rinses out the bottle under the tap, managing to get a faint pink hue to the bath water.

The end of the bath oil is another marker in the ongoing process of understanding that Granny has died. Maya's grandparents had managed their deaths with their usual under-stated efficiency and consideration. Hilary had wept uncontrollably at her father's funeral, embarrassing her mother and daughter in equal measure. Maya and her grandmother had subsequently agreed that a cremation would give Hilary less opportunity to perform her grief and eight weeks later they were proved correct. Granny had died, in her sleep, her clothes already bagged up and labelled for Oxfam and her harvest of onions, potatoes, carrots and shallots gathered and stored in the cool earth-floored outhouse. While Hilary was overseeing the transportation of her mother's pictures and silver candlesticks to Stoke Newington, Maya had filled her rucksack with her grandmother's vegetables to eat in her memory. Eating the last shallot, chopped with a tomato and parsley, had made Maya's tears course down her face. And thinking about it now in the last ever rose oil bath made her sniff again.

Balvinder

Why is Maya so cross? At Shakti we used to have a laugh, taking the mick out of Mrs K. No laughs now. I thought she might be a bit pleased to have company, seeing as she's all alone. And the baby doesn't bother her. I'm careful through the night to keep her quiet. Whenever she whimpers I feed her. And I cook her a good meal every night. Better than what she was getting before, judging by her food cupboards — ryvita, rice cakes, apples and weetabix. No cake, no chocolate, no ginger, no tunnocks. And I keep the baby's nappies out of her way, taking them down to the midden at the back. I go out when the baby's asleep and run to the bin and back up the stairs quick. My mobile is out of juice, so I don't know if anyone is trying to find me. I suppose they will be soon enough. Or maybe not. Maybe Kam has told them that she was covering for me and they're pleased that I've taken my shameful face away. Sometimes I think about my nephews getting born and how babhiji was fed panjeeri and looked after for forty days. And I greet a bit. Then I go to sleep. And when I wake it's OK again. When I see my wee bundle of joy. She smiles at me. Maya says it's only wind.

The housing officer asked what baby was called today. I said "I don't know" which sounded pretty thick. So she was put down on the form as "Baby Singh". Baby Lion. Fierce and proud. Better than baby rat. I don't know my National Insurance number either. I suppose my Dad knows what it is. The housing woman asked about where I lived before, and when I said my parents would kill me if I go back now she said, "is there a history of domestic violence?" And I said, "No, nothing like that. We just get hammered now and again." And from the way she raised her eyebrows she thought this meant "yes".

Baby Singh's eyes are beginning to look out towards people when she's not tired. But looking in, they're still cloudy-mud. I'm not sure if I'm more worried that they'll be blue or brown. Baby never has wind when she's looking at Maya.

Heather

"Fabby-doo!" (as Katie Morag would say on the Isle of Struay). Saturday morning. Blissy bliss bliss. I was so sensible to marry a man who likes getting up and out early. Doug wakes me with the Saturday papers, fresh bread and coffee. I wallow in bed until the last possible minute, before having to throw on my clothes, without even a shower, to get to the library for story time. The kids and I set out, leaving Doug preparing our roast chicken dinner to the sound track of his favourite prog rock. I push the buggy to the single storey red brick building with its fine frontage crafted when public buildings were a source of civic pride, and up the ramp through the wide double doors. As we approach the kiddie-corner I wish I'd brushed my hair properly and put on some lipstick. There's Ivy Codogan who used to be my father's secretary.

"Hello Heather dear. How are you?"

"Fine thank-you Mrs Codogan. How are your grandsons doing?"

"Och they're wee smashers. So they are." She smiles indulgently at two crew-cut laddies in matching denim jackets, punching each other. "So playful together aren't they?" she asks rhetorically. "And your parents how are they keeping? Such a shame they can't really enjoy their granddaughters isn't it? And Robin? Still the wild one? How your father used to worry about him. I still remember reminding him that boys will be boys." Her doughy face has kneaded itself into a sympathetic shape under its dusting of floury face powder.

It seems to be my turn to talk. I gulp and try to smooth down my hair at the back of my head, where it was rubbed up by the pillow overnight. The librarian in a coral twin-set has started to whesht us quiet. She's holding up a storybook.

"Now boys and girls, who knows this book?" A few hands go up but my little wonder-child calls out.

"Me, me, me. Magnolia boot." The baby claps her hands in appreciation of her sister's cleverness.

"Don't shout out please. It isn't fair on the other children. Now, who can tell me the full title of this book?"

"Mister Magnolia!" offers a girl with perfect plaits. "And it's by Quentin Blake." A proud tremor crosses her mother's shoulder blades. But before anyone else could get a word in, my girl has another announcement.

"I know it! In French! Iln'ac'uneboot!"

I catch her eye and put my finger across my lips. The story of Mister Magnolia's single boot keeps her rapt for the next ten minutes and the baby suckles. Afterwards the librarian remarks, "Very bright your little girl isn't she?" Clearly an admonishment. Perhaps its good for me to feel scolded. Keep me in my place. Remind me what it's like to be a supplicant in the educational process.

Maya

I had thought I would have Balvinder rehoused by now. The housing officer clearly thought that she was an emergency case. She said they had some flats available in Sighthill, Maryhill and the Gorbals. I looked up the areas on the street atlas. They seem reasonably close to the city centre. It's not like condemning her to a satellite housing scheme. I'm due to see them today. Mrs Kapadia has given me permission. The conversation, in front of the paper-wall-thermometer (which is yet to rise above freezing) went like this:

Mrs K: Did you talk to Mr Said about donating?

Me: He'd like to sponsor a sports team ... football or cricket. Perhaps establish a trophy to commemorate his late brother.

Mrs K: Tsk-tsk. No progress to report to the board next week. That University woman is coming to discuss the agenda this afternoon. She's got "strategy suggestions". Ugh.

Me: What sort of strategy suggestion?

Mrs K: I don't know. Perhaps she wants me to resign! Ha-ha!

And she laughed her tinkley laugh to show that she found the suggestion hilariously unlikely. I looked down at my boots, took a breath and quick before I could think about the consequences said:

"But I cannot raise money. I never even liked getting money for sponsored walks at school. It's embarrassing. I should do something else. Like the arts projects. I could do them very cheaply. Please."

And I realised my eyes were wide open in a beseeching-puppy expression. Mrs Kapadia was speechless. I suppose I hadn't really told her that I disliked the work before.

Mrs K: Well why don't you suggest a strategy to Mrs Professor when she comes in?

She turned back towards her office, her jewel-encrusted kitten-heeled mules clicking along the linoleum tiles. And since I was already flushed with embarrassment, I asked her if I could have the afternoon off to look at flats.

Mrs K: Moving are you?

Me: No, it's for Balvinder.

Mrs K: Oh yes. You went to see her. How is she?

Me: She's got a baby.

And Mrs Kapadia turned back towards me aghast. Her mouth was slack with her bottom jaw nestling down among her ample chins.

Mrs K: But no husband?

Me: Umm.

53

Mrs K: Are her parents knowing?

Me: No, only me.

Mrs K: Where is she? Still in hospital?

Me: No, in my flat.

Mrs K: Yes. Umm. Of course. Go and visit these places. Will you be moving with her?

Me: No!

I squealed this last bit, which probably seemed rude. Mrs K turned again, but her heels didn't click so jauntily now. Her parting shot was to tell me that I shouldn't tell the volunteer ladies on reception about Balvinder. I suppose I shouldn't have told Mrs K either. But it's done now.

Heather

I can't help but be annoyed when, having cut short a precious afternoon of proof-reading, I'm told at the Shakti reception that Mrs Kapadia is unable to see me, but that I should go and speak with the project worker Maya Paul. The annoyance dissipates quickly, when a charmingly smiley lady brings me a cup of milky tea infused with ginger, cardamom and loaded with sugar. Perhaps putting everyone's blood sugar up like this would make department meetings sweeter tempered …?

Maya Paul turns out to be a rather hot looking young woman with an extraordinary combination of curly red hair and almond eyes. I remember interviewing her, when she was wearing a purple linen dress and enthused about community participation in art projects. Today she looks rather squashed and, to my eyes, on the brink of tears.

"Mrs Kapadia says I've got to talk with you about strategy," she offers, sniffing.

"Oh aye" I reply warily.

"Well, I'm not sure what she means but I can tell you that this place is not working. We haven't made any resources available to black or Asian women, or their families, unless you count the reception volunteers and Mrs Kapadia. People wander in, sent by their GP or health visitor and all we do is tell them all the things we might do one day soon. But it's never going to happen since I can't persuade anyone to give us any money."

"And what should Shakti be doing?" I ask.

"We can't do much with just me as the worker. Especially since I don't even talk Punjabi. People come to gossip and drink tea. This morning three women brought in a picnic to celebrate Mrs Uddin's birthday. But just before you arrived, Mrs Kapadia said they were making the place look like Howra Station and told them to leave. Go and ask them. They'll tell you what it's like here."

The reception ladies agree with Maya Paul that plenty of women come through the doors looking for a chat and tea. They reckon that what women want is a safe place to learn how to use e-mail so they can write to their overseas relatives. And perhaps English classes.

"Have you talked to Mrs Kapadia?"

"No, no, no," the two ladies both reply, shaking their heads in unison. "She is not a common person like us. She is a big woman and has high ideas about our community. You tell her that we want e-mail computer and a chai shop and she'll believe you only." And they clutch each others' arms and fall about laughing.

Balvinder

Baby lion-singh has been asleep for three hours and won't wake even when I roll her over to check she's still breathing. I've looked at every book, box and album in the house and there's only Kilroy on the telly. If there was more milk in the fridge I'd make ras malai for tea. Will I make gajaarela? No. No almonds. I want to phone my Ma. I want to tell her that I've got a sweet wee babe and that she's got Dad's frown when she's got the colic. It would be worth a beating to see Ma smile at my little lion-singh. But I'd not be able to answer the questions that would follow the beating.

Maya

The good news is that Maureen is coming to visit! My own dear Reenie, to stay with me, even though Glasgow is definitely north of London. Vogue is sending her to research a special Scottish issue, so the staff writers can write the stories without leaving central London. The bad news is that the flats available for single, newly delivered mothers are, to use

Balvinder's terms bogging and minging. I so much wanted to tell her that the flats were fantastic and that she could move out NOW. I find her reading my old diaries when I get home. She isn't even ashamed. She just looks up from reading as I come in the door and says, "That fella you worked beside last year in London ... sounds gorgeous! What happened to him?"

But even though I want her out of my hair – big time – the flats that I have visited on Bal's behalf are the pits. The first one is on the seventeenth floor in a tower block in Sighthill, which is hemmed in by the M8, a cemetery and the trainline to Edinburgh. I have to cross a footbridge from the centre of town and walk along a path lined with bushes that provide perfect cover for lurking rapists and muggers. The lift smells of piss, masked by a recent dose of disinfectant. The threshold of the next-door flat is covered in blue gloss paint. The housing officer doesn't mention it, even though it is still wet and dribbling out into the hall. I point it out.

"Oh yes, he's a little confused the gentleman next door."

Sounds psychotic judging by the sounds coming through the inadequate walls. The flat itself is dirty, with no appliances but a fantastic view. The windows go right down to ankle level and swivel on a central hinge. We are admiring the stains of chip fat on the concrete floor of the cupboard-kitchen when one of the windows blows open and bangs in the wind.

"What do people do with toddlers in a flat like this?" I ask.

"Fit window locks," came the curt reply.

Even with a window lock it is only a pane of glass between you and half a kilometre of thin air. I felt sick as the housing woman walked over to shut the window again. She looks as if she's done this before, but what if she slipped? She coolly comments on the "high winds this far up."

The bathroom is the only place where the carpets have been left behind – aubergine shag pile tacked right up the side of the bath.

"What about furniture and a cooker?" I ask. "Balvinder has nothing."

"She can apply for an emergency grant of two hundred pounds in the first instance."

"What to get beds, a fridge, a sofa, everything?" I ask incredulous. "It cost me a grand and three weeks hunting the second hand shops to furnish my two rooms."

"The Salvation Army is very competitively priced. And they'll deliver." Perhaps you have to get hard-hearted to stick working in a job like hers.

"Why did the last lot move out?" I ask on the way out.

The housing officer indicates the blue-gloss-splatter and says, "Harassment".

I don't bother asking why the next flat has been vacated. The door frame of the neighbouring flat has been jemmied – split wood and the lock missing. A thin, pale, twitchy person pushes the free-swinging door open. Inside I can see three other similar people sitting disconsolately on a huge brown velour sofa with grease marks instead of antimacassars. Their feet are covered by a rubble of pizza boxes, newspaper, children's toys, disposable nappies and discarded clothes. I don't linger.

Heather

The babes are sleeping. Doug is on the sofa watching a James Bond film. One with Sean Connery, the mighty milkman. Doug's got a bowl of chilli-marinated olives, a bowl of pistachio nuts, a bottle of Merlot and two glasses. He's chuckling appreciatively and patting the place next to him. Watching cheesy movies together has always been a joint pleasure. I used to feel guilty about it, mistaking misogynist screenplays for the cause rather than a symptom of sexism. If I don't get those proofs done by next week I'll miss my production window and the book will be put back for six months. My man will wait for me but the publishers won't. So I go up behind the sofa, give Doug a quick shoulder rub before leaning over him to take a glass of wine which I reluctantly take off to the kitchen table where I spread out the contents of my brief case.

Maya and Balvinder

"That housing woman was here again today. Wanted to know whether I'd be moving into either of yon flats you visited."

57

"What did you say?" Maya is unable to keep a note of hope out of her voice.

"No, of course. I'll not live beside junkies or loonies."

"I don't **know** they were junkies."

"Maya – does your head button up the back?"

"What?"

"Or do you think mine does? I'll not have my wee babysingh falling out the window. Those blocks don't have a fire escape. And they all eat chips in there. So when a kitchen catches fire below you, you've to jump out the windie. But you'd have to throw your bairn out first."

Maya holds her peace while Balvinder's annoyance subsides. After some moments Maya asks "So will she find you a better place?"

"Don't reckon so," and Balvinder thrusts a piece of paper towards Maya.

"She made me sign this to say that I didn't want any of her flats. She's worried she'll be blamed if my Dad batters me to death!" Balvinder chortles. Maya blanches.

"Will he?"

"Mmmm" Balvinder considers for a moment. "Most probably" she nods cheerfully.

"Well then, if you can't go home, shouldn't you think again about the council flats?"

"Don't be dafter than you have to Maya. We people don't live in they flats. We're not welcome."

"But it's not all junkies. I met the residents committee in the Gorbals. They were nice white haired ladies in pastel acrylic cardies. Not threatening."

"Humph. Maybe not to you. Did any of them speak Punjabi?" Balvinder asks contemptuously.

"They want rid of the junkies. They want respectable mothers to move in."

Balvinder snorts. "My Dad's cousin used to beat his wife and after ten years of it she moved out to a council flat in Maryhill. She got put there to be close to Woodlands and 'cause there was another Asian in the block. A widow. Not a soul in the block spoke to either of them. Totally ignored. When my cousin and the widow took their weans to play on the swings, all the white folk would leave. They never said

58

anything racist, but they sent their kids to do the tormenting. Abusing them through the letterbox. Shouting 'Paki' and 'Your house is on fire,' or just chapping all the time. There's no way I'm exposing myself to that sort of nonsense. I can't be doing with it." Maya looks at the floor. But Balvinder isn't quite finished. "Breaks your spirit. That cousin has died now, by the way."

Since the matter seems to be closed Maya starts to clear the plates. The stuffed paratha that they'd just finished were delicious and Balvinder has put one by for Maya to take to work tomorrow.

Maya

Today I get home and the flat is perfectly tidy. None of my possessions are on the floor. Everything is where it should be, boxed or shelved. Balvinder is sitting with the telly on. She looks serious. My stomach lurches.

"Oh Maya. I'm that sorry."

"What for?" I ask, thinking "What have you done now?"

"I didn't realise that you minded me being here so much. I read your diary today. It was in the bag of sannies in your knicker drawer."

Yes, I think, wrapped up tight in a bag, at the back of the drawer, under the knickers, as an indication that you shouldn't read it.

And then I start crying. Standing just inside the door, plastic shopping bags bulging with unfamiliar vegetables. Weeping with shame and frustration. Shamed by the petty complaints I made to my diary. Sorry that I like Balvinder's food more than I like her. Mortified that it is so difficult to help someone. Resentful of Balvinder's ability to live in the moment in my flat. Jealous of her sweet little baby that she takes so much for granted. Vexed by her expectation that she will be looked after.

The tears dribble down my face. My neck is damp. The snot is running into my mouth and compounding my shame in front of Balvinder. She has only one set of clothes but always looks perfectly neat, even when she's just slept in them. She just does feminine better than me. She clucks gently and muttering "chalo" takes the shopping, removes my wet coat and wipes up my tears. She leads me to the armchair. Puts a blanket round my shoulders and the baby in my arms. "Countdown" is on the telly. A cup of tea arrives. The baby is swapped for a bowl of roti, dahl, and subjee. Then Balvinder gives me a letter.

"This arrived this morning. And I haven't even opened it," she grins naughtily.

It's from Maureen. A break-out of three prisoners (category C) from Barlinnie prison hit the headlines the other day and this, together with the derailment of a train south of Carlisle has led her editors to cancel her trip to Scotland. It's too dangerous. Reenie wants reassurance that I'm OK, since she's just read a Marie Claire in-depth report about drug-related crime and poverty in the housing schemes of Glasgow.

Heather

Proofs finally finished. Although I had to break my own rule in order to manage to get them back on time. Doug picked the kids up from nursery, fed them, bathed them and put them to bed two days running. I returned home at ten o'clock hungry, cross and tired. Doug fed me ricotta and spinach pizza (two for the price of one from the Italian deli) and a soft, soothing Chianti. I feel like a grumpy husband. Except that I feed the baby at four, then get up at six-thirty, out of the house by seven, before the others wake up. Back to proof-reading in my office with the door locked from the inside to prevent interruption. Finally get through to the last page. It was worth doing. I've found a dozen introduced errors. And now I'm heading home, in a taxi through the rush-hour traffic. I'm desperate to get back before the baby sleeps so I can feed her. Ease the hot heaviness of my breasts. Seems such a waste allowing milk to just leak through my shirt. A woman from the NCT class described how she kept sterilised nipple shields in her bra and emptied out the drips into a bottle for use by her husband in night-time feeds. Ergh. Thinking about it bring's my baby's face to mind and my nipples wrinkle and the milk starts to leak again. Quick! Mind over matter. Think about something else … Monday's lecture, the Shakti business plan, chairing the board meeting.

Maya

This morning as I was putting on my coat, I told Balvinder that I was going dancing and wouldn't be back until eleven. She looked momentarily downcast. Then she dodged back into the kitchen and reappeared with three tin foil parcels of food.

"Don't worry about me. It's the Eastenders special edition tonight." she said. I felt so pleased to be getting away from my flat and the television. I almost looked forward to the dancing. An escape from worrying about Balvinder. Or at least replacing that worry with anxiety about my lack of co-ordination.

I spend most of the day and into the evening filling out an application form for the Beaudessert Benevolent Fund. The University woman – Heather Cromarty – sent it to me, suggesting that I might be able to get the money for my art project. According to the explanatory leaflet Mrs Beaudessert was the Guyanese wife of an enterprising Glaswegian named Mr Ross who imported sugar and spices from Jamaica. They married in Jamaica and since her name was so much prettier than his, he took it. Together they brought up a family of Beaudessertlettes in contentment. Then after retiring, having made his fortune, old Mr Beaudessert developed a longing to return to his dear, damp homeland. Mrs Beaudessert had never set foot in Scotland, although she had always sported the Ross plaid at the Burns Night suppers she hosted in their elegant plantation-style home. They returned to Glasgow in the 1930s and she found it unremittingly grim. The riches that made it possible for Mr Beaudessert to go salmon fishing and play on the best golf courses did little to alleviate Mrs Beaudessert's sense of displacement. Being a resourceful and outward looking person, she channelled her sense of loss into establishing a benevolent fund to meet "the material and spiritual wants of women of swarthy complexion resident in Glasgow".

I've written my application about the mosaics and murals that I want to do in the Shakti building, describing the research I've done on Mughal miniatures and Bollywood film posters. On Professor Cromarty's advice I throw in a bit about setting up an internet café. She says the trustees like stuff about giving women "transferable skills and access to e-resources." She also suggested that I include a bit of biography to demonstrate my authentic Indian-birth to counteract my unfortunate Englishness.

Balvinder

I miss my Ma too much. I'm too lonely. I would go home now. I wouldn't mind getting a beating. It would be worth it to be back next to my sisters. Where is the joy in being alone? But would Dad beat the baby? I don't think so. I can't phone and check. Make a deal with Dad that he can hit me whenever, as long as he leaves her alone. Likely he would just ignore her. Pretend she doesn't exist. That might be worse. At least when you're being hit, someone's noticed you. You exist if you've annoyed some one that much.

Maya

"Partners please for the dashing white sergeants!"

A very small man comes to ask me to dance. His eyes are on a level with my shoulder. Or breasts if he stoops. This dance involves one partner – the bloke – holding the woman's hands above her head to turn her around. Since this little man was having trouble reaching above my head I offer to turn him instead. He chooses to interpret this as a joke and a joke in rather poor taste at that. So in penance I have to turn four times every eight bars with my knees bent. My quads are burning from the effort.

"And now find two other dancers and we'll strip the willow!"

I quite like this one and sit on the PVC banquette looking hopefully open to offers. The lovely Richie, who dances like an aerodynamic dream, is coming towards me and then, just as he's about to ask me to dance, two women from the advanced class cut across his path and bustle him off. Most unsporting of them, since they don't need Richie's skilful steering and steady footwork to make them look like they know what's going on. No-one is coming to proposition me, so I'd better be brave. I gather up two bodies, both looking terrified and we launch into the dance. The three of us stomp through the steps as Flora Macdonald calls them from the stage. I suspect we look more like rhythmic wrestlers than dancers. No matter. Afterwards one of them buys me a pint of seventy shilling (better than the eighty, not so thick), and we watch the advanced class tackle a Hungarian harvest dance. I gather some mean-spirited satisfaction from seeing the two Richie-snatchers getting in a muddle during a complicated three-handed turn.

Balvinder

No-one touches me. Maya doesn't even pick up the baby. I think she's worried that I might do a flit and leave her to bring up the child if she shows any interest. At home I get looked after properly. Ma massages my scalp and combs out my hair. My sister rubs my legs and I do Ma's with mustard oil for her varicose veins. I can even get a cuddle off my wee brother sometimes, as long as no-one else is looking. And now it's just me and my little babysinghlion. Alone. And no body makes my skin comfortable. I could live without ever having sex again. It was bearable, but not the fantastic head-rush that Rita-at-school had said. But I don't think I can live without the body comforts of my family. But perhaps I have to? Perhaps I just have to wait until babysingh gets big enough to rub my legs. The only body-pleasure left for me?

Maya

The confident dancers wear skirts with a pleat so they flare out as they turn. The green silk frock that Maureen sent up would whirl out a treat. But my balance isn't good enough. And neither is my underwear.

Shiv arrives just as the lesson is closing. Hamish and the band are playing the Canadian barn dance, so I ask Shiv to dance. As I'm turning towards the dance floor I clip the elbow of a dancer who's birling past. And on the way back round I stand on Shiv's feet. Oh I wish I were dainty and precise in my movements like Flora. Despite my gangleyness we do alright Shiv and me. His frame is big and solid enough to contain my limbs when they flail and keep our centre of gravity true and our axis of rotation steady. It's a slow and deliberate dance. I can imagine eighteenth century protestants plodding through it without feeling a single tremor of sensual pleasure.

63

The lovely Richie asks me to dance the Gay Gordons with him. Shiv is a good partner and we maintain a steady rhythm and never get lost. But Richie is a joy. He makes me feel "pretty and witty and gay" like Maria in "Westside story". He inspires confidence so I can let go of the routine and fly round the corners a little, syncopate the rhythm slightly. Or perhaps it's just the beer. Whatever the cause, it's a fantastic feeling of being co-ordinated and joined up with another human body. But when the dancing stops and the patter starts, Richie is a prat. His charm is embodied but not verbal.

"Do you move as well when you're horizontal?" he enquires.

I pretend not to have understood and thank him for the dance, while turning back to my place on the PVC bench, fleeing any follow-up questions. I park my bottom as close as I dare to Shiv in the hopes that Richie will be warned off. Shiv's talking to Hamish's wife about some trip "up west". That would mean Leicester Square where I'm from. But they're talking about boats and trains, so I guess it's not London's theatre land.

Shiv walks me to the bus stop again. We're looking across towards where the train line crosses the river and arrives into Central Station. The line that could take me south. Home. Except it's not. Where would I go? Granny's Leamington house has been sold to the man she always referred to as "that frightfully pleasant dentist" from along the road. He used to admire the wisteria and magnolia trees during Granny's summer garden parties. And now he owns them. Hilary might let me stay, but could I stand it? Maureen is still living with her parents, despite dressing like a trust-fund princess.

"Do you ken what they call that?" Shiv breaks into my thoughts. He points towards where the elevated train line crosses Argyll Street, on a wide bridge, sheltering a row of shops underneath. A burger bar and a pub are open, customers lurching between the two, their faces coloured by the orange street lights. I shake my head.

"The highlanders' umbrella. See there's a teuchter bar under there too." Shiv's pointing towards "The Gael". Funny to think of Scottish people feeling lonely in Glasgow. Imagine highlanders huddled under a cast iron multiple-rail-track-bridge, dazed at the prospect of the big city, with only the windows of some crummy fly-by-night discount shops for comfort. Where do they go next? Back on the train to their crofts? To the airport for a flight to the sun?

A group of young adolescents are hanging about by Macdonalds, on the other side of the road, flicking French fries, squirting milkshake and shouting at one another. But it seems that we're more interesting.

"Oi Paki!" one shouts. Shiv takes no notice and I look to see whether there's a bus coming, trying not to seem nervous.

"Paki-face! What you doing with one of our women?" shouts a tiny youth in a Nike baseball hat and Addidas jacket. He's short and slight with transparent opal-white skin and delicate-looking hands that are currently pointing at Shiv as he crosses the road towards us. I burst out laughing. What else can I do with the notion that I'm one of his women, when he looks not much over eight years old?

"What are you laughing at? Dyke!" the elfin-looking boy shouts. He's got the attention of his pals now and half a dozen are moving over towards us in a V-shape, like a flight of ducks with elfin-boy in the lead. Shiv pulls my hand and we both mount the steps of a yellow bus that he's flagged down.

"Where are you going?" Shiv asks the driver as the bus pulls back out from the stop.

"Quarrelton. Where are you going?" replies the driver.

"Just to Bellahouston." Shiv pays for two fares.

As I look out of the back window the youths have gathered in front of the Macdonalds window once again. They're back flinging discarded fast food at one another.

"Sorry," says Shiv as he sits beside me.

"S'not your fault," I reply.

"Aye, it's my fault for having the wrong face," Shiv pulls in his mouth in an expression of resigned exasperation.

"And mine for having sensible footwear. Anyway they were barely adolescent. Not really a threat." I try to sound convinced.

"Then why are you trembling?" asks Shiv. And he is right. My legs have gone to jelly.

"All that dancing," I say.

"They were neds. Wee baby neds, but none the less scarey.

65

At least they didn't find out you were English. Then we'd've been in real trouble."

We get off a few stops south of the river and start the long walk back towards my flat, in the hopes of finding a taxi en route. Shiv tells me he knows exactly where we are, since he's ridden every corporation bus route in Glasgow. He did voluntary work for a year, rather than sign on as unemployed. He got the same money as the dole, but the bonus was a free city-wide bus pass.

"So I'd sit on the top deck, smoking ciggies and writing rock lyrics. That was when you were still allowed to smoke on the bus like. And I knew for sure that one day soon I would become the new Bono."

"Have you got a band?"

"No, they've all fallen out with me."

"Did you play any gigs?"

"No, we just practised in Tim's Mum's garage. But our drummer, he's now gone to London with another group. They were on Top of the Pops the other night. And they've signed a record deal. And we used to drink in the same pub as 'The Pixies.' "

"Are you still going to be a rock star?" I ask.

"It's maybe too late for me now. I've not got the hunger any more. And I never could get the eye-liner right. Always looked more Alice Cooper than David Bowie. Now I'm gonnae be the first black poet laureate. Unless Jackie Kay gets there first."

I look at Shiv in his Cuban heels, his quiffy hair-do, pointy shaved side-burns and high cheek bones. His hands are plunged into his coat pockets as we trudge against the wind. He's looking down at the pavement. I can imagine his grainy photo on the front page of the "Times" when his laureate is announced in a decade or three. He turns sharply and catches me looking at him.

"Really Maya. I've had poems in Rebel Inc and one in a Black British anthology." He's mistaking my lack of response for disbelief. He wants me to believe in him. "It's a slim volume mind." And he's back in mocking mode. "And some of the writers are barely black. Deep yellow more like. Chinese who've been at the sun-bed too long. In fact, have you never

66

written a wee verse? Some dirty doggerel? Anyone can pass as
a coon if they've a creative streak. Could I put a word in for
you to get into the next edition?"

It's my turn to get serious. "I am a bit Indian Shiv. But I've
never written anything."

"Aye. Right you are Maya, with your bonnie red barnet,"
Shiv snorts, but I make him swallow his snort.

"No really Shiv. No bull."

It's only Maureen who's heard my story before. And
Granny of course, who helped to piece it together. Walking
along next to Shiv I don't have to look him in the eye.

"Do you want to hear about it?"

"Do you want to tell me?"

"Yes. As long as you don't ask any questions. And you
mustn't tell anyone else."

A taxi is heading towards us through the drizzle and the
driver is making eye contact as if expecting to get flagged
down. She's the first person we've seen since we got off the
bus, but we ignore her.

"OK," Shiv turns up his collar against the creeping wetness,
"You tell me Maya. I can keep it to myself." And we walk on
side by side.

Shiv stays silent as I talk. Perhaps he is surprised by how
my story comes out confident and certain. I'm repeating how
Granny used to recite it to me. The story felt more solid and
reliable when Granny told it to me.

"My mother was on a cultural retreat in Rajasthan staying
in a minor Maharaja's town house, to recover from the strain
of getting through her art history finals when she met a tabla
player. Ravi was the assistant music teacher. They met every
day at sunrise, because my mother wanted extra practice singing ragas. And because she wanted to seduce him. Once she'd
achieved this, Ravi stopped attending classes. Realising that
he wasn't coming back to work Hilary, my mother, persuaded
and paid one of the kitchen workers to take her to where Ravi
lived. They went on a bus out of the old, walled city and
beyond the low-rise sprawl into sandy scrubland. They got off
in a rubbish dump and walked until the plastic bags and
rotting vegetables gave way to sand and they could see a little
boxy hut the same colour as the sand. Out of the hut came

a small doughty woman in a bright sari. She saw Hilary and whipped back inside, only to re-appear banging two cooking pots together and shrieking. My mother claims to have asked 'Namastai-ji. Ravi kahan hai?' "

"Very good Maya, nice accent" Shiv can't resist commenting. I hold my finger across my lips as a warning to keep quiet.

"The woman just bared her teeth and battered the pots all the more. But Hilary could see Ravi leaning in the doorway, shrugging apologetically. If she only stood her ground, surely Ravi would come to her. But he remained behind his mother in the doorway, smiling. So Hilary had to leave, with the pot batterer following her until she'd got back onto a bus. Later, at the Maharaja's house, the sitar teacher took Hilary to one side and explained that Ravi's mother was worried about his corruption by a foreign woman that could ruin his chances of a decent marriage. Hilary was delighted at this view of herself as a dangerous woman." I peek sideways at Shiv who is walking, head down, into the surge of drizzly rain that we're walking through. I'm not even sure if he can hear me properly.

"My mother likes getting her own way. But despite not seeing Ravi again, she felt she'd had a good holiday, getting a more intimate vision of India than her fellow tourists. Four months later, she was back with my grandparents in Leamington Spa. She went to the doctor thinking she had a foreign microbe, to be told that she was actually nauseous because of a fertilised egg. Hilary assumed that once Ravi knew she was pregnant, she would be welcomed into his family. She imagined that she would be able to live as a daughter-in-law in the little sand coloured hut, learning to cook authentic curries, suckling her brown baby and perfecting her Hindi." My sour tone makes Shiv look up from the pavement. But I ignore him and keep going.

"My grandparents were shocked, but their neighbour's daughter had just come back from VSO, having married a Sandanista, so they felt that they had got off lightly. They mentioned adoption, but Hilary had other plans. She demanded an advance payment on her inheritance and returned to Rajasthan. She stayed in a modest hotel and tried to find Ravi. By now it was the hot season, and the Maharaja's house was shuttered and locked up. So was the boxy hut in the rubbish dump. My birth was brought on by a bout of dysentery. An Italian hippie, over wintering in the modest hotel, took Hilary to the hospital in a rickshaw. I came out quite easily and was washed clean by the hippie who then phoned my grandfather to give him the news: 'Que bella bambina!' We stayed in the hospital's private wing for a fortnight, thanks to my Grandpa sorting out an overseas money order. Hilary hoped that my pale, hairless state would be temporary and that I would turn into an exotically burnished little thing with time. But it never happened."

Now we've arrived at the doorway of my close. I turn to face Shiv. "Those racist baby-yobs couldn't see my Indian blood. Suppose I should be pleased about that." Shiv leans forwards and pats me on the shoulder.

"Well Maya, you've confirmed one universal truth for me. Everyone, even honkies, has an argumentative Indian granny. Although mine only bashes pots when she's cooking. It's a good story. Night-night." And he walks off.

I feel a bit stunned. Shiv really didn't ask any questions. Not about how much was true or whether I've ever contacted Ravi or anything. True to his word. But I've never really thought of the pot-basher as a Granny before. Indian or otherwise.

Balvinder

I was cosied into the bed recess when Maya got in from her dancing. But the baby needed changing, so I got up and once the baby was cooried in for a feed, ate some toast with Maya. She said she was sorry for weeping all over me the other day. And then she tried to hug me, but I was holding the baby so it didn't work very well.

"What are you going to do Balvinder?" Maya asks me very seriously. "You can't stay here forever. Even if your folks don't, won't the hospital come looking for you soon?"

"No, I gave them a kid-on address when I went in." I'd been terrified, not so much by the pains as by the realisation that I really was having a baby. But I knew I couldn't risk going back to my parents. "Specially my Dad.

"Well, how about the baby's father?" asks Maya.

69

"He's not the baby's father. He's just a bloke at a bhangra gig that I shagged. He's nothing to do with her."

"But if he knew then he could pay maintenance," Maya suggests brightly.

"Doubt it," I scoff. "He was just a laddie. He's no sense. Only works week-ends in his Uncle's shop anyway."

"Why d'you sleep with him then?"

"I didn't bloody sleep with him. I stood out the back of the hall next to a skip with him. I wanted to know how it felt." Maya drops her gaze. Sort of apologetically. I should be kinder to her. Perhaps she's not lost her cherry. The baby lets out a mighty fart, only slightly muffled by her nappy. "And um, now I suppose I know how it feels."

Maya doesn't say as much but she can't credit foolishness like mine. She doesn't understand my thoughtlessness. She's a planner. She thinks of consequences before they happen. She wouldn't end up with a baby unless she'd got a decent bidie-in. But she's not got a Dad from Jullunder. She can cock-up her own future. I'm not allowed to because it belongs to my family.

Heather

The Braidhead Hotel in Queensferry is not nearly as nice as it should be; all swagging and gilt mirrors but no creature comforts in the toilets. Just the job for a wedding reception in fact. The good thing about delaying marriage until your fifth decade is that you can afford decent champagne. But the off-the-shoulder white number is hard enough to carry off, even in your twenties. What is it about the big white frock? When do women grow out of wanting it? Still, there's no denying that Annie and her new man look very happy.

My girls eat a bread roll and some soup and are taken off by one of the bridesmaids to play in the garden. So I'm left to chat to Isabelle. We did SYS Physics together at school. As the only candidates in our girls' school, we had to walk over to the boys' school twice a week for a double period. I've not met Isabelle since those days, but I've heard about her from Annie. Some hot shot job in industry and a self-made man of a husband. We exchange platitudes about how beautiful Annie looks and what a lovely day for it, before there is a short silence, during which I feel greatly relieved that Doug is climbing in the Cairngorms with his mates. He doesn't do well with mincing chit-chat.

"So those two little ones are yours?" asks Isabelle.

"Yes," I try not to sound too proud of my delightful progeny in their matching pinafores.

"Annie tells me you manage without a nanny. Terribly brave of you."

"It works fine for us."

"But how do you ever go shopping?"

"I hate shopping. Doug gets most of our food in."

"Ah! And of course we have Johnnie Boden for all our emergency catalogue purchases." Isabelle eyes my skirt and top, perhaps looking for something comforting to say about my appearance. If that was her line of thought, she thinks better of it. "Well I simply couldn't manage without my nanny. It's a major domestic crisis every time one leaves us. I do admire women who can do the whole proper mummy thing, but frankly I couldn't get out to work in the mornings without hired help."

"Aye well. Universities don't generally start their working day too early."

"But however do you get your hair and make-up done?" asks Isabelle. I stare at her, not sure where to start expressing incredulity. Does my hair look as though it's been done? Does my face look as though I own more than a single tube of lipstick?

"Being well-groomed in University circles means chipping the congealed egg off your old school tie."

"Oh! You're still teaching are you? Annie told me you were doing very well. In charge of your own division aren't you?"

"Kind of."

"Splendid. I do so admire devotion to a calling. Of course I am so blessed in not having to work, because Craig was bought out a couple of years ago. But I do love the cut and thrust of a day's trading." She licks her lips in a greedy way. I'm stunned, unused to being the subject of pity. I'm more familiar with intimidating people like Doug's climbing friends because of my clever University job. Isabelle continues avoiding talking about the tragedy of my low pay and

71

non-existent status and congratulating me on my courage and fortitude on living in a flat in the inner city, using the NHS and not owning a car, covering up her pity with mock admiration.

At last the girls arrive back. The bridesmaid has grass stains on her pale yellow frock and is carrying the baby, yelling loudly, with a slight graze on her forehead. Her sister is crying in sympathy. What a relief to excuse myself from the table to wash the baby's head and calm her sister down. I can't face returning to the meal, so we ask the reception desk to call us a taxi and wait quietly outside the front door. I'll put a card to Annie in the post and blame the children for our flight.

Maya

At work, Mrs Kapadia comes to talk to me about Balvinder. She says she's been wondering what to do ever since I told her about the baby.

"I don't want to spread gossip. And this is number one, hot gossip."

Balvinder's mother, Mrs Singh phoned Mrs Kapadia wanting news of her daughter's whereabouts. Balvinder's cousin told Mrs Singh that Balvinder left London yesterday. But since, she never arrived at Mrs Singh's and she's not answering her mobile. Hence the phone call to see whether Balvinder had arrived at work. Mrs Singh was very worried and getting angry. What was Mrs Kapadia to say?

"I told Mrs Singh that Balvinder is fine and was planning to stay with me for a few days while we do some work together on a funding application" Mrs K smiles as though everything was sorted out.

"Did she believe you?"

"Why wouldn't she? I am a respectable woman!"

"Yes, of course, but ..." I peter out. I am trying to say that Mrs K wasn't really very friendly with Balvinder. But it seems impertinent.

"And since I am a truthful woman, I must now make it be true."

And that is how it came about that Balvinder and her baby were taken off my hands. Mrs Kapadia arrives in a large ivory Bentley with her driver who parks it on the double yellow lines outside my close. Mrs Kapadia puffs up the stairs, her turquoise dupatta catching on the bannister as she turns the corner. As her backdrop the stairwell looks so shabby with its battle-ship grey, piss-proof paint up the walls. Once she arrives inside my flat, I realise that I haven't enough cups to have more than one guest.

I'd warned Balvinder that Mrs K was likely to arrive to collect her when I got in from work. Given her resistance to contacting her parents or getting a council flat, I thought she'd be horrified. Quite the opposite. She showered herself and the baby, found the nicest outfit from the second hand hospital clothes for the baby and re-plaited her own hair smoothly. Then she set about making sweets, sending me out for extra sugar and milk.

Mrs K, enthroned in the only chair, is delighted with the baby, pinching her creamy flesh as though testing its consistency. She flips the baby over her shoulder and pats her rhythmically, her hands covering the whole of the baby's back. Oddly the baby seems quite content with the regular thwacking.

"You are a clever girl" Mrs Kapadia congratulates Balvinder, whose cheeks pink prettily.

I feel clumpy, ungracious and in the way.

Packages are brought out of the Bentley. Baby clothes wrapped in tissue paper, a new Moses basket lined in yellow lace, gift-wrapped velvety toys in primary colours and a complete layette in soft unbleached cotton. And for Balvinder a gold-coloured Punjabi suit with bright, silky embroidery around the neck and cuffs. She puts it on in the bathroom and emerges looking shy and lovely. With all the parcels opened and admired, Mrs K turned to me and raises her tea-cup.

"I give you a toast for Maya. Very many thanks for looking after our Balvinder. You were a friend in need! Hai-na Balvinder?" Balvinder smiles at me and nods her head. Mrs K gives me a parcel containing a magenta-coloured suit similar to Balvinder's.

"This is for you to wear when the baby is named. You will always be a special person for her."

Ugh. The horror. Mrs Kapadia's over-flowing generosity makes me feel inadequate and mean. I can't respond. I finger the embroidery around the neck of the tunic while they exchange news about the Shakti volunteer ladies and their husbands and children. Eventually the driver knocks on the door, warning that a traffic warden is approaching. He takes all the parcels except for mine back down to the car and Mrs Kapadia goes to sweet talk the warden. Balvinder follows, carrying her tiny amount of luggage in a plastic carrier bag. As she crosses the threshold she turns back to me.

"Thank-you for having me in your flat Maya. You've been a pal. I hope you won't miss us. See you at Shakti soon."

Balvinder

Balvinder stays with the Kapadias, living as a daughter of the household. After a month of seclusion, recovering from childbirth, she starts going out in public with Mrs Kapadia and quite soon Balvinder is accompanying her everywhere. Together Mrs Kapadia, Balvinder and the baby attend the launch of a mental health project, a homework club and an anti-racist arts website, displays of dancing and singing, performances of community voices poetry and warrior tales, private views of photography, junk sculptures and scissor-silhouettes. With Mrs Kapadia's support, Balvinder is delighted to show her daughter off. The notables of the Asian community, whom Maya had found so difficult to contact, are suddenly available for small talk, keen to view the novelty of the invincible Mrs Kapadia, accompanied by her shameless adopted daughter and grand-daughter of unknown provenance. Mrs Kapadia and Balvinder with the increasingly engaging baby, communicate their joint enthusiasm for the Shakti project and as a threesome lend it an unconventional glamour that draws others in. Mrs Karogi, wife of the travel agent and Mrs Bashir, recently widowed wife of the MP, both find time to attend Shakti board meetings, covenant funds and have rooms named for their husbands. Mrs Imran, whose long experience of the diplomatic life makes her a good match for Mrs Kapadia, takes it upon herself to furnish one room with computers and to teach internet and e-mail skills on a weekly basis. Mrs Jacob, who has the double prestige of being the daughter of a rich man and the wife of a holy one, runs a monthly tea party where religious matters are discussed over tea, pakora and spicy tomato chutney. The discussion is skilfully chaired to allow the South Indian Christians and Shia Muslims to contribute despite being heavily outnumbered by Sunnis and Sikhs. The debate frequently becomes extremely heated and nonetheless enjoyable for it, with all the women agreeing that only when men became involved does passionate disagreement lead to imputations of dishonour.

Mrs Singh

Mrs Kapadia rings Mrs Singh, and with Balvinder's permission, tells her about the baby. Mrs Singh wonders whether she will be forced to choose between Balvinder and the rest of her family. Despite fearing harsh judgement, she visits her newest grandchild. Balvinder sits next to her on one of Mrs Kapadia's butterscotch sofas and submits the baby for inspection. Mrs Singh notes the baby's milky skin and muddy-coloured eyes. She strokes the soft cheek and the baby turns towards her hand, rooting. Mrs Singh lifts the baby and embraces her. Balvinder lets out a breath that she's been holding involuntarily. Mrs Singh will not stay to take tea with Mrs Kapadia, but says she will return in three days time. And so she does, thereby establishing a pattern of twice weekly visits when she quickly takes over the care of her granddaughter, allowing Balvinder to do a few hours at Shakti. Balvinder works the telephones, following up the social contacts that she makes when out with Mrs Kapadia.

Mrs Singh eventually feels she has sufficient courage to tell her husband about Balvinder's daughter. Although greatly preoccupied by the increasing pain of his angina, he had begun to suspect something fearful had occurred since he hadn't seen Balvinder for nearly three months. He greets the news with just enough shouting and exclamation of outrage at his besmirched reputation to meet his family's expectations. But the gripping pain on his heart stops him short of making any threats that he would be unable to follow up. He resigns himself to never seeing Balvinder again.

Once the secret was out, Mrs Singh feels able to enjoy her granddaughter more openly. Acquaintances and neighbours indicate that they have heard about Balvinder by commiserating about the unreliable and feckless nature of modern girls.

Mrs Singh smiles in reply, shrugs and comments that "our girls have to be warriors in their own way." She is surprised that she is able to let the knowing comments and saccharine sympathy slide off. She does not feel shrivelled by shame, as long as she concentrates on the baby's lovely smile and Balvinder's quiet, defiant pride in her daughter.

The baby's eyes turn an unmistakably deep black-blue colour and Mrs Singh wonders whether the father was a Kashmiri or a white boy. Which would be preferable? And is either worse than having her daughter dishonoured by a sly Sikh? While the news of the baby's eye colour goes round, the shame is harder to contain and Mrs Singh finds herself unwilling to accept invitations for a gossip around a tea tray. But the excited speculation dies down again and when the baby reaches five months Mrs Singh offers to host a blessing for her at the Gurdwara. She sells some jewellery to fund the celebration and gently refuses Mrs Kapadia's offer to foot the bill. The morning of the blessing Mrs Singh gets her younger children washed and dressed in their prettiest clothes and they were watching at the window for the arrival of the taxi. She is having a fortifying cup of tea and wondering at her own daring. Yet no open defiance has been necessary. Her husband has not once asked her what she is organising, presumably for fear of finding out. She has heard that two of the Gurdwara elders have been very much against holding the blessing, but others have argued strongly that her parentage was hardly the baby's fault and that matters of honour are of secular rather than religious consideration. Mrs Singh's husband and the two temple elders have found that they have an important service to attend at one of the Edinburgh Gurdwaras and had taken themselves off early that morning.

A couple of the big families are absent from the blessing. Mrs Singh assumes that they were boycotting it. Other people quietly congratulate her on her courage during the langar. One little grey-haired woman, known for her piety and childlessness sits down by Mrs Singh at the long trestle table and describes in quavering old fashioned Punjabi how she had lost touch with her daughter after her husband had forbade her from ever returning home again. The daughter's sin? She had been spotted kissing a white boy. The brother had snitched on his sister as revenge for a disagreement over ownership of a record and had hoped she would be confined to her room for a day or two. Appalled by the dire consequences of his information, he regretted the loss of his sister greatly. His regret was felt most keenly as he realised that he too wanted to kiss a boy. Two years after his sister had been thrown out, the woman's son had left home of his own accord for New York, never to send a letter or to telephone.

"Men maintain honour and women pay the price sister-ji" the woman concludes and shuffles off to wash up in the communal kitchen. Mrs Singh's first impulse is to turn to her sister-in-law to pass on the story of how the woman they had thought tragically childless had actually lost her children as adults. But the knowledge that people are probably speculating over her granddaughter's conception around the same table stops her short.

Once her daughter's shameful behaviour has been widely discussed and has slowly begun to lose currency, Mrs Singh cautiously allows herself to enumerate what has been lost through the scandal. Her husband is the main casualty. Never the most communicative of men, after his angry outburst about Balvinder Mr Singh's discussions with his spouse have stopped altogether. Her husband's older brother's wife is no longer speaking to her either. An auspicious marriage that had been under discussion for Mrs Singh's nephew has fallen through and Balvinder's poor moral character is suspected to be the cause. A week after the blessing, Mr Singh was taken into hospital as an emergency case and his sister blames Mrs Singh for failing to prevent his ongoing heart condition. Despite serious concern about how long he has to live, Mr Singh refuses to see Balvinder or the baby. Still, his being confined to hospital means that the baby can come home and meet Balvinder's younger siblings. And Mrs Singh's sense of shame fades a little more as the baby becomes a more routine part of family life. On Sundays between hospital visits, Mrs Singh begins to show her face at the temple. A month after the baby's blessing a temple-regular called Jatinder Kaur, sits down next to her, bringing a cup of tea.

"Sat sree akaal. Helloji" they exchange greetings. An exchange of pleasantries and then news about children proceed. Jatinder Kaur asks after Balvinder in solicitous detail before going on to talk about her nephew in Colchester who has been left by his wife. Mrs Singh clicks her tongue disapprovingly, as is expected, but then surprises herself by asking why the wife left.

"Unreliable girls nowadays" comes the predictable reply. But when Mrs Singh fails to agree and a pause opens up in the flow of conversation, Jatinder Kaur goes on to say that the couple have had bad arguments. Mrs Singh assumes that the nephew has been hitting his wife. She dearly wants Balvinder properly married, but not at any price. She commiserates with Jatinder Kaur for her sadness in losing touch with her grandchildren. And then she steers the talk towards the difficulties of getting the council to issue an appropriate licence for the forthcoming mela. Some minutes later Jatinder Kaur goes to re-join her family, who are getting their shoes on, preparing to leave. No offers or proposals have been made and no face had been lost, but both parties know that Mrs Singh has refused an overture. And word must have got around since Mrs Singh does not find anyone else discussing their divorced or separated sons with her again. Gossip has its uses. Unfortunately, there's no talk of eligible, unmarried sons either.

Mrs Singh cherishes a hope that Balvinder will marry one of Mrs Kapadia's sons, both good looking and well-qualified lads. A marriage would conveniently sort out the impropriety of Balvinder sharing a roof with single men, but the idea doesn't seem to have struck anyone else. Given the elegance of her solution, she resolves to suggest it to Mrs Kapadia. Next time she is collecting the baby from the Kapadia house, she accepts the offer of tea. Balvinder goes to assemble the baby's changing bag, leaving her mother holding the baby with Mrs Kapadia pouring the tea.

"Yours sons are good boys," Mrs Singh begins tentatively. "They will need companionship soon hai na? My Balvinder loves you. Like a mother. Or mother-in-law perhaps ..." Mrs Singh is taken aback by the hilarity that her carefully rehearsed speech provokes. Mrs Kapadia is all dimpled and chuckling.

"Oh my dear Mrs Singh. I wish it could be so. Your Balvinder is perfect. Ideal daughter-in-law. But my sons are not the marrying types. They are good boys. But not marrying boys. One son prefers boys and the other is either writing his little poems or performing gori-dances."

This news is so unexpected that Mrs Singh can only blink. How can Mrs Kapadia carry herself with pride in society, having failed to raise her sons properly?

"But I very much hope that we can continue to share your beautiful granddaughter," Mrs Kapadia continues. Mrs Singh's nodding coincides with her blinking but she remains speechless.

Balvinder

Balvinder cannot disguise her delight at having gained a baby without losing contact with her Ma. She refers to Mrs Kapadia as her fairy godmother and names her daughter Meena in her honour. She has gambled everything and won. The relief at not being forced to leave Glasgow, lifts her spirits and renders her prettier and livelier than before, and also thrilled by the excitement of disrupting other people's expectations. Once the shock value of her husband-less motherhood wears off she begins to wonder whether she could marry Dr Soheil Sharif, the good-looking psychiatrist who sits on Shakti's board of managers, and still remain part of Mrs Kapadia's entourage.

Perhaps Mrs Kapadia senses Balvinder's roving eye. Or perhaps it is Mrs Singh's suggestion that brings her cousin Raj Jutley to mind. He is a recently widowed businessman based in Mauritius, who might be agreeable to contracting a mutually beneficial marriage. Mrs Kapadia feels that Balvinder's feistiness would complement her cousin's formal, old fashioned dignity, which, if left unchallenged, is in danger of coagulating into pomposity. She also hopes that since Raj lost his daughter in the same traffic accident that made him a widower, he will be willing to adopt little Meena.

Balvinder likes the idea of marriage to someone from outside Glasgow. None of the boys of her own age are bold or daring enough a match for her, even if their mothers would permit it. Having survived pregnancy, birth and early parenting, despite doing it in the least acceptable fashion, she feels pretty indestructible. She sees herself as a successful risk-taker, but she isn't yet ready for the long-term risk of a husband and decides to start with a more manageable project. Her father has been forced by dint of his heart condition to give up running his corner shop, so Balvinder takes over the lease. Initially she sticks to the stock that had kept her father in business for thirty years – white bread, bacon, sweets, ginger, beer and newspapers. If she can make a success of self-employment, her standing as a prospective bride for the Mauritian Kapadia cousin will go up.

Maya

Maya wants to feel pleased to have her private space back once Mrs Kapadia has taken Balvinder off her hands. She spring cleans her flat and tries to rejoice that everything will remain where she sets it down. She washes all the bed linen and dries it on the little back green by the midden. She scrubs the carpets, bleaches the kitchen and bathroom surfaces, wipes the dust from the top of the cupboards and the jam rings from the shelves. She moves the television back out of the kitchen. She sorts out the provisions, putting all the things that she doesn't recognise – saunf, haldi and moong dahl – into a bag to give to Bal. Surveying the muddy root vegetables in the bottom of the fridge, Maya makes a pan of what her grandmother would have called "a substantial soup".

Having eaten two bowls of the soup, Maya is able to contemplate tidying up her past. She gets down one of the cardboard boxes through which Balvinder rifled in search of diversion. This box had arrived for Maya at her student hall of residence, carefully shrouded in brown paper and string, two days after Granny had died. Inside were the dozen albums in which Granny and her mother before her had archived two generations of extended family life, plus an envelope of photographs and documents yet to be mounted. A note in Granny's careful, shaky hand:

Darling Maya
The enclosed is your history to do with as you see fit. I've sent a selection of her childhood photos to Hilary. I thought about burning the rest, but felt the decision to do

so should be yours alone.

From your ever loving and devoted Granny.

At the time Maya had stuffed the note into the box without examining its contents. It was too frightening. Maureen, visiting at the time, had enquired about the parcel and reacted: "Ugh, instructions from beyond the grave". Maya had not felt spooked by her Granny's last missive, but just unable to face the evidence of all that she had lost. She had moved house with the box three times and now, fortified with a strong coffee, she is ready to take over where her grandmother had left off. She empties out the envelope and reads the black-edged order of service from her grandfather's funeral that falls on top of the pile of photos. All Granny's favourite hymns. Granny had said there was no point in saving them for her own funeral. In amongst the photos of a picnic, a Warwick Castle, Hilary's cousin's wedding, there was a faded square of pink card, marked "Baby Paul", "norm. vag del." and "7lb 2oz" in blue ink. Hand-written Hindi script next to the English words, presumably says the same thing. Maya feels satisfied to have found evidence that she really was born in India and it wasn't just one of Hilary's fantasies. She sticks the hospital card and the funeral service in next to each other in the album.

The next day Maya is even more reluctant than usual to get herself to work. She anticipates having to explain her role in Balvinder's predicament to the volunteer ladies, aflutter with excitement. But as she sets her bag down on her desk and looks for her teacup, everyone is preoccupied with the meeting of the board of managers. The ladies are putting together an elaborate tea tray. Shuggie is arranging chairs and the overhead projector in the meeting room, while Mrs Kapadia is anxiously putting out pens and pads around the big oval table.

"Hello Maya," she calls. "Please to photocopy this agenda for me. And could you do something creative to make it pretty?"

The source of Mrs Kapadia's anxiety arrives in the form of Heather Cromarty who asks Maya to make copies of the new business plan that she'll be proposing to the board. The

meeting room door closes behind Mrs Karogi, the last person
to arrive who is apologising for being "on Indian time". Maya
wonders whether anything will have changed once the meeting is over. Shuggie is standing by the reception desk and
catches Maya's eye. His bristly grizzled eybrow dips in what
Maya interprets as a conspiratorial wink.

"That's our future they're away to discuss my friend. Our
conditions of labour. We should have a workers' representa-
tive on that board eh? Then again, what have the unions ever
done for you?" He pauses and looks Maya up and down.
"You'll never even have had a membership, will you?"

Maya shakes her head.

"You're a right posh spice aren't you. But then I paid my
union dues for twenty years and it didn't save my job or the
boat-building industry! Nae luck eh!"

Maya smiles apologetically. She'd read about red Clydesiders in an exhibit in the People's Palace one wet Sunday afternoon. Best not to mention that her grandfather had driven a
bus during the general strike after the war.

"There's no sense us waiting to hear if we've been
restructured out of a job eh! We'll away out to the pub shall
we?" Shuggie was ushering Maya out of the door and waving
to the volunteer ladies. "Back in a wee while ladies!"

When they return, Maya feeling disoriented from being in
a pub before noon and hazy from the pint of McEwan's that
Shuggie had felt she needed, they find the meeting breaking
up in good spirits. Heather Cromarty comes over to Maya.

"We've agreed a new plan. And the reorganisation should
release you from fund-raising." Heather was smiling over
Maya's shoulder to Soheil Sharif with whom she'd agreed to
discuss the Scottish Executive inclusive housing initiatives
over lunch. "You should be able to do the job you applied for
now. Let me know how you get on" Heather says by way of
farewell.

A few days later, Maya gets a letter from the Beaudessert
Benevolent Fund. The trustees have granted her an award. In
fact, they are giving her more than she had applied for. The
letter states that Maya's qualifications and experience, as out-
lined in her CV, mean that she should be on a higher wage than
she had specified. Everyone at Shakti is delighted. Mrs

Kapadia hugs Maya, the reception ladies make a celebratory cup of tea and Shuggie smiles. With Maya's wage being met for two years, there is money available to employ others. Balvinder is paid for the fund-raising work that she was doing anyway and two crèche workers are employed for five afternoons a week.

Maya's first project is the room to be used as a crèche. Heather Cromarty suggests that the board of managers should approve the decorative scheme "so as to avoid any unwarranted offence being caused."

"Did you think I'd be doing a Noah's Ark picture then?" asks Maya, confident that her Stoke Newington schooling was multi-culti enough to avoid the obvious pitfalls.

Maya works alone and quickly. The crèche workers are using the meeting room temporarily. Her design for the floor and walls features a Paisley pattern that she found in a book on the history of the textile trade in the Mitchell Library. She is pleased with the pretty asymmetrically curved tear drop, so familiar from her granny's bed quilt and, according to book, originating from India. When Maya's mosaic work frieze with plastic mirror tiles at toddler eye-level and swirly-patterned vulcanized rubber flooring are finished, Mrs Kapadia starts to plan a grand opening of the building. The computers have been acquired for the internet café and its decoration is Maya's next project. The board suggests that end-users should be more involved in defining future projects.

"End users?" asks Maya.

"It means those poor souls who we are meant to be helping" explains Mrs Kapadia. "We need evidence for the end-of-year report that we are improving people's quality of life."

"Well" says Balvinder looking up from her desk "Now that I'm getting paid, my quality of life has been improved to the tune of eighty pounds per week."

People are coming to the Shakti building in increasing numbers because the cups of tea laid on by the volunteer ladies have gradually expanded to full-blown tea parties. Competitive catering has led to an escalation from a couple of samosas to a cornucopia of plastic boxes containing fruit chaat, paneer pakora, aubergine pakora, ras malai and gulaab jamun. Under Mrs Kapadia's leadership the powerful urge to out-do one another in providing increasingly lavish catering is channelled into a cooking co-operative. A rota is drawn up so that several women per day use the little Shakti kitchen to prepare a couple of dishes to be shared out among the employees, the volunteer ladies and the increasing number of extra guests. The cooks have also made a special batch of Shakti chutney, cooked up when Mr Kapadia ordered too many crates of mangoes for the cash and carry. Jars of the chutney are on sale at the reception desk, carrying pretty Paisley motif labels designed by Maya.

Maya puts a poster up in the Shakti kitchen to recruit cooks to her art project. Then she goes off to explore the private collection of papers belonging to a family whose fore-fathers grew rich on importing cotton from India. Their papers are kept in a mahogany-lined library in their summer residence in the hills above Helensburgh. Heather Cromarty knows the family through her parents and has arranged for Maya to look through the samples of fabric and books of patterns dating from 1907. Every morning Maya goes out west of Glasgow on a train from Central Station. At lunch-time she eats her peanut butter sandwich sitting on a bench overlooking the Gareloch. Enjoying the sun on her skin, and the view of hills and water, Maya wonders whether she should go into holy orders. Solitude seems to suit her so well. The only person she speaks to is the housekeeper who lets her in, opens the library up, brings her a cup of coffee and a finger of shortbread at eleven and a cup of tea and a slice of ginger bread at four.

After a week, Maya returns to Shakti and is surprised that no-one has signed up for her project.

"You are a right daftie Maya," Balvinder laughs with some affection. "Who would respond to a poster?" Seeing Maya's fallen face, she continues, "The poster's lovely, it's just what sort of person gets into something because of a poster? Well, apart from you? You've got to go and talk to them."

So Maya goes and hangs about in the kitchen and gets in the way of the co-operative cooks. They are kind to her and find her jobs where she can do no harm, peeling vegetables and washing rice. She drinks tea, but can't really join in on the conversation, even when it's in English. She has no children, husband, mother-in-law or other household to report on. She has no-one to complain about. Or crow about. One particularly friendly cook persists in trying to find common ground with Maya until eventually in exasperation she asks

"Not even a boyfriend? So what do you do all day? Aren't you bored?"

Maya feels the scald of pity and goes to the kitchen less often.

Balvinder

I'm fair proud of my wee shop. Heather Cromarty reckons I should be signing up to study business economics and marketing in case I ever need a proper qualification. But I can read my customers and I know what they'll buy if it's put before them. The boys who appear of a morning with nothing on under their overcoats, trainers and no socks, will just as soon spend their grants on butter croissants as pan loaf. Especially if there's a dolly-bird waiting under the duvet. And the gap-clad couples who buy long-life naan bread for their post-pub suppers will pay fifty percent more for pre-packed dahl and roti dinner cooked by the Shakti ladies. Especially if they feel they're assisting a local oppressed minority. So much easier than actually getting to know your Paki neighbours. And I've got a lovely line of ethnic chutneys to complement your conscience-salving supper. It's like a game of ambush, watching my regular customers and planking the tempting products on the shelves. I have to hold back from punching the air when I get it right. Like the swithering of the English customers as they reluctantly choose between the "Herald" or the "Scotsman". Now I stock the "Guardian", and they buy the Scottish papers to feel in touch with us natives and the London paper to actually read. I could teach my Dad a trick or two. If only he was speaking to me.

The other cornershops have noticed I've arrived. Customers walk that wee bit further for my free-range eggs (from a farm near Milngavie – more suburban than country chickens and four pence off if you bring your own egg box), misshapen tomatoes (bought from the Allotment Owners' Association in season), mango chutney (from the Shakti ladies) and tablet (home-made by the wifie who kept the shop before my Dad).

The other shop owners have complained about my unfair business practices. My oldest nephew was showing off his new trainers and bragging how he'd earned them through his evenings and Saturdays behind my till. Now all the aunties agree that I'm paying him too much. The words "legal minimum wage" cut no mustard. Except with the Shakti board of managers who've invited me to stand for election at the next AGM. Will Heather Cromarty vote for me without an MBA?

Maya

Both Hilary and Maureen Oshanti write to say that they will attend the grand opening of Shakti, overcoming their prejudice against the extreme northerly position of Glasgow. Hilary had always been good at throwing parties and determined to attend any to which she is invited. When Maya was younger her birthday parties had always been fantastic and caused other children's mothers to mutter "upping the stakes that woman, with her fruit kebabs and home-made party bags". The food, decorations and games had showed the artistic and organisational flair that Hilary couldn't be bothered to put into her paid employment. A princess party with specially made sparkly frocks, a dracula party with blood orange juice and bat-shaped biscuits and a treasure hunt party with maps which led the way to a wooden box of pearl and cut glass necklaces buried in the sand pit. For a while after each glorious party Maya enjoyed a burst of popularity among her classmates. But it never lasted long. And Maya wasn't yet a teenager before she realised that to have friends interested in her simply because of her mother's parties was worse than having no friends. She came to dread her birthday. But Hilary was not prepared to stop throwing the parties. She told the other mothers that it was the only aspect of parenting that she enjoyed.

As Maya got older, Hilary's party themes developed. So when Maya achieved the necessary "A" level grades to get into Art School, Hilary threw a party in the subscription gardens to which her employer, the owner of the art gallery, held keys. It had a North African theme, as interpreted by Elle Interiors, rather than by Christian Aid. Tea lights in recycled, stencil-cut tin cans picked out the gravel paths and hung in the cherry trees. An embroidered awning covered a buffet of elegantly spiced finger foods laid out on brass hammer-worked trays. A beautiful young aspiring artist, of Hilary's acquaintance, dressed in a vibrant Kaftan served glasses of sweet mint tea and robust red wine to the guests.

While slumped alone under the awning after drinking too much wine too rapidly, Maya had resolved that this would be the last party that Hilary would organise for her. Maureen had gone to find areas of mutual interest with the beautiful aspiring artist, leaving Maya on the silk carpet, with a shawl tucked around her. Maya closed her eyes, not needing to watch Maureen charm the Kaftan-clad young lovely. And with her eyes shut, trying not to listen to Maureen, Maya had tuned into her mother's unmistakable tones instead.

"Well it has been a struggle, of course. Particularly during the eighties ... Yes, the political atmosphere, especially in north London was just so hostile to single parents. Not to mention ethnic minorities ... Not easy ... So much prejudice ... I've had to sacrifice my own work of course..."

Maya couldn't hear the other side of the conversation and it didn't really matter who Hilary was telling about her battle against exclusion and marginalisation. The aspects of her mother that Maya had tried to see as positive were recast. She saw how all her birthday parties had staged Hilary as the valiant heroine, coping jolly well with her frightfully difficult situation. Maya knew that it was Granny who arrived at two hour's notice to look after Maya when she was ill, who bought her school uniform and shoes, paid for music lessons and looked after her throughout the holidays. Inexperienced in the effects of red wine, Maya mistook her sense of maudlin doom for reliable evidence of the imminent collapse of her world. Even the thought of seeing Granny the next day in Leamington Spa had not comforted her.

Sitting on the train clanking out of Marylebone Station the next day, the sense of utter gloom had worn off, but Maya's resolve not to allow Hilary to stage another party had not. No more parties, not even when she would graduate from Art School with flying colours, as was her intention. The man sitting opposite her had fallen asleep almost as soon as he sat down. Maya watched as his jaw dropped and his head lolled forwards and wished that Hilary had handed her over to stay with Granny and Grandpa for ever when she was a baby. The man's mouth pulled shut as his head jerked backwards onto the headrest, but despite the violence of the movement he stayed asleep. Maya felt sure that she and her grandparents would have been happy together. The man's mouth opened again and a string of saliva descended slowly from his bottom lip. But Maya knew that Hilary's staging of her own noble struggle with the grave adversity of her circumstances would have been hampered without an illegitimate child as a prop. The saliva string was sucked back into the man's mouth as he breathed in noisily. Maya suddenly realised that she didn't ever have to live with Hilary again. This was her last summer holidays before going to college. Whenever Maya had protested about returning to Hilary's house at the end of the holidays, Granny had said that when she left school she could choose where she wanted to live. As the man's bleary eyes opened and he wiped saliva from his chin, he saw the red-haired girl opposite smiling a wide grin of satisfaction.

Before accepting the invitation to the Shakti party, Hilary phones Maureen and offers to pay for her fare to Glasgow too, thinking that this might increase the warmth of her welcome from Maya. When Hilary's letter comes announcing her arrival in Glasgow, Maya regrets her weakness in the face of Mrs Kapadia's expectation that she should contribute names to the grand opening guest list. Mrs Kapadia had insisted that she must know more than two people.

"What about your parents Maya? They will be wanting to see your pretty walls," Mrs Kapadia had stated. And Maya had agreed rather than explain that she considered herself an orphan now that Granny and Grandpa had died.

Holding the letter from Hilary, Maya phones her. "Mum you can't stay with me. Maureen will be here. It's a very small flat. Sorry."

Maureen has decided to visit far-flung Glasgow to demonstrate solidarity with Maya, to investigate a rumour among young London journalists that Glasgow might be the new Dublin and in the hopes that racism at an explicitly multicultural celebration would be minimal or at least witty.

On arrival, Maureen takes charge of dressing Maya up in her magenta suit from Mrs Kapadia, and taming her unruly hair with corn-rows plaited tight on to her scalp, each one finished with a gold bead. When they both go to meet Hilary at Central station, she is delighted by her daughter's appearance.

"Quite the little ethnic princess isn't she?"

Maureen, utterly used to Hilary's funny ways, agrees and adjusts her own vintage Jean Muir frock which, as she knows, drapes her elegant frame to perfection.

Mrs Kapadia has invited all the local councillors and members of the Westminster and Holyrood parliaments to the opening and a dozen have appeared. The recent stabbing of a Somali refugee in Sighthill has set public servants looking for easy gestures towards the promotion of good community relations. Maya's insides curl up as her murals and mosaics are praised by local bara sahibs as representing a harmonious marriage of the best of eastern and western traditions. She dares not speak, but stands smiling between Maureen and Balvinder, hoping to share their ethnic authenticity. Professor Heather Cromarty speaks on behalf of the board of managers to congratulate all those who have devoted their time and talent to making Shakti a place that people want to visit and urges the audience to introduce others to its resources. She holds up postcards, produced by Maya with help from the crèche that can be sent as invitations to visit Shakti. Heather takes a couple herself, sure that there will be a lonely or anxious undergraduate who would benefit from the warmth of the place. For all her deficiencies as an efficient manager, Mrs Kapadia strikes Heather as someone who could provide a sturdy and sympathetic shoulder to those time-consuming students who fall out with their families or boyfriends while trying to complete their studies.

After the speeches, the crowd moves through the building to drink mango-and-coconut-cup served from a counter decorated with paisley patterned cloths, to have their hands painted in henna and elaborate bindis applied between their eyebrows. Maya catches sight of Shiv leaning against a doorpost with Shuggie and finds the recent derby between Celtic and Rangers under discussion in a vocabulary so specialised as to be almost completely impenetrable. When Shuggie is called away to unlock a cleaning cupboard, Maya accosts Shiv.

"What are you doing here?"

"It's an open event isn't it? And may I say that I'm delighted to see you too," Shiv returns with his cheesiest smile.

"But how did you know about it?"

"Well, truthfully, I'm not here for the entertainment-value. I've to pick up my mum. Will you be coming to the dancing tonight? You were missed last week."

"Yeah. Well," Maya tries to tell whether Shiv is being ironic from his expression. She can't.

"I was trying to get this lot finished off for today," Maya waves her hand towards the colourful, shiny walls. "And my friend Maureen is up from London."

"Well, bring her too," smiles Shiv.

"Hello darling! Are you discussing your hiddley-diddley-music-dancing?" cuts in Mrs Kapadia, abundantly shimmering in her aqua marine shot silk.

"Ah!" Maya pauses for realisation to bloom.

"Shiv *Kapadia*" Maya states what is perfectly obvious given that Mrs Kapadia is holding Shiv's chin in an extremely maternal fashion. Nonetheless, Maya repeats the name with her intonation and her eyebrows raised questioningly.

"Shiv Kapadia?"

"Indeed. And your good name is?" replies Shiv with a heavily hammed Indian accent.

"Maya, as you know fine well. Paul is my surname."

"And so is mine," Hilary has butted into the conversation and is looking at Shiv. "But I didn't catch yours ... surely you're not Mrs Kapadia's son?" Hilary turns to Mrs Kapadia "You simply don't look old enough."

Maya is amazed anew at her mother's ability to shamelessly trowel on the compliments in order to get a social entrée. Why wouldn't she sit in the corner quietly and wait to be introduced?

"Because darling you'd never introduce me to any of your sweet little friends" had been Hilary's response when Maya had challenged her. And Maya could only agree.

And when would Hilary give up flirting with young men?

Shiv doesn't seem embarrassed by his own mother's cutesy fussing or Maya's mother's skittishness, even when Hilary asks "So, are you two special friends? Or perhaps I stand a chance ...?"

Maya was only grateful that Mrs Kapadia had gone to show the Maryhill councillor the outdoor play area, so couldn't witness such crassness.

"Yes" replies Shiv firmly. "We're special dancing partners."

"Ah. Hindu devotional dancing is that? It was mysticism that originally drew me to the east."

"Aye" Shiv ups the breadth of his accent and the speed of his delivery, "east of the Neuk and devoted to the bevvies." He winks at Maya. Hilary doesn't understand what he is saying, but at least she's been distracted from describing the extracts of the Mahabarata that she can recall from Peter Hall's production at the National Theatre.

"Has Maya told you about our dancing?" Shiv continues in a gentler accent.

"No, not a peep. She's always found my interest in other cultures a bit much. But you are following in my footsteps now, aren't you my darling?"

"Our dances enact courtship, fertility and humankind's relationship with nature, but they require great spiritual discipline and physical strength don't they Maya? Show your mother the bruises."

Shiv pulls up Maya's sleeve and above her elbows are the yellow-green remnants of a previously violet bruise. At the last dance class she'd attended, a pair of drunken brothers had enjoyed some competitive partner spinning during a 'Strip the Willow' which involved grasping the unfortunate birlee hard to prevent her flying off with centrifugal force. Regaining her balance once the music had stopped, Maya noticed that many of the experienced women had sat the dance out rather than join a game that they couldn't win.

Hilary draws breath to describe the blistered, callused feet of the Kathak dancers who taught her for a day in Rajasthan several decades earlier.

"Have you been battering young Maya again?" Shuggie has returned from the cupboard.

"Aye. But it's mutual" replies Shiv, pulling up his trouser

legs to show a bruised shin. "We were doing that reel with a stamp-kick step and Maya got me every other kick."

Hilary's expression falls. She can't quite understand what is under discussion but, alarmingly, it might concern hitting her daughter. However, Hilary's aversion to appearing out of the loop, especially in front of two new men, is stronger than concern for Maya and she urgently refocuses the talk back on herself. She turns to Shuggie.

"Hello. I'm Hilary, just up from London. I'm Maya's mother." The two missed beats that follow are, Maya knows, to allow an exclamation of congratulation for being such a youthful mother, or for showing such maternal devotion by travelling from the epi-centre of the country to this distant margin.

"She's a good lassie your Maya. No bother. Keeps herself busy."

"Why thank-you. She has always been a serious girl. Not like her gadabout mother. I've always been better at parties than working." Shuggie doesn't respond to this invitation to ask Hilary about herself. So Hilary asks, "And do you work here yourself?"

"I'm the jannie." Since Hilary is frowning her incomprehension Shuggie adds "The janitor. Care-taker. Most essential worker in the building! Anything that's clean in this building is thanks to me. They're a clarty lot these do-gooding women!"

"Yes, of course. How fascinating. Have you always done janitorial work?"

Shuggie shakes his head, "I was a spark on the ship-yards in my youth but there's no much call for that any more. I could tell you a few stories about those days."

"When you were a bright spark eh!" says Hilary, as Maya cringes inwardly.

"Aye, before my shine got dulled. What about you?"

"Oh me. Very dull. Manage an art gallery."

"What kind of thing do you show?" asks Shuggie.

"We specialise in young artists. Just graduated. I spend a lot of the summer going round the degree shows. We've got a good record of signing up people who then get recognised – six Turner prize nominations to date."

"So is it all that conceptual shite?"

"All concept, no execution" chips in Shiv, who, having had this conversation with Shuggie before is trying to short-circuit it.

"Well we don't hang bouquets of peonies rendered in pastels", says Hilary firmly and patronisingly.

"But that's a concept is it not? A concept that it's possible to represent flowers that look pretty. The trouble with that so-called conceptual art is that it's all concept and no craft skills." Shuggie's strong feelings on the matter are showing and Maya can see that Hilary is working herself up to defending her "lovely lazy-boy artists" with a passion that Maya cannot bear to witness.

"Come on Mum. Time to get your train," Maya jumps in before Hilary can regain conversational ascendancy. As Maya pulls Hilary away, waving goodbye, Hilary calls back to Shuggie.

"So I'll invite you to my next private view shall I? Then we can debate this further!"

Maya can hear Shuggie's growly Capstan-laugh as she collects up Maureen who has been sitting alone for the last half an hour.

"What charming young men!" Hilary witters as they leave the Shakti building. The sky is a deep inky-blue that never fades to black in the long mid-summer Scottish dusk. Dolly-mixture coloured fairy lights (put up by Shuggie up a ladder with Mrs Kapadia issuing artistic direction from ground level), pick out the angular lines of the Shakti building. Maya feels some satisfaction at showing Maureen and her mother the prettiness of her corner of Glasgow. Of course, her mother is focussed on something irrelevant.

"So will I be seeing my darling daughter done up in a red and gold sari soon?" trills Hilary, too loudly, just as they were walking past Mrs Abas climbing into her people-carrier. Frustration and disappointment well up Maya's throat as she suppresses the urge to groan "Muuuuuum". Maureen squeezes her hand sympathetically.

After putting Hilary on the night train back to London ("So romantic darling. Who knows whom I might meet in the buffet car after midnight!"), Maya takes Maureen to the Clydeside country dancing club for the second half of the class. As they walk along by the Clyde, Maya sees the grey river and deserted dockland through Maureen's eyes. It looks grim and unwelcoming.

At the club, Maureen sits down at a table sticky with spilt beer and Maya goes to fetch her a vodka tonic from the bar. As Maya walks back across the room, she sees that Maureen's high gloss finish makes her surroundings look grottier in comparison. Her polished limbs carefully folded to avoid contact with the dull chair and wobbly table. Her beautiful face has a switched-off dead-fish look, as though a membrane had come down behind her eye-lids.

Maya begins describing the peculiarities of the dancers whirling before them, but her enthusiasm melts under her friend's urbane gaze. It's a relief to be asked to dance by Richie. Maya returns, panting to Maureen, who has repulsed several requests to dance, resisting even Shiv's persistent entreaties. Sucking languidly on a cigarette, Maureen comments disparagingly "It's all so folksie, Maya-love. Where's the glamour?"

"I'm not sure I want glamour. That's not what I was born to. I'm a small town home-counties gel. Leamington Spa is my ancestral home."

"But even the Spa would be slicker than this."

Maureen seems to be referring to the rough décor of the club. The dusty old curtains patterned with 1950s-style tea-pots, the broken panes of glass and shabby chairs. Her voice has taken on a Yah-drawl, unfamiliar to Maya.

"Glasgow has cool places too, Reenie." Maya finds herself listing them off.

"The Glasgow School of Art, a fine example of Macintosh design."

"So twee," dismisses Maureen.

"The Gilbert Scott building at Glasgow University."

"Victoriana!" pronounces Maureen.

"The Museum of Modern Art."

"It's not quite the Tate Modern though, is it?" Maureen raises one eyebrow to mark a question hardly worth answering.

"Aieeeeeeeee. Whaohweee." A high pitched shout from the dance floor attracts their attention. Flora Macdonald and a partner with cropped grey hair are turning each other, breaking apart for a complicated set of stamping steps before whirling together again. They look great together – Flora is in one of her gypsy-style purple and green frocks with a tight bodice and panels in the skirt that fly out as she turns. But her face stays expressionless above her body's fleet movements. Her partner's face is the opposite – laughing, whooping and emoting for both of them. The band are speeding up as the dance continues, but Flora keeps up with such bold style and defiant flourishes that the dancers are clearly the victors of the musical duelling. The dance ends to stamps and cheers from the onlookers. Only Maureen remains coolly detached.

Maya has a final dance with Shiv, who persuades her to sign up for the annual club outing to the Western Isles. Maya phones a taxi rather than expose Maureen to Glaswegian public transport and they travel home in silence. Once back home and in their pyjamas they find themselves able to speak to one another again. The talk is of their shared school days, as Maureen shares news of their former class mates in London. Maya finds a bottle of Hock lurking at the back of her cupboard, a moving-in present from the old lady next door – "my son brings me one every Christmas, dearie." By adding a large slug of Crème de Cassis from another languishing bottle, the wine becomes drinkable. Maureen produces a tin of foie gras pate from her elegant soft-leather grip – "I was told the food here was appalling, so I brought supplies" – and Maya makes toast. When Maya puts Maureen in a taxi for the airport the next morning their common bond has been partially restored by discussing their past glories.

"Maybe I can persuade the features editor to send me up again. Perhaps to interview the owner of Skibo castle?" Maureen wonders aloud, trying to find something glamorous to redeem Maya's odd choice of location.

Balvinder

The Kapadia cousin from Mauritius has written. Raj Jutley. And sent a photo. He's a looker. Even with his shorn beard. I don't understand why men have short beards. Sikhs aren't meant to cut their hair, but scads of the young ones shave their beards. To cut your beard short but not shave it clean off seems like the worst of both worlds. Not properly Sikh and

95

not fashionable either. I wonder if his hair is shorn too? Can't tell under the turban. Might be bald. His letter is right old-fashioned. Like a proper suitor out of Jane Austen. Describing his estate, holdings and obligations to the local community. Seems he was much the youngest of eight children, and his parents and two older brothers have died. So no mother-in-law. Says he would be happy to move to Scotland. Just make the odd trip back to Mauritius. Doesn't mention Meena by name, but writes "I am not easily shocked and I love children. The death of my beloved daughter has left a great hole in my life."

Heather

Heather had looked forward to the opening party as one of the more attractive duties of chairing the Shakti board. Presiding at the party puts a seal on the weeks of complex negotiations necessary to get the new business plan drafted and accepted. She hopes to spend rather less time on Shakti business for the next wee while. Awaiting her attention are piles of exam scripts to look over before the examiners' meetings next week. Heather combines overseeing the meetings in her own department with being external examiner at Edinburgh University.

Mr and Mrs Cromarty live just off Prince's Street in the flat where Heather grew up, with a view out over roof tops and trees to the Firth of Forth. Heather would enjoy calling on her parents without her girls. The children had so little regard for the reasonable and adult world of the old couple that visits were inevitably stressful. Ornaments displayed on delicate tables, her mother's needlepoint and her father's thin legs were hazards towards which her daughters seemed to be drawn, at reckless speed. During the last visit with the children Heather had caught a Dresden shepherdess just before it hit the wood block flooring. Her parents were too old to re-arrange their home around juvenile needs so Heather stopped taking the children to visit. Perhaps if the senior Cromartys were still alive when the children reached the age of reason, they would find some conversational common ground. But until then her parents were quite content to hear reports of their grandchildren.

The examiners' meetings were over by two o'clock, and Heather walks down through the old town, letting herself into the flat with her own set of keys. She has an hour and a half before the four o'clock train to Glasgow. Her parents are stationed in faded tapestry-upholstered chairs on either side of a big window. For half a minute, when they haven't yet noticed her, Heather looks at them. She hasn't visited since before her trip to France and the increase in their frailty is marked. Her mother looks almost transparent. Her white hair had been gathered up into an undignified pigtail, presumably by the home-help. Her father's stoop had increased so his forehead seems to be touching his knees as he dozes in his chair. Heather moves towards them, greeting them louder than her normal speaking volume.

"Hello, Heather. Did you tell us you were coming?" her father asks, once he's managed to get his spectacles straight. "We do forget so many things nowadays."

"No, Dad. I just dropped by, hoping you'd be at home." She had, of course, talked to Mrs McFadyen last night, just to check that all was well.

"Oh yes, it's only Thursdays when we're away out," her parents nod their agreement to one another.

Heather makes a whiskey mac for her and her father and a cup of weak Earl Grey tea for her mother, enjoying the worn familiarity of the kitchen, unchanged since her childhood. The remains of her parents' salmon and salad lunch are on the table, ready for Mrs McFadyen to tidy away when she comes to make their evening meal. When Heather is feeling exhausted by the demands of work and home, she frightens herself by imagining that Mrs McFadyen has handed in her notice. Mrs McFadyen has been looking after the Cromarty household for fifty years and there is a careful, guarded inter-dependence and formal courtesy between Mrs McFadyen and the Cromartys which has stood the test of time. So far. Mrs McFadyen's great loyalty stems from the kindness and support the Cromartys offered when she had just arrived in Edinburgh from Inverurie, aged fifteen years and in search of work. And now, fifty years later, Mrs McFadyen has reached retirement age in good health and Heather's parents' depend-ence on her has never been greater. Heather reminds herself to send a large cheque for Mrs MacFadyen's birthday which falls next month.

Heather sits with her parents for an hour, talking about the latest theatre productions, book reviews and plans for the festival. Her parents get out to a play about once a month and have recently seen a devised piece at the Festival Theatre, directed by Mrs Cromarty's godson's daughter.

"The achievement was impressive. The writer had to respond to the improvisation of untrained actors. But why go to that effort when there are plays by Strindberg and Ibsen ready-made to perform?" Mr Cromarty asks rhetorically.

Mrs Cromarty diplomatically notes the excellence of the set design and the use of music, before moving the conversation deftly to a poetry reading they had attended which they both agreed had been quite enchantingly lovely.

"Do you know, as we looked around the bookshop, we knew every last Jock and Harry at that reading" Mr Cromarty smiles with satisfaction.

The Cromartys' central location, well-stocked drinks cabinet and delight in others' stories ensures that they are not short of visitors and they revel in their role as patrons of an informal salon. Neither has ever written or performed but they see themselves as the type of informed and engaging audience that every artist would wish for. They hope that the dignity with which they wield their literary knowledge has ensured that they won't appear as caricatures in the writing of those they patronise.

When they have run out of literary gossip, Mrs Cromarty asks after "the lovely Doug". He had been called this ever since Heather had announced that she would be moving in with him. The appellation had originally been intended as mockingly ironic, since Heather's parents felt Doug to be a most unsuitable partner for their brilliant daughter. He might be acceptable as a temporary boyfriend, to show how broadminded they were, but not for anything more permanent. Once they discovered that Heather had in fact married Doug, they were relieved that she had kept her own name, so at least when the divorce (that they saw as inevitable) came, she wouldn't have to alter her bank account or telephone directory listing. But now, after two decades of consistently referring to "the lovely Doug", it had become a sincere compliment. Doug's lack of a proper profession no longer seemed important, given Heather's dedication to hers and his ongoing devotion to the Cromartys' daughter and subsequently to their granddaughters.

"He's fine mother. Doing a few shifts in a fancy fish restaurant for a pal. And he's building the girls a new bedroom," informs Heather.

Having recovered from the initial shock of her parents' physical frailty, Mrs Macfadyen's dour description of her parents' being "closer than ever to their maker now, Miss Heather" did not seem any truer now than it had done three months ago. Heather had no doubt that if she returned to visit tomorrow she could enjoy almost exactly the same conversation. By keeping her visits well spaced the anecdotes at the forefront of the senior Cromartys' consciousness turned over. And their delight in one another's company continued unabated.

"Whenever we feel elderly dear, we just take off our spectacles and as if by magic my wrinkles disappear to your father's view and his to mine," Mrs Cromarty explained with a wrinkley-twinkley grin.

Still, enjoyment of their daily life together would not prevent death arriving some day. Then what? She would have to discuss it with Robin soon. Her brother had had little contact with his parents since his juvenile rejection of what he saw as his parents' excessive consumption, after joining the University branch of the Revolutionary Communist Party. The comfortable life of a recently retired civil engineer did not offer Robin the grittily authentic origins that he so desperately desired. Instead, he chose to emphasise his grandfather's feudal position as gamekeeper for the Earl of Elgin. Since abandoning the RCP's vision of utopia for one more concerned with circle dancing and sustainable housing, Robin had re-established infrequent communication with his parents. He visited them when he was down from the Northeast, bringing his own fennel and mint teabags. It seemed unlikely that he would want to care for one parent if the other died.

Heather would to talk to Robin tomorrow. He would be in Glasgow for a day conference on community-led recycling initiatives and Heather has suggested that they meet in the Shakti café.

Balvinder

The letter and photo from Raj Jutley lie in Balvinder's pocket for a fortnight. She knows that Ma and Mrs Kapadia are very much in favour of the match. But Ma hasn't met the man and Balvinder knows how much her mother wants to get her errant daughter tidied into a respectable union. Mrs Kapadia's approval is more persuasive, since she's made it clear that Balvinder and Meena are cherished guests in the Kapadia mansion.

"You are the daughter that I never had," Mrs Kapadia says when laid out on one of her huge brocade sofas as Balvinder massages her leg. According to her, Raj Jutley is everything that he says in his letter – rich, hard-working and serious about his business. Mrs Kapadia also feels he could be loving.

"What about his wife auntiji – how was she?" Balvinder asks, as she starts on Mrs Kapadia's other leg.

"I only met her once, at their marriage in Cape Town. Sweet girl. Very shy, a village girl. I think Raj loved her, but she wasn't a partner to him. He couldn't discuss business with her."

"She feels like my rival."

Mrs Kapadia clicks her tongue disapprovingly. "She's dead Balvinder. And Raj wants to move on. He's grieved for two years. You are smart and pretty. So is your daughter." Mrs Kapadia gives the cradle on the floor next to the sofa a push to set it rocking. "Only write to him to see if you have an understanding."

Balvinder's cocky flirtatiousness has evaporated now she's faced with the prospect of an actual man. Particularly one who is ten years her senior. She resolves to talk to Shiv next time he's around. There's no side to him, he'll tell her straight.

"So what exactly are you asking me, Balvinder? Whether to marry him?" Shiv and Balvinder are sitting on a teak bench next to the agapanthus bed in the garden, having eaten Mrs Kapadia's speciality 'Angrezi-Sunday-lunch' starring Yorkshire pudding and roast lamb for the meat eaters. The rest of the Kapadia household has retired to watch the cricket on the satellite channel.

"No, no. I just want to know whether he seems OK, decent."

"Aye, I suppose so. Just ordinary really. Old fashioned maybe."

"Could I trust him?" Balvinder is trying to work out what she wants to know from Shiv. "Is he like my Dad?"

"What, you mean grumpy with a pot-belly?" Shiv queries.

"No, I mean foul tempered and free with his fists."

"No, I don't think so. How can I tell? I've only met him a few times. At weddings and that. Last time was during the world cup. We talked football." Shiv taps his fingers on his chin while he tries to remember Raj Jutley. "He didn't support the one team, knew about the whole tournament. Open-minded. Oh, and I remember he was drinking pints of milk. Not beer. Some of the uncles were teasing him. He said it reminded him of his village days."

"So, would you marry him?" Balvinder asks, expecting Shiv to laugh at her.

"No. But I might write to him," replies Shiv quite seriously.

Heather

Young Balvinder from the Shakti centre comes to find me at work today. I don't recognise her for a minute. Is she a student from the Thursday morning seminar? Then she smiles and I recognise her. She has her baby on her hip – all dimpled knees and gummy grins. A sweet wee tumshie-girl. Whenever I get those broody yearnings, I remember that I'll be nearly fifty when my babies start at primary school. And retiring by the time they leave school.

Balvinder wants to talk about marriage. Specifically arranged marriage. She expects me to disapprove.

"It's no very feminist is it?" she points out.

"What, marriage?" I ask.

"No, arranged marriage."

"Depends how it's done," I suggest, not sure how personal her inquiry is. Balvinder is nodding so I continue cautiously. "One of my students is writing about South Asian marriage systems. She says all marriages are arranged. By someone.

Matchmaker, parent, pal, whoever." Balvinder is still nodding. I continue, "Individually arranged marriages or family-arranged marriages. Neither type is superior. Either type can go wrong. In fact, there's more divorce among white people than Asians." Balvinder has stopped nodding.

"But that's 'cause the Asian women are too feart to leave!" she says crossly.

"That's the negative spin. But perhaps it's also because their families work harder to keep the marriage together ...?"

"If it's yourself that's choosing, how do you know? How did you know that your man would be OK?" There's no doubting the personal nature of Balvinder's question now.

"I didn't know, really. Not with absolute certainty."

"But you're still together aren't you?"

"Aye."

"And are youse happy?"

"Well you'd have to ask Doug too. But I think so. Content, definitely."

"Why did you choose him?" She's not letting go of this topic. I'd throw her out as a nosy bisum. But she's so earnest. And she's really seeking some kind of answer.

"Because I was lonely without him and my parents disapproved. The mystery is why we're still together two decades on." But Balvinder isn't concerned with staying married. She doesn't want to hear about the wee compromises that we've both made to keep our joint life chugging along.

"Did you ever swither about him?"

"No. Not when the time came. I'd been abroad teaching at a summer school and I'd missed him so much. It seemed cracked to be alone, when I had a man at home who I loved. He was just waiting for me to say the word."

"So you married him?"

"Aye, well, no. First of all I moved into his flat in the Gallowgate. Once my parents had calmed down from that shock I decided we should marry properly, although Doug wasn't fussed."

"So why go to all the bother?"

"To show that we meant it. For ever. That it wasn't just a phase."

"Who would your folks have liked you to marry?"

102

"Not sure. Maybe a lawyer from Edinburgh or Fife." Which means of course a Protestant or at least an atheist, but not a Catholic. If they could've chosen for me they would have picked a QC who wrote esoteric poetry in his leisure time. And read French and Italian. My attention drifts as I think about the Tuscan holiday home that my parents would, under ideal circumstances, have liked me to have gained through marriage. I see Balvinder waiting for me to finish. "With a liking for poetry."

"And did they introduce you to anyone like that?"

"There were plenty of poets about the place. But since they were my parents' friends, I automatically discounted them."

"And what did they say about your choice of husband?"

"They didn't ken for a long while. I didn't tell them. They found out a couple of years later at the theatre. I'd booked the tickets over the phone."

Balvinder frowns "How?"

"I'd stupidly used Doug's credit card. He'd made me a signatory of it, in my married name, which then got printed across the ticket stubs."

"Were they raging?"

"No. No. It was fine. By then they could see that even though I'd married beneath me, as they saw it, I hadn't ended up in a high rise with a squad of weans." And then I look at Balvinder with her illegitimate, fatherless daughter on her lap. The baby was smiling at her own delightful fists. I feel a right numpty. And a rude numpty at that. I apologise, but Balvinder just asks "What for?". So I say that I have to stop our chat because I've a senate meeting to attend.

Maya

Research by someone in Heather Cromarty's department has shown that Muslims are the poorest Asians in Britain. So the Shakti board wants us to get more Muslims using the building. And poor ones if possible. Mrs Kapadia suggests that I go to the mosque women's group to recruit participants for my paisley project. I think Balvinder should come too. At least she speaks Punjabi. She says "no way".

"It would look like I was taking the piss. But you'll be

alright. You're white. There's loads of white converts. Just don't tell them you were born in India. OK?"

So, as part of my employment duties I am to visit the women's group at the mosque and ask whether art is missing from their lives.

Heather

After the girls are asleep I go and put my cap in. I'd a pal who said the cap ruined the spontaneity of sex. But that can be a good thing. If Doug and I had to wait for spontaneous passion to overcome us, given the competition from utter exhaustion, we'd be celibate. But once I'm capped, sex has got to happen, otherwise it's a waste of all that slippery effort. I put on my prettiest nightie and a black thong to give Doug something to peel off me. Talking to Balvinder today did make me look at Doug when I got home and realise what a lucky woman I am. I go to snuggle up with him on the sofa. He's admiring Kirsty Wark interviewing some minister on Newsnight. I never wear a thong, except at home. The cheese wire between the cheeks doesn't help in daily life, but it acts as a clear signal of intentions to Doug. "Mmmm" he murmurs into my hair "you must give that young woman relationship counselling again, if this is the effect". And then we fall into bed and into our familiar and delicious routine.

Balvinder

Balvinder takes no offence at Heather's reference to the reckless reproduction of the plebeian classes. Why should she? It's white trash who fecklessly drop babies whereas her people have big families who are loved. And anyway Meena wasn't a squad. She was a pearl. A pearl of a girl.

Heather's equivocation about marriage convinces Balvinder that she might as well enter the lottery of lifetime partnership with the man who has been picked out for her. Mrs Kapadia has Balvinder's best interests at heart and cares for cousin Raj too. Mrs Kapadia's judgement has to be better than Balvinder's, given the runt of a man who, amazingly, sired baby Meena.

And so Balvinder writes a letter to Raj Jutley on blue airmail paper. She tells him about the joy of Meena and her hopes for her little shop. Within a week she gets a reply which is reassuring, interested and friendly.

Heather

Over a bowl of creamy chickpea curry, Robin agrees with his sister that neither of their parents would want to go into a home. Heather complains about the impossibility of speaking to them about their frail future. When Heather attempts to edge carefully up to the topic, Mrs Cromarty invariably closes down discussion with, "Well I won't be aware of what you're up to, so whatever is least bother dear." Mr Cromarty's response is even less helpful: "Put a bullet between my eyes when I become a burden!"

Heather tells Robin about her visits to homes for the genteel elderly in the Edinburgh area. They all smelled of institutional humiliation. Even the most expensive home couldn't mask the smell of boiled brassica and urine despite the pot pourri and bees wax furniture polish. Even the one run by the sweet Australian woman who ran mental gymnastics groups and oral history afternoons, still relied on the televisual entertainment for hours at a stretch. Heather couldn't bear the idea of her parents parked in adjacent PVC chairs, bringing their critical faculties to bear on "Sabrina the teenage witch".

Heather fetches two cups of chai, and, on smelling the mixture of clove and cinnamon, Robin decides to make an exception to his dairy-free dietary rule. Having listened to Heather's worries, he proposes his suggestion for managing their parents. First, they should clear all the rooms of their flat in Prince's Street except for the three rooms that Mr and Mrs Cromarty occupy. Second, they should sell the Jacobean furniture and Edwardian silverware and with the resulting money, pay for the junk to be removed. With the rooms cleared, cleaned and cheaply refurbished, there would be space to have paid help in from the nursing agency when the time came. Robin even says he'll stay with his parents, providing the accumulated clutter of nearly six decades is removed. Heather isn't sure that it will work as a plan. The whole notion of her parents becoming dependent on her to the extent that she has to take such difficult decisions is hard to take. But she has no real alternatives in mind. She agrees with Robin that she will ring around auctioneers and antique dealers to get quotations.

Talking to Mrs McFadyen is going to be the most difficult part of effecting any change. Heather is worried that Mrs McFadyen will feel that the senior Cromartys are being treated dishonourably. Ideally, Mrs McFadyen would remain part of the household but will she tolerate having others in her kitchen? Robin assures Heather that he can handle Mrs McFadyen who's always had a soft spot for him, as he gathers up his hemp shoulder bag to return to his recycling conference.

Maya

"Are you coming to Islam now?" is how I'm greeted every week at the Mosque women's group. I try to explain about Shakti again. And how we want women to come and join in the projects. And eyes glaze over. I'm ignored in a friendly way for the rest of the session. I like going. It's soothing. The mosque looks like an ordinary semi-detached house from the outside. I wouldn't have known it was a Mosque, apart from the knot of men with their heads covered, gathered around the front door. Usually it's only men who use the building, but one afternoon a week, women get the upstairs to themselves. The group of men always stop talking when I pass through them. Last week, I had to walk past on the other side of the road twice before I got my courage up to go in. But it's worth the discomfit to get to the airy sanctuary upstairs. At the top of the stairs are three shoe shelves and a washroom. After cleaning my hands and face, I open the door onto a room which has windows round three walls. The other is bare and white, covered in leaf-dappled sunlight. Cotton sheets cover the floor where a dozen women sit with their children around them. They assume that I must have a Muslim boyfriend. Three of the regular attenders have married men from Pakistan and converted. Except they call it reverted. Because Islam is the natural state.

The children play and sometimes talk to me.

"Are you a Muslim?" they ask. I feel embarrassed to have to shake my head. It seems rude.

"Are you a Christian then?"

"Not really" I have to admit.

"So what are you doing here?" a bright little girl called Aysha asks. Good question. I'm not sure of the answer. Aysha has just started wearing the hijab. It's tightly pinned round her head. She's so pleased with it and rather scornful of my inability to keep my own hair confined to my headscarf. Some weeks, she brings her next-door neighbour Kylie. Kylie loves the dressing up, borrowing Aysha's clothes and telling everyone that she'll be a Muslim as soon as she's old enough to leave home.

Someone calls the group to order, usually Samira, an earnest girl who is studying for a BSc in Pharmacy. The chatting stops and we all move to the far end of the room. Copies of the Qu'ran are carefully collected from the table and laid respectfully on jumpers and coats to keep them from touching the floor. A passage is read out in Arabic by Mrs Hamida and then we turn to the English translation. The significance of the passage is discussed. I get distracted by pins and needles. My legs won't remain crossed underneath me for long enough.

Sometimes a prayer call comes across the tannoy, interrupting the lesson. I move to the back of the room where coats and bags are slung on hooks and a couple of babies are sleeping on the floor and I try to melt into the wall. The sing-song call is nasal and beautiful. It pricks at my tear glands. To the others, I suppose the sound is as familiar as church bells. In line, women and girls do their prayers, the little ones imitating the older ones, kneeling and standing up. Kylie goes through the movements precisely and elegantly without needing to copy anyone else. I want to join in too. I want to be part of the line rising and falling, held together by common words. I want to be part of the wave of prayer that is traversing the globe. Perhaps if I followed the movements of prayer for long enough the faith would follow?

Well, I won't be finding out here. After prayers today, Samira approached me. Had she been shoved forwards by Mrs Hamida and Aysha's mother? They certainly watched intently as she walked over to me. Samira explained that none of the women objected to my coming. Quite the opposite, they

107

welcome all-comers. But the committee that runs the mosque feels otherwise. And the committee could deny them the use of this room.

"A couple of the lassies who used to pray with us have got mixed up in politics. They sell the 'Socialist Worker' in town on a Saturday. You might've seen them?" Samira wants to know.

"No. But so what?" I don't see that left-wing politics is necessarily incompatible with the way that Islam advocates respectful and fair treatment of all.

"Well, they also go to Shakti."

"Oh. I see." I don't see. But I know the girls she means now: Sameena and Rubina who hang about with two blokes in donkey jackets and woolly hats. I've talked to them at Shakti. They aren't interested in doing art. "Have they stopped being Muslim?"

"No, that's the problem really. They maintain that they understand the Prophet's message. Peace be upon him. But they disagree with the committee." Samira sighs. She looks too tired for a young woman.

"What about?"

"They think we women should have free access to the mosque. Like the men. And not have to pray at home," Samira is spelling it out for me.

"But there is a prayer room at Shakti. Doesn't that solve the problem? It's not very big, but they've made it nice with carpets."

Samira is getting exasperated at my not seeing the problems that are clear to her. Clear and constraining.

"No. The problem persists and Shakti is part of it. It's splitting us up," her voice has got louder. One or two people turn around. She takes a deep breath. "The committee wants to stop our meeting here. They think we're all about to follow those lassies. We have to be beyond reproach. Devout. Serious." Samira comes to a halt but her unspoken words are hammering in my ears. I don't force her to say them out loud. As a hanger-on I impede the group's claim to being soberly engaged with Islam. I make them disreputable. I'm not accountable to a husband or a father. Or even a mother. This much I understand. And I nod.

"Sorry." Samira touches my elbow and turns to get the group back to the Qu'ran.

So the refuge of passive prayer is denied to me. I turn to leave, quietly.

Heather

Robin is impressed by the excellent Shakti snack that he enjoyed with his sister. The next day, having established that no animal suffered production of the chick pea curry, he takes a fellow conference delegate who happens, in addition to her recycling interests, to be writing one thousand words on 'top ten vegetarian bites' for "Scotland on Sunday". After publication of her article, visitor numbers to the Shakti café increase ten-fold. Heather chairs a meeting of the users' forum where the cooking co-operative reluctantly agrees with Mrs Kapadia that they need to charge realistic prices for their produce, even though this goes against their ethic of hospitality. (At the same meeting Rubina and Sameena lead an alliance of devout hijab-clad Muslims and leftie, feminist, pierced, wild-girls in a move to make Shakti a women-only space. But since it would be Shuggie that would have to police such a policy, pragmatism wins the day.)

Heather writes some customer questionnaires and gets Maya to put them out on the café tables every day for a week. Maya collects the completed questionnaires and sends them on to Heather's keen postgraduate student who puts together a little consumer profile report for the Shakti café. Her report suggests that the increase in food prices does not deter customers, especially not broadsheet-reading vegans. The rave review of the jelabis consumed by Robin's freelance friend seems to have inspired a broader people to visit the Shakti café. The same freelance suggests that a book of Shakti recipes would make the ideal mid-winter festival gift. The contract between Shakti and the freelance is drawn up by the professor of commercial law who is Heather's running partner (twice round Queen's park, thrice per week). Maya is commissioned to illustrate the recipes that the freelance manages to deduce from hours watching the co-operative cooking enterprise. Sales of the book, published by a small independent house, start slowly. Then the freelance friend sells an article to "The

Herald" entitled, "Samosa so close to ya", profiling Mrs
Kapadia and plugging the book. The article is picked up by
the Observer Food Magazine and book sales pick up. The
book goes to a second and then a third print run. Heather gets
advice on investing the book revenues from a banker whose
children also attend Noah's Boat Day Nursery and Shakti's
financial future looks promising.

Maya

Thank God, Maureen can't see me now. I'm stepping carefully into her green silk frock in a drafty barn. When Shiv said
we'd be staying in a bothy I imagined something far cosier.
Perhaps a wood burning stove, warming rustic bunks with
fluffy blankets and lashings of creamy hot chocolate. The reality is far more ravaged by the elements and rodents. All the
other Clydesiders make like they're enjoying the fresh-air fun
of performing their toilette at an outside tap. When Shiv said
there'd be dancing, I imagined more glitz.

In the pub, I listen to Hamish's misty-eyed stories of how
thirty years ago he would cycle up through Clydebank and
Dumbarton to Loch Lomond's east coast on a summer Friday
night to drink cider with his pals. He describes a fabu-
lously innocent time when they would all sleep in a ditch
together under a tarpaulin, then leap up at dawn to eat a
hearty breakfast and yomp up Ben Lomond. Valuable oral
history, no doubt, but marred as an experience by his aston-
ishingly virulent halitosis. So I move to talk to Flora who
introduces me to the cropped grey-haired woman as "Norma,
my partner". Judging by the low simmering argument they
are conducting, in between exchanging small talk with me,
they're partners in more than just the dancing.

At midnight, the publican goes to bolt the door from the
inside, which panicked me; what about fire escapes? Shiv tells
me to, "Stop fretting, hen". I'm not sure that "hen" is any less
oppressive than "chick" when applied to a woman. At least
not when spoken by a bloke. I complain that I am tired, so he
gets me a whisky sour — equal parts of whisky and freshly
squeezed lemon juice. Quite revolting and very bracing.
Hamish pushes back the velour-topped bar stools, clearing a
space for the snare-drum player, and gets out his accordion;

and, I imagine, the night will begin. But the musicians are too far gone to care whether anyone dances or even listens to their music at first. After several mournful numbers, they remember there are other people in the room and start to pick up the tempo. Norma and Flora dance crossly together. Flora looks as though she doesn't trust Norma to catch her as she spins and turns. Half way through a tune Flora stops spinning and marches Norma out of the back door of the pub. I had been thinking of sneaking out to try to sleep in the damp bothy, but since we're all sharing the same barn, I just stay put.

Hamish and the snare drummer descend into melancholy once again. The drummer sings some gloomy songs about the clans massacring each other and everyone stares into the middle distance. I feel dreadfully English and hope not to be noticed, grateful that at least my hair is appropriately red. Eventually the lock-in ends and we were released as the soft low cloud is turning from dark grey to light grey with the dawn. I struggle into my sleeping bag on a wooden platform hoping the spiders will stay out of my orifices while I sleep.

After a few hours unconscious, we escape from the methane filled bothy into the rapidly fugged-up mini-bus. Everyone but me sings a song about flinging jeely pieces from tower block windows to children below. But I know "If it wasnae for your wellies" because I saw Billie Connelly sing it at an Islington pub when Hilary was going out with a stand-up comedian. At the Drover's Inn, hangover-curing dog-hairs are consumed and Flora explains the plan for the weekend.

"We're headed for the Isle of Lisemore, where my cousin lives. We've a kindae rivalry going with the dancers there."

It seems that every summer the Clydesiders go and dance in the Lisemore village hall as near to the shortest night as they can manage. Sounds kind of gladiatorial. At least we're going to sleep in Flora's cousin's house which has a telly and fitted carpets.

"My auntie and uncle built the house when they first married and took up farming their own sheep. Now they're the oldest generation and they've moved back to the old farmhouse. They let this one to the holiday-makers."

On the ferry, I'm leaning on the rail around the deck, next

to Norma, watching the gap of water between us and Oban widen.

"What is that bizarre building?" I ask pointing at what looks like a Roman ruin on the hillside, just emerging from the cloud. "The Romans didn't get beyond Hadrian's wall did they?"

Norma thinks it's a folly built by one of the rich folk who retired to Oban. She says there's plenty of them, including Princess Diana's mother who used to be spotted cycling down to the Co-op to buy her Beefeater's. We carry on talking as the outcrops of land slip past us. At one point, we see seals' heads looking at us, quizzically. Norma is talking about how she loves this part of Scotland.

"It's like breathing again after a few months in the city. Really breathing."

"Have you thought of moving here?" I ask.

"Oh aye. Me and Flora had a fantastic holiday here with her cousin a few years ago. We were staying in a wee cottage up a track. We swam in a sweet loch everyday and caught fish for our tea. It was a slice of paradise, so we started making plans to move. But there's no much call for a dancing teacher and a feminist handywoman on Lisemore. Even a handywoman with a some basic librarian skills. So we thought about moving to the Isle of Skye and doing bed and breakfast."

"What stopped you?"

"Well, we went on a exploratory research trip, staying at every B and B from Lochalsh to Trotternish and realised the horror of it all."

"What horror?" I prompt.

"The horror of trying to live your holiday all year round. We met half a dozen middle-aged couples from Cumbria or Yorkshire, who'd sold up and moved to Skye after a couple of happy holidays. And condemned themselves to a life of changing drip-dry nylon sheets for other happy holiday-makers. We decided the escapist dreams were more fun than the reality."

Norma looks out, shielding her eyes against the sun that's just come out, and points, "Look that's Ben Cruachan."

I can see the smudgey blue outline of hills and mountains in the distance. I don't know how she can tell one blue

smudge from another. After some minutes gazing at the
horizon, Norma asks me why I moved to Scotland. I tell her
about my job at Shakti and it turns out she knows a bit about
the place, says the idea for it started at a discussion group at
the women's library, where she spends her days.

"The library's a lovely place, you should come and visit. It's
just around the corner from Shakti. In the Trongate." Norma
is taking off her woollen hat as the sun is staying out and
keeps her eyes on the horizon.

"I applied for a job at Shakti. One of the few jobs that I ever
really wanted."

"Mrs Kapadia's job?"

"No. The jannie's post."

"Shuggie's job!"

"Yes, but it should've been mine. I'm a qualified plumber
and not a bad chippie and I've done site-management. And
they liked me at the interview, but then I said the L-word. Or
maybe the F-word was the problem." She looks knowingly at
me. But I can't pretend I know what she's talking about.

"What?" I ask.

"Describing myself as a lesbian feminist."

"Oh. Right. Um. What's wrong with that?"

"Some of them didn't mind, or so Heather Cromarty was
telling me afterwards. But a couple of the ladies felt that I
would frighten the horses. Or the husbands, to be precise. So
Shuggie got it instead. And he's a good man, but he's no
feminist."

"I get on OK with him" I say apologetically.

"Aye. He's a nice fella. And you two have something in
common. He's right knowledgeable about art. You should get
him to take you to the Burrell some day. He knows all about
the paintings there. He does a bit of tour-guiding at the
weekends. But I'd still like his job," she looks at me with a bit
of friendly defiance.

"Why?"

"I could've made a difference. Working at the women's
library is, you know, preaching to the converted. Folk only
come if they're already pretty feminist in their thinking."

"Mmmm," I make a non-committal noise.

"But Maya! I'm really serious about my feminism. You see,

113

it saved my life." I giggle. I had to because Norma looks so solemn. But I immediately wish I hadn't. Norma continues, "No, really. It did. The women's movement people called it then. People who didn't like it. It was Heather Cromarty that taught me about feminism. In an evening class. Thanks to her I didn't get battered to death by my husband. See, I was getting a doing every Saturday night after closing time. It was Heather that showed me that it wasn't just my problem with a man, it was a bigger problem. More general. Gendered power and that. Women all over the world and through history have come off worst. I began to understand a wee bit about how gender works. And then I understood that I couldn't fix the marriage. Or him. So I left him. Bill. Bastard. Poor Bastard." Norma's looking out to sea. Talking to herself really.

"Was Flora married too? I mean before she met you?"

"Och noo!" Norma laughs. "She's far too sensible." She turns to face me again, "You're lucky, Maya."

"How am I lucky? Shiv calls me 'Maya no mates.' "

"Take no notice of him. He's got an equal opps policy on insulting folk. Thinks he can get away with it because he's black. Or at least not white. No. You're lucky because you don't need feminism. You've been to University. You'll know what gender means. And inequality. At your age, I was that ignorant. I really needed feminism as a way of thinking about the world. And I think other women do too. I'm certain they do. And Shuggie's certainly not going to give it them is he?"

I have to agree with Norma. Norma apologises for her outburst. Says she's pre-menstrual and a bit emotional. She promises to fetch me out for lunch sometime. Show me the women's library. And she'll talk to Shuggie about taking me round the Burrell collection too. So there. Another possible friend in the making. Or at least a lunch date.

Heather

Heather breathes out heavily and returns her gaze but not her attention to the dissertations that she is meant to be second marking. She has come round to Robin's plan for dismantling their parents' flat while leaving them in situ. It is probably the kindest thing. But how much to tell them? Can she and Robin pretend that nothing untoward is happening? Perhaps she could take the batteries out of their hearing aids when the furniture-removers come? Even if they could clear the flat undetected, what are the chances of one parent getting a burst of curiosity and taking their walking frames down the corridor to a guest bedroom only to find it void of memories? Would that finish them off? Is it robbing them of their past? One thing is for sure, given Mrs McFadyen's pivotal role in their lives, the whole thing will only work with her approval. "So don't go doing anything rash," Heather tells herself. The whole business will have to be tackled slowly-slowly, gently-gently. Such caution goes very much against Heather's organisational style, which is to take rapid decisions and execute them precipitately before anyone can object. Doug calls her the queen of slash and burn management. Her super-speedy decision-making gets results in a University with financial problems and a centralised power-base. But it isn't going to work in managing her parents' worldly exit. Heather picks up her red pen and thanks the fates that Doug has four sisters to worry about his parents.

Maya and Balvinder

Maya and Balvinder are working together at Mrs Kapadia's faux marble kitchen work surface. The occasion is the Kapadias' annual divali party to which every Hindu in the west of Scotland, many of the Sikhs, some particularly prominent Muslims and a fair number of Catholics, Protestants, atheists and agnostics are regularly invited. Balvinder has been delegated to puri-cooking, deftly flipping the golden puffs out of a pan of boiling vegetable oil. Maya, having proved herself incapable of kneading puri-dough into smooth round shapes, is washing up, cleaning the plates of the waves of guests who eat from Mrs Kapadia's heaped buffet.

Baby Meena is sleeping face down on her grandmother's spreading bust, arms akimbo. Mrs Singh's big comfy body seems to meld with the sofa in which she is immersed. By contrast, at the other end, Doug is holding himself stiffly to prevent a sofa swallowing, while balancing his two girls and a plate of gajarela on his knees. Doug is relieved to have his daughters as a human shield. He seems to have achieved honorary-woman status as the men have stopped trying to usher him into the front sitting room where whisky is being discreetly sipped from heavy crystal tumblers, usually stored in a glass-fronted cabinet with integral lighting. Sometimes he wishes that he followed the football, just to have easy conversation at gatherings like this. The lack of scars on the knuckles and inner forearms of the other guests suggests there isn't a serious crag-hopper or chef among them, with whom Doug might be able to swap stories.

Heather is standing in the hallway, half-way between the men's room and the women's room, talking to a delightful clinical psychologist with whom she has just discovered a shared research interest. They are discussing where Heather might apply for funding to evaluate the psychologist's specialist clinical work in Ruchill.

Maya is telling Balvinder about her recent triumph at the Highland Dancing Endurance Trials. In a clapboard hall on the Isle of Lisemore, Maya and Shiv danced for fourteen hours, with only two breaks for tongue sandwiches and cups of tea served on pale-green ridged crockery. Maya was presented with a "Miss Endurance Scotland" satin sash and, wearing a gold plastic tiara, had her photograph taken for the Oban Times. She couldn't work out whether the Islanders really were serious about the trials, or if it was an extended exercise in heavy irony. She will send the cutting to Maureen, when Flora passes it on to her. Maureen will tease her on the phone by imitating her mother's tone in asking whether the Prince of Endurance is, after all, a super-special friend?

Maya is not telling Balvinder that Shiv had asked her if she would marry him, on the deck of the Cal-Mac ferry as they returned to Oban. Maya's spluttered response had been that she couldn't possibly marry the boss's son.

"It would be too horribly clichéd," she had said as she stared wide-eyed with alarm full into Shiv's face. "And any-way I'm still enjoying having a friend and a hobby. Why would I trade that in for a hubby? If you were my husband and we danced together, we'd have a shared obsession. It wouldn't be healthy. Whereas now, it's good clean fun."

"OK then. I'll ask you again in a year's time. By then you

116

might be working some place else. And perhaps you'll have made yourself another friend."

Just then, a man in a Cal-Mac jacket had pointed out dolphins swimming along parallel with the boat. The energetic arcs the animals described as they whizzed out of the water looked like joy riding. The fun the dolphins were having was contagious. Shiv and Maya had laughed out loud and left the topic of marriage in their wake.

When the dolphins had dived out of sight, Maya looked out towards the mainland and thought she might be able to see Ben Cruachan again. The view was a beautiful mixture of mountains, sea and sky. No wonder Norma and Flora had thought about moving here.

"It feels like we've been on a foreign holiday, Shiv. I feel as though I must be abroad. It's too dramatic, too scenic for the humdrum British Isles."

"Well, you are abroad, you soft southerner!"

"Mmm I suppose so. But I keep expecting people to speak a foreign language, an alien tongue. Norwegian or something, not just English with a funny accent."

"On yourself Maya. You know fine well it's you with the comedy sassenach accent," Shiv laughs.

Maya doesn't tell Balvinder that she was disturbed by Shiv's proposal. It upset her sense of security. It was fine dancing with someone who treated you like a sister, but to dance with someone who has proposed ... did that mean he fancied her? He didn't behave as though he did. Lurking beneath Maya's distrust of being fancied is the even less palatable suspicion that Shiv feels sorry for her being so alone and is trying to join her up with his family.

Maya does tell Balvinder about the agreeable feeling she had as the Oban train drew into Queen Street Station. The high rise flats, the tenements, the city centre civic buildings had a familiar, friendly look. The easy, short walk to the number 66 bus stop, the speedy arrival of the bus which took her to her own little flat, had conspired to make her feel that she knew her way around. Maya had arrived home and shut her flat door behind her, knowing that Heather Cromarty would be knocking on it in a few hours time to give her a lift to the Kapadias' party.

"It's worth going away, just to be pleased to come back again. It's beginning to feel like home I suppose," says Maya.

"There's no place like Glasgow," Balvinder agreed as she flipped another golden puri out of the steel pan of boiling oil onto a bed of kitchen roll.

"Have you lived anywhere else?" Maya asks.

"Not really. Why would I want to?"

"Just to check that Glasgow is the best place I suppose."

"Oh I know that for sure. We stayed England-side for a couple of months. Dad was to go into business with a man in Dudley so we let out our flat here and moved down."

"Did you like it?"

"It was amazing. You know how here Asian folk run corner shops or restaurants? All of them. Well down there, Asians do everything. They're builders, electricians, bankers, everything. We even saw a Sikh policeman. And one of my Dad's pals was arrested and said the prison was full of Muslims."

"What, there's no Asian criminals in Scotland?"

"No way. The lads don't dare do anything really bad. They'll get bawled out by the aunties. So it is safer here."

"Is that why you came back?"

"No. Well yes. The Dudley man ran away with a big bag of my Dad's money. Disappeared. So we had to flit back. The man wouldn't've got away with it up here. It's too small. But down there folk get away with all sorts. It's out of control. Girls in mini skirts, smoking. Everything."

Maya shoots Balvinder a look. But there's no irony or mickey-taking on Balvinder's face. She's serious. Glasgow's miles better.

Balvinder

I'm e-mailing Raj now, to get his replies quicker. I've got all his letters in a packet under my bed, tied up tight with string. His handwriting is elegant and regular. On account of his strict primary education in Mauritius, he says. I've told him everything. Well, more than I've told anyone ever before. Because it's just writing I've not felt embarrassed. He knows about Meena; he knows I'm soiled goods, and he's still interested. He asks really funny questions, like "Would you wish to maintain a vegetarian kitchen?" and "How do you feel

about alcohol?" and "In a British election, would you vote for
the socialist party or the right wingers?" And he's really
interested in my answers. I don't even mind if he is bald any
more.

I did want to tell Maya about Raj at the Kapadias' party.
But it felt like bragging. Her having no-one. No brothers,
no sisters. No grandparents, aunties, cousins, nothing. Her
pal Maureen seemed a bit snotty like and her Mum's pretty
useless. As a mother anyway.

Maya

Returning home late after the party, Maya feels terrible
and wonders whether her achy limbs could be due to the
dancing that started up in Mrs Kapadia's kitchen after all the
food had been cleared away. Maya was leaning on the breakfast bar next to Mrs Kapadia.

"This is our peasant dancing, Maya" Mrs Kapadia laughed
as she clapped her hands in time with the young men bouncing about to the music, their hands raised up and their faces
tilted to the ceiling. "It's more fun than that Scottie dancing
that you do with Shiv, isn't it?" she teased. At which point
Shiv had danced over towards them.

"No, no!" Maya squealed as Shiv pulled her arms. "There
aren't any other girls dancing."

"That's because they're Asian lassies. They cannae. You can
though. You're allowed. You're white," Shiv insisted, and his
mother smiled and moved her head from side to side. Maya
obeyed Mrs Kapadia's affirmative wobble-nod and got up
to dance. None of the Clydesider dance-steps worked to the
Punjabi music. She felt even less graceful than usual and as
soon as Shiv took his attention from her, she sat down quick,
hiding in the shadow of Mrs Singh on the sofa.

"Shabash. Good girl."

"Sorry?"

"You are nice girl. Not show-off-lady-small-skirt."

Mrs Singh didn't expect any more conversation so Maya
enjoyed sitting and watching, protected by Mrs Singh's bulk
and approving inertia from Shiv's entreaties to dance.

Maya feels shivery and tearful. There's nothing to do but
put herself to bed where she dreams fitfully of waltzing with

Balvinder who turns into Shiv, while Shuggie marries Hilary. She wakes up with a start. It's morning and she lies feeling the relief of escaping fom her dream. Then she feels the heavy ache in her limbs and telephones Shakti to excuse herself from work before returning to her sweaty bed. She hears Granny's advice in her head "Keep up your fluids, keep away from the doctor and you will keep your health". But her legs are too wobbly to get out of bed again so she doesn't drink anything. She drifts in and out of hot hallucinatory sleep through the day. Until roused by a battering at her door.

"Hiya, Maya. You look dreadful." Balvinder is standing on the landing smiling. Maya tries to smile back, but the effort makes her legs give way beneath her. Balvinder picks her up and helps her back into bed.

"You're freezing," Balvinder says as she lifts Maya's legs up onto the bed. She lays a palm on Maya's forehead. "And hot too."

The cool dryness of Bal's hand is lovely. Maya is sorry when Balvinder removes it. Maya finds herself being propped up against her pillows and given sips of iced water, followed by ginger tea sweetened with honey. A little revived she takes some paracetamol. Balvinder wipes down Maya's face, neck and arms with a wet flannel. Through her fever, Maya notices that Balvinder has managed to slip her into a clean nightdress while keeping her body hidden under the quilt. Balvinder gets all the sticky tendrils of Maya's hair off her neck and tied into a plait, by which time Maya is exhausted again.

Heather

Robin was not mistaken about his hold over Mrs McFadyen. She phones me at work.

"Robin came to call. He and I were discussing your parents, Miss Heather, and we're worried."

"Yes" I reply, swallowing the sense that I am being admonished for neglect of my filial duties.

"They're not getting any younger, are they?"

"No", I have to agree.

"And neither am I." Would it be rude to agree with her? I stay silent just in case and implore the God in whom I have no faith to prevent her from resigning. "So I'll be needing more help with looking after Mr and Mrs Cromarty."

"Of course," I am delighted to agree emphatically. I realise that my fingers have been crossed. I don't approve of superstition. Mrs McFadyen goes on to explain that, with my permission, she will start on a spring clean of the flat to get a gentleman's guest room sorted out for Robin who'll be visiting more often. She is ticking me off. And if any extra expense is incurred, Mrs McFadyen could perhaps pick out a few wee items. A couple of antique dealers attend her bowling club and she could get advice from them. So it's all in Mrs McFadyen's capable hands. Robin always did get his own way. Thank God. Or the fates. Or the chakras. But mainly Mrs McFadyen.

Balvinder

I can't leave Maya alone in her flat overnight. And I don't want to bring Meena here. Too many germs, so I phone my wee sisters. Ma says they can come as long as they bring their maths revision with them. They're pleased for a reason to get out of the house. My big brother drops them off. We all three sit and watch Maya's tiny telly for a bit. Then I need to get back to feed Meena.

We all go through to the other room and look at Maya. She looks pitiful in her bed, surrounded by her pretty bed linen. I try to talk with her, but she's away with the fairies. She's too ill to leave on her own. Best place for her is with Ma.

Maya

Balvinder and her sisters get Maya into a taxi, carrying her in a fireman's chair-lift down the wide close stairs. They pay the taxi driver and carry her up more stairs to their flat. She is put in the girls' bedroom, where Balvinder used to sleep before she moved to Mrs Kapadia's. Maya is very ill. Ill enough that the GP agrees to do a home visit. He prescribes antibiotics for bronchitis. Through the heat haze of her fever, Maya calls Mrs Singh "Granny". She knows that it isn't her own Granny but recognises that she is being cared for. Whenever she opens her eyes there is someone sitting by the bed, giving her sips of water, keeping her bedclothes straight. One night she coughs up blood. Mrs Singh wonders whether they should inform Maya's mother of her illness. She asks Maya the next morning and gets no reply. Mrs Singh doesn't know whether Maya cannot or will not respond. Balvinder goes to Maya's flat to look for Hilary's address, but can't find it. Why would it be written down, since her mother's Stoke Newington address has been constant since Maya was three months old? There are no numbers stored on Maya's mobile. Balvinder looks out the application form Maya submitted for employment at Shakti, and finds an address and phone number in South London. She telephones the number that turns out to be the school where Maya worked before moving to Glasgow. Balvinder gives up.

After a week of being too ill to eat or talk, Maya begins to surface back into the conscious world. Her bedside companions, whom she had taken to be different versions of Balvinder, separate out into two different people, neither of whom are Balvinder. Jasvinder and Harminder are only a year apart in age and share the same clothes, but Maya can tell them apart: Jasvinder has a mole on her cheek and her hair doesn't reach quite so far down her back; Harminder makes dirtier jokes. The two girls nurse and entertain Maya, overseen by Mrs Singh, who in between taking her son to school, is up and down to the hospital visiting Mr Singh in the Coronary Care Unit.

As Maya begins to sit up in bed, Mrs Singh prepares food to tempt her back to eating. Her appetite returns and Maya longs for a soft-boiled egg with toast soldiers. But Mrs Singh doesn't eat eggs. Maya drinks lassi and eats stuffed paratha and stops losing weight. Mrs Singh is relieved. Since Balvinder left her flat, Maya had not bothered cooking meals and had become thin. Too thin. Maya hadn't noticed her shrinking body size, although she was pleased to have gone eight weeks without a period. It saved on laundry bills.

Jasvinder tells stories and sings songs. She teaches Maya the words to a lullaby, and when Meena is put for a nap in Jasvinder's bed, Maya sings it softly. Harminder's favourite song mocks a groom's prowess and is sung by the bride's family before marriage. Every time Balvinder comes round, Harminder starts singing it, under her breath at first, then getting louder until silenced by a clip round the head. Maya notes that Balvinder, who had always seemed so calm and collected is an irascible big sister. Her main means of communication, especially with Harminder, is to scowl, bark and slap. When not teasing her older sister about her marital status, Harminder enjoys teaching Maya how to swear in Punjabi, claiming that no language compares for expressing earthy obscenity.

"See, my granny in Punjab, well, she's a peasant. Grows things out of the mud. She says Punjabis are the bravest, rudest people alive!"

Jasvinder tuts at Harminder's coarseness. To have one shameless sister is bad luck, but to have two is ominous. She tries to balance her sisters' immodesty by her own efforts. She tells Maya the stories of peaceable Guru Nanak, the first Sikh Guru, whose portrait hangs over her bed. With his big white beard, Maya had taken him for Santa Claus during her delirium. Harminder counters with stories of the tenth Guru Gobind Singh, a dashing warrior who took on the Mughal armies and whose rakish good looks are shown in a portrait hanging in the kitchen. Guru Gobind Singh's combination of handsome and wholesome reminds Maya of a 1930s movie idol.

Sometimes, Balvinder's older brother visits, with his wife and children. Until four months ago, they too had lived in the flat. Now, they're in a newly built house on the outskirts of Maryhill. The children have been told to keep quiet for the sleeping invalid. They peek round the door and ask in shouty-whispers, "Is she going to die?"

"Well am I?" Maya asks herself. "It would be good to see Granny again, assuming that there is an afterlife. But no," she tells herself, "I think I will recover."

Maya's second course of antibiotics finishes and the sick line that Balvinder had organised from the doctor runs out in four days time. Although her legs feel less wobbly, Maya doesn't want to get out of bed. She doesn't want to leave the cocoon of Mrs Singh's flat. She wants Jasvinder to rub her back with mustard oil and Harminder to massage her scalp with jasmine oil, and for daily demands to stay in retreat. She doesn't want to phone her mother or write a report for the

Beaudessert foundation trustees. She's not sure how long she's been here, but suspects that the rent is due on her own flat. And so, reluctantly, Maya gets out of bed to phone her landlord. Harminder and Jasvinder have taken Meena out in her pram to put her to sleep. Maya had thought Mrs Singh was on the round trip to visit her husband in the hospital, before fetching her younger son from school. Instead, she finds Mrs Singh in the kitchen, weeping over a pile of red bills. Maya gets a toilet roll and offers it to Mrs Singh, who blows her nose and wipes her tears while Maya pats her on the back. Ineffectual affection, but better than just watching.

"Poor Mrs Singh," Maya says with feeling.

"Beta, too many bills. What to do? My English is too bad, and husband is too ill." Stating her case provokes Mrs Singh to start crying again. When she has stopped sobbing, Maya picks up the bills and tidies them into a pile, away from Mrs Singh's view. Then she makes tea.

"Only English tea. I can't make chai. Sorry Mrs Singh." Mrs Singh doesn't look as though she minds, as she adds four spoons of sugar and sips. The skin on her broad face looks grey and onion-skin-brittle. Maya finds an orange acrylic blanket and leads Mrs Singh to the kitchen sofa wedged into what used to be the bed recess. She lifts up Mrs Singh's feet and tucks the blanket under her legs. Maya turns on the wall-mounted television and finds a syrupy-looking Hindi-language film on the cable channel. Placing the cup of sweet tea in Mrs Singh's hands, she takes the bills away to the sitting room.

All the rooms lead off a central hall and with the departure of Mr Singh to hospital and his son to the suburbs, two remain unused. However, the sitting room has always been unused. It is laid out formally with the armchairs covered in plastic wrap to preserve their pristine cleanliness facing each other, ready for small talk. It's hard to imagine when the Singhs would use this ceremonious room. Since Maya has arrived, almost all domestic activity is conducted in the big kitchen.

Maya spreads out the bills on the plate-glass and gilt coffee table and kneels on the spongily underlaid carpet to examine them. Gas, electricity, water rates and council tax amount to nearly two thousand pounds. Maya wonders whether the television is licensed. She acquired a horror of debt from her grandmother, together with a taste for the satisfaction of keeping finances orderly and in the black, thereby denying unearned payment to the bank. Hilary had found her daughter's precocious interest in domestic accounting infuriating, since she equated chaotic personal finances with a liberal mind and a free spirit. She had accused Maya of being a control freak, when, aged fourteen, she took over collection of the child benefit and payment of the essential household bills.

When Balvinder returns to collect Meena in the afternoon, Maya takes her through to the sitting room to discuss the bills. Balvinder is puzzled by the accumulated debt and goes to interrogate Mrs Singh in impatient, rapid-fire Punjabi in the kitchen. She returns to the sitting room and pulls out the drawers of a camphor-wood chest in the corner. She lifts out a dozen heavily embroidered saris, kurtas and Punjabi suits. The inter-leaved tissue paper rustles and the gold threads and sequins glint. Balvinder sighs.

"I've been paying Ma every month out of the profits of my shop," says Balvinder mournfully as she strokes an inky blue sari with a silver border. "That money should've covered the bills. But Ma's been squirreling this lot for my wedding instead."

Balvinder groans as she lays the clothes back in the drawer.

"And if I marry then there's the sisters to get kitted out," Balvinder's pretty face looks worn down. "My brother isn't paying anything to Ma the now. He's got his new house to pay off and he has to keep his missus happy," she smiles wanly at Maya.

"Balvinder. Can I live here?" Maya demands.

"Yes, as long as you need to. Ma likes having you here." Balvinder slides the drawer slowly back in and turns back to Maya. Her face has lifted, levity dancing around her eyes. "You might be wanting to get back to work, mind."

"Why's that then?" asks Maya more sharply than she means to.

"Rubina and Sameena have been minding your arts group while you've been off. The internet café now has 'Agitate! Educate! Innovate!' painted, three foot high, black on a red background," Balvinder laughs as Maya's face takes on a

125

slightly disgusted look. But Maya won't be distracted by such matters of taste. She shakes her head.

"No, I mean move in here, not just a stay."

"I thought you liked your wee flat. Your private space."

"And so I do. But I'd miss your sisters and your Ma. I'd miss their kindness. I'd feel cold on my own. Besides Harminder hasn't taught me all her swear words yet."

Balvinder smiles, then turns back to the bills. "Of course. You don't cost much in food. There's no way I'm ever living here again. And I'd feel better if there was another adult here, now my brother's away."

"No, but if I lived here, I could pay my way. The three hundred a month I pay in rent alone would cover most of the monthly outgoings. What does the mortgage cost?"

"Nothing. My Dad bought it outright twenty years ago. Cost nothing. Back then no-one wanted old flats."

"Well there we go. Money problems solved. Even if your Dad never earns again." Maya is grinning with triumph. She could be useful to Mrs Singh and help Balvinder.

And so it happens. Maya gives notice on her flat and moves her modest number of cardboard boxes into one of the Singhs' empty bedrooms. She buys a tin trunk in which to store her diary and albums under lock and key. Mrs Singh sells the last of her jewellery to pay off the outstanding bills. Maya pays her rent monthly into Mrs Singh's account and Balvinder sets up direct debits to pay the bills.

Slowly, over the course of the next few weeks Maya recognises a growing feeling of safety. As safe as she had felt during her childhood summer holidays in Hunstanton. She knows when she wakes up that she won't have to meet any strangers or explain herself to anyone unexpectedly. At work, Sameena and Rubina have taken over the recruitment of people to join Shakti's activities. They have fallen out with the Socialist Workers and given up selling their paper. Having reaffirmed that Islam has all the liberatory potential necessary for a revolutionary movement, they have returned to the regular women's meeting at the mosque. There they conduct vigorous discussions with Samira and Mrs Hamida on interpreting the Qu'ran. Their readmission and Maya's departure has led the mosque committee to ignore the women's group once again.

Liberated from the need to talk to people, Maya is able to concentrate on decorating every suitable surface in the Shakti building. She has helpers who join her in the painstaking labour of painting, applying sequins, decoupage and varnishing, but mostly she works alone. Sameena and Rubina offered to paint over their vivid slogan in the internet café, but Maya has taken up the idea of words as part of her decorative scheme. The kitchen will feature recipes painted in various scripts – Gourmoukhi, Bengali and Dev Nagri. Stories and sayings of the gurus and prophets on the importance of learning are being collected by women from their aunties and grannies to adorn the internet café.

Maya goes back to the dancing class just once. Shiv had come into Shakti to persuade her and she reluctantly agreed. But returning to Mrs Singh's flat later in the evening, Maya feels acutely self-conscious of carrying the smell of ciggies and pubs into the flat. Mrs Singh does not make any comment, but Maya knows that she has polluted her safe, clean refuge. So when not at work she stays at home with Mrs Singh, watching Hindi movies and drinking chai. In the evenings, Mrs Singh butters Maya's dahl and urges her to take just one more roti and as a result Mayas cheeks and hips are filling out. When feeling light-hearted, Mrs Singh is wont to pinch Maya's cheeks with proprietorial pleasure. Maya's embarrassment is quelled as she submits to Mrs Singh's benign pleasure in her wellbeing.

Maya helps Balvinder's little brother with his homework and the sisters with revision. She takes her turn washing up and has learned to make a passable tarka dahl. Sometimes on a Saturday, if Mr Singh has already been visited, they all go to a Bollywood film screening. Maya wears her Punjabi suit and is introduced by Mrs Singh as "my new daughter". On the streets, and providing she keeps her eyes down and her dupatta well-wrapped, she can become invisible to passers-by. Occasionally Harminder wonders why Maya doesn't get herself a boyfriend.

"It's such a waste Maya. No-one could stop you getting a boyfriend. So why not?"

"They're not good for much, boyfriends," Maya says. "Apart from annoying your parents. And since my mother would be relieved rather than annoyed, why bother?" Another reason is that she hopes that Mrs Singh would object if she got a boy-friend. Not that Maya has any intention of jeopardising her asylum by finding out.

If he gets a bypass done, Mr Singh might be fit to return to his flat. Then maybe Maya will move on. But since his blood pressure is far too high he won't be coming back yet awhile.

The end

Balvinder's wedding to Raj Jutley takes place in the temple where Meena was named. After the religious ceremony, Mrs Singh provides a simple meal in the communal dining hall downstairs.

Mr Singh has given his blessing to the couple from his hospital bed. He spoke to Raj as one man of business to another. Balvinder cringes as her father describes the chal-lenges of self-employment in his little corner shop as compar-able with Raj's export empire. But mainly she is relieved that Mr Singh has accepted their union. Her husband's acqui-escence gives Mrs Singh's celebratory mood legitimacy. She is delighted. Of course a mother and daughter should weep when they are to be parted by marriage. But to lose a single-parent daughter in marriage to a successful businessman is not so bad.

After leaving the temple, the party continues in the even-ing in the Shakti building, hosted by Mrs Kapadia. Everyone that Maya knows in Scotland is there and, as she stands behind the drinks table, distributing fruit juice and fizzy pop in stainless steel beakers, she adds them up and wonders whether it's enough. By the end of her life, Granny had three friends. At least that's what she claimed. And after the big turn out of the Leamington Spa establishment for Grandpa's funeral, there were only half a dozen mourners at Granny's cremation. Three good friends seems like something to aspire to for Maya. Three real friends would be better than being best chums with whomever you happened to be standing next to, like Hilary.

Guests are crowding into all of the rooms in the building, each lit by night-light candles in small coloured-glass jars filled with water. Shuggie's worries about fire-hazard have been countered by Mrs Kapadia's assertion that no-one would be smoking indoors, "So why not have candles as our riskiness tonight?" This leap in logic floored Shuggie leaving him flapping the air with his hands in gleeful annoyance at the preposterousness of women. The flickering soft light lends an air of romance to Maya's workplace. It reminds her of the last party that Hilary threw for her in the gardens in London. Except this time, Maya can take credit for the prettiness. The low flickering lights together with the bright coloured clothes of the guests set off her wall paintings and mosaics a treat. Maya conjures up Jaipuri palace parties, where her father might entertain Rajasthani princesses with his tabla-playing. She has a clear image of an elegant man in a silk kurta with the callused hands of a serious percussion player and the haughty profile of a man of honour. He would carry himself into a trance by his own playing and not notice the admiring glances of the audience. He must be a glamorous and feckless character otherwise Hilary wouldn't have fallen for him in the first place. Perhaps she can at least thank Hilary's irresponsible attitude for having offered her the licence to invent her own father figure.

Mrs Kapadia and Mrs Singh have insisted on inviting Hilary to Balvinder's wedding, against Maya's wishes.

"How rude would we look, if we failed to include her?" Mrs Kapadia had demanded of a recalcitrant Maya. The invitation had forced Maya to phone Hilary to explain that she had moved house. She had expected Hilary to be offended that Maya had found a replacement mother in the form of Mrs Singh. But Maya should've known better. Hilary was ecstatic.

"But that's lovely darling. I always said you should get in touch with your Indian roots." Maya didn't bother explaining that the Punjabi village where Mrs Singh grew up was now part of Pakistan. Maya would not allow her mother to stay at the Singhs, insisting that Hilary book herself into a hotel. But Hilary would not be put off from attending the party. Having been alerted to some splendidly quaint ways of life on her previous trip, she knew that greater familiarity with Glasgow could only be to her advantage on the North London dinner party circuit. Hilary stands next to Maya, scanning the crowd, pronouncing them "such colourful, exuberant people."

129

SKINFULL

Heather Cromarty arrives alone, having left Doug at home to put the children to bed. Doug insisted that the children needed to go to bed at their normal time, and not be kept up for the party, relieved that fatherhood offers a reason to stay in and watch television on a Saturday evening. Heather is discussing with Norma and Flora how to have her parents' collection of first editions bequeathed to the women's library. Heather's desire to realise the maximum pecuniary value of her parents' belongings has been overcome by her deeply felt conviction that books should not be traded as items of value. Mr and Mrs Cromarty are not aware that their daughter is parcelling out their possessions in anticipation of their demise. But as Mrs McFadyen noted to Robin, while packing up a selection of pictures and silver trays for a dealer's consideration, "What they don't know cannae harm them," adding for good measure that "what's for you won't go by you." Perhaps the senior Cromartys will never notice the loss of the books, since their ability to read small print and to explore the outer reaches of their large flat is waning fast. Norma is tickled by the idea that an Austen first edition would share shelf-space with copies of the Pink Paper and Spare Rib. But, despite Heather's insistence that the first editions should be read by ordinary library users, Norma is not convinced that the library would be able to obtain suitable insurance.

Flora disengages from the library discussion and wanders over to talk to Shuggie who is lurking, unable to join in with the party: the stiletto heels are damaging the floors and the drinks leave sticky marks on the window sills. Hilary recognises a kindred spirit when she sees Flora's bright velvet frock and clunky silver jewellery. And then she sees Shuggie.

"Maya darling, can you introduce me to her?"

"No," Maya answers automatically and then adds, "Who do you mean?"

"The one in the frock talking to that bloke who gave me the come on last time I was here."

"Mum! He's called Shuggie. And he did not!"

"Of course he did darling. He was simply bristling with it."

"No Mum. He's just interested in art. He takes Japanese tourists around the Burrell collection. He knows loads about it. He's written about this year's Turner short-list, actually."

130

"Nonsense darling. I've never heard of him."

"How do you know? You don't know his name, mother."
Maya finds Hilary's extreme self-belief offensive.

"Where's the article?"

"In some literary review."

Hilary is making her way over to Shuggie and Flora anyway, so Maya gives in and accompanies her.

"Promise me that you won't flirt mother" Maya pleads.

"Only if he doesn't start first!"

Within minutes of joining their group, Hilary establishes
that Flora and Shuggie are half-siblings. Despite the lack of
alcohol, Shuggie gets into a joking dispute with Flora as to
whose father had been the most dissolute.

"Mine was an utter shite!" declares Shuggie.

"That's right enough, but mine was a devious shite" insists
Flora.

Maya returns to her post at the drinks table. Hilary is, of
course, flirting with both Flora and Shuggie. But at least
they're her own age. Maya hears Shuggie, Flora and Hilary
agreeing that single mothers had it harder in their day. From
across the room Maya can see that Hilary has Shuggie in her
sights: her hand is clasped on his forearm and her eyes are
opened extra wide as she shrieks with laughter at whatever he
has just said.

Balvinder's cousin Kam bustles up and asks for six half-full
beakers of Irn Bru, with an exaggerated wink. She then pro-
ceeds to top up each drink from a clear bottle that is quickly
slipped back into her copious handbag.

"A wee voddie top-up. Do you want one pal?" Kam asks
Maya kindly. Maya shakes her head. It's the Irn Bru rather
than the vodka that puts her off. Kam makes off towards a
group of cousins, each equipped with mint breath-freshener
for when they have to embrace the aunties.

Shiv mooches over and Maya tries to locate Mrs Singh to
hide behind. No luck. Mrs Singh is just disappearing into the
ladies to change Meena's nappy. Maya has to face this one
alone.

"Hello Shiv."

"Hello stranger."

"Would you like a drink?" asks Maya brightly.

131

"No, ta. I'd like to know why you've given up on the dancing."

Maya shrugs apologetically, "It's not me Shiv. Not now. I need to sit about quietly."

"So why not marry me? We could sit about quietly together."

"No, no Shiv. You're embarrassing me." Maya blushes hot.

"I know. I try it with all the lassies, but you're the only one who responds," Shiv smiles sadly. "I'll be asking you again next year, you know. About marriage."

Maya tries hard to laugh as if this is a joke. "If I ever do marry, I'll be asking your mother to fix me up with someone." Maya nods towards the door where Balvinder and Raj are just arriving. They've been to their honeymooners' suite at the Hilton to get changed into matching oyster-coloured silk outfits. They look so pleased with one another.

"She's made a good match there." People are flocking round the newly weds to congratulate them.

Rubina and Sameena have connected a CD-player to a set of amplifiers and started dancing to disco-bhangra music with Jasvinder and Harminder. Others are joining in. The group spots the arrival of the bride and groom and dances over to surround them in a circle, smiling and whooping as they jog up and down. Mrs Singh emerges from the toilets with a newly fragrant Meena and laughs at the sight of her daughter and dignified new son-in-law surrounded by a group of over-excited youngsters. Maya takes Meena from Mrs Singh, to prevent anyone prevailing upon her to dance. Mrs Singh joins the group, dignifying the dance step by performing it half as fast as the younger people. Meena cannot protect Maya, as Shiv takes the baby and hands her over the heads of the dancers to Raj Jutley. Meena is held up in the crook of her new father's elbow, patting his bearded chin and crowing joyously. Shiv catches up Maya's hand and pulls Hilary away from Shuggie, leading mother and daughter in a dance he calls "strip the Punjabi willow".

Why did I long to reach my eighteenth birthday so? I had done ever since I could remember. Why did it matter? I'd been able to order drink in bars since I was sixteen and I didn't want to have sex with men anyway, especially not after I'd met Jo.

Jo, of course, was a girl. Well, a woman really. But her usefully ambiguous name meant that I didn't have to explain this to anyone until I was quite sure that the fuss would be worth the bother. Not that anyone could have complained since I've never pretended anything different. My mum prided herself on being able to speak to anyone that I brought home to her – a useful skill when you're a social worker. Even after she gave up work to look after me, she kept her skills alive with the freaks that I brought home from school. In fact it was more than a useful skill, it was a point of honour. And I suppose I was drawn to types who might test my Mum's small-talk skills.

She couldn't get a word out of mysterious Malcolm, but that was no great shame on her abilities; no one else could either. He was always at the bus stop, morning and evening, not speaking but sometimes shaking his head. He never got on or off any buses because he lived at the vicarage, bang next door to school. He wouldn't even headshake when asked about his parents. But Malcolm's hair was the same brown ringlets as the vicar's wife, and social work never appeared at the vicarage, so I guess they were his parents. My mum managed to talk to Yasmeen, no bother. Or rather she listened. Yasmeen had been the first in our class to get a mobile, but the last girl to get a period. She decided this placed her perfectly for prostitution: she could talk to her punters without her parents knowing and she couldn't get pregnant. Mum tried to explain that fertility wasn't always signalled by a red-letter day. But Yasmeen was too busy talking about her business plan which involved tapping the market of men who fancied Asian babes and rested on the legendary premature ejaculation of white men, meaning she could manage a high throughput. Probably, she told Mum, she wouldn't even have to have sex with most of them as they'd not even last that long. Then she moved on to describing the endless list of things that she was going to buy with her pure-profits enterprise: mini-disc stack system, a Prada suit, Fendi baguette.

Mum was always the person who got the conversations going; on our annual holidays to Cyprus in train compartments, ticket queues and on the beach she always had exactly the right opening question that was innocuous and non-threatening. Dad finished the conversations by sharing out our picnic, issuing invitations for barbecues and beers, or starting five-aside games, but it was Mum who got them going.

But Jo was a tougher proposition for Mum than Malcolm or Mediterranean tourists.

"How lovely to meet you!"

"And you Mrs Fort."

"Would you like a cup of tea?"

Clearly something was up because we never drank tea in our house – only coffee (black and strong), juice (freshly squeezed) and alcohol (new world). But Mum had bought tasty tips golden brew to make the right impression. An impression of homey comforts I suppose, even though Mum had always said the tannic brew epitomised the worst of the British history (colonial) and taste (insipid). So without her anti-tea touchstone, I should have known that Mum was adrift. But I didn't figure it out, at least, not for a long time. I was so insulated in my duvet of delight with Jo.

"Please. Aye. Milk and three sugars." Jo smiled at Mum and asked me about my clinic placement the day before. I had just begun to tell her about a complicated road accident case when Mum cut me off.

"Surely you shouldn't be giving us confidential patient details darling!"

"But I only told you his first name!" I protested. She carried on pouring tea and proffering bourbon biscuits across the pine kitchen table, scorch marks disguised with a floral cloth. So then Jo tried asking about the petunias in the kitchen window box.

"I just bought them at B&Q. They practically grow themselves."

Jo tried another question about the cat, which was firmly closed down too. Mum didn't ask Jo about herself. None of the usual probing questions mantled in soft, maternal interest. Nothing. Just gazing into the middle distance, sipping tannic liquid.

That night, after the stilted tea-sipping, when we were both sitting on the sofa, watching an Attenborough-voiced programme about coyotes, I asked:

"So what was that tea business Mum?"

"I thought there was enough for Joanne to deal with already, without introducing our prejudices about hot beverages" she said with heavy intonation on "enough". "And anyway I always quite liked tea before I met your Dad. It was him who loathed it."

"Mum, Jo knows all about me. Everything. She's not bothered. She's cool about it. In fact she thinks it's interesting. She asks about it."

"About what love?" Mum asked in a carefully light, neutral voice.

"You know ... whether I knew my real Mum."

"Your birth mother darling?"

"Yeah. And if I'm bothered about looking different from you."

"But you don't! People comment on how similar we look."

"But that's mannerisms isn't it, like how we both pull our earlobes when we're thinking and swivelled our eyes at Dad's jokes." Mum didn't laugh. I could've gone on about the twitches and reactions that I'd learned from her and Dad, but she clearly wasn't in the mood. And neither was I, really. I wanted to gaze at pretty pictures of coyotes running their loosely jointed limbs across the screen and bask in the knowledge of Jo's adoration. Mum wanted reassurance that I still treasured my learned family traits more than the crudely biological links that I had lost. It was family lore that it takes no parenting skill to bequeath your offspring red hair, but some dedication to pass on a gloomy disposition. But I couldn't be bothered to convince Mum yet again that I am a secure and happy individual and that I bought all of her propaganda about being special because I'm adopted.

"So when are you seeing her again?" Mum asked.

"Tomorrow. She's picking me up from college on the way to the climbing wall."

"That's where she works is it?" Mum asked with synthetic interest.

"She manages the whole leisure complex, but she climbs there too."

"What a clever person she is!" More bright maternal sheen.

"Yeah. She's reached the regional semi-finals." I thought this would make Jo seem more respectable somehow, not just locked into the lesbian ghetto, but competing in the straight world and winning.

"Of what?"

"Ummm. Freestyle amateur I think. Not sure."

"Lovely."

We left our brittle consensus that Jo had a talent and returned to the coyotes who were now nuzzling a red and ragged ruminant corpse. The voice-over was noting the evolutionary pressures that led female coyotes to fight off their own offspring for a meal during times of scarcity. I got embarrassed watching the slurping desperation next to Mum and went off to play k.d.lang's "endless yearning" and think about Jo's muscled shoulders.

My longing for Jo was muddled up with longing to reach my majority. Why? Lesbians don't have an age of consent. And I loved every aspect of my life then: college, mates, home. Turning eighteen wasn't meant to change any of it.

Jo had climbed two new routes on the wall and named one of them "Sappho" and the other "Dorothy". "Sapphic ladies"

136

had been Dad's respectfully mocking term for the women's healing tent at solstice camp, but Jo had to explain the queer claim on the Wizard of Oz. Bizarre. Why claim a kiddie-film when there's the whole world of avant-garde and cinema noir out there? When Jo had claimed and named her routes, she came to watch me grasping my way up a grade two pitch.

"Not your knees, Fliss! If you can reach it with your knee, you can get a toe in!" she hollered.

I was charged up by her gaze on me. The next reach was too far up and too wide for comfort. I had to fling my weight towards the little lump of plastic screwed to the wall and pinch my fingers around it. Falling off the wall means humiliation as your belay-partner holds your weight and you dangle on the ropes for the whole club to see. The boys don't take you seriously if you fall off. You're meant to struggle for every reach as if you're on a Himalayan mountainside clinging on above cloud level, despite the backdrop of badminton mixed doubles.

"Keep three points of contact, lassie!" Jo reminded.

My last five moves flowed one from the other, like dancing upwards. Superhero sexy I felt, knowing my movements were admired. I got the rush as I scrambled onto the upper platform. I looked down: Jo had taken over my belay from Tim. The pressure from my harness suddenly seemed erotic rather than restrictive. I climbed carefully down the fixed ladder as my legs and arms were trembling after the full-body concentration of the ascent. "Elvis legs" Tim called it. At the bottom, Jo grinned and hugged me around the shoulders.

"Well done doll-face. Nice climbing." She pushed me away as a sinewy type came to congratulate her on her virgin route. The extreme wall had only been installed a couple of weeks ago and the serious climbers were competing to name each combination of moves up it.

Later in the pub, Jo left the beards' table, where she was planning a trip to Fontainebleu and joined me and the other baby climbers. Her welcoming open-faced grin was beamed round.

"Which of youse are coming along then? To Paris?" We all shook our heads uncertainly. The other old-handers had made it clear that the trip was only open to the experienced climbers.

"Aaach go on! It'll be magic. We did a trip to north Wales a few years ago. We brought back the same number of bodies that we started down the road with."

"I'm not sure that I'm up to climbing all day for a week" ventured timid Tim. His puny body was so slight that gravity could barely get a grip and, even with arms like boiled celery, he could hoist himself up the most unlikely of reaches. He was a doddle to belay.

"You're right there, son" Jo nodded seriously. "Your arms hurt like buggery after the first day. You de ken how you're gonnae lift your tea to your face in the morning. But you have tae climb again cause there's fuck all else to do in that forest!"

In the face of this hard sell, a couple of us juveniles said that we would go and Jo went off to find parental permission forms. She was looking over my shoulder as I filled in my nationality and date of birth.

"You'll no need your Ma's permission for the trip" she commented and I looked up frowning. The others had gone to get another round in. I was drinking ginger beer mixed with bitter, in a pint glass so I wouldn't look like a wuss, or, as Jo put it "a raving poufter". I was feeling light-headed. She put a finger on my date of birth and raised her eyebrow. I looked down at her beautiful, capable finger: the muscles which held her against the rock face were visible on the first two joints; the skin on her knuckles bore the scars of having been wedged into nooks and used to bear her weight while she searched for another cranny. The fingernail was filed, following the contour of the callused flesh.

"You'll be eighteen by then, Felicity", she pointed out. And more quietly she added, "I'm sorry your Ma didnae like me." I drew a breath to protest that of course my mum liked her because she was so broad-minded she liked everyone. "What did you tell her I was?" asked Jo.

"A climbing instructor, of course! And a champion climber", I smiled.

"No, you daftie. Not ma job. What did you tell her about us?"

"What do you mean?"

"Did you say, my naïve wee pal, that you were bringing your suitor and prospective lover round for tea?"

"Yes, well no" I said hopelessly, feeling that both answers were probably wrong. I had always felt utterly confidently queer, until I met Jo who somehow made me feel a fraud. She had suffered; she had been refused access to her stepchildren when she came out and then lost a job because she would not keep her appetites for women invisible.

I have never suffered for being a girl who prefers girls. I don't remember any pressure not to express this desire. The only problem I recall was convincing anyone to take me seriously. My first fantasy-girlfriend was Audrey Hepburn, but this went unnoticed, since all the girls in year nine fancied her after *Breakfast at Tiffany's* became the video of choice in the common room. In year ten I started calling myself a lesbian, mainly as a defence against the spotty year eleven boys looking for opportunities to practise their moves. That must've been about the time when Josh made his confession of true love to me which only helped to make lesbianism seem like a blissful refuge. Even at college I didn't get any trouble. The other first year physios were divided between well-scrubbed home-counties gels, hopeful of a doctor husband and hearty, sporty capable women who preferred squash to sex. All of them were far too dedicated to learning muscle groups and manipulations to notice my sexuality.

In sum, I simply hadn't suffered for the queer cause. Jo had assured me that my time would come, which didn't feel very comforting. Similarly, her mocking smile as she waited for me to settle on "yes" or "no" was not meant to offer succour.

"No. I haven't ever called you my girlfriend 'cause I don't own you and you're not a girl", I tried. Involuntarily, the sentence took on an upward intonation which sounded horribly pleading.

"Oh, so you're not out to your Ma after all then?" Jo pounced, making Tim, carrying a tray of drinks, jump and slop the beer. He edged the tray onto the table and returned to the bar to fetch a cloth.

"Yes I am. She's always known I'm not straight." I looked Jo full in the face and dared her to query me. Which she did, sarcastically.

"Aye, aye, sure. That's why your Ma was that pleased to see me the other day."

"She was nervous because she knows you're important to me."

"But not important enough to be claimed by you!" was Jo's sharp response. Tim scuttled off again to join a huddle round the fruit machine.

"So, are you my girlfriend? Is that what you want to be?" I asked Jo, pacifyingly.

"Och we're not getting anywhere. Sup your beer." And she took herself back to the beards to pore over Michelin maps of the environs of Paris.

On my free study afternoon I helped Mum with the weekly shop. As an indulged only child my preferences had always governed the household menus. Now I'm doing my "nutrition and healing" module, Mum has to eat broccoli (folic acid), apricots (vitamin A) and brown rice (thiamine and riboflavin).

"At least the Barbie-yoghurt phase was cheaper", Mum smiled ruefully as we left the organic veg shelf behind. "Do you remember how much Dad used to try to enjoy your favourite foods? Picking at fish fingers and crinkle cut chips. He so wanted to be the perfect Dad. You know that don't you, love?"

"Of course, Mum" I muttered. Dad had been dead two and a half years, but Mum still needed to talk him alive. They were so much made for each other. I had taken it for granted that all parents glowed with contentment in one another's company and delighted in everyday tasks, if they were undertaken as a duo, but Yasmeen assured me this was deeply abnormal.

"If only we'd eaten more of this type of food", Mum sighed as she dropped a bag of bean sprouts into the trolley, "then maybe ..."

"No, Mum. It's inherited. You couldn't have stopped his heart attack by force-feeding him greens. He wouldn't't've thanked you, anyway. Remember how he loved his cheese." Nick Parks must've modelled Wallace on my Dad: "Cheese! You cannae beat it!" he used to tell us as he tore open another industrial pack of economy mature cheddar. Packing for our holidays would be Dad getting a fortnight's worth of cheese into his rucksack. By the time we reached the Mediterranean it would get a bit sweaty and he'd have to make a lot of cheese sauce over a youth hostel stove, to use it all up. Dad said the cow was God's way of making greens palatable. When we ran out of cheese at home, I gave him some lawn clippings on a Tuc biscuit. He had roared with laughter and said I'd be the next Billy Connolly if I kept that up. I must've been three or four and recall it as the first time I realised that grown-ups didn't always say what they meant, even straight-talking honest people like my Dad.

We were drifting down the dried fruit and home-baking aisle. Glacé cherries and desiccated coconut usually soothed Mum so I broached a tricky topic.

"Thought I might go climbing with the club in Whitsun week."

"Oh! How nice! But what about your birthday?"

"They don't leave until the Monday."

"I was planning a special dinner party for you. A sort of surprise ..."

"I really want to go climbing Mum. Jo says I've got potential."

"I dare say she does" said Mum tartly, weighing up some citric acid. "But there's someone I very much want you to meet. Someone who has a real interest in who you are."

"Jo is interested in me Mum. It's not just my climbing."

"Yes dear."

"Do you like her Mum?"

"Of course darling. I like all your friends."

"But she's not just a friend."

"No. She's your climbing instructor. And she's twice your age I would guess." Mum's lips were pulled tight. As she let them go to smile "Good afternoon" to the vicar, I could see where her coral lipstick had seeped up the pucker lines.

"More than twice. Thirty-nine, she is", I told Mum unnecessarily.

"Old enough to be your mother."

"And I don't need another mother", I said, patting her arm.

"I agree."

We surveyed the biscuit aisle in silence until we reached the two-for-the-price-of-one Belgian-chocolate-coated vanilla wafers.

"Not with your diabetes, Mum" I reminded her.

"I was thirty-nine when I got you", Mum said quietly as she dropped a virtuous packet of garibaldi in the trolley. I nodded. "Just in time before I got too old", Mum smiled distantly. " 'Our own bonnie wee lassie' your Dad said. He used to be up twice a night for the first year, just to check on you. Couldn't believe his luck. Do you think about her a lot?"

"Well I'm seeing her tomorrow." Mum turned from the pasta display, to look me straight in the face and then her taut muscles relaxed.

"Oh! Jo!" she gasped.

"Who did you mean?"

"Yes, that's right. Jo" and she swung the trolley towards the cash desk unexpectedly.

"But Mum, we haven't done the crisps or oat cakes yet", I said, annoyed because we'd run out of both at home. And distracted by my disrupted snacking scheme, I didn't note the twitchiness that had taken hold of my usually serene mother. She, too, was anticipating my eighteenth birthday but with trepidation, not pleasure.

"Out of budget love", she responded. She's always kept a running total as we toured the supermarket. We've always been short of money. Or rather she has and I've usually been cushioned from all hardship. "Cosseted", Jo reckoned.

I was going to college in a Jo-flavoured dream-fantasy on the top of the bus.

"Hello stranger!" An elbow in the ribs and there was Yasmeen sitting next to me. She didn't look like a girl who'd left school less than a year earlier. She looked like the MD of a global corporation: shimmering suit, spiked heels, well cut coat and enough make-up to look glam but not over-done.

"You look good", I greeted her.

"I know", she replied. "You look pretty fit yourself. Like gym-toned, not like 'I fancy you'. Are you still doing the lezzie thing?" she asked impertinently.

"Oh yes. It's for life. So you needn't ask again, Yas" I said firmly as I bared my teeth in a grimace warning-smile at the granny who had turned around to cop to a look at a real life pervert.

"What about you? Still turning prozzie tricks?" I asked slightly louder than necessary.

"No way. That's a mug's game. Have you heard about chlamydia?"

"No. Is she any good?" I thought I could see the biddy's pleated acrylic hat trembling with suppressed rage. Well, I hoped.

"Doh! It's a horrible lurgey that rots your women's bits so you can't have babies."

"Well that would save on condoms, eh Yas!" But Yasmeen wasn't doing irreverent this morning. At least not about herself. She was serious.

"But I would really mind if that was me. So I've taken the pledge", she told me, her big brown eyes holding mine in a sincere gaze. I could see the subtle slick of mascara on her outer upper lashes.

"You never drank anyway did you? Remember that Christmas when the lads had White Lightening, you were the only sober one among us."

"No. Not drink. Sex. I'm a born-again virgin."

"What your hymen's grown over again?" I said spluttering with laughter. Yasmeen was the queen of sexual know-how when the rest of us were still trading top trumps. Her forswearing sex was just bizarre.

"It might do. Some women's do. But the important stuff is in my soul.", she emphasised the last word by thumping her chest. "That's what my Imam says anyway."

"You're doing this at the mosque?" My incredulity had got beyond laughter.

"Well, he's not actually allowed in the mosque. The committee doesn't approve of him so we meet in the community centre. He's the man Fliss. You'd love him," she said, misty eyed like a J17 photo-romance.

"Not sure he'd love me though. Apart from atheism, there's the small matter of homosexuality which the most liberal of organised religions finds hard to accept." Yasmeen took no notice and launched into a description of the dream-boat Imam's caramel twinkling eyes, manly whiskers and authoritative ways.

"And he really knows Islam Fliss. Like, he knows the

difference between tradition and religion. He talks to us. Really talks. Not like 'it's tradition, so you must!' or whatever."

"But you never bought that tradition stuff anyway did you?" I asked. "Why would you need some bloke to help you understand Islam? Just get a book out the library!"

"Because he is so fit Fliss. I mean like ghugh!" Yas let her jaw drop and her eyes widen in crazed admiration. "And if I had him in my life, I would never need speed or tabs again. He is …" and she kissed her fingers like a French chef.

"Yas, what if he really just wants to save your soul? You know, strictly spiritual fervour?"

"Oh ye of little faith!" she imitated the Welsh lilt of our old RE teacher. "Have you already forgotten that Yas always gets her man?" she admonished as she stood up.

"Or her Imam?" I added. With a lascivious chuckle, Yas made her way off the bus to Top Shop where she had just been promoted from sales assistant to deputy manager.

"Yas for Prime Minister!" I said with a closed-fist salute to the bisum who had turned around to goggle at me again.

"This is what we had always planned for you darling. Your Dad and me." Mum was arranging the stock of fancy food delivered from the deli. Posh food that never usually graced our modest kitchen surfaces. "We used to talk about it every year on your birthday. It was one of the last things he mentioned in hospital." She was stacking bottles of sparkling chardonnay on the lowest shelf in the fridge. "The money was put away for this dinner by the time you were five years old," she said as she loaded almonds in the cupboard and marinated kalamata olives in the larder. I broke up the cardboard boxes that the food had arrived in, stacked them and tied them up with string for recycling.

"Can I invite Malcolm, Josh, Phil and maybe Jo?" I asked thinking about the birthday meals that I'd had over the past fifteen years. I had been eighteen months old when Mum and Dad had got me and Mum's photo albums document every birthday celebration since then. Maniacal and defensive record keeping is inevitable if you've been a social worker Mum said. Aged two I had big cheeks and a mystified expression as other kids are blowing out two whopping great candles. "Who are they?" I had asked Mum. "Oh neighbours' kids," was her vague reply. From three years until fifteen years old there was just the three of us gathered round a big cake, our expressions expectant and stuck, captured by the automatic timed flash on Dad's camera. On my sixteenth, Mum suggested inviting some friends to distract us from Dad's absence. Malcolm, Yas, Josh and I had played at being grown up with wine and candles and linen napkins. We all got the giggles after the first bottle of wine. Even Mum. And then Mum had gone to bed and we'd watched *Pulp Fiction*, all squashed up together on the sofa, chanting our favourite lines out loud. And for my seventeenth we did exactly the same, except Phil was there and Yas wasn't, because her father had banned her from leaving the house except to go to the library.

"No, love. This is a serious rite of passage. There'll only be one guest apart from us two."

"But that's not ..." I started to protest.

"I'll cook you another birthday dinner if you like darling." But she was thinking about the serious dinner, checking off a list of ingredients for my favourite dishes: mushroom soup; spinach ricotta lasagne; lemon sorbet with hazelnut cookies.

"She was a colleague of mine in social work. A great friend. We haven't seen each other since." Mum gazed unseeingly at a packed of dried porcini mushrooms. "I do hope you like her darling. I know she'll like you. She'll be proud. Proud of us both. And of Dad too."

"Did she know him then?"

"Oh yes. She introduced me to him. She walked out with him before I did in fact."

"What? You took her cast offs?" Mum put down the eggs she was breaking.

"I didn't mean to ... I was just doing her a favour."

"By setting up home with him?"

"No, by taking your Dad out for a coffee when Stella had ditched him. He was broken hearted and she asked me to show him some kindness." She gazed out of the window at our strip of garden, her head slightly tilted to one side.

"So you married him?" Mum was tipping a yolk from shell

to shell to separate it from its white. It seemed a few moments before she understood what I had said.

"No love. Listen!" She put the eggs down again. "She was my colleague and best friend and she was very political. Very active in the women's liberation movement. And she loved your Dad. Really. A lot I think. They had their future together mapped out ... a commune they were going to set up in Herefordshire ..." she trailed off as she disappeared into the past again.

"So what happened?" I took over separating the eggs.

"Stella started reading Andrea Dworkin's stuff. You know, 'all men are rapists', or at least 'heterosexual sex is often violent and oppressive to women'. That kind of thing. She was working in the battered children's unit at the time, doing good work. Pioneering. Exhausting. All her cases were also being sexually abused."

"But that wasn't Dad's fault was it?"

"No darling, of course not. He had nothing to do with it. He was busy designing city-centre pedaestrianisation schemes. No. It wasn't his fault. But Stella's work was ahead of its time. She knew that battery and abuse went together and she knew both things happened in the shelter of the family." Mum took a tray out of the oven. "People still thought that only dirty, suspect strangers abused children in those days. You know, men in macs. Stella could see that abuse happened in families."

"Not all families" I pointed out, picking a warm hazelnut out of the roasting tin. "Not ours."

"No, of course not. But in most of the families that Stella worked with. She only met families where the men were doing awful things to the children and where the mothers were letting their men away with it. And your dad was a bloke. And he was the bloke that Stella was thinking of making a family with..."

"So she left him because he was a bloke?"

"Yes I suppose she did. Because that was how we understood it then. Male power was the problem." We were both gazing out of the kitchen window at the bird table in the garden where a pigeon was failing to get into the peanut supply. "And because of separatism I suppose."

146

"Locking abusers up?" I asked.

"No, love. Separatism. I mean women living separately from men. Apart."

"What like a harem?"

"But not under a man ... away from all men. Escaping power play, violence. That was the idea. Like a feminist kibbutz. Seemed like a solution back then." Mum shrugged. "Stella and me, we lived together with other women in a big rented, ramshackle house. We learned plumbing at one evening class and 'managing domestic electrical wiring' at another so we didn't have to rely on tradesmen. It was fun. Idealistic. We had huge arguments about whether a man could be a feminist: whether it was possible to have an equal relationship with a man." Mum sighed. "Some of them decided it wasn't, so stuck with each other. Political lesbians they called themselves. Having contact with men was like consorting with the enemy. You felt apologetic."

"But Dad was super-gentle. He never hurt anyone."

"I know love. And Stella knew that too. But when you see that stuff every day, you look for a reason. And we all agreed that men or at least male power was the reason."

"But to hold Dad responsible ...? I don't think I want to meet this woman. Specially not on my birthday."

"She didn't exactly hold Dad responsible. She just couldn't keep it all going at once. Her work, coping with the consequences of men's brutality, was the evidence that women were looking for to support separatism. Stella was condemning the men who were wrecking children's lives and she didn't feel able to go out with your Dad as well. It sounds foolish, simplistic now, but she thought that looking after those children was important and she had to choose them over him." Mum started whisking the egg whites slowly and methodically. She was always careful not to wear out her muscles before reaching the stiff snowy peaks. She refused to buy an electric whisk, claiming that food didn't taste so good when mechanically mixed. I started rough chopping the hazelnuts.

"I suppose we should be pleased though. That she didn't want him, otherwise we wouldn't have got him would we Mum?"

"No. That's true. And we also have Stella to thank for you."

"What?" I put down my chopping knife.

"She gave you to us. Me and Dad."

"She's the Cypriot?" I asked, rather loudly. Why had Mum rambled on about feeble-minded feminists if she'd really been trying to talk about my birth mother?

"No, no, love. Not your mother. She was the social worker" said Mum putting the whisk down and resting one hand on my shoulder to reassure me. Her head was slightly to one side, waiting for my next question.

"Social worker?" I asked.

"For your adoption."

"Oh. Yeah." Mum was still looking expectant. "Cool. I'm glad she wasn't my mother. That would be too weird. Especially if Dad had been her boyfriend." But I thought I'd check that I had understood Mum's story so far. "Is Stella Cypriot?"

"No, no. Definitely not. I'm not sure that anyone is. I'm not making a very good job of this am I?" said Mum more to herself than to me. "Stella said we should be led by you. That you'd instinctively ask, if we were always open."

And I was going to ask more about Stella, but I was also quite relieved for the distraction of Yasmeen's face that appeared at the kitchen window. She had her tongue stuck into her lower lip, bulging it out. She was bouncing up and down and had started swinging from the lowest cherry tree branch by the time I got the back door open. The cat ran up the tree onto Mrs Ashkenazy's shed roof and was giving Yas a glacial stare. Mum's face was quite neutral through the window. She was still in her feminist house-share, falling in love with my Dad, I guessed.

"Hiya Fliss." squawked Yas, a bit out of breath when she'd finally stopped her monkey impression. "Hiya Mrs Fort! Awright?" She waved and shouted. Mum smiled distantly.

"Yeah we were until you showed your daft face. You big tit! What you doing here?"

"Just came to see if you still live here. That's all. I was passing like and ..." Yas brought her face up close to mine and made her eyes big and sincere and drew a deep breath "and I wanted to ask you something." We were sitting on the bench under the cherry tree watching the cat watching us. "Felicity, why you don't invite me to tea anymore like you used to?" I snorted out the breath that I'd held in anticipation of a real question.

"Yes I miss watching Blue Peter with pink wafers and orange squash, too." I said sardonically as I patted her knee. "But you've got your new Imam-hunting hobby now, haven't you? In fact that would explain why I don't even see you in the pub any more."

"True. He doesn't drink. He lives down this street you know."

"Your holy man?"

"Yeah. He rents a room from the Haqs on the corner. You remember their geek-boy son?"

"Naw. What d'he look like?"

"Black hair, brown eyes, brown skin, thick glasses. Doh! Like a Muslim you prat!"

"So you're only visiting me in the hopes that you bump into your Imam-man?"

"Mmmm", Yas looked unusually coy.

"Coffee, girls?" Mum called from the back door. We both nodded and stuck up our thumbs. Mum's face looked faded and saggy in the bright sunshine, despite her welcoming smile.

"She's always been nice to me, your Mum," Yas said thoughtfully. "Even when I was being even more obnoxious than usual."

"Yeah."

"You're lucky, you know."

"How do you mean?"

"Well, white kids are embarrassed by their parents and Asian kids are harassed by theirs. Black kids don't have to worry because they're all in care. But you, you get on with your Mum."

"Josh isn't in care," I protested.

"Yeah, but he's posh black innit? All the black kids on my street are in care."

"That's 'cause you live next door to a children's home you div." I cuffed Yas round the head.

"Humph. Fzat, fzat, hisss." Yas made fighting noises at

the cat, still on the shed, to distract from the flaw in her argument.

"But you're right. I do get on with my Mum," I said conciliatorily. "Except, she doesn't like Jo."

"Jo from the sports centre?" Yas asked.

"Yeah."

"How did your Mum meet her?"

"Cause I brought her round to tea."

"You really do miss wafers and squash on the sofa!"

"I thought Mum ought to meet her. Because you know. We go out together a lot. And. Well. I fancy her."

"She's a dirty great bull-dyke, Fliss! What did you expect? Your Mum's not meant to like her!" Yasmeen had stopped her cat-teasing to berate me for my stupidity. "Still," she carried on more gently, "it could've been worse. Imagine if she'd been all over her – they must be about the same age."

"Euyerch! Yas! Don't be gross. Jo's in her thirties and my Mum's nearly sixty!" Yas merely smiled knowingly and wobbled her head annoyingly from side to side to imply "well exactly" but without actually saying anything. She waited before baiting me further.

"Imagine that, your Mum copping off with your girlfriend. That would confirm all that my father thinks is wrong with this country."

The back door clunked open and Yas jumped up to take the tray that Mum proffered.

"How is Mrs Mohammed, Yasmeen?" asked Mum. I was amazed she could remember Yas's surname. It was a full year since she'd been round. Those social work skills again.

"Yeah. Fine, thanks, Mrs Fort. Busy. She's going on haj, you know, pilgrimage, next month. To pray for her wicked children."

"Oh but she must be proud of you Yasmeen, with your pretty face and cleverness!" Mum smiled.

"Girls shouldn't be clever, Mrs Fort. That's boys' business. Anyway, it's my brothers that need divine help."

"Send her my regards, Yasmeen," said my Mum, preventing the listing of the Mohammed boys' narcotic-related sins, as she turned back to the house.

"Will do, Mrs Fort."

Yasmeen walked back to the bench, sat down and balanced the tray on her knees: two coffees with hot milk and hazelnut biscuits fresh from the oven. The crumbly buttery biscuits burned our tongues and the sun heated up our hair.

"But they never really mortified you did they, your folks? Not properly. Not like mine do." Yasmeen whisked crumbs from her kameez. "Mine never stop discussing marriage prospects and salaries. Like that's all there is to life. Even now I've got my promotion. Your parents never made you cringe so much you were practically inside-out did they?"

"Ummm" I had to think. "Well, once maybe."

"When?" asked Yasmeen putting the tray on the grass.

"On solstice camp" I replied.

"You used to get a week off school every year for that camp didn't you? And you'd come back looking like a Paki."

"I assume that's a compliment, Yas."

Yas didn't answer but instead asked "So, what about this one and only cringe?"

"Some of the hippy campers did drumming, in a circle, round a campfire, stoned and a bit shamanic. Well, more shambolic than shamanic. One time my parents got up and did a cha-cha-cha round the circle. They thought it was hilarious. I had to hide in the healing yurt. And that's when I realised the pure joy of being adopted. Even in the pits of parent-cringe you have a way out. You can refuse the shame!"

"Do what? So you ran away to join the circus?" suggested Yas, flinging herself into a cart-wheel.

"No. There were too many circus performers on that camp already. I just told everyone I was adopted, that they weren't my real parents."

"But you are adopted aren't you?" asked Yasmeen.

"Yeah, spaz-head, that's the point. If my Mum is embarrassing, it's not my problem. I haven't got her mouldy genes so I'll not necessarily take after them. I've got a choice!"

"I'm not going to be like my Mum ... no way" Yas said, her mood dropping like a stone. "Nothing but breeding and eating all day."

"What about Leila, did she get away?" Yasmeen's big sister had been the most glamorous girl in school. Defiant of

151

uniform, attendance and smoking rules. Haughty, tall and unafraid.

"Nah. She fell in love. She's married. One son and a baby on the way. And she eats. All day."

"Well you could always take after your Dad."

"What gambling, drinking and swearing about the government?" Yas was shredding the leaves of the shrub that overhung the bench.

"No I was thinking more of running a business." I raised an eyebrow knowingly at Yas.

"S'only running until he's busted for passing hot goods. He's only ever a back-hander away from the law." Her nostrils were flared and her eyes narrowed. "Stupid wanker" she muttered.

"Have you seen Malcolm at all?" I tried to distract Yas from cursing Mr Mohammed.

"Nah. You?" Yas asked, her face was turned down as she twisted her long sheeny hair around her left hand and into a bun that sat prettily at the nape of her neck.

"Saw his Dad in Asda."

"Did you ask if he's broken his vow of silence yet?" Yas smirked.

"Perhaps he talks at home. We don't know."

"Mmm" she assented. "Did you fancy him? At school I mean."

"What does a girl have to do to be gay around here?" I asked in exasperation.

"You can fancy both you know. What about Madonna and Courtney Love?"

"They don't do it for me. Too much plastic surgery." I wrinkled up my nose in disgust.

"No div-brain. They're bi aren't they."

"Dunno. Who cares? Anyway, I don't fancy boys. Never have done. Specially not Malcolm."

"But you liked him. You were the only one who talked to him."

"Yeah. 'Course I like him" I nodded. "But Yasmeen love, here's the funny thing about me" I laid my arm with patronising concern on hers. "I don't have sex with every one I like. I prefer a chat and a cup of tea."

"Oooooh! Missy pure! And who was it explained to you how to do it? You didn't know shit! It's a good job one of us had done our homework and figured it out innit!" Yas punched me on the bicep and rubbed shredded leaves through my hair. "You daft dyke."

"Slapper!" I accused as I rolled her on to the grass and stuffed her mouth with daisy heads.

"Not any more" Yas said as she triumphantly pushed a handful of grass down the back of my shirt and stood up smoothing her dupatta. "That was last year. Right. Off for namaz. See you later."

"All right girls?" my mother called down the garden.

"Yes thanks, Mrs Fort. Just off to say my prayers at the mosque women's room. Thanks for coffee. Catch you later Fliss. If you're lucky!" Facing away from Mum she winked at me and ran the tip of her tongue over her upper lip in mock-seduction.

"Jo's here for you darling." Mum's voice woke me. "I told her you like your lie-in after the week at college." I opened one eye and squinted up at Mum's head and shoulder around my bedroom door. "Says you're expecting her, but I could ask her to come back later." Mum's voice had an unfortunate pleading tone. My somersaulting tummy flipped me out of bed. I pulled on a dressing gown and mumbling thanks stumbled down stairs and out the front door.

"Got bikes doll!" said Jo by way of greeting. She was astride one bike in her shorts and helmet, another leaning up against the front fence. She looked so awake and energetic. "C'mere!" She was nodding down at the bike as if wanting to show me something. As I got within reach she put an arm round my waist and breathed in the hair behind my ear and growled deep in her throat. The hairs on my forearms stood up and my innards melted. "I could eat you whole" she said low as she manoeuvred me round into a more wholesome hug.

"Won't you come in for breakfast Joanne?" asked Mum from the front door.

"Thank-you, but we should get away up the road. The forecast isnae so good for this afternoon."

"Are you going then Felicity?" asked Mum. I nodded in

response while still looking at Jo. "I'll make you up some sandwiches then love."

An hour later and the houses were thinning out. We cycled past terraces, mid-rise estates, semi-detached prestige estates, detached houses with gates and, finally, scattered farmhouses guarded by a mess of outbuildings. The bikes Jo had brought from her work were new, tight and smooth. Free-wheeling down the hills put me in mind of the summer of my first bike when Dad took us to Centaparks and I spent eight hours a day in my new saddle. I had thought then that I would never walk again since cycling was such a superior form of locomotion. But at senior school only the swots cycled and you couldn't hang around the bus stop with a bike, especially in the helmet and fluo jacket my Dad imposed. Way uncool.

But there I was chasing Jo up the road, Jo who was beyond cool; she was cynical and hard and uncompromising. And she wanted me. How lucky was I that Sunday morning? To be seventeen, in lust, cycling in the sunshine with gay abandon after a woman with a firm grasp of life's pleasures. And I thought it was only going to get better once I reached eighteen: I thought Mum would snap back to serenity and find some gentle chit-chat to make with Jo who would become my proper girlfriend and that we would be as delighted in each other's company as Mum and Dad had always been.

Jo must have planned the route beforehand, although she pretended it was all "gallus serendipity" that we ended up at lunch time on a bank of violets and celendine, sheltered by a beech coppice, looking south down towards the plain covered with the sprawl of the city in the distance. She produced Cornish pasties, Hoegaarden beer, Pellegrino water, sun blush cherry tomatoes and root vegetable crisps fried in virgin oil. We ate listening to the song thrush venting her fury at our arrival, before flopping backward on to the cool, spongy bank.

Jo's hand found mine and stroked up the inside of my forearm. She lifted my wrist and took my watch off.

"You take a tan quick," she said as she looked at the white watch silhouette she'd revealed. "You've no been under a lamp have you?"

"No. I've always tanned. One of my many talents."

"My swarthy beauty!" Jo trailed her fingers up my arm across my shoulder and neck to my face. She traced my jaw, cheek and brow bone, circling the pads of her fingers in the middle of my forehead. I felt supercharged and sleepy. "And your eyebrows join up in the middle," Jo commented.

"Mmmm. Yas said I should pluck," I said without opening my eyes.

"Pluck, you? No. k.d. lang was never the same after she'd depilated."

"So you like my one eyebrow?"

"Oh aye. Makes me wonder what your Ma looked like."

"Probably about the same as she did when we left her two hours ago."

"Very good, Ms Knife." I could hear Jo smiling.

"I mean your other Ma."

"I haven't got another Mum."

"OK then. Your biological mother. Her." Jo was not prepared to let the topic drop and I was reluctant to come out of my doze.

"What about her?"

"Well. How many eyebrows did she have?"

I opened my eyes and propped myself up on one elbow. "I don't know. She gave me up remember."

"But you must know something about her. Are you no curious?"

"She was Cypriot." I dropped down onto my front with my cheek in a patch of moss.

"Is that it?"

"Mum and Dad never hid that I was adopted, but they never much talked about it either. Why would they? Nothing about my birth parents has ever mattered, 'cause my real parents are perfect." I could feel Jo looking at me to check whether I was being sarcastic. "People only go looking for an alternative when they're dissatisfied I reckon." I settled my limbs comfortably on the bank again hoping that the topic was finished and that Jo would start stroking me again. Instead, her mouth arrived on mine, her breath smelling of yeasty beer and we kissed for a long time. Until then, anticipation had seemed the most delectable part of enjoying her. Watching her stretch her sinews up the climbing wall, feeling

155

her thigh next to mine under the pub table had my nerve ends jangling. The zingy, alert, in-touch with the world feeling. Kissing her, all the jangley excitement seemed to focus down into a hot, luminous core that joined my mouth to my cunt. Jo brushed her fingertips over my open palm and I felt dizzy ... I couldn't concentrate on the outer reaches of my body as well as the intensity at the centre. After a while (how do you measure time when you're snogging? Number of lip contacts? Fluid ounces of saliva exchanged?), Jo stopped and looked down at me still sprawled on the bank. I was expecting her to say something soppy to me, but she didn't. She just looked at me, neutrally, dispassionately until eventually a Clint Eastwood smile pulled across her lips.

"What?" I felt compelled to ask.

"You're a privileged lassie."

"I know. To have my own personal trainer paying such close attention to my facial work out," I said smugly. Jo snorted with what might have been amusement.

"Do you have no guilt?"

"Well it is hard to deprive men of my desirable body, but it's a small matter compared to centuries of misogyny ... no?" Jo was shaking her head in mock despair.

"Ya cocky wee sod." She gazed out towards the city. "Come on. We'd best be getting you back to your Mammy."

It was down hill all the way home. My legs pumped and I listened to my lungs while watching Jo's lycra-clad gluteous maximus ahead of me.

"That was a good winching," she said as she left me outside my gate and double-biked down the road. And perhaps that was when I enjoyed the warmest moment of our relationship.

What a fantastic Friday: the best of my life! Although, looking back, it seems like I was living in la-la-land. First thing, Mum was smiling over the breakfast table, a real smile, not just her mouth tensed up around the corners. She'd laid the table with our special red birthday crockery and made a stack of pancakes. I drizzled them with real maple syrup chanting "just like Laura Ingalls Wilder used to eat" in memory of my younger, sweeter self. Mum laughed and we sang my birthday song together without missing Dad too much. Mum hugged me and kissed me on both cheeks.

"Congratulations on your majority my beautiful, clever daughter!" she said. Then we drank coffee and ate pancakes and I opened three parcels from Mum, two from the cat leaving the one from Mrs Ashkenazy-next door to one side. "I am so proud my love," Mum smiled at me. "And your Dad would have been too. So proud." I grinned at Mum as I peeled an orange. My Dad loved birthdays. He would transform the kitchen into a birthday bower with streamers, chains and fans made from pretty paper and I would sit bathed in parental affection opening parcels from each of my numerous soft toys. "She is our own wee faery-bairn" Dad would beam at my Mum as she nodded in agreement. Not until a month after Dad's funeral, on a wet Wednesday evening when the vicar was in the front room talking to Mum, had I learned that Dad hadn't always been so big on birthdays. I had been finishing off some homework at the kitchen table when the cat had nosed her way through the kitchen door, leaving it ajar. I had stood up to shut the door again, in the hopes of keeping the cat in the kitchen for company, when I heard Mum say my name.

"Felicity changed our lives Reverend. Especially his. She gave him back his joy." The vicar's deep, rumble encouraged Mum's talk. "Like birthdays. When I first knew Bill he wouldn't celebrate birthdays. Not even his own. Birthdays were grim: he'd lost three brothers by his ninth, his father by his tenth and his mother by his eleventh. He was always amazed that he lasted as long as he did. He'd convinced himself he'd be dead by thirty like his mother and then by forty like his father. It was after we had her that we really, really fell in love with each other. I'd been caring all my working life. But loving a child and loving your husband loving that child, well, that was quite different. It was a virtuous circle where everything just got warmer and safer and sweeter and funnier. Until now." Mum had gulped and sobbed and blew her nose while the vicar rumbled warmly. And I had closed the door quietly.

As I was unwrapping the mint-and-peach coloured shoe-holder crocheted by Mrs Ashkenazy, the letter box rattled. I went to hang the crochet-creation in the down stairs lavatory next to the princess-toilet-roll-cover and decorative cistern cover from previous birthdays. Three letters were waiting on the door mat. I opened a red hand-made envelope containing a watercolour of a bunch of poppies with "See you at the pub tonight? All love from Josh" written inside. I stuffed a creamy soft package addressed in Jo's regular script into my pocket and looked at a lilac envelope. Mum had stopped clearing the plates and admired Josh's painting, and was now watching me too closely. An anodyne pastel reproduction of a cat on a windowsill emerged from the lilac envelope and inside it said "Wishing you every happiness on your birthday. Looking forward to meeting you soon. From Stella." I stood the card up on the breakfast table.

"May I read it?" asked Mum.

"Course. She's your friend anyway. Nothing to do with me." I said shrugging as I found my college bag and checked for my bus pass.

"She's coming on Saturday night" said Mum. "So you'll meet her then."

"I'd rather not Mum. I could go out and let you catch up with her."

"No!" Mum swung round from where she was putting the flour away. "No love. Felicity, I need you here too. You need to be here." Mum looked frightened. Ever since Dad had died, Mum had stopped going out. Stopped socialising. Their dancing days had stopped when his angina got too bad, but they'd carried on going to the jazz nights, even when Dad couldn't play any more. Josh's Mum used to babysit. But even listening to jazz had stopped when he got really breathless and then after the funeral she hadn't been able to face other people. She didn't even bother going to church any more, saying it wasn't the same if Dad wasn't there to be annoyed by it. "It's really you she's coming to see, love," said Mum.

"OK. I'll stop in. Thanks for the delicious breakfast and the lovely presents." I said kissing Mum's cheek. "In fact I think I'll wear this one now." I pulled my tee shirt off over my head and took the one Mum had given me out from its tissue paper. It was deep brown to match my eyes and had gold angel wings embossed on the back. In discreet script around the waist and arm hems "angel" was written over and over, so it looked like a mediaeval pattern.

"Felicity! Mrs Ashkenazy's son might be mowing the lawn! Cover up!" Mum never liked me undressing, even though she said the human body was nothing to be ashamed of. I pulled the shirt on and admired my reflection in the hall mirror before calling goodbye to Mum.

"I'll be at the pub until late. See you tomorrow!"

Yas was on the bus again and she gave me a big smacker. Of course the bint with the acrylic hat was sat watching.

"How did you remember it was my birthday?" I asked.

"I know everyone's birthdays from our class. Dunno why. Praps because Pitaji said it was unIslamic so we weren't to have birthdays. Anyway, Malcolm's is next month and Josh's was a fortnight ago."

"Oh bollocks. I forgot Josh's. And he sent me a lovely card this morning. Really pretty." Then we got separated as a load of school kids got on the bus and it was a few stops down the line before I could talk to her again.

"How's your campaign going?" I asked.

"I'm getting extra Qu'ran reading lessons tonight."

"What just the two of you?"

"No, with the other girls too. But he's dead brave, 'cause the mosque committee is spitting nails."

"Why's he doing it then?"

"He says the prophet, peace be upon him, was the first feminist and wanted women to hear his words too." Yas's voice had gone soft and dreamy. "Fliss, he asked me not to wear make-up the other day. Said God had made me beautiful enough. So he's noticed me."

"What do you mean he's noticed you? You made it sound like you were practically shagging the other day. Does he know your name?"

"He calls us all 'sister'."

"Oh Yas. Why don't you come down the pub tonight? It'll be good. Josh's coming. We could get Malcolm along too."

"Thanks Fliss. No. I don't need the pub anymore. D'ja get any good presents?" I let my jacket drop off my shoulders to show her the gold angel wings on the back of my new T-shirt.

She admired it and knew which designer boutique Mum had bought it from.

"And Jo sent me this" I pulled the creamy package from my pocket.

"What is it?" asked Yas.

"I dunno. Didn't dare open it in front of Mum. Just in case."

"In case it's a bloody great strap-on?" Yas sniggered, winking at the school girls sitting opposite us. "Well go on then." So I tore open the velvety paper to reveal a lavender book. "The wise woman's book of daily words" read the title in purple. I thrust the book at Yas and held my forehead in my hands.

"Why are lesbians so full of hippy humanist shit?" I asked Yas. "Even the cynical Scottish ones."

"Have a lovely day pumpkin and remember" Yas said holding the book open and ostentatiously reading "woman's love moves mountains". She tucked the book in my bag before squeezing my knee and weaving her way to the front of the bus.

I felt superior all day at college because none of the students or staff knew it was my birthday. I knew that I had reached the height of maturity since I resisted the urge to squeak "and it's my eighteenth birthday today, you know" even when I got 91% in a physiology test. Later, over chips and brown sauce in the canteen, I pretended to my classmates that I'd got 70%. They were speculating on the questions that would come up in the end of year exam and worrying about next year's placements. I wasn't listening properly, drawing Jo's name in brown sauce on my empty plate until a spiteful tone made me listen up.

"Old clever clogs isn't worried, are you Felicity!"

"Mmmm?" I pretended not to have heard her nastiness.

"Leave the girl-wonder alone, Camilla!" said Jilly, a big-hipped woman who'd failed the test. "S'not her fault she's bright. Pick on someone with the same IQ as you. Like me!" She snorted with laughter at her self-deprecating insult.

That night in the pub I got my first legal round in. I lent

back in my chair and looked round the table. Jo and Josh, who had just met for the first time, were comparing their experiences of camping on the Isle of Skye. Josh had recently returned from a geology field trip looking at layers of rock. Jo used to go climbing in the Coolins when she lived in Glasgow. Tim from the climbing club was hovering on the edge of their conversation, nodding and smiling and next to him was Malcolm, who, as usual was silent. He'd changed since the bus stop days: his silence wasn't awkward anymore, in fact it was the opposite, soothing in contrast to the competitive trading of expertise between Jo and Josh. Then Phil arrived with her latest girlfriend – a punkette in stripey tights and a mohican – and presented me with a bunch of gerberer in orange and hot pink. She wrapped me in an attention-grabbing embrace, squashing the flowers, and announced in her thespy tones:

"The prettiest little dyke in town has just grown up. Well done precious. Now you can become the biggest bull-dagger there ever was." The punkette sniggered into her pernod and black and Jo looked like she might be offended. I laughed aloud. Phil's determination that everyone around should notice her queerness had not got her beaten up. At least not yet. Phil set about establishing mutual acquaintances with Jo who was testy, but unable to resist Phil's insistent fruity enthusiasm. Both had belonged to a women's running group "ragged runners" and shared a loathing for the feminist resource centre librarian. Having found some common ground, Phil and Jo settled down to less aggressive pub chat.

The punkette fiddled with her dog collar and safety pins while an argument rollicked around the table about feminism and a sense of humour.

"Well, do you know a funny feminist?" Jo asked no-one in particular.

"Phil was pretty hilarious last time we had a beer race," suggested Josh.

"I think our friend Jo means intentionally amusing rather than drunken buffoonery," replied Phil and turning to the punkette, assured her, "Have no fear: I'm not proud of recreational vomiting. Furthermore," she turned back to the whole table, "I'm not sure that my feminist credentials are quite intact."

"How d'ja mean?" I asked.

"Well, only last week the city-centre sisters accused me of being too competitive in our fanny-fart fugue." She lowered her head and looked over her gold-rimmed glasses for extra effect and after a pause added, "It's a devised piece."

"Oh Philly!" The punkette spoke at last. And with a surprisingly posh accent. "What about the confidentiality?"

"Sweet-heart, until you spoke, no-one knew who else was there!" Phil replied. "Now, who would like to explain to Josh and Tim about fanny farts?" Tim was crimson and feverishly flipping a pile of beer mats off the table edge with the backs of his fingers, to catch them in the same hand.

"The term's self-explanatory isn't it?" asked Josh sweetly. "Funny farts make you laugh!"

"No, a cunt" grunted Jo.

"Don't call my best pal a cunt!" I chipped in.

"It's a fart out of your cunt that Phil's talking about. A fAnny fart" explained Jo patiently, but clearly enjoying Josh's discomfit.

"Shall I show you darling Josh?" enquired Phil with pre-tend concern, patting his forearm. Seeing that this could only get more embarrassing, Josh nodded. Phil had started to get down on the floor into a shoulder stand before the punkette begged her to get up. She was pale-faced with fear.

"Oh all right then." Phil relented and instead challenged Jo to tell three non-sexist, non-racist jokes in a row.

"A man goes into a doctor's surgery with a duck growing out of his head!" announced Jo, unable to resist the challenge, "So when did this start?" asks the doctor. "Well it was just a pimple on my bum to begin with" says the duck." Jo grins triumphantly. Everyone but Malcolm laughed. "What do you get if you cross a sheep with a kangaroo?" asked Jo rhetorically.

"We don't know, what do you get if you cross a sheep with a kangaroo?" we chorused.

"A woolly jumper!" Everyone groaned together. "What's red and lies upside down in the gutter?" and without waiting, Jo told us "A dead bus." And Malcolm laughed out loud, with noise in his throat. Everyone else was groaning so loudly that they didn't hear.

"So I think that proves my point" said Phil with some satisfaction. "Jokes have to be tasteless in order to be funny." And, having made clear that her Mum was Irish, she told a string of Paddy jokes. All of which encouraged Tim to get stuck into a sheep-shagger shaggy dog story, justified by having lived near Dartmoor for a while. When he'd final got to the punchline, which involved an elbow being mistaken for a testicle, Jo shook her head.

"Is that no disgusting or a meringue?" she said.

"What?" asked the whole table. After two repeats she wrote the joke on the back of a beer mat AM I WRONG? A MERINGUE?

As Phil tried to imitate Jo's accent to make "a meringue" sound like "am I wrong" Jo held her head in her hands in what I took to be mock despair. "It's not often that I miss Scotland, but this would be one of those times," she sighed.

"Time gentlemen please! And ladies too!" hollered the publican.

We stumbled out, along the shop fronts and into the park. There we smoked two joints that Phil had brought ready-rolled and gift-wrapped in gold foil. Silence fell on us as the spliffs went round. It was broken by a reedy voice.

"There was this nun sewing and sewing on her singer machine. After a while she said: 'I think this is becoming a habit'." It was Malcolm. Jo hooted with laughter and couldn't stop. Which started everyone else. I dug Malcolm in the ribs, so he knew that I knew that he'd spoken.

The final birthday ceremony was "stoner bumps". Under Phil's direction I lay spread-eagled on my back looking up at Orion. Everyone else lay on their bellies in a circle with their hands underneath me. Phil called out

"OK my lovely friends, on my count. A one! A two! A three! …" And on each count gentle upwards pressure from twelve hands was applied the length of my limbs and torso. I was floating around the heavens, attached to some of my best people. "A seventeen! A eighteen!" I was the luckiest woman alive.

Mum started getting ready for her serious dinner party first thing on Saturday. By ten o'clock the persistence of her kitchen noise was no longer bearable. This was the beginning of my disenchantment with being eighteen. I pulled on my tracksuit and sloped out to the swimming pool. I knew I was a bit hung over, but that didn't explain my bad mood. I didn't like the feeling that here I was, having reached long-awaited legal adulthood, able to drink, vote and (God forbid) marry, but things were nonetheless out of my control. This cosy little dinner party with Mum's wierdie friend who had rejected my Dad, was happening even though I had made it clear that I would rather be rolling up my sleeping bag and counting out my climbing socks.

I stepped out of my tracksuit in the warm chlorinated air of the communal changing room and felt better. My razor-back costume looked good: the cut-away shoulder-straps showed off my lovely glossy black armpit hair and the so-called boy-legs, kept my equally black, but irredeemably shamefully proliferous pubes hidden from public view. Saggy women struggled with grey knickers rolling against sallow skin. Bodies bent in apology for their nudity, half-hidden by a damp towel clutched between chin and chest. Thank the Lord for my parents' liberal upbringing and for my careless progenitors' toned muscle and dark olive skin. I enjoyed the admiring or envious looks from my fellow changers. The cringers looked sideways at me as they struggled into their damp jeans while a couple of the regulars with their square swimmers' shoulders openly admired my brazen delight in my own body.

Two steps through the verruca-exchange footbath and over to the fast lane where there was only one other swimmer. I stood on the side stretching my arms behind my back. The swimmer looked too slow to share my lane. I could never resist diving in for the first length, even though it meant leaving my goggles off. My well-drawn arc broke the surface with barely a splash, and I came up five strokes down the pool to slice through the remainder of the water, executed a tumble turn and powered down another length. This was all it took to scare the slow fellow out of the lane, leaving me alone to settle into a steady rhythm of pushing the water away and under for the next thirty minutes. The excess alcohol worked its way out of my pores and dissolved into the pool.

I spent the rest of the day avoiding Mum by starting and finishing a college essay on diagnosing and treating sports injuries in the upper limbs. Her expectation about the evening was bubbling around her. She came and gazed at me sitting at my desk.

"What are you going to wear tonight darling?" she asked after too long a pause.

"This" I said ungraciously shrugging my shoulders, still clad in my grey track suit.

"I would like to make it more of an occasion" Mum smiled hopefully. I looked at her in disbelief. She was usually completely cool about clothes.

"What about 'don't judge the book by its cover'?" I asked.

"Stella will have things to tell us. Important things. I'm apprehensive."

"Bout what?"

"About whether we'll all be the same afterwards." I had to check Mum's expression and she was super-serious. No messing. "Like getting an exam result, but less certain."

"So clothes are the least of your worries. Why not just put Stella off?"

"No love. We can't do that. It's important we see Stella. Perhaps the right clothes will be like a uniform. You know, stop any bad stuff getting at you."

This didn't make sense to me. I was unassailable. Unshakeably confident. Nothing could disrupt me. "I know you're nervous Mum, but now you sound barking."

"Uniforms protect the private person beneath. Honest, they do. So wear your smart suit will you love? Please?"

"Won't your friend think that's a bit odd?"

Mum said "She always said that we had to set the rules when this moment came. Us. You, me and Dad" as she stroked the back of my head.

"OK. Whatever."

That was why I was sitting in my own front room, watching the evening news in my best suit. I was stroking the cat

165

but trying to keep her hairs off my suit, when the doorbell rang. I'd only ever worn the suit once before at Dad's funeral, but I liked the way it fell back into place, draping from my hips and shoulders when I stood up. Through the glass I could tell that it wasn't Jo or Josh and Mrs Ashkenazy always came round the back.

"Hello Felicity" smiled the ordinary-looking woman on the other side of the glass.

"Hello. Come in. I'll get Mum."

The woman was wearing a dusty blue skirt with a denim jacket and blue tee-shirt underneath. She looked about Mum's age but not so pretty or so worried. She didn't even try to make small talk, just came in the front room, put her brief case down on the floor and sat on the sofa. Her face was open and friendly but she did not look as though she cared whether I liked her or not. Afterwards, a long time afterwards, I realised that she must have done plenty of those visits. It was part of her job.

Mum came in, threw her arms around Stella and burst into tears. My usually self-composed mother was sobbing into the blue denim shoulder within three seconds of meeting.

"Get your Mum a tissue Felicity" said Stella, bossily I thought.

When I arrived back in the room Mum was saying "Oh I've missed you, Stella."

"Me too. But we decided, didn't we? And for all the right reasons." She looked from Mum to me and smiled. "So, how shall we do this?"

"I've cooked. Shall we eat first?" Mum asked tentatively.

"OK. Perhaps best not to do these things on an empty stomach." Stella was nodding at me as if I knew what was going on.

"Mmmm" I agreed, loathe to admit my ignorance. Loathe to cede any ground to this woman who had walked in and, after a lifetime, my lifetime, had Mum's confidence.

We sat in the kitchen and Mum opened a bottle of wine. It was still odd to see her wielding the waiter's friend cork-screw. It used to be Dad's job.

"Happy birthday, Felicity" toasted Stella gravely.

166

The soup was too hot to eat and as we spread butter on our bread, Stella was asking Mum about someone called May.

"So you haven't seen her since?"

"Who's May?" I asked abruptly.

Both women stared at me and then looked at each other. Mum's face was ashamed and defensive at the same time.

"Marjorie?" queried Stella.

"May hasn't spoken to me since the summer when Felicity was two." Mum drew a deep breath, and answering a question that no-one had posed, went on "May is racist."

"Ah!" said Stella. Why was Mum accountable to this woman? And why wasn't she answering me?

"Is this a good time to tell Felicity about her?" asked Stella.

"I would think so", I said as gently as possible, looking towards Mum who was blowing her nose. She tucked the hanky back up her sleeve.

"May is my sister. My younger sister. She lives in Essex." Mum's voice was soft and sad but quite certain.

"Harlow", I said. "Harlow is written under that photo of my second birthday."

"Yes, love. Those children are your cousins. May has four. Or did have last time we spoke. I keep hoping that the kids might get in touch. I used to change their nappies. They'd be in their twenties now. John will be thirty soon."

"Anyone else I should know about?" I asked.

"No love. Just May."

"Why haven't we seen them? Why did I think we didn't have any other family?" I could see Mum was braced for anger, but I felt just mildly curious.

"They didn't approve" said Mum with deliberate calmness.

"Of what?"

"Of you."

"What? Being adopted?"

"Yes, partly that. They felt it was odd and hard to explain to people."

"But they came to my birthday party" I said rather petishly, trying to understand.

"Yes, but that was before they knew. Well before we knew too" said Mum turning slightly towards Stella. "This is the only lie Felicity. The only falsehood that I knowingly

167

continued." She took a deep breath. "You see, Stella told us that your birth mother was Cypriot. It seemed right. You had a mop of black shiny hair and light skin. But in fact your birth mother was white, and your father was black, from Guyana." This just seemed odd. I turned to Stella with palms upturned and my shoulders slightly shrugged.

"It was the right thing to do at the time", Stella sighed. "It was extremely important to get you placed in a loving home and a race match was impossible. Your birth father was a mixture of Chinese, African, Scots and Welsh. We always want parents to fall in love with the child before they find out the hard stuff."

"You were deciding who could be my parents?" I asked.

"Yes" said Stella unapologetically. "And sixteen years ago having a black father was a problem." She paused waiting for me to digest this. "And now you're eighteen you have a right to know all about the circumstances of your placement. If you want to." Stella smiled tentatively.

"Birthdays are usually meant to involve joyful celebrations and gifts from friends, not strangers turning up to make your mum cry", I said coolly.

"Yes, I'm a little taken aback too", said Stella, her smile fading. "I had thought that Marjorie would have prepared you, so that our meeting made sense." She was looking at me, but her comment was for Mum.

"I always answered her questions", Mum broke in. "I never lied, but I didn't force the issue. Like you said." A pause as she watched her hands scrunching up her napkin. "I was frightened, Stella. And you said that providing we loved her enough everything else would fall into place." Mum's face was reddening. "You said you were going to handle telling her. That's why you never told us the details. You promised." Mum was close to tears again. Stella's face was composed and slightly inclined towards Mum. She looked like the demonstration of "active listening skills" in the clinical communication video at college.

I reached my arm around Mum's back. "I'm chuffed to be black. Loads of good role models. Every R&B act and decent athlete in the country in fact. S'no big deal. Still me innit?"

Mum had started crying again. "Perhaps she should go?" I suggested, patting Mum's elbow.

"No. No. We need her to tell us. Tell us about you. When you were a baby."

"Marjorie, I don't think Felicity is ready for this. Really I don't. Perhaps it would be better if I came back another time." Stella was pushing back her soup bowl and folding her napkin.

"You said you'd do it. I need to know. Me. The mother." Mum's voice was muffled as she wept into the crook of her arm.

Stella was looking quite uncomfortable now, which was something.

"Felicity, do you wish to ask me anything?" she had turned to face me.

"Umm" I bit back a facetious question about whether she thought denim was ever appropriate on a middle-aged woman. "Why did you come here?" I asked as neutrally as possible.

"I thought I was doing a placement de-brief with my old friend Marjorie and the grown-up daughter that I had given into her care."

"But you never found out whether I wanted that de-brief, did you?" I asked.

Stella's open-listening face flinched. "You're right. I should have found out. I assumed. And, to be quite honest, I was curious as to what had happened. On reflection, perhaps not very professional."

"Let me assure you that the adoption has been a total success" I told her, doing my best not to sound smug. "Thanks to the absolute dedication of my mother. We're fine." This made my mother sob harder than ever.

"But aren't you curious about your origins? Children have the right to know" chanted Stella as if quoting from an adoption handbook.

"You're in my origins: semi-detatched suburbia in all its glory." I opened my arms expansively, like Dad used to after a good meal. "I can't remember anything earlier than Mum and Dad. Nothing you could tell me is relevant." I managed to stop short of telling Stella she was irrelevant. But her face looked as though she'd understood. She looked appalled. "I think you should leave now" I said.

"Yes, of course." Stella's face snapped back into professional niceness. "I'll leave you my phone number." She handed me a business card: "Stella Bouchier, Chief Placement Debrief Coordinator, Ecumenical Adoption Agency". "So if, after you've looked through your file, you have any questions, you can get in touch." She fetched her brief case from the front room and lifted out a buff folder bulging with papers depositing it on the table.

"I'm sorry you weren't ready for this yet, Marjorie" Stella remarked, rather sourly as she turned to leave the kitchen. Mum was blowing her nose into a piece of kitchen towel. I went to check that Stella really had left and locked the front door to keep her out.

Later, after I'd tucked Mum into bed, with the radio tuned to the world service and a sleep-eze homeopathic tablet under her tongue, I returned to the kitchen table. I put all the food away and washed the dishes, but still hadn't decided what to do with the file. I wanted to move it in order to shake the bread crumbs off the linen table cloth, but it felt difficult to touch it. I really didn't care what was in the file so perhaps I should burn it? On the other hand, Stella knew what was in it and I didn't like her knowing something that I didn't know. And what about Mum? What would Dad do in these circumstances? He would've opened a bottle of beer and lit a ciggie; he would have hovered at the back door, flailing his arms about occasionally, pretending to keep the smoke outside. He would've wanted to protect Mum and me. He did protect us. He protected us from his illness. Right up to when he failed us by dying.

I opened the back door, and stood on the threshold, looking out at the lupins and roses – his roses – trying to picture him. I puffed my chest out and pulled my shoulders back and muttered "it's a piece of nonsense" under my breath like he used to when vexed. "And she's a right bisum, boogling about in our business" I said louder, imitating Dad's Ayrshire accent. "How dare she? Coming round here, stirring up strife? She's no right!" Even if Dad had loved Stella a long time ago, he wouldn't've allowed her to upset Mum.

With Dad's blustering sense of righteousness behind me I was able to pick up the file with two hands to stow it in the highest kitchen, the one that was only ever opened at

Christmas for the cake ornaments and plum pudding bowl. Standing on a chair, I reached over my head to pull the cupboard open and one sheet of paper escaped from the top of the file. It slipped past my hand to the floor. Curse Stella Bouchier's inadequate paper storage methods. I tried to retrieve the letter without looking at it. I should have screwed my eyes shut. But I didn't. So even though the page was upside down, the words "… pornographic images of baby …" vibrated out at me. As I stuffed the page into the folder a carefully inked signature "Stella Bouchier" disentangled itself from the page. I pushed the whole folder into a black bin bag and sealed it up with packing tape, as though I could keep the words confined, stuffing the parcel into the back of the cupboard, underneath the fairy lights.

I found Mum's cooking brandy and knocked back a glassful before falling into bed with my headphones blaring Nirvana into my brain.

I woke at dawn and before I could remember anything, twitched the curtains aside to see a golden pink sunrise spreading across the sky. In the optimism of a new day, as yet untroubled by human stupidity, it seemed possible to keep Mum safe from the nastiness. I went to wash myself clean and pure under the shower. Drying in front of the bathroom mirror I looked at myself wrapped in nothing but my new knowledge. Was I more café au lait than olive-toned? Was my cute nose more African or Scottish? And what about my lips? I put my hand in a clenched fist and saluted my own black power. My hair was still undeniably straight and smooth despite my new found parentage. The sound of Mum stirring in her bed got me back on track. I dressed quickly and made breakfast which I carried up on a tray to Mum's room. Placing the tray on Dad's side of the bed, I drew the curtains, turned off the radio and got under the duvet with my legs crossed to pour the coffee. Mum's bleariness cleared with her second cup.

"How do you feel love?" she asked me.

"Fine Mum. How about you?"

"Shocked." I let this sit in the air for a few moments, thinking about all the different things that might have shocked Mum.

"I'm only shocked that kids are entrusted to Stella's care. What an eeejit." I shook my head in disbelief.

Mum wasn't listening. "What are we going to do about your file?" she asked.

"Umm burn it?" I tried out.

"You might regret that later" said Mum staring into the middle distance and clutching her cup.

"Possibly. Lock it in a bank vault?"

"If you're sure you don't want to go through it now. Stella's due to retire shortly. She might not be around much longer. Professionally, I mean."

"What could I want with her though?" I asked, not too rudely.

"I don't know love. It depends on what's in that file."

"But you must know."

"No, really I don't. That was the deal we had with Stella. She thought we'd bond better if we didn't know how you'd ended up in care. She was ahead of the times with attachment theory."

"But you were a social worker too. And you knew I'd black in me didn't you?" I pointed out.

"Yes, but only after we'd had you for a while. Stella told us your birth mother was Cypriot and then you got ill. May, my sister, what with her having nursed, she was worried. Worried you might have thalassaemia. She'd seen plenty of kiddies with it when she worked in north London. So I asked Stella. And she said it was more likely to be sickle cell than thalassaemia. Didn't make sense to me at the time. I just passed on the information to the doctor. And then you got better with iron supplements and antibiotics. It was anaemia on top of tonsilitis. Only recently, since your Dad died I suppose, when I was going through papers, all our pre-adoption medicals, sorting out the past it began to dawn on me that sickle cell is a black disease." Mum sighed long and mournfully.

"But why ask Stella, why not just look up my file?" I asked, a bit exasperated.

"I worked in another division love, with the oldies. All I knew was that you came from another city and Stella couldn't find a placement for you. She knew that your chances were running out as you got older."

172

"Why couldn't she place me?"

"That's what we agreed not to discuss, on the understanding that when you reached eighteen she would reveal all."

"Like the bad fairy."

"Good, we thought, allowing you to escape your past."

"It's not my past Mum. It's Stella's. I'm not interested in it." I watched Mum picking at her cuticles absent-mindedly and filled her cup to distract her. "Were you looking for a baby?"

"No, not at all. Your Dad and I had agreed to devote ourselves to our work because the world was too over-populated already. Stella persuaded us. We were apparently your last chance before going into long-term fostering, which would've meant no parents of your own." Mum swallowed hard. "I think several families rejected you before she tried us."

"And she told you nothing more?" I asked.

"No" Mum shook her head. "I just guessed it was bad because Stella was pulling out all the stops in her search." Mum paused. "We trusted her."

I manage to stay silent for two beats rather than explode about Stella. "Mum, do you mind that I'm black instead of Cypriot?"

"Oh darling!" Mum put her cup down and wrapped both her arms around me. She smelled of lavender water and honeysuckle talc. "Of course not. I love you. You are my perfect daughter. Mind you, if I'd known I might not have taken those Greek evening classes for so long. But we had good holidays didn't we?"

Of course! That was why we went so often, even though Dad would rather have been keeping the green fly off his roses all summer, not expiring of heat in Mediterranean youth hostels where you couldn't buy decent cheddar. "Yeah Mum." I snuggled down and we both subsided to recover from the emotional overload in a sleepy fug of mutual appreciation.

The mini-bus thundered down the feature-free French roads towards Paris and I savoured the increasing distance between me and my home. I didn't want to have to think about Stella or adoption or that file of papers for five days. Mum had always been good at letting me go, always clear that she was looking forward to my return, but urging me to go out and discover the world. Whatever I discovered on this trip at least it wouldn't be about me and my past. The flat plains of northern France went on and on. So much space, so few people. I tried out my school French at the service station and got a nod towards the toilets in return. The ladies' was closed for cleaning. The woman with a wet mop exclaimed, indicated the gents' and eventually pushed me in through the door. I dived into a cubicle, hardly daring to see whether any of the backs at the pissoire were beards from our mini-bus.

We arrived at the campsite as dusk was gathering. We put up our mismatched local-authority-loaned tents which looked extra scruffy next to the pristine continental European equipment. The other campers were enjoying fragrant well structured meals eaten in an orderly fashion.

"Bon appetit!" I called and enjoyed the predictable courteous reply of "Merci Mademoiselle!" How could they tell I was a Mademoiselle rather than a Madam in the gloaming? Tim and I had been commissioned to scrabble around in the bottom of cardboard boxes and kitbags for stoves, billies and water carriers. Night had fallen to shroud our culinary shame by the time we had found enough bent forks to eat our plain-boiled pasta.

The following morning Tim and I were sent out to find the camp shop. The sun was filtering down through early summer leaves as we left the beards counting out caribiners and re-coiling brightly coloured woven ropes, discussing which rocks we would be tackling, who would accompany the gumbies and awaiting their breakfast. It felt as though we should be leaving a trail of pebbles to ensure our return, since the mixture of tents, trees and grass, interspersed with boulders seemed to extend indefinitely in all directions.

"Y'alright?" asked Tim without making eye contact, once we were out of earshot of the others. I'd slept with Jo and he'd been with the beards in a six-man tent. Jo hadn't tried anything on, just a friendly hug before we pulled our arms into our sleeping bags. "Good barrier method contraception eh!

Three season bags. You can't be too careful." she had chuckled as she turned over, her shoulders hunched away from me.

"Yeah." I replied. "You?"

Tim nodded. "They fart like cart horses," he giggled. We wandered on enjoying the sight of campers getting ready for the coming day. From a big orange tent a party of men emerged in hard-hats and heavy moustaches, dressed for duty on a building site. Queuing up by the sinks was a group of white-blond and beautiful teenagers, all clutching wash-bags. What could they need to clean when already so gleaming? I couldn't stop staring at them, not so much because of their beauty, but because, all sporting similar bowl-cut hair, their gender was fascinatingly unreadable. Tim instigated a game of "spot the nationality" naming the blond androgynous beauties Dutch, but possibly Danish. The construction workers we agreed were Rumanian or perhaps Estonian. The easiest nationality to spot was the British, who were embarrassingly distinctive: mottled flesh, too short shorts, socks with sandals and frying bacon the same colour as their noses. During our great summer treks south, Dad had regularly insisted on being Scottish not, he had said, that he was proud of being a Scot, but it was less shaming than being English. Mum always said I could choose: English like her, Scottish like Dad, Irish since she had two Irish grandparents, or Greek Cypriot. Guyanese was never on the multiple-choice list. Until now.

Eventually we came upon the well-stocked log cabin shop and stumbled through the shopping, resorting to pointing when our pronunciation of "beurre" failed to get any helpful response. As we re-traced our steps, the forest seemed less endless. I recognised a big gnarled oak that stood out among the pretty, light coloured birches just before we passed the Brits who were shaking ketchup on to their bacon butties. The construction workers' orange tent was zipped up with their pans and cups stacked neatly on a wooden orange box. The blond androgynes had started a wholesome game of volleyball in a clearing.

After a breakfast of salt-free sweet French butter on fresh spongy baguettes, Tim and I were sent off with the McKinley brothers, both experienced, who hadn't climbed in Fontaine-bleu before. We started with the easiest climb in the forest so the only way was up. We settled quickly into a routine whereby the McKinleys climbed each route first, while Tim and I belayed. Then it was our turn to try to imitate their moves up the boulders and cliffs. Each ascent was treated as revision of the climbing instructors' handbook and each mistake we made was their failing. They had to pass the instructors' exam in order to get a summer of climbing at a brat camp in the Rockies. The instruction was monosyllabic: "Left!", "Up!", "No!" and worst of all "Knees!" Towards the end of the day I managed an ascent without any knee contact and got a congratulatory back slap. After that I had to sit out with my muscles liquefying around the joints. I didn't even feel safe to belay. Looking around at the idyllic woodland scene as the light faded and the temperature dropped a few degrees to a comfortable warmth, I wondered whether similarly sylvan glades existed in England. "Perhaps", said Tim, when he joined me on my rock while the McKinleys took themselves up a couple of difficult climbs to close the day, "But the place'd be covered in crisp packets and condoms in Blighty!"

Back at the camp, Jo rubbed Raljex into my arms and legs and assured me it would only really start hurting when I tried to move the next morning. The beards were more relaxed after a day at the rock face. The one they called Socks noticed that Tim and I were knackered and, despite mocking that we'd not even been climbing, only bouldering, offered to cook his signature dish of Irish stew. This was achieved by combining a tin of meaty lamb chunks, a tin of tomatoes and a tin of baked beans. Amazingly it tasted good. But, as the others pointed out, so would horse dung after a day of climbing.

By the third day the lactic acid build-up in my muscles had dissipated and my climbing was becoming more fluent. Tim's ability to pull his meagre body weight up on the least likely of finger holds improved with his confidence, and my determination not to be outdone kept me right behind him. The McKinleys had become almost proud of us, reporting our achievements to the rest of the camp in the evening.

"Y'know that bastard overhand on pitch 67?" Grunts from around the paraffin stove. "Fliss did it in five moves." Grunts of a positive texture. "And young Tim was up the witches chimney in seven."

"Nice one Tiny Tim."

Me and Tim were chuffed to pieces and even washed up without complaining. I was annoyed that these hairy men with zero social skills thought that I wanted to climb as well as them. And I was even more annoyed that, at that moment, they were right.

After our sweet-corn and tuna surprise, "the surprise is Doug, that there's last night's pasta in it too!", I asked if we were going to visit Paris before we went home.

"Only if they've installed a climbing wall in the Louvre, love", Socks said laughing at his own wit. Jo laughed too slapping him across the shoulders. I stood up in annoyance. I wanted to protest, object, draw attention to my knowledge of things other than climbing. We used to stay overnight in Paris every summer. Dad used to find little "Routiers" restaurants where we would have the "prix fixe" menu with a carafe of the house red. The drop that Dad poured into my water made it a glamorous pink with a slightly acid taste. Those meals marked the start of the real holiday, the adventure and excitement. I wanted to say "My Dad would call you a philistine." He took me to the Rodin museum to gaze at "The Kiss", the Picasso museum to be horrified by "Guernica" and the Pompidou Centre for a laugh at a building with its innards hanging out. He loved Paris because it showed town-planning as an art and the French because they understood that art was for the people. Jo and Socks were discussing their favourite pitches in the Peak District. I moved away from the group towards the forest and the rocks that we'd climbed on the first day. If only I smoked, this would be the moment for a moody ciggie, sitting on one of the boulders, to make a sultry silhouette against the twilight. I scrambled up the easiest rock face, the darkness covering my less than perfect moves. From the top I could see the bright spots of stoves and lamps dotted about. I wanted to leave the climbing philistines, but the escape routes were limited.

A shadow was moving along the base of my rock. For a moment I thought, or perhaps I only hoped, that it was Jo, come to claim me and kiss me and laugh at the beards. But it was Tim. His pale face appeared up out of the gloaming.

"Fliss?"

"Humph."

"What you doing?"

"Trying to grow a beard" I said sulkily. "And develop an over-inflated sense of the importance of climbing up lumps of rock. What you doing?"

"Checking you're OK" said Tim sweetly. "And whether I can borrow your toothpaste. Mine's disappeared. I think it might've been the secret ingredient in Doug's bolognaise."

By the time I'd got back from the washroom, Jo was asleep. Or pretending to be. I reached out to her arm that was outside her sleeping bag, and stroked it. She snuffled and pulled inside the sleeping bag. As she moved, I caught a whiff of the Aramis cologne that she used. Her breathing was slow and steady. Last week that spicy sweet smell had been enough to make me catch my breath with excited anticipation. I remembered the dizzying feeling of brushing past her at the climbing wall and sensing her not give way. I had thought that we'd be onto full frontal frottage by now, but there we were our fourth chaste night lying next to one another under canvas. What was going on? Had something changed? Had my sex-appeal disappeared? Someone walked past with a hurricane lamp and the filtered light illuminated Jo's cheekbones and lovely jaw-line. I got a little lurch in my stomach seeing her handsome face, but it disappeared again when I thought of her laughing at me with Socks. Any residual lust trickled away as I pondered that she had not spoken to me properly since the trip had started. In fact, I realised that she'd spent more time talking to Tim over the washing up than to me.

Tim and I were the kids on this trip – not even low status, but no status. We were slight and unskilled and smooth chinned. Whereas Jo was, according to the McKinley brothers, the most skilled and technically adept climber, although sometimes a beard outclimbed her on length of reach or brute shoulder power. As I allowed myself to appreciate that Jo had ignored me for three days and four nights, I felt furious. What happened to her desire? How could she have stopped wanting me? And then I felt sorry for myself. Tears welled up in my eyes with the realisation that I would be back home the following day. None of the problems had disappeared and I had not been whipped up into a froth of lust which I had hoped would shield me from them. I zipped my sleeping bag up to my tonsils and pulled the hood over my eyes. Perhaps, I thought resignedly, I would have to sort out the problems before the lust would return.

Mum looked terrible. As though she hadn't slept since I had gone away. The skin around her eyes had gone crêpey and sand-coloured and her eczema had returned and created a crack between her thumb and index finger. We avoided talking about her dermatological disintegration, or the black bin bag that glowered in the highest kitchen cupboard. I showed her the new calloused skin on my knuckles with pride before emptying my smelly kit into the washing machine.

I was pegging my sleeping bag to the washing line immersed in my thoughts about the file in the overhead cupboard.

"D'ye fancy a drink doll?" Jo's question made me jump. Mum's face at the kitchen window looked wan.

"What are you doing here?" I asked evenly. "Haven't you got a job to go to?" When we'd all left the minibus at the sports centre a couple of hours earlier, Jo had barely said "good-bye", she had been so busy cataloguing equipment in thick camaraderie with Socks and Doug.

"Signed off for today" Jo shrugged, as she helped me fold out the sleeping bag to get the sun. I went to replace the peg bag to the shed and she followed me. As I closed the door behind me she pushed me gently against the shed wall with her hands on my shoulders and kissed me. Instant molten intestines. I wanted to dive into her and never emerge again, except that the nugget of annoyance was still there in the middle of the lusty lava. I was still narked. I flicked her off me with my hips and moved away from the shed, back into full view of the kitchen window.

"You ignore me in France and now it's all back on!" I squawked, trying to keep my outrage as quiet as was compatible with my pent-up fury at her presumption.

"How did I ignore you? We were with each other non-stop!"

"You never snogged me though did you?" I realised how whining this sounded as I was speaking.

"You're just embarrassed tae dae it with your mother about! You're an uptight, wee lassie. Let me know when you're out of your closet and want tae know about being a grown up lesbian in the real world." She turned from me, walked back down the garden, out of the side gate and round the corner.

I sat down on the log pile behind the shed. My knees were wobbly. Jo had imparted a knee-trembling mixture of arousal and insult. How dare she? Being a dyke (or dyklette as Dad had insisted) was, together with my high regard for my parents, the bedrock of my identity. I loved to shock my mates with tales of my happy, calm home life. I don't even have a coming out story: I'd never been in. I had just always liked girls. Really liked them: enjoyed how they move, talk, laugh, smell, really fancied them. Not that I had ever disliked boys: they can be funny, sexy, generous, interesting too, but they don't have that lithe mixture of uncertainty and braggart that pushes my buttons. And my parents always knew this. But lesbian wasn't the right word for me. I had yet to find someone else who called themselves a lesbian and who felt the same way about girls as I did. Doreen, my Mum's mate who ran away from her husband and children and, more specifically, their expectation of a full domestic servicing, called herself a lesbian. But she didn't fancy women she just found them marginally less awful than men or children. Shireen was the student chair of the school council and a political lesbian: her incisive analysis of gendered power meant that she had rejected men as potential partners before even snogging one. Phil perhaps? When we first met at the pub she had explained her hope that a little queer experience would help tap her own hitherto blocked creativity and give her something interesting to discuss with interviewers when she broke the big time. By her own admission she was more pretentious hipster than lesbian. It was only Josh who understood exactly how I felt about girls, because he felt it too. Unfortunately he felt it about me. And ever since he admitted his love for me – the love that dares not speak its name indeed – he had ruled himself out as a confidant. We could no longer share our girlophilia. Perhaps one day when we're both settled down with Ms Right it'll be OK again. One day.

There, on Dad's log pile, in the midst of my lust-fever, I think I knew that Jo wasn't Ms Right; she had been too dogged in her initial devotion. Even through the exhilarating excitement of being the object of her desire, I was too much aware of the allure that my youth held for her. It was too easy. Where's the virtue in having peachy skin and tight muscles? But even if I had realised I didn't want her forever, I still wanted her to worship and long for my body. I wanted to be wanted. I wanted to feel that power.

"So go and bed her, girl!" was Yasmeen's (loud) advice on the bus the next morning. "At least you don't have to worry about contraception, innit!"

"Mmmm. The thing is I want her to bed me."

"I want to be seduced!" Yas was singing in a Dublin accent until I slapped my hand over her mouth. "Mmmmph gerroff." Yas stuck her tongue out between my fingers to make me let go. "That's my best Mary McCoughlan impression!" she feinted indignation.

I started another line of thought to distract her, "So what about your little campaign?"

"He's coming round for tea tonight."

I asked incredulously, "What with the whole Qu'ran class?"

"No, just him. Mum wants advice about her haj. And she's hoping he might put the fear of God into my brothers." Yasmeen looked really, genuinely pleased.

I realised it wasn't just her expression that looked different from usual. "Is that why you've no make-up or earrings on today?" She nodded and looked almost demure. Amazing.

"They'll kill me at work. We've got a three-line glamour whip from the area manager. Here's my stop. Good luck with that dyke, Fliss."

Worrying about how to manoeuvre Jo into seducing me kept my mind off worrying about Stella Bouchier's poisonous file, all day at college. Perhaps the students' union gay, lesbian, bi and transsexual officer would have some useful advice? At lunch I visited the union building but the receptionist said all

181

the exec officers were on a team-building away day and would I like an appointment? No thanks. By the end of the afternoon's "Team Management Skills" lecture I had decided that I would just wait and see how things went. But perhaps at the next session at the climbing wall, I would go straight from college so I had to get changed at the sports centre, hopefully at the same time as Jo. Maybe my crisp new black sports bra and turquoise lycra shorts would tip the balance and she would be unable to resist me. But I'd feel a prat if I fell off dressed like an athlete. Perhaps baggy trackies were safer, if less seductive. But if we were to get undressed together, maybe that would be a moment to remind her what she was missing? Trouble was we usually went home in our climbing gear. Sigh.

None of my sartorial strategising mattered in the end anyway. I had just put Mum to bed because she looked so ghastly, when the door-bell rang. Jo was on the lintel holding a dozen red roses, like an old fashioned suitor. I grinned and asked

"Have you come to ask for my hand in marriage?"

"Aye. That'll be right hen. Where's your Mammy?" Jo sounded riled and looked predatory.

"Upstairs. Asleep. Or unconscious."

"Good." And that was all she said for the next forty minutes. She silently led me into the front room, closing the door behind us. She sat me on the sofa, closed the curtains, turned off the top light, took off her Levi jacket and seduced me, thoroughly, by the light of the television.

As the jingley bars of the Eastenders theme tune faded I felt able to speak again.

"So that's what lesbians do in bed ..." I giggled.

"Aye. And would you like to be one when you grow up?" replied Jo with a self-satisfied smile.

"Oh. I'm not sure. Perhaps you can show me again. Perhaps in a bed, rather than on a sofa?" I suggested coyly.

"Only if your Ma sleeps like the dead" said Jo.

I asked "What about your place?" but the only answer was a "hurumph" as Jo pulled on her jacket back and left the house.

And after that first time we fell into a weekly pattern:

climbing on Tuesday and Thursday nights, when Jo barely looked at me; pub on Friday night when she sparred with Josh about geology or Phil about feminism. And every other night she would come round once Mum had gone to bed and leave me breathless, without room in my head to think about anything or anyone but her. So much so that it wasn't until one sunny Sunday morning several weeks later that I realised Mum might be in trouble.

Jo was away on a climbing competition with other climbers. She wouldn't let me go: said I'd put her off her stride. I wasn't sure whether to be flattered or outraged. But in the warm sun, with Yas for company, it was hard to feel cross about anything. Yas insisted that we sit in the front garden just in case the object of her desire strolled past. I was idly weeding the cooch grass and ground elder out of the spikey mombresia clumps. I'd passed on all the pub gossip: Phil had been dumped by the punkette and had picked up one of the barmaids, which meant that she never left the pub. Josh was going off on a field-trip to Iceland and Malcolm had taken to laughing out loud on a regular basis, but could only tell jokes in the dark. Phil's barmaid informed us that he could speak to order drinks OK. I squinted into the sun to where Yasmeen was sitting on the flagstones.

"What about you then Yas? Have you reeled in the dream-boat yet?"

She shook her head. "No. Not even a nibble. Dunno what to do." She turned to look at me. "He's the real thing Fliss."

"Well, just bed him, girl!" I offered, imitating her cocky tones. But she wasn't doing cocky.

"I don't think I can. None of my old tricks work. What's worse is, I'm not even sure if I want to." The seriousness of this news made me stand up from my weeding and step over to sit next to her.

"What, you've gone off him?"

"No. No. Definitely not. He is perfect. He's too good. He's pure and high-minded. He never comments on what we wear out loud. But see, if I go to class in heels or lipstick he just looks sad, disappointed like."

"Mmmm". I was trying to imagine Yasmeen the sex queen being shamed by mere lipstick.

"I can feel it. So can the other girls. And he tells us how in the eyes of Allah we're good as we are, without adornment."

"But what about your work?"

"S'like being back at school. I go to work dolled up and then get changed in the loos before class. Feels hypocritical." Yas sighed and looked glum.

"So give up work. Your Dad would be delighted."

"I know. I've thought about it. But I love Top Shop. They're giving me day release to do my management qualifications." Yasmeen was solemn. I hadn't seen her this troubled since her inability to hold a tune denied her the role of Rizzo in the school production of "Grease". At that time, she was Rizzo in real life: feisty, sexy and way ahead of the rest of us. She threatened to sue the drama teacher for race discrimination and then decided that seducing the lad who played Danny Zucko would be more effective revenge. But this time she was just bewildered. I put my arm around her shoulders and she leaned into me.

"Poor Yas." I stroked her hair and looked at the ants on the garden path. Yas was at a loss, without a plan or a scheme to fox the world. It was peculiar. "Come on. I'll make you a cup of coffee."

Mum was at the sink with her back to us.

"Hello Mrs Fort" said Yas, having regained her poise.

"Oh. Oh. Um. Hello." Mum shuffled around to face us. She had tipped out some pills on the draining board and was trying to swallow one of them. "Hello Yasmeen dear. Are you well?"

"Yes, fine thanks" said Yas her voice had dropped a tone, subdued by seeing Mum's dishevelled state.

I took Mum's arm to walk her up the stairs. She got back into bed.

"Just a few more minutes darling. Another snooze. You don't need me to get up do you love?" she muttered, her face already pressed into the pillow.

In the kitchen, Yas asked "Do you think she was going to take an overdose?" pointing to the pills that I was tidying back into their pots.

"Be pretty hard to do much harm with Evening Primrose Oil and homeopathic sleeping remedy!"

"She looks dreadful. Wrecked. Is she ill?" Yas persisted.

"Dunno. She sleeps all the time and cries at night some-times. I make her soup and tell her jokes. I don't think she's ill; not like infected with anything." I warmed the jug and spooned the coffee grounds out of the caddy – Dad's caddy featuring Troon golfers. "One for you, one for me and one for the pot."

"But she's not right is she? Your Mum's usually pretty and smiley. But now she's just pale."

"She's white" I suggested, wishing Yasmeen didn't look so concerned. It made me feel as though I had neglected Mum.

"Yeah. But she's ill-pale, not honky-pale, you dumb dyke." I didn't know what to say. Yasmeen was right. Ever since Stella Bouchier's visit Mum had been falling apart, dissolving into tears and disintegrating under her duvet. A few weeks ago, just before I became immersed in Jo, I had suggested again that I dispose of the adoption agency file. But Mum hadn't been able to answer, except by weeping. So I had con-tinued to ignore it.

"There's a file Yas. That's the problem." And while I poured coffee I explained about the dreadful birthday visit. "The social worker woman lied to my Mum. Said I was Cypriot, when actually I'm Guyanese."

"Eh?" said Yas.

"Scared I spose. Scared that my Mum wouldn't take to a black baby. But thought olive was fine."

"Guyanese, dirty knees. There's all sorts there: Chinese; Asian; whites. My cha-cha's married over there. What sort are you?"

"Um, well my blood Dad was black. Among other things."

"Are you black then?" asked Yas smiling.

"Apparently so. Well, according to my unwanted social worker."

Yas jumped up and flicked the radio on "Course you're black. I knew that Fliss. Cos you've got rythmn innit?" She was dancing around the kitchen, trying to pull me to my feet.

"Yas! This is serious. I'm trying to tell you. My Mum's worried about what else might be in the file."

"What, in case you turn out to be the bastard child of a Prince and disappear to pursue your inheritance rights?" Yasmeen said sarcastically, sitting down again.

"Um. No. More like what kind of hideous things my birth parents did before I was taken off them."

"Oh. Yeah. Mmm. But does it matter? You're alright aren't you? Not damaged like?"

"Damaged? Me? I'm perfect! Ask Jo! I said that to Mum: "Look at me! Whatever they did, I've come through pretty cool." I licked my little finger and smoothed down my right eyebrow in a King-of-the-Hill-kind-of-way. Yas smiled faintly at my mime, but was thinking about troublesome mothers.

"The last time my Mum was going a bit bonkers with my brothers, we got a social worker. Didn't sort the boys out, but made Mum feel better. Made her worries legit. But mostly she liked the social worker 'cause she talked Urdu really well."

"So do you, don't you?"

Yas shook her head. "No, I talk like a peasant, not full Urdu."

"So, did she discuss her troubles?"

"No way. That might get spread. She talked about the cricket and Zee TV."

"Yeah well. It's a social worker that's caused Mum's trouble," I sniffed. And then we sat silent for a bit. I could hear Mum's snuffley snores. We finished our coffee and stared at the grounds in the bottom of the mugs.

"Being grown up is shit." Yas announced. "Welcome to the land of compromise and disappointment. You can't stop your mother weeping and I can't choose between following my fashion muse or my Muslim teacher. S'rubbish." I smiled across the table at Yas, fearless Yas who always got what she wanted. But now she couldn't work out what she wanted. I knew what I wanted. I wanted Jo to come round and to reduce the world's complexity to a single core of hot hunger in the centre of my body.

"Mmm. But at least I'm getting shagged at last." I grinned at Yas. "You were right what you said, back then."

"When?"

"When you were banging that kid in the drama group, you said that sex was more entertaining than a Simpsons double-bill and more satisfying than a chess game."

Yas laughed "You remember that rubbish?"

"I didn't believe you then, 'cause I really loved chess."

But it wasn't only sex that I wanted. I also wanted Mum to un-scrumple, to get up and to cook hazel nut cookies again, to fill the house with vanilla smells and quiet, unvoiced disapproval of Jo.

After Yasmeen had expressed concern about my poor creased and flaking mother, I noticed that Jo never mentioned her. She always came round at 9pm and never even checked whether Mum was safely tucked up in bed before getting down to business. And then she seemed to get bored of the sex as our sofa sessions climaxed quicker. I was moaning about this to Phil at the pub on Friday night, waiting for Jo to arrive from the climbing wall where she was intensive training for another competition.

"Oh that's normal darling" Phil assured me, breathing her smoke out over her shoulder and winking at her barmaid at the same time. "Lesbian bed-death."

"But we haven't even made it to a bed yet," I said gloomily.

"Get yourself some suspenders and crotchless panties," was Phil's next jewel of advice. "It got us past the week seven low."

"Phil! This is me we're talking about. My quadriceps are delicious and nylon lace would not show them to any better advantage than the light sheen of coconut oil that they currently receive", I said firmly with a pretend frown. Phil squeezed my thigh rather suggestively.

"No, you're right. You're already irresistible, so Jo must be a fool. Perhaps she's just tired ... coming up for the change maybe?"

"Changing what? The clocks went back ages ago."

"Change of life. S'what my dear mama blames all her troubles on. Has done for fifteen years, if my Pa is to be believed." Phil shook her shaggy well-cut hair back off her face and sucked thoughtfully on her cigarillo. "Perhaps we need to stoke up her possessiveness. I know, we'll have a fabulous party. A dee-pee."

"A tee-pee?" I asked.

"A dinner party with scintillating conversation, plunging necklines and sensuous food" said Phil, her eyes narrowed in thought. "And we must find some young lovelies to drape themselves about your fabulous frame. That'll get Jo going again. You'll see." Phil looked towards the door to check who had just arrived. It wasn't Jo. "I reckon she's the old fashioned misogynist-lesbo-type. You know, likes you as a geisha, but probably not looking to settle down and visit Ikea with you." I was used to not understanding Phil, with her fondness for long words and pretentious sub-clauses.

"I don't want to be her wife, if that's what you mean" I ventured.

"No luvvie. I know. You'd be a child-bride anyway." Phil pinched my cheek patronisingly. "But, wouldn't you like her to hold your hand occasionally, here, in the pub? Or call you 'my darling'?"

"No Phil. You do quite enough of that. Anyway, Jo says she doesn't do public displays of affection because they're possessive and heterosexist."

Phil snorted derisively. "Or it might be that her stoney Calvinist heart wouldn't permit such frivolous pointless affection."

I felt I ought to keep going in Jo's defence. "And she says you and the princess pint-puller are chancing your arms with your Sapphic carry-on."

"Yes, yes I know. And if only we'd been at the Stonewall riots, like her, we'd know what homophobia is really all about. Bless. She's an oral history project. Maybe we could get lottery funding for her?"

Tim and Josh tumbled in, having been at the AGM of the croquet association. They were the only two members under sixty and, during the Treasurer's report, Josh had calculated that together they had reduced the average age of the meeting by forty years. He had played croquet for years and channelled any competitive feelings into viciously smashing coloured balls off the smooth corporation green, to leave him calm and chilled for daily life. Tim's experience of the game was limited to childhood summer holidays playing on his grandparents' mole-hill ruptured back lawn. This was enough for Josh who needed to recruit young players to ensure that his favourite past-time didn't die out with the octogenarians.

"It's Josh, the lad with balls of mahogany" announced Phil

to the pub in general. Josh took no notice, concentrating on getting a round bought and transported to our corner table.

"How was Iceland?" I asked.

"Yeah good thanks Fliss. Specially the hot springs and Bjork look-alikes. Yum." Josh slurped the top froth off his Guinness. "It's good to get back to a pint that costs under twenty quid." But that was all the air-time that Phil allowed the boys, before launching into detailed planning for the big DP.

The telephone noise nudged into my dreams and eventually shoved me out of sleep and out of bed. Saturday morning. In Mum's room I found the telephone under a pillow on the floor. Mum was asleep. Of course when I pushed the button to take the call, the ringing stopped. Ugh. Back to bed to try to pretend I was still asleep. No point in getting up yet. Mum wouldn't be up at all. Jo was cross training all day. "Like you need any tips on grumpiness" Phil had wittily quipped in the pub. Just as I settled the bedding back around me, cutting out all of the annoying little drafts, the phone went again.

"Good morning Felicity. Stella Bouchier here. Sorry to call at the week-end, but your mother left a rather desperate message last night."

"She's asleep."

"It was you I wanted to talk to. About your origins."

"What?"

Stella slowed down her talk to idiot-pace. "To offer you a chance to talk through your early origins."

"I think I told you that I have all the origins I need thank-you."

"Yes, but you've had time to think about your African-Caribbean heritage by now I expect ..."

"It doesn't change anything. I still get called a Paki by the estate kids. And I've always liked spiced bun and Bob Marley."

"Now I know this isn't strictly my business, but as an old family friend, I am worried about your wellbeing and your mother's."

"Did you come to my Dad's funeral?" This stalled Stella Bouchier's professional pursuit of wellbeing and I heard her swallow.

"It did not seem appropriate."

"Aaah. Well now. I don't think it's appropriate for me to see you just now. Good-bye." I turned the ringer off on the handset, just in case the old bat persisted. I went through to look at Mum, still sallow, still sleeping. The wooden framed picture on the wall above her dressing table reminded me that my Mum hadn't always been asleep. The summer after Dad had died we visited the Lakes for a long week-end of walking and recuperation. The vicar had recommended a non-profit making Christian hostel and with Dad and his vehement atheism gone, we were free to go. We had never been to the Lakes with Dad because he insisted that if you'd got as far as the Lake District, you might as well carry on up the road to some real hills in the highlands. The picture showed Mum and me at the top of Helvellyn, our cheeks rosy from the upward climb and our hair whipping around our heads in the breeze. It was taken by a lovely lad who had arrived at the summit at the same time as us. He was impressed that we had managed to get to the top with no more than a packet of egg sarnies, a cagoule and a map by way of equipment.

I turned to look at Mum in bed: her cheeks had hollowed out since that summer and her hair had lost its burnished coppery colour and was fading to ashes. A glance over at my reflection in the dressing table mirror showed that my face had thinned out too, losing the childish curve in my cheeks and showing up the high cheekbones that my Dad used to say would "break a sailor's heart one day". When I had told him to shut-up he would protest his political correctness: "Sailors can be lassies". I looked at his picture in the silver frame on Mum's bedside table: bright red hair, wide set pale blue eyes embedded in smile lines. I couldn't help smiling back at him. He wouldn't've minded Jo. He always said he was delighted not to have to worry about a man stealing his daughter's heart: "I'm with you Fliss-hen, I would choose a woman every time" and he would enfold me and my Mum in a squeezey hug.

Mum turned over, opened one bleary eye and half smiled.

"Hello Mum." Mum didn't answer, she just shut her eye again, with its bruisey shadows all around. "Come on Mum. Wake up. S'morning" I turned on the radio and went to open the window. As I was tucking the curtains back, I saw another photo on the floor behind the dressing table. I picked it up and wiped a layer of dust from the picture. It was Mrs Ashkenazy sitting in our garden with a Milly Molly Mandy book open in her hand. I am sitting on her knee, smiling and Mum is lying stretched out on a lounger with a blanket over her legs. Mrs Ashkenazy used to come round a lot. Every day in fact. Her shiny dress material skidded over her nylon underwear, so I used to slip about on her lap. And she smelt of cinnamon and fried meat. She read to me every afternoon, in the garden usually but on the sofa when it rained. All the Rudyard Kipling stories that her son had enjoyed were good, but my favourite was "The Family at One End Street"; the chaotic life of a big family was so exotic. And Mum was always lying down. Always tired. Mrs Ashkenazy would go home when Dad got back from work. When did it stop? I suppose when Mum got less tired and perhaps Mrs Ashkenazy got more tired and I learned to read to myself. But whenever Mum took to her bed Dad would say to me "She's just a bit feek and weeble, Fliss. It'll pass. Let's go and feed the ducks." And to Mum he would say "Don't come over all Victorian again, Marj. Please. I don't think I can bear another nine months of neighbourly goulash."

I put the photo back under the dressing table. Best not to remind Mum of that time. She still didn't or wouldn't stir.

Monday morning and it was raining. And the bus was full of school kids so I couldn't see a seat anywhere.

"And good morning Ms Felicity Fort. It's so kind of you to join us this morning. Allow me to introduce you to Ms Fort, ladies and gentlemen. She is a sex addict. And on the show this morning, she's going to tell us what it's like when you have to be shagged senseless once a day in order to keep going. However, judging by her appearance this morning, there's been an interruption to ... bumphherg." I had managed to sit down on Yas's knee and put my hand over her mouth to silence her piercing nasal drawl and stymie her Oprah-style charade.

"Morning, Yas. I am so **not** in the mood for any of your bollocks."

"No bollocks on me, love" came the muffled reply.

The school kids were still staring, uncertain as to the appropriate reaction. Only the tallest, hardest looking girl was laughing. I smiled serenely back at them and noted with satisfaction that acrylic hat woman was absent.

"No bollocks, but balls of steel" I said. "You know, most people have grown out of humiliating their friends by the time they've reached adulthood."

"Ah-ha, but I'm still seventeen" spluttered Yas pulling my hand away from her mouth.

"Hmm. Well I'm thinking of divorcing you before you reach eighteen" I muttered as I slid into the seat next to Yas which had just been vacated, beating the tall hard school girl by seconds. The prerogative of age.

"How's your Mum?" asked Yasmeen, once she'd straightened out her hijab. "Any better?"

"Has your mum arranged a betrothal to the immaculate Imam yet?" I asked, to avoid answering. Mrs Mohammed was regularly feeding the dreamboat on pilau, stuffed paratha and puffed out puris. Yas shook her head gloomily.

"Nah. They were discussing how geek-boy Haq needs a good wife. Apparently he's going off the rails. And then he, teacherji, only went on about what a devout and scholarly person I was. And how I would make someone a lovely wife. But I don't think he meant himself. If the Haq boy is suggested, I will definitely have to start with the mini-skirts again." She smoothed out her hijab over her shoulders with dignity.

"Your Mum likes him then?"

"No, she says the Haqs were sweepers and cobblers in Faislabad."

"No, the dreamboat."

"Yeah. Devoted. Giving half her pension to his educational fund. Dad's livid." Yas said as she stood up and pretended to give me a big good-bye snog for the benefit of her juvenile audience.

As I emerged from the changing rooms into the sports hall, there was no-one on the climbing wall. I was longing to tell Jo or Tim or even the McKinleys that I'd been given my next clinical placement and it was in the Sports Injury clinic.

Yipeee! My glorious career was starting at last. My college tutor had tried to be discrete, but I knew that loads of the girls wanted that placement, especially Jolly-hockey-thunder-thighs Camilla. "We thought you would be well placed to learn both the academic and the practical lessons available from working there." So doing well in tests and essays was paying off at last.

But there was no chance to glory in my achievement since all the climbers were gathered around Socks who was reading aloud from a magazine. "And although modest about her own achievements, anyone competing in next month's regional finals would be well advised to watch out for Jo McMann!" A collective "Wah-hey" rose up from the blokey group. Several men peeled off towards Jo, who was sitting to one side looking abashed, and clapped her on the shoulders as they sauntered over to the wall. Socks was holding "Amateur Climber" open on a full-page photo of Jo stretching around an overhang, with her shoulder, back and thigh muscles taut and clearly defined.

"Nice one Jo" I offered as I sat down next to her to put on my climbing shoes.

"Thanks, doll. Will you be celebrating with me tonight?" she said quietly, while concentrating on re-lacing her own shoes.

"You bet your taut ass I will" I replied as I strapped on my harness.

At ten o'clock, rather than waving me off, with all the others, Jo let me into the passenger seat of her boy-racer car and drove me home. And on the leather sofa of her converted mill-house apartment, we celebrated our achievements. In the safety of her own home, Jo was prepared to cede a little of the control of proceedings: she allowed me to trace her major and minor muscle groups and she seemed to be enjoying my anatomical explorations, judging by her breathing. But suddenly, she was back in charge.

"Come on Cinderella, let's get you home to your mammy. I don't want the child abuse squad kicking my door down." There was no point in arguing when she was in management mode. Besides, the erotic charge of watching her drive was good compensation for being kicked out. And then Jo invited me a little further into her life. "My best pal's girlfriend is in town tomorrow night. Do you want to come out for dinner with us? You'd be doing me a favour, I never know what to say to her."

At home the house was still, but holiday brochures were strewn about the front room. Perhaps Mum was coming out of her hibernation at last. I tidied them into a pile while I made myself some marmite toast.

"It was Stella's idea really, darling" announced Mum the following morning. It was the first time she'd been up for breakfast for ages. She had brushed her hair and changed into a clean nightie. She looked thin.

"What was Mum?" I was caught off guard. I hadn't realised Mum had been phoning anyone. Thought she was too tired.

"Going to Guyana."

My muesli went down the wrong way and it was some minutes before I managed to expel an organic oat flake from the top of my oesophagus.

When I stopped coughing, Mum continued "We could sit in the sun, drink in the local atmosphere and admire the plentiful wildlife, according to the brochure."

"I thought our next big holiday was going to be to Venice, before it sinks. That's what we decided."

"But we've never been to Guyana."

"We've never been to Venice either. Or Timbuktu, Mum ... oh I get it. Stella's idea. She wants me to get to grips with my roots."

"And she thinks I could do with some sunshine and a change of scene."

"We could do that in Cornwall or Marseilles."

"Yes, but we don't know anything about Guyana. It might be fascinating."

"Exactly, we don't know anything about Guyana, because we've never wanted or needed to know."

"Because we didn't know, darling" Mum said patiently.

"We don't know anything now, Mum. Only what Stella told us."

"She suggested it might be lovely for you to be part of the ethnic majority, instead of a minority ... you know, to look like everyone else."

"Mmph" I grunted as I chewed on an especially tough bit of sun-dried fair-trade apricot. "S'pose that might be quite funny. But I could just go down to the Baptist church on a Sunday morning instead. It'd be cheaper. Josh's mum goes." I really didn't feel interested in the bloke or the woman who made me. I could see that I might be one day. Maybe. But there was a queue of people ... Mum's lost sister, the cousins who blew out my birthday candles, Dad's family (what was left of them) who were all violent oafs according to Dad. Some Guyanese bloke who carelessly made me was not a priority and, as far as I could see, never would be. I was too busy trying to figure out who I was now and I didn't have time to consider who I might have been, if things had been different. But if Mum was busy planning a trip to Guyana, it probably showed that she didn't know anything about any kiddie-porn. Or didn't want to know. And at least she was out of bed and talking about something other than just going to sleep again.

"Have you eaten anything Mum? I'll make you some toast." She sighed. And slumped a little in her seat. I fetched the loaf and the pint of semi-skimmed from the front door step, cut the crusts off a slice, toasted it lightly and spread a thin scraping of the cashew butter that had been bought as part of my birthday feast.

"Thanks, darling."

"At the week-end, Mum, I'll have a look through that file and see if it says anything interesting about Guyana. OK?"

"OK, darling. That would be lovely" said Mum, but I didn't believe her. She sounded tired, not delighted.

"But tonight Mum, I'm going out. Will you be all right? Shall I ask Mrs Ashkenazy to come and heat you up some soup?" I lifted a tin of Scotch broth from the store cupboard.

"Oh no, love. I'm not ill, just tired. I'm fine." And as I was getting my bag and leaving the house, she trudged back up the stairs saying she just needed a few more moments in bed.

The girlfriend of the best pal and Jo were meeting up in Lillith's, a premises handily located for the station and perfectly situated for queer bashers, being off an ill-lit alley in a commercial quarter of the city centre.

"How was your journey down?" Jo was asking a small

woman wearing her long hair plaited and a floaty skirt beneath a velvet jacket. The woman looked more like a bohemian auntie than a proper lesbian. Jo had sat down, so I was able to wrap my arms around her neck and land a kiss on her cheek and then her mouth as she turned. Gruffly she introduced us to one another.

"Flora, like the low fat spread" I said, immediately wishing that I hadn't.

"Hello Felicity. Felicity, like happiness. I am pleased to meet you", Flora said. Jo got up from the table to order food and drinks and I got over my embarrassment by prattling on about the Karaoke nights that Phil and I had enjoyed in Lillith's.

"It's not really a Karaoke night, it's a variety show. Three or four women hog the floor and no-one else gets a look in. Phil's one of them in fact. Or she was before she started going out with a barmaid from another pub. She'd spend all week rehearsing her four numbers, planning her outfit, getting all her pals to come along and clap for her. It was mad. They had to close them down in the end because fights kept breaking out between rival camps." Flora was nodding amiably. Jo brought a bottle of wine and three glasses and excused herself for a smoke. "So, um, have you known Jo long?" I asked.

"Aye, well, a fair wee while" said Flora in a merry voice, as if there was a big joke to be told. "But I don't really know her, if you ken what I mean. Ma bidie-in, Norma, she's big pals with Jo. In fact the first year we were walking out together, all I'd hear was 'Jo this' and 'Jo that'. I was that jealous." Flora smiled in affectionate remembrance of her former foolish self. "And what about you? Have you known her long?" she asked.

"Few months I spose. Feels like longer" I said, feeling gauche and exposed in Flora's benevolent gaze. I was embarrassed about my relationship with Jo: she'd barely mentioned Flora or Glasgow or anything about her life in Glasgow. She'd barely mentioned anything, since talking wasn't what we did together. "Um. Are you just visiting?" I changed the subject.

"Aye, well, I'm running a workshop in the art gallery. Frisky folk dancing for beginners or some such. It's part of a festival. It was a good excuse to come and catch up with

Jo. Check she hadn't lost touch with her Caledonian quines. Norma was a wee bit worried. But now I know that she's distracted by a lovely young thing like you, we'll stop worrying."

I shot a look at Flora: she was being friendly and sincere not snidey. So I thought I'd better keep trying to make conversation. I was my mother's daughter, I should be able to talk to anyone.

"Umm. Glasgow, what is that like? Deep fried Mars Bars and Rab C Nesbitt probably don't quite sum it up do they?"

"D'you ken, I've never seen one on sale. I quite fancy the idea. Like baked Alaska."

"My Dad used to talk about Glasgow as the most exciting place in the world."

"Was he from the dear green place?" Flora asked.

"Not born. Ayrshire he was from. But went to Glasgow as soon as he could get the bus fare out of his village. Stayed with an aunt when he was doing an apprenticeship."

"Where abouts was that then?"

"Um. Not sure. Somewhere you can see the Clyde from your bedroom window."

"Doesn't narrow it down much!" Flora laughed. "East or west?"

"Dunno. S'pect Mum knows."

"And is she Scottish too?"

I shook my head. "Oh no. She's the reason that Dad never went back."

"Just like you and Jo?"

"No, I don't think so. If Jo's being kept here, it'll be her climbing." We both glanced towards Jo who was smoking and chatting to a waiter at the other side of the room. "Are you persuading her to go back?"

"Well we keep telling her the women's scene has improved. And the queer stuff."

"Is that why she left then?" I asked.

"I'm no sure. It was afore I knew Norma."

"She's never talked to me about Glasgow."

Flora carried on "I ken there was a right stushie when she left. And she's not been back much since."

Jo arrived back at our table at the same time as the pizza. I

197

concentrated on eating while Jo and Flora worked their way through a list of mutual acquaintances in Glasgow. Jo's accent got more pronounced with each glass of wine: ballachulish, peeley-wally, eccelfechen, hoaching, and blairbuie might have been dances or places or insults. I couldn't always tell. Why didn't my Dad teach me properly, instead of going on about Billy Connolly and his beige turds? I managed to gather from the flow of talk that someone called Margot had gone to prison for battering her husband to death with a brick, her self-defence plea having failed, whereas Sonali was in hiding. Women's Aid weren't sure how long they could hide her for, if a criminal prosecution was brought. Norma's dad was still alive and still refusing to tell Norma's ex-husband her whereabouts. Flora's Dad had died at last, and Flora had felt nothing but relief. Flora's mother had wept at the funeral, despite having been "beaten black and blue by the old half-wit". The second bottle of wine was finished; Jo ordered three double Glen Morangies and Flora turned to include me.

"It's pretty gloomy stuff, eh Felicity. No wonder Jo's no for visiting very often. I'll need to find some good news. Wait and I'll think ..." she sipped her whisky. Jo smiled. She was looking more relaxed. "The women's library is doing great. New collections being donated all the time. Moved to a bigger place. A big old town house. It's full ae fantastic oak book shelves and the original fire places. Norma's restored them all and it's smashing in winter. Pure dead romantic. Like a Stevenson novel."

"Norma'll enjoy that I daresay" said Jo.

"What about your folks? Any news?" asked Flora.

Jo shook her head, knocked back her drink and called a taxi which she directed to drop me off first. No frolics on the leather sofa then. She kissed me good-night chastely and Flora shook my hand warmly. "Come and visit us in Glasgow soon Felicity. We've a lovely spare room. Here's my mobile number, just in case" and she took my phone out of my hand and entered her details. Bit of an imposition I remember thinking. But I was quite impressed that she knew how to do it.

I should have gone straight to bed. Of course I should have done. But I didn't. Instead I climbed onto a wooden kitchen chair and pulled out the taped bag full of adoption correspondence. Shutting the cupboard door and replacing the chair, in case Mum should come down in the night, I carried the bundle up to my room and began to try to make sense of all the bits of paper.

By 3 a.m. I felt sick, frightened and confused. I hadn't found any reassuring explanation about how to be black or any useful stories about Guyana for Mum. Nothing easy. Just difficult questions and horrific suggestions. I felt sick because this was sort of what I wanted to find. But it was messier than I had expected. Jaggier. I wanted something easy to prove to Jo that I had suffered too. I wasn't just a piece of pretty stuff to distract her from life's difficulties. But I wanted it in a neat package not a sprawl of unresolved nastiness. I put the papers under my bed with a bag of dirty washing to hide them and crept into Mum's room to slide under the duvet on Dad's side of the bed. Her breathing was slow and calm and I followed its rhythm to soothe myself to sleep.

Next morning, I had more or less managed to bury the chaos of questions that my late night reading had raised. It was exam results day at College and I anticipated the comfort of success, delivered in terms of percentages. On the bus Yasmeen was subdued.

"What's biting your bum Yas?"

"My Mum's gone off to Mecca" she said.

"But that's good isn't it. At least she can't marry you off to the Haq geek this week."

"Mmmm. But she can't cook for us either. And my dahl-brained brothers think it's my job."

"But you work all day: they're at home."

"I know. And I wouldn't mind that. I quite like making roti-salaan. Makes me feel safe. But those useless boys just complain about the shape of the roti. Spoils the whole meal. Bastards."

"What about dreamboat? Are you cooking for him?" I asked

"No. Mum offered. He said it'd be improper" Yasmeen replied sulkily.

"Ah-ha. Is that's what's really eating you?"

"Maybe." She looked out the window.

"Come round for tea at mine will you?"

"I'm not that desperate Fliss!" Yas punched my upper arm. She'd never rated my ability to heat up tinned food as real cooking.

"No. I know. But I am" I said seriously. "I need some help figuring some stuff out."

"Oh. OK then. Sorry. Not tonight. It's Qu'ran class."

"I'm busy too." Tonight was Phil's blessed dinner party. She'd got everyone involved and it would be impossible to miss. "Tomorrow?"

"OK. Please, can I cook?"

"Are you insulting my way with baked beans?"

"Yeah. They're always tepid."

"Mmm. Maybe that's how I like them." I gave Yasmeen a quick hug before she pushed the stop button and made her way down the aisle.

I had been to Phil's house once before. Back when she had first made her appearance in the pub, she had hosted what she called "an intimate little soirée, darlings". She lived in a scruffy terraced house, shared with an indeterminate number of others. One of them was certainly her brother and another one her girlfriend of the time who had, before Phil moved in, been going out with one of the other housemates. Phil's stories at the pub were of internecine warfare over every aspect of domestic order from who slept with whom to whether vegan or vegetarian margarine was bought with the communal food fund. But the evening we had visited, everyone was on best behaviour and the sitting room had been hung about with fairy lights. Guests had been instructed to wear evening dress and to prepare a "short turn". Yas, Josh and I had sought clarification in the pub.

"Oh come on darlings. You know. A party turn. A skit. A song. A poem." Phil had shaken her head and despaired of "the sad lack of culture among the younger generation".

She was probably only seven or eight years older than us, but it certainly seemed like a whole generation. We had sat on her saggy sofa, decorated with an Indian bedspread and listened to Phil's friends and housemates recite soliloquies, odes and sing medaeval lovers' laments. In between we drank peach juice and Prosecco, which Phil had insisted was "simply divine, nectar for the Gods". We had nodded and drank and gawped at the women in their chiffon frocks and charity shop beads squeezing, congratulating and patting each other with evident pleasure. One of them perched on the sofa next to me and told me all about herself: her job as a set designer, who she had slept with (the housemate who'd been jilted by Phil's arrival), who she'd nearly slept with (almost everyone) and who was on her hit list (anyone not already mentioned). "And what about you. What do you do?" she had asked leaning in too close.

"I'm doing biology, maths, French, history, English, chemistry, art and design" I had replied truthfully. She had promptly stood up and gone to ask Phil whether it was wise to have her daughter at a party where there were drugs circulating.

Phil certainly hadn't invited us for the quality of our cultural input. Josh, who was the only male, apart from Phil's brother, had said he only knew one poem, when invited to take the floor. He had taught it to me and Yas, as he was too shy to say it by himself. Phil had pulled Josh to his feet, his long legs threatening to fold under him after the three doses of Prosecco and, flanked by his gal pal chorus we had recited:

> The following words of wisdom
> Were marked on a toilet wall,
> Declaring in indelible pen:
> "God made MAN first of all."
>
> Underneath, in a different hand,
> Which betrayed uncommon focus;
> "She made him as Her early draft,
> Before Her final magnum opus."

I cringed thinking back: the three of us lined up, the exotic innocents in varying shades of brown, three monkeys who had yet to sleep with anyone in the room. Even Yasmeen, who claimed to have done every position in the Kama Sutra had been a bit subdued. The assembled ladies clapped us, but the rhyme, which had seemed such unadulterated wit when we had committed it to memory, seemed like puerile nonsense as the next performer launched into an epic of love, loss and tequila of her own composition.

But this time was to be different. I was going as a paid up member of the lesbian club with my real grown-up girlfriend. Yasmeen wasn't coming because the Qu'ran class gave her a chance to see her Imam. And Josh, along with Tim and Phil's brother, had been persuaded by Phil to don dinner jackets and serve the assembled ladies at table.

Jo picked me up in her boy racer. I was wearing the suit buttoned up over a black sports bra and had oiled my hair, slick against my skull. Deep red lipstick and a diamanté collar prevented me from looking too butch and stealing Jo's thunder. I looked good. Really good. Like one of Madonna's Latin American pretty boy dancers. Jo obviously thought so by the way she whistled through her teeth. Mum was watching "Eastenders" and kissed me on the cheek. "You look gorgeous Felicity love. Look after her, won't you Joanne dear."

"Yes Mrs Fort. Good night."

Jo drove too fast across town to Phil's house. At a red light I asked her "So did Flora get back to Glasgow OK?"

"I would imagine so, since Norma hasn't phoned in a fantoushie yet" said Jo with a half smile.

"I didn't know you smoked, by the way."

"I don't, by the way" Jo said shortly

"Well you did at Lilith's."

"That's what talk of Glasgow does to me."

"Makes you smoke?"

"It's a coping mechanism hen. You'll understand when you've got stuff going on."

I bit back the desire to suggest that an implication of child sexual abuse in the first two years of life might be stuff, and asked "What're you coping with?"

"All the shite that families leave you with" said Jo gazing out the window.

It was hard to imagine Jo having any family; she was so self-contained and sure of her own judgement. "What family have you got there?" I wondered.

"None that I care to talk about. That's why I left Glasgow so I don't have to smoke and I don't have to think about family."

We were greeted in Phil's front hall by her brother who tried to take Jo's leather jacket from her.

"No offence pal, but I'll keep it on. I need it to keep the vegans at bay."

The brother smiled good naturedly and ushered us through into the back room where a long table had been put together with ivy along the middle and mismatched gold rimmed glasses, around which the barmaid was fluttering, folding napkins into pretty shapes.

"Drinkies, darlings?" asked Phil after she had extravagantly embraced us both. "Thought we'd start with a sparkle!" she said pouring cava into teacups.

"What have you done with all the housemates Phil?"

"They were banished to the pub, so that they could arrive like proper guests. And so you can eye them up as they arrive, young Felicity." Phil gave an exaggerated wink.

When the "lovely ladies" were announced by Phil's brother, they had evidently been briefed since each of them came and gave me very lingering greetings. Jo didn't seem to notice, although she did stay at my side, restraining her conversation to words exchanged with Josh or Tim as they re-filled her glass.

We ate guacamole, cherry tomato salsa, blue corn chips, roasted red peppers and rocket warm salad with sweet potato cakes accompanied by a Vouvray and a Côtes de Ventoux, our appreciation of which was encouraged by a brief lecture on viniculture from Phil. After Tim and Josh had cleared our plates with a great show of subservience, Phil stood up and tapped her knife on her glass. The ting-ting silenced the seated women, while Josh, Tim and the dirty dishes took themselves off to the kitchen where the brother was washing up.

"Ladies. We hope to have assuaged your appetites for food and wine, but left you fresh for other sensual pursuits." Phil's suggestive tones were met with a collective "wooooOOOO" from the table. "Namely gossip and conversation" she continued over the cat calling. "But before you throw yourselves into social intercourse, we have two small announcements to make. First, I would like you all to raise a glass to the lovely Felicity, whose expression of her desires inspired this modest little gathering. What a peach of a girl! You're one lucky lesbian, Jo." I turned to look at Jo's expression as she obediently raised her glass to me. She was wearing a neutral mask, the same one she keeps on when she's on duty at the leisure centre. When the congratulatory hub-bub had quietened down Phil carried on "And it is partly the vision of hope and youthful loveliness that is Felicity's version of dykedom that has inspired me and the loveliest of my ladies ..." Phil took the barmaid's hand, kissed it ostentatiously, and then laid a trail of kisses up her bare arm to the back of her neck, while her audience cheered. "to get going on the next generation of dykelettes and pretty boys." Phil pulled the barmaid gently to her feet and placed one hand on her belly and an arm around her shoulders. "With the help of my dear brother, we are now pregnant!" Silence. But Phil is unfazed. "So would you please raise your glasses to our gloriously queer pretended family!" There was an initially ragged but then rousing roar of amazed and surprised approval. The bar maid lifted her glass of apple juice to toast Phil's brother as he was led from the kitchen to make a shy bow before retreating quickly. "Oh bollocks. I forgot the champagne!" Phil dived after her brother and returned with two chilled bottles, Josh following with clean teacups. Phil caught the surge of fizzing wine and handed it to her lady announcing: "An act of faith in the future."

"A good excuse for bed-death more like", muttered Jo.

The excited chatter broke into smaller groups. The women nearest to Phil and the barmaid were discussing baby clothes and where to buy organic cotton vests in colours that weren't too sludgey. The cluster of lovelies being served champagne by Josh were asking whether he would consider donating his sperm.

"Only if you take it via the old fashioned method" he said soberly and softly, provoking drunken giggles.

The group on the other side of the table were agreeing on the superiority of women-only households. "You know of course that 90% of child abuse is perpetrated by men. They shouldn't really be allowed to parent at all."

"I'm not at all sure that I would be brave enough to have a baby. Even once you're past the messy business of conception there are so many things to go wrong."

"My neighbour lost her baby in the 9th month. The day she told me, I was wearing that yellow T-shirt, you know the CND one. 'The only safe fast breeder is a rabbit'. Mortifying. I hate bumping into them, don't know what to say."

"Did you see that copper who's been prosecuted for indecent images? Porn. Kiddie-porn. He was part of the vice squad."

"Yeah. Claimed it was case research. All 1,500 images."

"Ugh. Filth."

"How? How do they do that."

"S'only thing that would justify the death penalty."

"How did his wife not notice?"

"Said in the paper she thought he was playing a lot of online poker."

Jo snorted in derision at the last comment, made by the pretty, glittery lady to her left, who didn't notice.

We left an hour or so later and Jo still hadn't taken off her jacket. Jo offered to drive Josh and Tim home, since their duties had finished. The table had been dismantled into its constituent parts and the card tables, desks and picnic tables had been pushed to the sides of the rooms. Two women were demonstrating the Finnish tango, using the boys as their demonstration partners. It looked enjoyable, silly, pointless fun and the boys didn't want to leave. Phil and the barmaid were looking on, with amusement, standing in the doorway. With the kitchen light behind them and Phil's arms wrapped protectively around the barmaid they looked like a holy family in the making.

"Congratulations to you both" said Jo. "And thank-you for a ..." she paused, swallowed, took a breath and, failing to find the appropriate adjective to describe the evening ended with an abrupt "Good-night."

Phil wrapped one of her arms around me, without letting go of the barmaid. "Good night young Fliss. When you're bored with Calvinist strictures, come and join the wicked wenches and sybaritic old soaks. We'll show you a good time!" But Jo wasn't listening to the wind-up having headed off for the front door.

"Thanks Phil. I've enjoyed it" I said sincerely as I disentangled myself from her and placed her arm back over the
barmaid's belly. I left, shrugging apologetically at Josh and
Tim who waved goodbye over the shoulders of their dancing
mistresses.

It was lunch time in the college canteen and I didn't realise
it was my phone for an embarrassing half dozen rings. It never
usually goes, since I haven't given the number to anyone but
Mum, Jo and Yasmeen. I see Yas most days on the bus and
neither Jo nor Mum ever phone, so it's been pretty silent. It
was especially annoying that the phone should go at that
point, since I'd just been doing an anti-mobile phone rant:
"Everyone I know I see here at college, the climbing wall or
the pub, so why would they need to phone me? There's nothing that urgent in my humdrum little life that won't keep a
couple of hours until I get home. In fact, I'm thinking of
getting rid of it." I said, for effect.

"Oh no!" said one of the sporty doctor-hunting gels, as if
I'd suggested rhinoplasty to her pretty tip-tilted nose, "I
couldn't live without my mobile. I might miss something."

"Like what?" I asked, perhaps with too much challenge in
my voice.

"I dunno, a party invitation or a tasty piece of gossip. Or
a proposal" she giggled, glancing sideways at another doctor-
chaser.

"I think that's your phone ringing Fliss, with some very
non-urgent news", smiled matronly Jilly with the big hips.
I scrabbled in the bottom of my bag, holding my breath.
Mum, Mum, Mum, Mum was all I could think. I fumbled on
the key-pad to take the call and then gasped, "Mum, are you
OK?"

"Hello. Felicity? Is that you?" came a voice I couldn't place
for a minute.

"Yes. Hello. Oh. Flora. Hi." She must've taken my number
when she was putting hers into my phone in the taxi. "How
are you?"

"Aye, I'm fine myself. It's Jo I'm worried for. Has she said
anything?"

"About what?"

"Well, it's a mite difficult to explain. Kindae about her father. Well her mother."

"She hasn't mentioned them" I said tentatively as I moved away from my class mates to an empty table.

"No. Well." Flora paused awkwardly.

"Is it bad news?"

"Aye, well. Norma has tried to tell Jo herself, but she won't have it. She cuts the call when her family's mentioned."

"Oh."

"Her Da's dying, so could you maybe ask her to come to Glasgow?"

"What now this minute?"

"Well it is likely to be a matter of days not weeks."

"Oh. OK. Yup. Um thanks for phoning." Although gratitude was not at all what I felt.

That night, after our session on her leather sofa, when Jo was driving me home, I tried to tell her.

"Jo?"

"Mmmph."

"Flora phoned. Says you should go and visit your folks."

"Ha! Did she now. Nosey bisum."

"Says your Dad is ill. Very ill."

"Good."

"No, really ill. Like might not recover. Ever."

"Mmm. Like I said. Good."

"I could go with you."

"Why?"

"I'd like to go to Glasgow. Flora invited me remember."

"Well it'll no' be wi' me pal."

But two days later Jo changed her mind. She won the regional heat of the climbing championship and the next round was to be held in the Kelvinhall indoor sports arena.

"You can come as my groupie if you like, doll" she offered magnanimously.

"She's helping me with an essay" I said to Mum as Yas and I went up to my bedroom after supper. As an excuse it was less implausible now that Yas was doing her management qualification. I couldn't tell Mum it was easier to look at the file with Yas than with her. In any case, Mum had become completely fixated on the idea of a Guyanese voyage as the way to make everything better. She was getting out of bed more often, and had started to watch travel programmes as well as Eastenders, just in case Guyana was featured. She had been through our box-file marked "travel" to find whether our passports were still in date and come across some unused travellers' cheques left over from the last holiday before Dad died. In the face of her engaged activity, I couldn't tell her that my birth father's birth place was the least perturbing aspect of Stella Bouchier's unwelcome birthday gift.

"Look Yas. Here are the letters that the social worker wrote about me as a baby" I said as I fanned out half a dozen pieces of adoption agency headed note paper. We sat on the floor, surrounded by bits of official paper, most of which I had put in an "irrelevant" pile ... reports from the GP, child psychologist, short-term foster mother, paediatrician, play specialist, nutritionist and social worker all saying what a normal baby I was. Reassuring perhaps, but not riveting reading. "But they don't make sense."

"Sense of what?" asked Yas.

"You know, why I got adopted off."

Yasmeen read through the letters one by one while I fiddled with the tassels of the rug. As she looked up from the last one, I continued "The story isn't all there is it?"

"No. This is just the official stuff. Social services and the adoption people covering their arses. Aren't there some case notes or something?" Yas leaned back against my bed.

"Yeah, kind of. There's the placement case notes, but they miss out the scary bits."

"Eh?" Yas looked puzzled.

"Look, read this." I handed her the letter that had first fallen out of the file on my birthday encounter with Stella Bouchier.

"OK, so baby A is you, right?" asked Yas after her first quick scan through. Then she read out loud, slowly and deliberately "Due to the discovery of a number of pornographic images of baby A in the home of her father, she was taken into care by the local social services. The nature of the images was such that it was felt impossible to return baby A to this domestic setting with any degree of confidence for her future safety." She paused and adjusted her hijab under her chin. "So what was it then? A few nudie shots or the full split beaver?"

"I was one year old at the time. How do I know? Pre-memory innit. Thank God."

"Pretty fucked up though. Twisted."

"Mmmm." I assented and Yasmeen was silent for a few moments.

"Does it hurt you?" she asked quietly.

"What?"

"Thinking about it?"

"Um. Not exactly. Uneasy but not hurt. It doesn't really feel as though it's me."

Yas looked at the floor for a few seconds before looking up to ask "So what do you want me to do? I mean I'm sorry and that, but what can I do?"

"Well look at this" I handed Yas the memo headed "Pre-placement assessment" signed by Stella Bouchier and dated a month after the letter that Yas had just read. "No mention of porno, just 'break-down of family setting due to abusive father.' That could be anything – a slap, shouting, neglect, sexual stuff, anything."

"So why not ask the social work woman?"

"She dumped my Dad and lied to my Mum. Why would she tell me the truth?"

"Yeah. True." Yasmeen agreed and fell silent again.

"Well" I prompted after a few beats. "What would you do?"

"I'd be bloody delighted to find that me Dad wasn't me Dad. Even if he was an abuser. Better than a bully and a crook."

"Yaaaas."

"No really. I hate my Dad Fliss. He's a nasty man. Not like your Dad. I mean Mr Fort. He was good. So yeah. I'd be delighted to discover that my Dad hadn't made me. 'Cause worse than turning into my mother would be becoming my Dad. Far worse."

"Why does your Mum stay with him?"

"She says men take and women give. That's just the way it is."

"But what if your birth Dad had been, I dunno, fiddling with you? And getting off on it? What then?"

"Mmmm. Dunno. Doesn't your Mum know what happened? Can't she tell you?"

"Don't think so. Hope not. Can't risk finding out. It'd finish her off if she knew this stuff. She's just getting over the shock of me being black."

Yas put her long elegant fingers over her temples and pressed her head as she thought. "Scars? Have you got any scars?" as if pursuing a cross-word clue.

"Only where I fell off my bike onto my knees."

"Is your cunt normal? Does it look like its been messed with?"

"I dunno. I've not seen many to compare with."

"Aaah. Young innocent carpet muncher. Give it time!"

"Yas! You are gross."

"Not as gross as your old man, by the sound of it."

I shoved Yas with both hands on to her back and sat astride her. My Mum's voice interrupted before I could thump Yasmeen as hard as she deserved. "Girls do you want a drink before I go to bed?"

I yelled back quick "No thanks Mum, Yasmeen has got to go."

On the doorstep, Yasmeen said "Sorry Fliss" and patted me cautiously on the shoulder.

I took advantage of her contrition and asked "Will you come and find him with me?"

"Who?" she asked.

"Him. You know, the man." I couldn't say "father" since he wasn't.

"The pervert? The porno-producer?"

"Yeah." I nodded, unable to think of a more satisfactory name for him.

Yas raised one finely shaped eyebrow in incomprehension "Why?"

"To find out."

"Find out what?" Yas shrugged her shoulders up. "That men are shit? We know that already. That's why you're a lezzer innit? It's certainly why I need religion."

"I'm a dyke because I fancy women. Lesbianism has nothing to do with men."

"No shit! Although, that's not what my brothers would say."

"I'm not interested in what your pervy brothers say. About anything. Will you come with me?"

"OK, whatever, no problem. Have you got an address?"

"No, but Stella Bouchier probably has."

"OK, let me know. I could do with a day trip. And I'm owed holiday. TOIL I've gotta take before I lose it."

At a suitable moment, when she'd eaten her soup and had Eastenders to look forward to, I told Mum that the Guyana trip was off.

"He wasn't very Guyanese Mum. He came to this country when he was five years old. To Liverpool."

"What else was in the file?" she asked anxiously.

"Nothing much Mum. The mother died and I suppose they thought he couldn't cope on his own. P'raps it was a bit racist."

"Is he still alive?"

"Doubt it. He was fifty-five when I was born."

"He'd only be in his seventies then."

"Yeah but he wasn't well then. S'partly why I was taken off him."

Mum was biting her fingers. "No other surprises?"

"No Mum. Very dull. In fact I've shredded all the paperwork."

"Oh. Didn't you want me to look through it?"

"No Mum. S'my responsibility. Like Stella said. Now I'm eighteen."

"OK love. I'm sorry."

"What for?"

"Sorry I've been so hysterical. I was convinced there was something horrible lurking in that file that was going to spoil everything. And I've been so worried that if you were troubled, I wouldn't be able to keep you safe. I miss your Dad so much." And of course, once my brave, strong mother had said that, then I knew that I couldn't let anything be spoiled. It had to stay intact. And only I could keep it together.

211

Mum was fine about me going to Glasgow. And although she was better at getting up and eating now, Mrs Ashkenazy promised to keep an eye on her. I said that she was under doctor's orders and, fearing the offer of the speciality ghastly goulash, lied that she had been put on a vegan regimen.

Jo bombed up the A1, enjoying putting the car through its racey paces, shouting insults at the drivers who weren't playing as fast and loose as her. As we got into the hills of southern Scotland, she became more morose and wanted to listen to the same "Cowboy Junkies" tape over three times. I suppose I had imagined that in a car, unable to do sex, we might talk to one another. But, apart from the odd thigh squeeze and a request to find her fishermen's friends in the car pocket, there was no chat about us, about Scotland or even about climbing.

I thought about Dad as Glasgow came into sight: tower blocks and church towers against a backdrop of hills. I would have liked to tell Jo about him, but she was busy cursing taxi-drivers and their inadequate road sense. Jo parked behind a parade of shops in front of an ill-lit crescent of tenements. We pulled out our rucksacks from the boot and picked our way over piles of rubbish that had spilled from the shops' dustbins, into a dark doorway and up some damp, wide stone-flagged stairs. On the third floor a nameplate announced "MacDonald and Bruce." Flora swept us out of the grimy close and into her lush fantasy of a flat. There were so many textures, colours and delights that, in my over-travelled state, I was unable to speak as well as concentrate on taking it all in. Jo and I were embraced, relieved of our jackets and guided to deep armchairs in front of a fire in a room hung about with pictures, carpets and swathes of heavy fabrics in rich red shades. Almonds and olives in murano-glass bowls were placed within reach and ceramic goblets of mulled wine in our hands. With the wine fumes warming my nose and the fire scorching my shins, I allowed Flora and Jo's talk to lap around me. Two cats came and sat by me in the big chairs and I was sinking into a sleepy trance when Norma's arrival changed the atmosphere. Where Flora reminded me of a bohemian art teacher we'd had in the third year with her layers of clothes, hair and silvery jewellery, Norma was spare. She had short silver crew-cut hair, and a well-made, definite sort of face. She wore standard dyke uniform of jeans and denim jacket. She kissed Flora, embraced Jo and shook me by the hand.

We ate in another big warm room, a kitschy kitchen that looked like a film-set. The cooker, fridge, pots and pans had clean uncomplicated lines, like in a cartoon. Pretty cups and saucers were arrayed on shelves and all of the messy products of modern eating and cleaning were hidden away behind cupboard doors. Norma conjured up a cartoon-style meal: lamb chops, smooth mounds of mashed potato, peas and neat hemispheres of grilled tomato all sitting separate on big plates. Jo poured bisto-gravy over hers, joining up the little food-islands. She refused stout and drank Irn Bru instead, saying she needed to keep a clear head for her climbing. I followed her lead and admired the contrast between the muted green formica table-top and the implausible orange glow of the drinks.

"So" said Norma, clearing the plates and putting a plump kettle onto the gas ring, "you're finally going to tell your folks 'cheerio and thanks for all the memories'?"

"No. I telt you, I'm here for the climbing. Mind I said I'm in the national semi-finals."

"Aye, but now you're here, you'll be wanting to tidy things up, will you no?" Norma asked while spooning tea into a stout pot. She arranged a dozen shiny-wrapped items on a plate with some curranty bun and put it on the table. "Caramel wafers, tea-cakes and bannock, to remind you what you're missing down south!" The kettle whistled.

Flora had already excused herself to "get ready for ma teaching". She had asked me a few questions about college and climbing while we were eating, but Norma didn't seem to bother with small talk. So I held my peace and enjoyed the opportunity to admire the collection of 1950s implements shelved in a lit alcove to my left. I recognised an egg-slicer, a spong mincer and a potato-snow-maker from helping out in Mrs Ashkenazy's kitchen.

Flora's head came round the door. "Awreet women. I'm away out the now, but I'll bring some oysters back when I'm finished. S'only a short class the night. See y'after." She disappeared, only to re-appear. "If you get bored with their

old-time bleathers, there's a telly in the guest room Felicity"
she said conspiratorially, before leaving again.

Norma was pouring tea through a stainless steel strainer
shaped like a mermaid and carried on as if Flora had never
spoken.

"I'll run you round the night." Norma turned to me "Do
you take tea Felicity?" I nodded while Jo was shaking her
handsome head.

"I'm no going anywhere Norma. Except to ma bed, with
ma groupie."

"They'll mebbe be deid next time you're up. In fact, from
what Mrs McWhurter in the post office says, they'll mebbe be
deid the morrow." Norma was insistent with a flush creeping
up her neck. "This isnae a rehearsal!"

Jo just shrugged.

I felt I should probably assert myself as a girlfriend, despite
being called a groupie, and said "I could go with you. Um, if
that'd help." Jo glanced at me and rolled her eyes. Norma
smiled briefly and apologetically before turning back to Jo.

"I ken you cannae forget, but if you dinna forgive them,
they'll aye keep their hold over you" Norma said in a low,
calmer voice with her elbows propped on the table and her tea
cup held in front of her face.

"They watched me getting a doing and what did they do?"
asked Jo.

"Fuck all, Jo. But what could they have done? Even by
the time you arrived at Women's Aid you were still besotted
with her."

"She was perfect" said Jo quietly, adding "almost" a few
seconds later. I felt completely invisible now. Not just
irrelevant.

Norma was nodding with her eyes narrowed against the
steam from the tea. "Aye, devastating in every way. Especially
when stocious. But your folks would never have seen her three
sheets to the wind."

"No bugger did. Except me" said Jo grimly.

"So they were only as blind as the rest of us."

"No. I telt them." Jo looked accusingly at Norma.

"Straight out like?"

"Uh-huh. Hard to avoid. I was discharged to them from

the Southern with a muckle great interal laceration." Norma
had, without getting up from the table, reached a bottle of
whisky and three glasses from the cupboard. The liquor
looked like piss and smelt like petrol.

"I mind. I mind. And mind, I said you should've prosecuted
at the time."

"Aye Norma. That'd be right. 'Hello officer. I've been
raped by my girlfriend. And yes, I'm a Taig dyke. So when
you've finished tugging yourself off, and got through the
standard issue sectarian homophobia, perhaps you could take
down my particulars.' Aye that'd be just grand." Jo tipped her
head back and poured the whisky down her throat before
refilling her glass.

"It was assault", Norma stated.

"I ken that. But I mind your coven who didnae."

"Aye, you're no wrong. And if feminist folk couldnae
imagine you being abused by that sweet-looking lassie, how
could your benighted parents?"

"What, them so sorely lacking the insights of feminism?
Ha!" Jo barked out a very un-amused laugh. She knocked
back another glass of whisky. Perhaps, I thought, you have to
drink it like that, throwing it down your throat, so the foul
liquid can't touch your taste buds. I was clutching my glass
with both hands, but felt no temptation to take a second sip.

I was washing up the dinner dishes, slowly and methodically, hoping that Jo would be unconscious by the time I had
finished, when Flora arrived back. She was carrying a paper
bag that she started unpacking on the table.

"Fancy an oyster Felicity?"

"No thanks. Shell fish and me don't get on."

"Nooo!" Flora rippled out her girlish merry laugh. "Ice-
cream." She held up a dough-nut sized pair of curved wavers
stuffed with ice-cream. "From the Queens Park café. Best in
the world." She was right. The smooth vanilla tasted of cool,
sweet, creamy, fragrant milkiness. There was none of the
greasy after-taste of the yellow Walls' soft scoop that Dad
used to call "whale fat dessert". The oyster-wafer contained
what Flora called "nugget": super-sweet glue that attached
itself to your teeth. While we were both licking out the

shells, Norma reappeared, kissed the top of Flora's head and put the paper bag in the freezer. She sat at the table and uncorked the whisky again.

"Messy business eh Felicity" she commented with finality and without looking at me.

"Um. Yeah" I said lamely.

"Is Jo sleeping?" asked Flora neutrally.

"She is that. Log-like" said Norma examining the bottom of her glass through the liquor.

"You know them then, Jo's parents?" I wondered.

"No exactly, but they stay in the same scheme as ma family. So I hear about them. My Ma sometimes calls for their messages. When the home help's off like." Norma drank, refilled and stood up. "I'm going to catch the news headlines." Flora was clearing the wooden draining board of the washing up I'd piled there.

"Be through in a minute, ma treasure," she said absent-mindedly.

"What about the girlfriend?" I asked quickly before Norma returned. It was easier to ask Flora than her brooding partner.

"Who's that then?" Flora said.

"Jo's. Who beat her."

"Oh her. A right nippy sweetie from what folk say. Before my time on the scene hen. Jo was only a bairn, barely eighteen, still at home. Came out to her parents for the lassie. Canadian she was. Over here with a bank. She's away again now. Left a trail of broken hearts along the M8 and then disappeared on a jet plane from what I hear. Not a steady lassie like yourself." Flora turned from the dresser where she was replacing crockery to give me a broad smile. "Does Jo talk about her then?"

I shook my head dolefully. "Jo doesn't talk about anything to me."

"She's the strong silent type. A granite girl, like ma Norma."

"And why won't she speak to her parents?"

"I suppose she doesn't trust them."

"But if they're dying..."

Flora nodded. "I know. That's what we think."

216

Norma returned to the kitchen saying "One typhoon, a train crash and an underground strike."

"Why won't Jo talk with her folks, Normy?" asked Flora, reaching out her hand to stroke Norma's bottle-brush hair.

"Habit partly. It's twenty years that she moved south and all that time she's been incommunicado." I was frowning and shaking my head, trying to make sense of the fact that the woman with whom I shared my body had not spoken to her parents for longer than I'd been alive. "They hated her being a lesbian. But that Genviève charmed them. She charmed us all. She was rich, sophisticated, good-looking, sexy, raunchy. Us wee schemie lassies didnae know what had hit us. We'd all have jumped intae bed wi' her. But it was Jo she wanted." Norma's attention snapped back onto me. "You should ask her Felicity. She might even tell you about it." She paused. "I'm needin' ma bed. G'night."

Flora handed me a clean towel and a water glass and, before she followed Norma, said "S'all a bit grim, eh doll? But it's history. You're the future. You're the first lassie Jo's brought to visit. She must think the world ae you. Sweet dreams."

Jo was rolled up in the spare room double bed with her back to me. I got under what remained of the quilt without disturbing her and lay tensely in the darkness. I thought about getting a train home first thing in the morning, using my emergency credit card. Mum would be pleased to see me. But it seemed pathetic. Babyish. And then I'd have to explain to Jo.

When the morning actually came, a breakfast of potato scones, sausage meat patties and eggs all fried up together restored my courage. Jo had already gone out to Kelvinhall. Apparently she didn't want me with her. Flora made Norma and me a grease-proof parcel of sandwiches each.

"Take your jelly pieces and Norma'll chum you into town."

I got on the bus with Norma and accompanied her to her work at the Women's Library, from where she pointed me east towards the People's Palace. I wandered about the elegant building, admiring the select artefacts that the museum curators felt summed up their city's character: Billy Connolly's banana boots, a scold's bridle and a kitchen range. The place was empty except for me, so I settled onto a little plastic seat in the kiddie-interactive zone, hidden from the security woman by a big display case, and keyed in the number on Stella Bouchier's calling card.

"Can you put me through to Stella Bouchier please? ... It's Felicity Fort."

La Bouchier sounded irritatingly pleased that I had phoned. But she didn't want to tell me anything over the phone, insisting that we meet up in person.

"I would be failing in my professional duty Felicity, if I allowed you to meet your birth father without a careful briefing beforehand. And a debriefing afterwards. I am sure that your mother would agree with me."

"Thing is Stella, I've moved to Glasgow with my girlfriend. Did Mum not tell you? And um, we're planning a commitment ceremony some time next year. But we think that it's important to explore my, um, origins together. You know, tidy up the past before we start our joint future, properly. And um, she's a trained social worker and she was a CPN too. So we feel she can handle any issues that might come up."

And in the end it only took a few more minutes to convince Stella that the responsible and anti-homophobic thing to do was give me my information. Perhaps she couldn't fit a drive up to Glasgow into her professional schedule. I scribbled down the address and promised that I would phone her afterwards, without any intention of doing so. She couldn't make me could she?

The bit of paper was in my pocket and my fingers kept closing around it. He was living only an hour's drive from home. Stella had said that he had been alive two years ago and assumed she would've heard had he died. I tried to feel the momentousness of the occasion: I told myself "I have the key to my past in my hand." But it didn't feel true. My past was my daft old Dad and my careful, sweet Mum. I felt as though I ought to burst into tears or laugh out loud or spontaneously hug the museum staff. I might've done if Yas had been there to share the joke. But she was shifting shifts and flogging frocks 600 miles away. I would save my emotion until I was back on home territory. In the mean time, I got back to exploring Glasgow's attractions.

Flora had insisted that I visit the Barras on the grounds of its being choc full of fantastic bargains. I admired the knocked-off tellies, cheap leather jackets, junk shop jewellery and second-hand bedding. There was a whole stall flogging items that hadn't been picked up from a dry-cleaners and another with repaired shoes that had been abandoned with a cobbler. It made me wonder whether all the goods in a tiny cake shop next door had failed a health and safety inspection elsewhere.

Meandering back towards the women's library, I was hoping to find a steamy café underneath a railway bridge arch where I could sit still for a while. I crossed a piece of open ground and passed a couple of people squatting by a stained blanket spread out on the ground. Laid out on top were three pairs of grubby Y-fronts, a PVC belt and an acrylic sweater. Several more blankets were laid out: one had clothes piled high and as people rummaged through them they fell off onto the wet ground; another had what looked like the contents of a child's toy box. I was funnelled down an alleyway where the discoloured, misshapen goods, which I had now realised were for sale, were hung up the walls of the overhead railway line. Everything looked not just second hand, but third, fourth or fifth hand. And there was the café that my stomach had been growling for, but I didn't dare go in case the bacon rolls had had previous owners so I carried on past the selection of hearing aids and dentures, bras and pirated tapes. No wonder Flora was excited about the Barras if this was the competition for the discerning bargain-hunter.

My mobile vibrated in my pocket but I decided not to answer it. It seemed rude to flaunt a £50 phone when people were trying to trade charity-shop rejects around me.

Down the road, I returned the call I'd missed from Jo. She'd just been knocked out of her heat and was on her way to the city centre. She directed me to the queer-friendly surroundings of the Tron theatre bar. Half an hour later, I'd finished reading Diva and drinking my cappuccino and Jo appeared at the bar. She looked elated and slightly self-conscious in her climbing gear as she brought over two pints of Guinness. As we were drinking the first draught of dark beer through creamy foam, plummy tones from over Jo's shoulder asked "How the devil are you Joanne?"

"Fuck me, Lynda!" said Jo when she'd recovered from inhaling her beer and turned around. "What have you done to your voice?"

"Been to RADA. Damned expensive way to get elocution lessons." Eventually, when they'd embraced, laughed and lit up a cigarette each, they noticed me.

"This is Felicity. My ..." Jo paused "travelling companion."

"Delighted to make your acquaintance", said Lynda as she kissed my hand. I smiled and sat back while they reminisced about a string of names that meant nothing to me. Suddenly, Lynda sat upright in her chair and cried "Oh bollocking bollocks. Must go, my friends. I've got a show to pull down. The others'll be cursing my good name. Haste ye back, darlings."

Jo was beaming as Lynda's back disappeared through a "Staff Only" door.

"School pal. Good yin too" she said and went for more beer. With a fresh pint in front of her, she didn't seem to want to speak much, content to bask in the ebb and flow of the activity and chat around us.

"Jo?" I intruded.

"Aye."

"Why didn't you tell me about Genviève?"

"Why in Christ's name would I wantae talk about her? She damn-near killed me."

"But you loved her didn't you?"

"Aye. Sure I did. But she wasnae a psychopath when I fell for her."

"When did she change?"

"De ken. Couldnae say. I was that delighted at myself for my cleverness at winning a sleekit girl who had her own wee housie and that my parents liked. In the end, they liked her mair than me."

"Is that why you won't visit them?"

"Kindae. I'm just needin to find a wee smoke" Jo said and she went off to the bar to ponce a fag from the pretty bartender. "What's it to you anyway?" she asked on her return.

"Um. I thought I'd a right to know."

"A right!" Jo hurumphed. And as she sat drinking and

smoking, this could've been the moment where I told her my worries about my murky past. I drew a breath, but realised that I was not prepared to tell her. I didn't trust her with my stuff. So perhaps I shouldn't ask about hers. Perhaps I couldn't understand her stuff. Was she worried that I would read too much into her having been raped? I shuddered slightly to think what with.

"Cold, doll face?" Jo asked.

"No. Fine." I looked at her. She was as handsome as ever. Her jaw line firm as she watched the clutch of folk who'd just arrived at the bar. And the thought of sex with her still made my stomach lurch. But I got a bigger lurch realising that this was probably it: Jo had brought me back to visit her oldest pals. This was probably the most intimate we would get. Drinking beer together with occasional sessions of mutual masturbation.

The next day we left Glasgow and I admired Jo's profile all the way south.

"How was your holiday with Caledonia's answer to James Dean?" Yas asked sarcastically. We were in the park, enjoying the sunshine during her lunch break.

"I've been a right muppet haven't I?" I was lying on the grass on my jacket staring up to the sky through the dangling branches of a willow.

"How's that Fliss?"

"With Jo."

"No more of a muppet than anyone searching for love's young dream" said Yas, as she turned over onto her front and cupped her chin in her hands.

"She's not young. And she doesn't love me, does she?"

"D'you love her then?"

"Dunno. I fancy her. And she seems to fancy me. S'not enough though is it?"

"Dunno. Depends. Some people'd be pretty pleased with good sex," Yas pointed out.

"Yeah. Maybe. But being a couple is not just sex, is it?"

"Guess not. But it probably helps."

I complained, "She never tells me stuff. Important stuff. It's you that listens to my stuff. Not Jo."

"Are you propositioning me Felicity?" Yas mock-simpered, fluttering her ample lashes.

"I don't think you're soft-top material love. Too enamoured of the puppetry of the penis."

"No way am I soft. You ask my slaves in Top Shop!"

"No. Soft-top convertible. Convertible to the homosexual lifestyle, luvvie," I camped. I expected Yas to agree heartily that she was not muff-diving material and to call me a daft dyke.

"Probably not Fliss. But I've been giving it some serious thought. I mean, how many happy straight women do you know?" Yas asked, as she passed me the bag of cheese puffs we were sharing. Her complexion stayed peachy and her figure willowy while eating rubbish.

"Um. Mmm. Mrs Ashkenazy seems quite content" I said.

"Is she straight?"

"Depends what you mean. Her first love is cats and her second is crocheting. And there's no Mr Ashkenazy." I thought some more. "How about your sister? She's all blissed out with her bloke isn't she?"

"Yeah. But she's got mother-in-law troubles."

"Ah. Sorry."

"S'OK. She's not getting hit. Yet. She thought she could escape all that stuff with a love match."

"My Mum was happy before my Dad died," I offered.

"My Mum would be happy if my Dad did die," said Yas gloomily.

"Ice-lolly?" I offered, as the Mr Whippy van tinkled its way towards the pond.

"Mmm. Something really phallic, please", said Yas. "Remind me of the straight and narrow" she winked. When Yas got bored of licking her Zoom suggestively, she asked "So when is our big day trip then?"

"What day trip?"

"To see the old porn-producer."

"Eh?"

"Your old man. The bio-dad."

"Oh. Yes. Soon." But not too soon. It had seemed so urgent to find him when I was in Glasgow. But back on home territory, surrounded by comforting normality and the every day routine, it seemed like an indulgence. A dangerous indulgence. "I'll let you know."

Yas went back to work and, reluctantly, I left the sunshine and trudged up the stairs of the college library to the third floor health collection. Two pieces of course work demanded my attention. My phone vibrated. The number on the screen was unfamiliar so I took the call.

"Hello Felicity. I got your number from Flora. Is it OK to talk the now?" It was Norma's uncompromising voice in my ear.

"Um. Hang on. I'll just go outside", I said and took the steps back down three at a time. "OK. Fire away." It was good to feel the sun on my skin and leave behind the stale air of the library with its peculiar paper-dust smell, the antithesis of outdoors, for a few moments longer.

"I need to ask you a favour, Felicity." Norma, utterly competently grown up, ask me a favour! "And before I ask you, don't forget you could refuse. I'm only asking because there's no other way, short of driving down myself."

"It's about Jo", I guessed.

"Aye. So it is. She cuts me off when I try to speak to her about it and if I send a letter she'll deny all knowledge. And for my own sake, I need to know that she knows."

"Knows what?"

"About her Da.", Norma paused. "This is a lot to ask a young lassie like yourself."

I waited. I wasn't going to beg to be allowed to run Norma's errand.

"Would you tell her that her Da has died? And would you tell her that it's next Tuesday he'll be cremated? Up beside Sighthill."

"Oh" I let out an involuntary gasp.

"I ken lassie. It's a shock." I felt a fraud, since I hadn't even met, let alone known the man. "Death's always a shock. Even," Norma said more to herself "even when you've long wished the bastard dead."

"She won't want to hear, it will she?" I was beginning to understand what Norma was asking me to do.

"No. You're right there. But she needs to know. Or mebbe

I need her to know. I cannae collude, pretend she's accidentally lost touch. Especially after youse were here visiting. She's choosing not tae see them. So, will you dae it?"

"Um. I think so."

"Y'are still seeing her like?" Norma asked.

I wondered: was I?

"Are ye?" Norma asked again.

"Ummm" I said noncommittally. We were still seeing each other. Or rather, Jo was seeing bits of me. But not often. Jo had stopped visiting my house because the coast, or rather the sofa, wasn't clear any longer. Mum's lassitude was receding and she was staying up later, watching the telly, cooking and generally inhibiting Jo's sexual expression. So sex only happened occasionally and always at Jo's. "Yup. We're meeting at the pub tonight, after she's finished training."

I didn't get much work done in the library that afternoon. Too many dead dads in my head: Jo's, mine and the Guyanese bio-dad that I had never missed. Two definitely dead and one possibly dead. Although Jo wasn't so sure that her father was dead. She got to the pub late, as usual, straight from the climbing wall. Everyone else was ensconsed around a sticky table, swapping trifling pub talk. I went up to the bar with Jo, but a suitable moment to announce her father's death with due respect and solemnity did not present itself. So we returned to the table where Malcolm was pulling over a velour-topped stool for Jo.

"How was your return to Mother Alba?" asked Phil archly. Josh put down his pint to listen to the answer. Phil had accused him of being "an indiscriminate Scotophile" in the past when he had spoken for too long about "Belle and Sebastian", "Travis" and "Franz Ferdinand". Josh had pointed out that "Franz Ferdinand" were mostly English, but had agreed that he loved Scotland and launched into an explanation of the significance of the Cambrian divide for quaternary geology. Or something.

"Fine thanks", I said smoothly while Jo kept her face in her beer glass.

"Did you see the Burrell collection?" asked Phil.

"Only if that's what they call the assortment of used underpants next to the barras," I replied.

"MOMA?" asked Phil.

"Don't think so." I shook my head and carried on shaking as Phil continued

"Delmonica's? Babbity Bowster's The Macintosh House?"

"No" said Jo, joining in at last. "We were staying with old friends. They fair took to young Fliss" she said, putting her arm around my shoulders.

"So they should" retorted Phil. "Did you take her to Gretna Green and make an honest woman of her?"

Jo sighed. "As you well know, Phyllis, I'll not be aping hetero-rituals any time soon."

"What, not even for Fliss?" Phil persisted.

Jo started a counter-attack "Will you be getting a queer curate to pronounce you 'woman and wife' with your pregnant princess?"

"We'd thought of a spot of light hand-binding to tide us over until after the birth. Nothing too S&M mind, darlings. You'll all be invited" Phil swept her arm to include everyone in the pub "when we've located a suitable wise woman."

"Ah well" grunted Jo "at least you'll not be shoring up an establishment church riddled with hypocrisy and corruption." She looked up and caught Malcolm's eye. "Er, with exceptions, I daresay," she added.

Phil was bored of taunting Jo and got stuck into Tim instead, specifically his devotion to Aston Villa, despite their poor performance. Relieved to be on safer conversational territory, Tim defended his team with gusto. I took cover under the football talk and turned to Jo.

"Norma phoned me today."

"Oh aye" said Jo, without taking her eyes off Tim. "Is she a'reet?"

"She wants me to tell you that your dad has died."

"Oh aye. That'll be reet then", Jo said with heavy sarcasm.

I had anticipated anger, belligerence, jubilation or even tears, but not disbelief. "You don't believe me?"

"Aye, I do. It's Norma I dinnae trust. She could be kidding on, just tae get me up there, to the old fucker's death bed."

I shook my head and tried to think why Jo should believe Norma's message.

"I don't think so."

225

I shrugged as I admitted to myself that I couldn't prove whether or not Jo's father had died. But I could finish Norma's errand. "She said to tell you the cremation's on Tuesday, near Sighthill. She seemed sincere."

"Oh aye. She is that, our Norma. Dead sincere. Well-meaning. Ken, road to hell, good intentions an' a' that." I didn't bother asking Jo what she was talking about, since our subdued talk was drowned out by the others' intense discussion about some footballer. Or his wife.

What else could I do? I had told Jo. She distrusted the message. And her suspicious cynicism got to me. It was creeping and ugly and unsettling. Her refusal to see her father, dead or alive, seemed cowardly and unimaginative. As the possibility that Jo might be gutless crept about my mind, I stopped fancying her, or at least I started to stop. I started looking at her, sizing her up, without being so distracted by lust.

That night, when I got home, I found the jacket that I'd worn to Glasgow and fished out the bit of paper with the old Guyanese bloke's address. On the bus the next morning I told Yas that I was ready for our day trip. I wanted to find bio-dad before his health gave out. Or confirm if it already had done.

"No worries" Yas said.

"Easy for you to say" I replied.

"I just meant, I'll get a car," she smiled ruefully.

"Good afternoon. Felicity is it?" he said as soon as we approached him, sitting on a vinyl chair, wreathed in the smell of piss and boiled cabbage. He could not have known I was coming that day, or any day. We hadn't known we were going to visit until the day before. Yas had just passed her test and her brother's latest court appearance resulted in him being banned for a year. So she had her brother's battered Fiat panda, reeking of dope and due an MOT which it would fail. Having got the bottle up to make the visit, I was unwilling to phone ahead, in case they said "no". So we just went. Yas said we could go for lunch in a country pub, if we couldn't find him. Stella Bouchier might've phoned the place and warned them, but I don't think so. The nurse who unlocked the heavy oak front-door was surprised when we asked to see him.

"He's not had many visitors. Well, you're the first actually. Daughter you say."

But he wasn't surprised, or said he wasn't.

"I was hoping you'd come and find me one day," he said. His face was softly lined with high cheek bones and a calm smile. His hair was tight white curls high up on his forehead. He put me in mind of the angel, Gabriel. His voice had a faint Guyanese lilt, and he spoke in short, breathless sentences, more like reciting than conversation. It was as if he had been working on this speech for a long time.

I can only remember all these details because clever Yas recorded him on her i-pod (won for shifting more sparkley frocks than any other branch of Top Shop). I've listened to it over and over again, so often, in fact, that I could now reel it off, should the digital recording disintegrate. But straight after the visit, when Josh asked me, all I could describe was a round, brown face with eyes that were disconcertingly like my own.

"What has that wicked woman been telling you? Upsetting your sweet countenance? It was she who stole you away from me. She will have told you harsh things as though they are the truth. As though it will be good for you to swallow bitter medicine."

There was no-where to sit down, so Yas and I stood before him. He continued, with his eyes shut.

"Your mama was a beautiful woman. Lovely to behold. But troubled. Troubled by djinns and devils. She came off the drugs when she got pregnant. She was so young. And she wanted to do right by you. But the demons kept calling her off. And when she was away with them, you would cry and cry. You needed your mama for feeding. I didn't know what to do. Except I knew what I loved even more than food, so I stroked up your lily flower. And just like your mama liked it, so did you. You used to smile and gurgle and not miss your demon-chasing mama any more. Aaaah. Ha, ha, ha. And because you used to smile so serene, I took your photo. I put it up on the wall. It was my pride that I could keep you happy. That was our downfall, my girl. I was going to get my oils out. Paint the baby in ecstasy. But then the devils took your mama away and a demon took you too. And I was left. Alone.

Alone. With the people that suck your brains out." He sighed, opened his eyes and smiled at Yasmeen. "I'm ready for my dinner now, girl."

And that was it. He didn't speak any more. As his face settled into stillness, his skin suddenly looked papery thin and his brown eyes took on a milky hue. Yasmeen took my elbow and guided me out. I turned as we left, to see a care assistant spooning in dinner and holding a feeding cup to his slackened mouth.

We never really broke up. But then, since we'd not exactly been going out together, how could we? Jo came round to the house a few more times. We sat in the kitchen and drank coffee. Mum came and asked some polite questions about Jo's climbing before going back to the television. I went back to Jo's after climbing a few more times. The leather sofa sex was still breath-taking, but I had become detached from it, looking down on the sweaty wrestling from above. And during my out of body experiences, I couldn't help remarking that whatever ruses I tried, Jo remained clothed throughout proceedings. One night as we left the sports centre, Jo strode off towards her car, expecting me to follow. I hesitated and called "Got to get back home" to her back. I suppose I was hoping that she might persuade me, but I think I also knew that the seduction rather than the repetition was what she loved. She didn't come to the pub again after that.

With Jo gone, there was more space for Josh. The evening after I'd visited the old porn-producer, he asked "what've you done today then?" If he was taken aback by my reply, he didn't show it. "Visited my half-dead, abusive birth father." I described the institutional stink and the strange feeling of looking at a face like my own, albeit darker and more lined. And then Phil arrived with news of the barmaid having gone into labour. And my introspection was curtailed with more hopeful news.

I had to phone Stella Bouchier, even though it would fulfil her expectations. What was I expecting? Some type of apology I suppose: an apology for busting into my calm life, reducing my precious mother to a tearful heap and giving me a great many worries that cannot be resolved. I suppose I am pleased to have seen the man who was my father before Dad took over the job. It was interesting to see his face and hear his voice. But it doesn't mean that I know what happened back then: I still don't know if he really loved me and if he really abused me. Reading the terrible file and then finding him hasn't made me feel more myself. Or less. I wanted to explain this to her and get her to admit that my version of reality was more complicated than hers and that she couldn't understand it. But she wouldn't. She cut across me in a brisk professional tone.

"Felicity. The man is a manipulator and a liar. Always has been. Charming, but highly deceiving."

"No, Stella, he was a shrivelled up husk in a loony bin."

"He was manipulative then and he's manipulating you now." And then she started to spill the beans, as if she wanted her version of what had happened to over-write whatever the old fella had told me. I suppose this is what she had wanted to do on my eighteenth birthday, but Mum's tearful fear and my hostile indifference had robbed her of her revelatory moment. And now it all came tumbling out. I wanted to put the phone down and cut off her interfering, self-righteous flow, but I was fascinated by the unprofessional way in which crucial details of my early life were tumbling out. "He met your mother in hospital, where they'd both been sectioned. He got her pregnant. She was barely sixteen, but her parents decided not to prosecute, since that would have meant everyone knowing that they had an illegitimate black grandchild, as well as a mad daughter. They preferred to confine her to the hospital. It was them who wanted adoption before you were born. But they hadn't counted on him getting himself discharged and finding a priest who was prepared to marry them, to save you from being born out of wedlock. They claimed they were tricked into giving permission, but perhaps he simply convinced them that he could make everything disappear and they signed her away, instead of signing you away. I'm not sure: it was before I was allocated to your case. So you lived with him while she was in and out of hospital. And he abused you. Sexually. He photographed himself masturbating you and made copies of the pictures for his friends." Stella paused to draw breath.

"He says I liked it and it stopped me from crying."

"That's what all abusers claim. That the victim wanted it. Otherwise how could they live with themselves? Enjoyment is irrelevant to the abuse of power. We discovered the pictures when your mother committed suicide in the flat. Your father was out at the pub and a neighbour heard you crying. The photos were seized as evidence but no prosecution could be brought at that time, since there was no evidence of harm inflicted on you. Things were different then. People didn't know about paedophiles. It wasn't recognised as a problem. Nonetheless, I managed to get you placed for adoption while he was on bail before the trial." Stella's tone of triumph seemed to expect me to congratulate her.

"His alcoholism and mental health problems undermined any claim he had over you. And all his family were overseas." I had known that the birth mother had committed suicide. It was written in the case notes about her "taking her own life". But I hadn't known that I'd been with her at the time. This news hit me in the stomach, got me in the guts and knocked the wind out of me. It made me want to cry. But still not really for myself. I wanted to cry for a baby, a baby who was rejected, whose sweetness and neediness couldn't keep her mother's attention, couldn't compete with psychotic illness and depression. But that baby who I wanted to cry for wasn't me, it was any baby, an idea of a baby, essence of baby. I gulped and, with my hand over the phone blew my nose. I couldn't let Stella hear my upset. She might want to come round and counsel me.

"Why am I hearing this stuff from you? Why isn't it in my notes?"

"It was Felicity. But when you joined my case load your previous social worker destroyed the ante-natal and post-natal case notes."

"My notes."

"Yes."

I asked "Why?" and there was no response from Stella for a few moments.

"I'm not sure, Felicity. A nervous break-down I suppose. She was unwilling to let you go."

I didn't bother to say goodbye. I put the phone down, went

out to the woodpile behind the shed and cried long and hard into a hanky. Then I came back into the house and arranged with British Telecom to have our phone number changed. I did not want Stella Bouchier dropping any more of her truths on my mother.

My mother. My dear, darling, dissolving mother who was now beginning to reform herself, to coalesce again around the idea of being a widow with a grown-up adopted daughter with an uncomplicated history. She has suddenly aged, with her diabetes taking its toll on her kidneys and eyes. Sometimes we still share giggly, carefree times, but mostly Mum has withdrawn into a dignified, level contentment. She doesn't despair under the duvet any more, but she doesn't seem to have soaring delight either. Perhaps we needed Dad to be our ballast to let the nonsense really take flight.

We have talked about contacting Mum's sister, but it seems too risky to me. If the long-lost aunt turns out to be uninterested in meeting her black bastard niece, it might send Mum back to her bed in tears. But perhaps once Mum's used to me being black, then we'll send a tentative Christmas card: "I'm dreaming of a white Christmas."

Yas says I should sue. Sue social services. She pulled all the papers out from under my bed and read them through carefully again. There is nothing referring to me before the age of 9 months and no mention of a previous social worker. All the important details are missing. The letters are meaningless. What would I sue for? A full set of notes that I didn't want in the first place? Emotional distress? Unprofessional conduct, Yas says. But I'm not sure that even super-smooth professionalism could have made the last few months easier. I can't sue Stella for thinking she knows best. Or the previous social worker for cracking up. And anyway, things are back together again now. What's made it OK in the end was nothing much to do with social workers or their record keeping. No, in the end it was the fourteen and a half years of prime parenting that Mum and Dad gave me.

So here I am. I've made it to my 19th birthday. And life is sweet and calm. This morning, I took Mum her breakfast in bed. She still finds it hard to get up in the morning. We ate apricot museli and drank black coffee and talked about birthdays past. Mum wept a little when we got to thinking about last year's birthday dinner with Stella Bouchier. "Your Dad would've berated me for my foolishness, Felicity," she sobbed.

"S'OK Mum. We've found our way through it. S'alright. I'm glad I know all that stuff." And I thought to myself, imagine if I hadn't found out until after that old fella had died. He might've seemed really scary. I might never have known that he was just a dribbling, old, institutionalised man.

Then Mum pulled a package out of her bedside table. It was a mini panettone with a candle in the top. We lit it and sang together. But not "Happy Birthday to you" which Dad always hated, ever since he realised that even when translated into French or Italian or Hindi, its tones remained dreary. He refused to sing it, even for his perfect little daughter. So we had each chosen our own favourite song for rendition on the appointed day. Mum's was easy: "Non, je ne regrette rien" was the song that preserved her from organised religion as it celebrated all that was indomitable and admirable about the human spirit without recourse to the supernatural. Dad chose "On the sunny side of the street", the first tune he'd learned on the trombone that he'd stopped playing on account of the heart condition and that eventually finished him off. My song had always been "I went to the animal fair" until I reached the age of eleven, when I changed my mind once a week throughout the year and several times a day in the week before my birthday. But even when I settled on annoying, ephemeral chart toppers, Dad bought the sheet music and had them note perfect on the day. On my sixteenth and seventeenth birthday Mum sung "We all live on a yellow submarine", which had been my choice when I turned fifteen and the last birthday song that Dad had sung. I had discovered the album in his vinyl collection and had thought the druggy hallucinogenic connotations to be the height of dangerous sophistication. So that's what me and Mum sang in bed together, both letting tears leak down our cheeks as we remembered Dad's enthusiastic singing.

And here I am in the pub. Sitting quietly in the corner, waiting for everyone to turn up. Malcolm will arrive late with Phil's former squeeze, the Punkette -- his first real girlfriend.

Malcolm still doesn't talk much, but then neither does the Punkette. They mostly snog. Seeing them mooning over each other makes me realise what a prat I must've looked with Jo. But nobody holds it against me. Phil will be in later to wet her baby's head (again). The baby will be with the barmaid's mother for the evening, snuggled up on a respectable draylon sofa, watching "Vintage come dancing" since the barmaid thought she'd better come along and keep an eye on Phil.

Yasmeen might look in for a grapefruit and tonic water on her way home from the station. She's been at a Top Shop management residential course. She texted to say that they're looking for a manager for the West Midlands region. She needs a good excuse to leave home, especially since her Mum's going on Haj again this year, and taking Yasmeen's older sister and the two children, as a means of escaping their unpleasant men folk. The Imam, perhaps inspired by Yas's brothers, has announced his intention to start a mission to save British-born Muslims from losing their faith. Yas still isn't sure whether it's her Mum's stuffed parathas or her own long-lashed eyes framed by the hijab which keep him visiting their house.

Tim has grown a beard. Or at least a skinny moustache and a goatee and has taken his climbing instructor's exams. He and the McKinley brothers are leading a climbing expedition of kids from our old school to North Wales. Tim's barely taller than most of the pupils, but he gets up those rock faces like greased lightning. Stylish greased lightning at that. I've given up climbing since things cooled with Jo. Seemed better to leave her be with the beards for comfort. I've joined the croquet club instead. I'm pretty rubbish at it. But they have excellent midsummer and midwinter parties, so says Josh, with all sorts of strange old English solstice customs. And being inept at croquet helps me to practise modesty, which I need, since, if I can keep it up for another year, I'm due to graduate from my Sports Science and Physio degree with a distinction. Yipee. I've got a placement with a US women's soccer team lined up, but really and truly I want to work with the British Olympic team. How cool would that be? Imagining being in the British strip is my main fantasy now that Jo's stopped trembling my knees.

But the best thing about this birthday is that I've got Josh back. The old Josh. He came round this morning, after I'd finished the singing breakfast with Mum, to bring me a big bunch of gladioli. And, after some coffee, he announced that he's fallen in love. With a girl from Guyana who he met in Iceland. He's been writing to her ever since the field trip. His Mum approves of her because she's a Methodist, which, while not quite Baptist, is better than nothing. Josh showed me a photo and I expelled a huge sigh of relief to see that she doesn't look like me. She has big, curly hair, round eyes and a round face. She's the only other person I know from Guyana, apart from the old fella. It would be good to have an excuse to visit the country without the trip being about me. So I'm hoping for a wedding next year and then I can visit the land of my fore-fathers.

"She's lovely Josh. Has she got a sister?"

"Yeah, she's got five. There must be one you could fancy, then we could be in-laws!" Josh was smiling his lovely open, generous smile.

"Will you do something with me Josh?"

"Sure."

"But don't ask any questions about it?" Josh mimed zipping his mouth closed. In silence, he helped me gather up all the bits of paper from under my bed and together we made a fire at the bottom of the garden and kept it stoked until there was nothing remaining but pure, sterile ash.